Fall From Grace

The Grace McDonald Series
Book 1

SUSAN KRAUS

Flint Hills Publishing

Fall From Grace: The Grace McDonald Series, Book 1 © Susan J. Kraus 2014

Revised Edition 2020

All rights reserved.

Cover Design by Ashley Honey
ashleyhoney.com

Flint Hills Publishing

Topeka, Kansas

www.flinthillspublishing.com

Printed in the U.S.A.

Revised Edition
ISBN: 978-1-953583-99-4

"Some marriages end with a bang,
some with a whimper.
But in every marriage,
without exception,
the beginning of the end
is a secret."

Grace McDonald

"Some marriages end with a bang,
some with a whimper.
But in every marriage,
without exception,
the beginning of the end
is a secret."

Grace McDonald

1

Mandy's pulse quickened as she climbed the front porch steps to the therapist's office. She wasn't used to talking about herself and she'd never done *this* before. Ever since she'd picked up the phone to make the appointment, she found herself thinking of what she might say and where to start. All she knew was that after twenty-nine years of living on autopilot, always doing what other people wanted from her or expected, Mandy wanted something different.

From her window, Grace McDonald watched the young woman come up the walk. She was at a half-run, breathless. *It's the good girls who run*, Grace thought. God forbid they keep anyone waiting.

Grace had been a therapist for over twenty years. Her office was in a converted house, a weathered gray structure with crisp white trim and a sweeping porch, set back from the street. She wanted the space to feel welcoming, where people could take off their shoes and curl up on a paisley chair or comfy sofa as they tackled the difficult work of sorting out their lives.

This young woman had called last week. When Grace asked if she'd ever been in therapy before, she'd said no. When Grace asked what the current issues were that motivated her to pick up the phone to make the appointment, she'd hesitated.

"I'm tired of being worried all the time," she'd answered after a pause. "I want to know who I am."

Hearing the front door close, Grace walked to the waiting room to greet her new client. In her hand was a packet with the usual forms: contact info, a HIPPA release, insurance data. Once Mandy completed them, they would move into the office and get started.

Mandy was standing by the door as if uncertain where to go and what to do.

Grace extended her hand with a smile. "I'm Grace McDonald," she said. "And I assume you are Mandy?"

Five minutes later they were seated in the office, the forms signed and filed.

"Where do you want to start?" Grace asked. "Is there anything you've been thinking about that has moved to the top of your priority list?"

"I don't know where to start," Mandy answered. "I can usually solve a problem once I know what it is. But my head is a jumble."

"That's how many people feel. They don't need answers as much as someone to help define the problem. They want to be happier, but don't know which direction or what sorts of changes will accomplish that."

"That's about right. I need to decide on a direction and I've been stuck for a long time. I'm afraid to do anything because I worry I'll regret it later."

"How about I ask you some questions to get us started?" Grace asked, reaching for her pad and pen.

"Yes. Ask away."

Grace started with the easy ones: Where did you grow up? Are your parents alive? Did they divorce or stay together? What kind of work did they do? Do you have siblings? Where do they live now and what did they do? Where did you go to school? What kind of work do you do? Are you married? And on and on. . .

Mandy answered quickly, as if relieved to be able to provide the right answers. Then there was an almost invisible shift.

"So, Mandy, how old were you when you met your husband?"

"Nineteen."

"And you got married?"

"A year later."

"What attracted you to him?"

Mandy hesitated. She knew but had never said it out loud. When Danny had tossed back a shock of his blonde hair, she'd felt dizzy. How his skin tanned to buttered toast. She'd luxuriated in his possessiveness. Even thinking of that time made Mandy blush.

"So I presume it wasn't his intellect?" Grace asked, noting the blush.

"He was a hunk."

"And what was it about you that Danny fell for?"

"He says I was the right girl in the right place at the right time."

Grace felt a slight shiver at the disproportion.

"Tell me about your wedding," Grace asked.

"It was pouring, but I didn't care. I was so in love," Mandy replied.

"And what about it do you remember the most?"

"Dancing. Danny dancing," Mandy said, her eyes shifting to look away from Grace and out the window at the sky.

Mandy continued, describing a spring morning so rainy that water filled the street in front of Cornerstone Christian Church. When they ran from the church to the waiting limo, under a barrage of slick, damp rice, water soaked Danny's shoes. As soon as they got to the reception hall, he'd peeled off his wet socks and shoes. He spent his wedding reception barefoot, dancing with his bride, dancing with all the women, his feet arching upward as he waltzed around the room.

When friends described the wedding, it wasn't Mandy they remembered, but wild-man Danny dancing barefoot.

So, the guy likes to be the center of attention, Grace thought. She started to speak, then stopped.

Time was almost up.

But then Mandy spoke, for the first time posing a question instead of answering them.

"How do you know if a decision is right?"

"Right for who? For you? For your husband?"

"Start with me."

"Well, I think it helps to write stuff down. List the costs and benefits. First, the short term, but then try and imagine your life in ten years with each choice."

Grace sensed that Mandy was talking about her marriage, but she kept her response more generic.

"And if I'm still not sure?" Mandy asked.

"Do it again. It often takes months, not a few days. And, really, in the end, you may have to go with your gut."

"Go with my gut?"

"Yes. We have instincts for a reason. If your instincts are telling you what to do to survive, pay attention."

She wants out, Grace thought after Mandy left. *But she'll need to see that on her own.* Regardless, there was plenty to work on.

"This new one seems so damn young," Grace told Gil, her husband, later that evening. "She reminds me of Molly. Tries hard to be good and make things right. Rationalizes and tries even harder when they're not."

Molly was their daughter, a college freshman. Alex, their son, a junior at a university in Texas, was two years older.

"How is that a problem?" asked Gil.

"I think she puts up with a lot. Like in her marriage. Keeps hoping it will get better."

"And will it?"

"If she sticks with therapy, she'll change. That could be good or bad for her marriage."

It was hard for Grace to leave work at the office. Sometimes it helped to use Gil as a sounding board, never using names or identifying information, of course. When she spoke out loud, she could sometimes see the client or the issues in a different light.

2

That night, in the middle of the night, more asleep than awake, Grace reached out to touch the security that was her husband. She absently patted at the quilts until her synapses connected to form a thought—*Gil is gone.*

His side of the bed was empty. Grace felt his pillow. It was cold.

She squinted at the yellow light of the digital clock: 2 a.m. Pushing back the covers, she stumbled towards the hall. She peered into the children's empty bedrooms. She checked the bathrooms.

"Gil?" she called in a stage whisper. "Where the hell are you?"

Only after checking the living room and kitchen did she see him sitting outside on the deck. Moonlight outlined his back, but his face was in darkness. Grace saw a flicker of light and realized he was smoking a cigarette.

Grace felt a creeping sense of unease.

Gil hadn't smoked in years.

She softly opened the back door and slipped out onto the deck. Gil startled at the faint sound of her bare feet on the wood. He moved to put out the cigarette.

"What are you doing out here?" she asked.

"Couldn't sleep. Just thinking."

"When did you start smoking again?"

"I'm not smoking again, for God's sake. I'm just having a cigarette."

"What's going on, Gil?"

"Nothing. Really."

"Want to talk about nothing?"

"Drop it, Gracie. I'm just distracted with work."

Grace looked at her husband in the darkness.

"You never could lie worth a damn," she said.

In the silence of the night, from the other side of the river, they listened to the wailing of a siren.

At that moment, on the far side of Kaw Valley, an ambulance burned rubber as it came around the curve. Directly ahead, two police cars sat at angles by the side of the road, their headlights illuminating the overturned car in the culvert below. Danny Rivers flipped off the sirens as he slid the ambulance forward, then backed up efficiently between the two cruisers. He was out in an instant, pulling open the back doors, calling instructions to the other paramedic.

A boy lay twisted in the tall weeds. His head was angled back as if he were trying to see the stars.

He looked about fourteen.

"No seatbelt," said one of the cops. "These friggin' kids think they're immortal."

Danny dropped to his knees, reaching to check for a pulse. His hand jerked back involuntarily.

The body was cold.

"He's long gone," Danny said. "When did this happen?"

"Don't know for sure. A trucker reported a car in the ditch. Can't see it from the road unless you're up high."

"Any ideas what caused it?"

"Maybe a deer. Maybe booze. The coroner can sort it out."

"You need more here, or you want me to take him in?"

"Go ahead." The cop coughed and looked away.

Danny's hands were gentle as he and his partner moved the boy's body onto the stretcher. Returning, he drove slowly, sirens silent.

Later, standing in the entrance to the Emergency Room of Kaw Valley Hospital, Danny shivered in the night air. He looked at his watch: 3:10 a.m.

He liked the intense shifts, the big accidents, even the fires. His adrenaline pumped and the hours flew by. And even a slow shift was better than a fucking office.

If it hadn't been for Mandy, he thought, he still might be stuck with some boring 8-to-5 desk job.

"You're like an ambulance," Mandy had told him after her epiphany. "I was standing on the balcony, and one went by, and all of a sudden I knew." Then she'd placed the brochures for the Vo-Tech program for paramedics down on their oak kitchen table.

Mandy was right. In the midst of chaos, blood, the moans of the injured, Danny felt in control while making split-second decisions.

Danny had two more runs before his shift ended. In-between, he took a detour past their apartment. He parked for a few minutes in the street and looked up at their darkened windows. He imagined his wife asleep under her quilt, his son snoring softly.

It was all he needed to feel safe

3

Four months later, Mandy Rivers was still coming to see Grace. Mandy felt that she was taking apart her life, piece by piece, and reconstructing herself. With each session, she felt minute, incremental shifts in how she saw the world, how she saw herself in her world.

Grace once used the image of a cocoon, telling her that she was growing a new self, that there would come a day when she would emerge and not quite recognize who or what she'd become. But Mandy felt more like a snake that was slowly, painfully, shedding its skin, leaving behind a hollow, brittle shell—a mold of her former self.

"If your mom were still alive, what advice would she give you?" asked Grace.

"Stand by your man. Grab one while you're young and cute and hang on for dear life."

"Do you agree?"

"I never questioned it. But I also resolved to never end up like my mother—bitter and unhappy. I'd make my marriage work no matter what. And I'd never walk out like my Dad did. Too many people get hurt."

"Do you see how that makes what you're thinking so painful?"

"What do you mean?"

"*You're thinking about leaving.*"

If I don't get hit by a car because I'm so fucking distracted, then the guilt is gonna kill me for sure, Mandy thought after the session. She'd seen therapy as a way to *fix* herself, to make herself a better wife. But it felt like the *self* was going in the other direction.

The ambulance was stopped at a red light when Mandy's maroon Honda Civic passed directly in front. Danny started to wave, a reflex, but her car was gone. *What's she doing at this end of town? She never comes downtown in the middle of the day.*

"What'd you do for lunch?" he asked her that night.

"Nothing."

"Stay at the office?"

"No. Grabbed a burger. Did an errand."

"What errand?"

"Just an errand already. I needed tampons. Satisfied?"

But he wasn't.

Mandy surprised even herself with what came out of her mouth in her sessions with Grace.

"I hate my job," Mandy said a few weeks later, sounding as if she'd just made a discovery. "I really do hate going in every day. But I don't know what I'd be good at."

She worked for an insurance agent, answering the phone, filling out forms. Her boss never blatantly harassed her, but he put his hand on her shoulder in a way that made her cringe, and he left soft porn magazines in the office's cramped, unisex bathroom.

"Go with what makes you happy," Grace said. "If you truly like it, you'll do fine."

"I got a new job," Mandy told Grace a month later.

"That's wonderful. Tell me how."

"I came home from work last Friday and my son, Ross, was sitting on the front steps crying, cradling this mangled, half-dead dog. Some damn hit-and-run. So I called around for a vet and ended up with Dr. Emmesch at VetPlus."

"And?"

"There was this notice in her waiting room."

Mandy described seeing the word, "WANTED," in big print, followed by,

"Caring, competent individual to be a medical assistant and office support for veterinarian's office. Must love animals and people. Will train the right person."

"It's like a light bulb went off," Mandy continued. "I'd never thought about it, but I do love animals. And I like most people."

"And you're caring and competent," Grace added, "which was pretty obvious as you'd just gone to all that trouble to bring in a dog that you'd never seen before."

Mandy told Grace how, when Ross had emerged from the inner office, red-eyed yet proud that he'd stuck with the dog, stroking its head until the end, she'd stood up and asked about the position.

"Did you have to fill out an application?" Grace asked.

"No. We just talked right then and there. She asked me a bunch of questions, then asked when I could start," Mandy continued. "It happened in twenty minutes."

"She's lucky to get you." Grace paused, then continued. "So, what does Danny say about all this?"

"I haven't told him," Mandy replied. "I'm waiting for the right time."

"There may not be a right time. Just tell him. And don't apologize."

"I think it has to be today. I already gave my two-week notice."

"Danny? Guess what? I got a new job." Mandy's voice on the phone was breathy.

"What are you talking about?" Danny was at work, at the station.

"A job. At a vet's office. She just called. I wanted to share the good news."

"I thought we didn't make decisions that affect the family without talking them over first."

"Danny, it just happened. Pure luck. I fell into it."

"We can talk about it tonight. I'll swing by when I get a break."

Hanging up the phone, Danny felt a tension in his neck. Something was different with Mandy. When he'd complained about the messy kitchen last week, she hadn't apologized like she usually did. She'd just looked at him, her eyes unreadable, as she loaded dishes into the sink.

Danny remembered when he'd first met Mandy. Then her eyes had been eager. She was trim, with lush auburn hair and a generous smile. She was pretty enough, but not the sort of knockout that Danny had dated in the past. But he'd been burned by one of the truly beautiful ones, a girl whose ambitions extended beyond what he had to offer. She'd left him, the only one who'd dumped Danny before he could dump her.

And so he was bruised when he'd first noticed Mandy. He didn't like being hurt. He never wanted to be left again. And Mandy had looked appealing, cute yet indistinguishable, a girl who would never leave. With her, he'd thought, he'd always be the one who was loved more.

Even so, marriage was no picnic. After Ross came, she'd gotten so focused on the kid. Simple requests, like to pick up his uniform shirts from the dry cleaner, she'd forgotten. She was too tired to cook. They'd argued often. And now there was this job thing.

It just didn't feel right.

Mandy started her new job 10 days later.

VetPlus was different from any job she'd had before. Every day she received compliments: how she was the only one who'd ever kept Ginger quiet for a shot; how she got Petey-bird from his cage without ruffling a feather. She mastered the technical aspects of the position with ease. She could handle bookkeeping and scheduling while calming a frightened kitten.

"You are truly good at this," Dr. Emmesch told her. But the connection, from job performance to feeling competent, was difficult for Mandy to make.

Danny jotted down the numbers on the odometer of Mandy's car. Ever since Mandy had caught him off guard with that job change, he'd been edgy.

He could see that she was happier with the new job, which should have been a good thing.

But there was something else. She usually brought sandwiches or salads to work and ate in the break room. But he'd called a few times at the vet office, around lunchtime, and she'd been out.

Was she seeing someone? Impossible. His Mandy would never do that. But it couldn't hurt to keep track of her mileage. A pattern was emerging. It had something to do with those Tuesdays.

He'd looked through Mandy's Day-Timer when she was asleep. There were the usual scribbles about their son's soccer practice, Cub Scouts, jotted bits of grocery lists. But on Tuesdays there was a small neat notation.

Not every Tuesday, but at least twice a month. "G.M." Right next to 12 noon.

What was "G.M."?

"I feel like I'm cheating," Mandy told Grace at their next session. "He

doesn't know I come here. I've never lied to him before."

"Sure you have," countered Grace. "Every time you kept your mouth shut so you wouldn't rock the marital boat."

"That's different."

"How? You weren't honest about what you really thought or felt. In my book, that's a lie."

"That was to keep the peace, keep the marriage," Mandy replied. "But this?"

"Why don't you tell him about therapy?"

"I'm scared to."

"Is that why you held back your real feelings?"

"It was just easier to go along."

"But it wasn't a lie?"

"No. A lie is covering up something, an act. This was more like a secret. I knew my own feelings, but I figured it was better not to share. That's different."

"A secret is different than a lie?"

"It was just thoughts and feelings."

"Just?"

Mandy started to develop a timeline in her head.

When *had* Danny changed?

Had *it* started when she got pregnant? Mandy wondered.

They'd been married for just two years. She'd been so huge with Ross, her belly button poking strangely up through the soft clinging fabric of her maternity nighties. It'd been a struggle to lift her pregnant body off the bed. She remembered how Danny had looked away, not offering his hand to help. He'd found her swollen feet, the waddling manner with which she walked, unappealing.

"The timing is bad," he'd told her. "My priorities have got to be with school."

"Danny has a very important exam," she'd explained to the other couples when he failed to show up for their third birthing class. "He has to study."

She hadn't really known that, but she'd wanted it to be true. So she'd said it three or four times, and then, at least to her, it was.

At that point, if anyone had asked her, Mandy would have said her marriage was good.

"What do you mean that things changed?" Grace asked. "How did they change?"

"He just started calling me names."

"What kinds of names?"

It was hard for Mandy to say out loud, but she did, often hesitating, sometimes crying, tell Grace what had happened in her marriage.

"You're eating like a pig," Danny had noted casually during dinner one night, as Mandy had reached for a second helping of the pasta.

She'd frozen, as though he'd reached across the table and grabbed her arm.

"I'm pregnant, Danny," she'd said softly. "I get hungry."

"Well, you're gonna be a blimp if you don't stop stuffing your face," he'd replied, sliding off the chair and walking out of the room.

It was hard to remember exactly how or when the teasing started.

"My little pumpkin," he'd say with a grimace. "My watermelon girl." The images would be food, big food, and always accompanied by "my," always in the possessive.

She'd tried to laugh them off.

When Mandy went into labor, Danny was at work, his third day on the new job. Hours later, as Mandy screamed her way through transition, Danny arrived. He wore his blood-stained uniform and looked like he'd come directly from battle to be with the woman he loved. He charmed the nurses, while holding cold, damp compresses to Mandy's forehead. But he didn't look her in the eyes. He didn't share that moment when their son slipped into full, breathing life after one last wrenching push.

They'd named him Ross, for Danny's grandmother's family, an Irish legacy. He was a cheerful baby, except for the hours from 4-to-8 p.m. when he had colic. Then he would scream, hot barking screams of gassy pain. They drove Mandy crazy. She would rock him, walk with him, sing, try to nurse. He would grab on to her swollen breasts, sucking desperately, then wrench away to howl.

Danny did not stick around.

"You're more patient than I am," he'd say on his way out the door.

Mandy knew that it had nothing to do with patience. She'd begged him to stay, but he'd looked through her and walked out.

The name-calling was intermittent, but the first slap didn't come until two years later, when Ross was a toddler. The living room was strewn with toys and baby paraphernalia. As hard as she tried, Mandy could never quite remember what precipitated that first slap, whether anger from banging his toe on a toy left in the middle of the room, or if she'd said something that made Danny lash out.

"I must have done something to start it," Mandy said to Grace. "He wouldn't have changed out of nowhere."

"Maybe it wasn't such a big shift for him," Grace observed. "Perhaps the difference between using demeaning words and a slap is just a choice of tool—words or hand. They both hurt, and they accomplish the same results."

"She wants to find reasons for his behaviors," Grace said to Gil later that night. "She thinks if she can figure out what she did to cause them, or what the triggers are, then she can fix it."

"Don't we all do that?"

Grace didn't reply. He was right, of course. She'd always thought that if she could just put her finger on what started Gil's distancing, his withdrawals, she could make them stop.

"Yeah," she said, "but most of the time it's magical thinking."

Danny came into the apartment almost on tiptoe. It was the middle of the night and he was on his break. He edged down the hall and looked into the bedrooms. Mandy was asleep, curled up, hands tucked beneath her head. Ross lay sprawled, his comforter kicked on to the floor. Danny went in, picked the comforter up and gently covered his son.

Mandy's purse was on the kitchen counter. He flipped through her checkbook. He looked in the compartments of her wallet. Then, mixed in with scraps of paper on the bottom of her purse, Danny found a card. "Grace McDonald" it read. "Individual, Marital and Family Therapy." On the back was scrawled a time, and a date. 12 noon. Next Tuesday.

He'd found "G.M."

Grace believed there was a point when the emotional tide could turn in a marriage, like the invisible moment when rushing ocean tides hesitate, freeze, then begin to ebb. It may not be momentous, nor even memorable, but from that moment on, there is no going back. She was beginning to feel that time had passed for Mandy.

"Is there a particular incident that caused you to lose trust?"

"Yes."

"What happened?"

"Danny and I were arguing on the phone. And he said, 'You're going to regret talking to me like this.' Then he hung up."

"And then?"

"When I went to get Ross from daycare, they told me Danny had already picked him up. But when I got home they weren't there."

"And what did you do?"

"I just sat there, all night, waiting for the phone to ring."

"Did you think of calling the police?"

"Yes, but what could I say? That my son was with his father? Danny knows most of the cops anyway."

"Then what happened?"

"They came home the next day. It was a Saturday. Danny had flowers and bagels. He pretended like nothing was wrong. He said he just figured from the way I acted and sounded on the phone that I needed a break from him and Ross. He said, 'Didn't you see the note? I left you a note.'"

"But?"

"There was no note. I never found a note."

"Where did they go?"

"I don't know. He never told me. When I asked, he said 'What difference does it make?'"

"And what did that teach you?"

"That Danny could really hurt me, really scare me. That I better not cross him or I might end up paying in ways I never imagined."

"Have you told him how you feel?"

"I tried once, to explain how scared I'd been. He just said, 'Too bad you couldn't enjoy your time off.' And he laughed."

Grace wanted Danny Rivers to come in. If she could get him to understand how his actions hurt his wife, then maybe there was a chance. But every time she suggested it, Mandy put her off.

"I want a divorce," Mandy announced one day. "But just saying it makes me feel like a criminal."

"So, tell him," Grace answered. "See if it makes a difference."

"That's what I'm afraid of. That he'll change for a little while. But it won't be for real, and then I'll be a year older and feel weak," said Mandy. "Now I feel strong enough that maybe I can go through with this."

"Then how is what you're doing a crime?"

"Because it's premeditated," Mandy said. "Premeditated divorce. I feel that I owe him one last chance, but I also feel that he has forfeited that chance. I shouldn't have to walk out to get his attention."

"It sounds like you're afraid to get his attention."

"I am. I'm afraid of what I once wanted more than anything," Mandy said. "Now I feel anxious just hearing his footstep. I just want out."

With Grace's guidance, Mandy planned her leave-taking. She made lists of their belongings, taking pictures of the rooms of their house to document. When she bought food, she would write the check for ten dollars over the amount and put the change in a secret savings. With each and every act, she felt a wave of guilt, like nausea in its intensity. But she also felt her resolve harden.

With Danny, Mandy was accommodating, making no waves, no demands. If Danny didn't come home for dinner, she left a plate of food, covered with plastic wrap, next to the microwave. She went to work, cleaned and cooked and supervised Ross's homework. On the surface, their relationship appeared untroubled.

"Hey, Mandy, let's go to Kansas City on Sunday afternoon and look at open houses," Danny said. He was at the kitchen table, reading the morning paper as Mandy washed up the breakfast dishes.

"Where did that come from?"

"Just been thinking. We have some savings and a tax return coming soon. And I heard they're recruiting paramedics over there, with bonuses for signing on. I'm getting itchy for a change of scene."

"What about my job?"

"You can always get another job. Or I might make enough that we could afford for you to stay home."

"Danny, I'd go nuts staying home all day with nothing to do. Ross is in school now."

"We could take care of that. Ross isn't too old for a baby sister or brother, you know. You've always wanted another kid."

"I can't pretend much longer," Mandy told Grace at their next session. "I need to get out or I'll be stuck, like one of those animals caught in quicksand. I'll struggle to free myself, and then choke and die."

"Then it's time to leave."

Mandy put a deposit down on a small apartment close enough that Ross could walk to school. She went to an attorney. She had to hold her right hand steady with her left in order to sign the papers without shaking, but she signed them.

She arranged for Ross to spend the night at a friend's house.

And then she told Danny.

"I want a divorce," she said. "The papers will be filed tomorrow."

She stumbled through her catalogue of reasons, of why she needed to not be married to him anymore, of how they were hurting each other, hurting Ross.

Danny did not respond. She waited for his rage. At that moment she would have welcomed it to confirm the rightness of her decision. She needed him to call her names, to feel the burning sting of his open hand on her face. She needed him to help her leave without regret, without second guesses.

Danny put his head in his hands and cried.

4

"Remind me again why we decided to have a big party?" Gil grunted, pushing the wheelbarrow over a small rise.

"Because we just love to entertain," Grace replied. She leaned against a tree, rake in hand, waiting for him to dump the mulch so she could spread it. "We owe a lot of people. It's part of the social construct. Pay-back time. And it happens to be our 27th anniversary."

"We never had an anniversary party before. The 25th would have been more appropriate. 27th sounds so . . ."

"Ordinary. Boring. All the more reason for a party."

"And our guests will be disappointed if there's no mulch?"

"It's an outdoor party. I've rented a tent, for God's sake."

"A tent that would make Barnum and Bailey proud," Gil added.

"Okay, so it's big. But people will be all over the yard and I want the garden to look nice. Just haul. . . "

"And both the kids are coming home?"

"Hope so. Alex may back out. Molly wouldn't miss it."

"How'd we get such different kids from the same genetic material?"

"Haven't I ever mentioned the mailman? He had this cute ass and this smile that could melt. . ."

Grace ducked as a handful of wet leaves flew past.

It hadn't always been this easy between them. For years, when the kids were young, they'd been consumed by family duties: homework, Scout meetings, piano lessons, sports. She and Gil had been chronically rushed and irritable. Arguments flared easily. There'd been no time for quiet chats, no time to garden. No time.

But that was long past.

Grace had never really fantasized about mid-life. She wondered if anyone did. But, like an unexpected gift, there was just enough time in each day to appreciate the sky, the trees, the feel of a breeze. The seasons felt intense to her, uniquely gratifying. Yes, sometimes she missed her kids, but she luxuriated in the absence of demands.

The party was a success. Long tables rimmed the tent, each covered with a yellow sheet for a tablecloth. Grace had, for the first time since her wedding, hired a caterer and food appeared as if by magic. Gil set up a well-stocked bar on the deck.

Molly had showed up a day ahead of schedule with two girlfriends from college in tow. Alex called to say he wouldn't be able to make it.

The big surprise of the day was the dance floor.

A truck pulled up at noon and two men got out. Grace went to see what they wanted.

"Where do you want the floor?" they asked.

"What?" Grace asked.

"You ordered a dance floor. Indoor-outdoor. 12 by 16."

"What are you talking about?"

Gil came up behind her.

"In the tent, guys. We may need to move a few tables."

Grace's jaw dropped. She looked at Gil.

"Can't have a party, especially an anniversary party, without a few dances," he said, moving his arms as if to sweep her into a cha-cha.

"Where did you get it?"

"These wedding rental places have everything. You're lucky I didn't fall for the seven-foot Grecian fountain."

People started coming at 4 p.m. and stayed until the moon was high. They ate, drank, and danced.

Gil had put together an assortment of music, from polkas to waltzes to oldies-but-goodies, and the boom-box boomed. People who hadn't danced in years found themselves laughing and crying. Some friends had brought their instruments, and by 10 that night, there was a bass, guitar, fiddle, and a snare drum in sync.

But Grace's favorite memory was a private one. Rubbing her hair with a towel as she walked naked from the shower, she saw the box sitting in the middle of their bed. It was wrapped in silver foil.

She unwrapped it. Inside was a blue vase, a Blenko, solid yet graceful, with a note.

"Every Friday, for the rest of your life, this vase will have fresh flowers. Maybe only a few stems, but forever. Always. Love, Gil."

5

In the weeks after Mandy moved out, Danny's nightmare returned. It had plagued him in his early 20's but abated after he met Mandy. He was a child. It was dark. He was crouching, arms wrapped around his knees. Hiding. He could feel his heart beating. He was in a closet, crowded with clothing and boxes. He was so small he felt he might be invisible.

A door slammed on the floor below. He heard voices. Raised. Angry. He couldn't quite make out the words.

"Where have you. . ."

I'm not taking this crap from you anymore. . ."

"If you think you can just. . ."

Then a crash. A splintering sound. The voices again.

"Please, don't. . ."

"That'll teach. . ."

A pounding. A thud of fist on flesh.

Silence. Another slammed door. And then the wailing started far below. A hopeless, unremitting sound of anguish. Like a baby who knows it will never be warm.

"Stop it," Danny screamed, choking into the blanket that covered his mouth. But he couldn't stop it. He couldn't move from the closet. Even when he had to go so bad he peed through his pajamas and onto the cold tile floor, he couldn't move.

Danny would jerk awake, trembling, in a cold sweat, his body on the brink of urinating. Then he would stumble to the bathroom.

The Rivers' divorce hearing was scheduled for July.

The interim three months were awful. Danny called Mandy at work or left messages on her answering machine at home almost daily. When it was his time with Ross, he would come early, or late, or not at all.

"We need to talk," he'd say, in front of Ross.

Mandy did anything he wanted, except come back. She

accommodated his midnight urges to tell her what she'd done wrong in the marriage. She declined to argue when he contended that the furniture was his because he'd bought it, all the credit cards being in his name. She listened as he raged at her for destroying their family.

Mandy went to garage sales on Saturday mornings. Nothing matched, but she bought a sofa, chairs, and table. She found discounted gallons of paint and spent an entire weekend making the living room walls soft blue, her bedroom a buttery yellow. She found a sheet in a wild pacific print to cover the $25 brown tweed sofa.

She stopped by the side of the gravel roads that twisted through the farms outside of town and cut wildflowers. She filled glass jars with purple coneflowers and yellow coreopsis, wild orange lilies and lavender.

There were daily hang-ups on her answering machine. Sometimes, late at night, she sensed Danny's presence. It was as if she could feel his eyes probing through the concrete and drywall.

She slept with a baseball bat under her sheets, and would awaken sometimes at night to find she was curled around it, fetal position, holding tightly. She would awaken in a sweat, and have to calm herself, taking in long, slow breaths through her nose, exhaling through her mouth. She smelled the amorphous stench of desperation hanging in the air, but she thought it all came from her, that she owned it all.

The hearing was on a hot, drizzling July morning. Mandy sat next to Mr. Robinson, her lawyer, and Danny next to his, Mr. Grimes.

Danny and Mandy had each dressed for this ritual of dissolution. He wore a gray suit, a checked tie. She'd given him that tie for their fourth anniversary, with a joking note about how she'd "never untie the knot."

Mandy wore a long, slender skirt, and a coral scoop neck top. She'd discovered them at the garage sale of an art professor with eccentric tastes and an eye for color who was clearing out her closet. In an impulse of transformation, she'd bought twenty-two items, at a dollar each, and then returned home and cleaned out her own closet.

In the courtroom, feeling Danny's scrutiny, it was all she could do not to cringe. She felt herself floating, detached, distracted by an overlay of voices.

The judge was talking, and Mandy forced herself to pay attention.

"So, sir, you are contending that your wife is not making this decision of her own free will, that she has been brainwashed?"

The judge was not addressing Danny's attorney, who had been speaking, but Danny. The words didn't make sense to Mandy, because they were so unexpected.

This was to be a *run-of-the-mill* divorce.

The property was basically settled and the judge would make whatever final decisions remained. Joint legal custody was the assumption in Kansas. Ross would live with her, spending Wednesday nights and alternate weekends with his Dad.

"Yes, sir, I am," replied Danny to the judge. "We had our troubles, just like any couple, but what is happening here isn't right. She was influenced to go behind my back, to plan all of this out so there was no hope of reconciliation or change. I'm willing to do whatever it takes to make this marriage work, if she'll just give me a chance. But she can't."

"What do you mean by 'can't,' Mr. Rivers?" asked the judge.

"She's so wrapped up with this therapist person, in doing whatever she tells her to do, she can't make a free choice. She went in secret for months. She's being manipulated."

Danny's voice was pleading. Mandy had no idea at that moment if he truly believed what he was saying, or if this was just one more game.

"Objection, Your Honor." Her attorney's tone was indignant. "This is irrelevant nonsense, with no basis in fact. Mrs. Rivers is hardly incompetent."

"Overruled, Mr. Robinson. I will hear what I think needs to be heard. I do not want to see this matter again in my courtroom, certainly not through any future complaints against this therapist. I would rather resolve it now."

The judge consulted his calendar.

"A case scheduled to be heard next Tuesday at 9 a.m. has just been dismissed. We will adjourn until then, at which time I want the therapist present."

Mandy's mind struggled to focus. She was not going to get divorced today. All this time she'd focused on this day, this hour. She didn't have the strength to keep it up, even for another week.

A plaintive wail began deep in her chest and rose up her throat. It emerged as a keening, a sound so primitive, so out-of-place in the contemporary courtroom that it caused everyone to abruptly turn and stare. A part of her, the part that watched from the outside, knew that this was not the sort of behavior that would help her case. But she could not stop. She held two hands to her mouth, as if smothering herself, and the sound diminished to low, choking moans.

The judge threw one final, assessing look in her direction as he walked to his chambers.

The week was a blur. Grace McDonald was subpoenaed. Mandy went to work every day at VetPlus, tending to the sick, giving booster shots and heartworm pills to the healthy. But she would walk to the storage room for a certain medication, then stand in confused bewilderment staring at the shelves. She was told by the other staff, especially Dr. Emmesch, to go home, to take time off. But Ross was at Scout camp for the week, and being alone at home made her feel vulnerable. She was safer at VetPlus, surrounded by other people. She went home only to sleep.

Danny inserted the key into the car lock and softly opened the door. Even so, it made a noise in the quiet of the night. He sat down sideways on the seat, his legs still on the ground. He'd made a copy of Mandy's car key before she'd moved out.

He looked in the glove compartment. Then he sorted through the catalogues and papers left on the floor. *She really is messy,* he thought. He'd brought a flashlight, but the moon was strong enough.

Danny had also come by during the day, while Mandy was at work, to check the mail. A few times there had been letters that looked personal. He'd taken them to steam open.

"So sorry to hear about your separation," one girlfriend had written. "Can't say I'm surprised. Just want you to know I'm here for you."

There were more like that. He felt hurt that Mandy had talked to people about their private business. He tore the letters up.

"State your name," the court reporter said.

"Grace McDonald."

"Do you swear to tell the whole truth and nothing but the truth, so help you God?"

"I do." Grace's voice was tight with an unanticipated anxiety.

"Please be seated."

Mandy's attorney, Robinson, went first. There were the usual requests for clinical expertise and experience. Grace related her years as a therapist, academic degrees, post-graduate training at the Menninger Clinic. She duly noted her list of publications and university teaching experience. She felt her composure return.

"Is there anything that would cause you to question Ms. Rivers's ability in making this decision to separate and divorce?" he asked.

"No," she replied. "Ms. Rivers is an intelligent, articulate individual, who has arrived at this decision after much painful soul-searching. She spent months struggling to determine if her marriage was workable."

"And what has your contribution been to this process, Ms. McDonald? Have you attempted to persuade or coerce Ms. Rivers in this decision?"

"No, I have not attempted any such thing. My role was to assist Ms. Rivers, as I would any client, to determine her own values and needs, and to act accordingly."

"So, this divorce action was not initiated or coached in any way by you?"

"No, it was not."

"No further questions, Your Honor."

Danny's attorney approached the witness stand.

"Ms. McDonald, do you generally see couples together when there is a marital issue?" he began.

"Yes, I do, if the couple seeks counseling. But if one partner comes in, it is up to that partner to decide if they want their spouse involved."

"Do you encourage spousal involvement? Or do you just coach people in how to dump their husbands?"

Robinson was out of his chair, "Objection."

"Sustained," said the judge. "Mr. Grimes, restrain yourself in this cross examination, please."

"I'll rephrase the question, Your Honor."

He turned to Grace.

"When do you bring in the other spouse, Ms. McDonald? Under what circumstances?"

"I encourage spousal involvement if I think it would be useful and if the client desires to work on the relationship. I cannot demand such involvement, from my client or the other party. It would be an ethical violation to ever make contact without the express, written permission of my client."

"Why exactly did you choose not to encourage spousal involvement in this case?"

Grace felt trapped. Mandy had asked her to not say anything that could make Danny angry. But his abuse was the very reason that Grace hadn't pushed harder. And she was under oath. Did this idiot lawyer know what he was asking?

"I do not encourage spousal involvement when the client is afraid of the spouse in question."

"Are you saying that Ms. Rivers told you that her husband had been abusive?"

"Yes"

"Was this physical or merely verbal?"

"Merely?" Grace's voice was tight.

"Answer the question, please."

"Primarily verbal, some physical."

"Have you ever worked with other couples where abuse was present?

"Of course I have."

"And were some of these marriages salvaged? Were the spouses capable of change?"

"In some, yes."

"But you determined that Mr. Rivers was incapable of change?"

"I respected the stated wishes of Ms. Rivers," Grace replied.

"Did you ever present Ms. Rivers with data on the detrimental impact of divorce on children, or attempt to persuade her to work on her marriage rather than walking away?"

"I don't recall."

"Isn't it your professional responsibility to share research data with your clients?"

Grimes had walked back to his table as he spoke. He turned now, holding a sheaf of papers, and returned to stand inches from the box.

"Do you recognize this, Ms. McDonald?"

Grace saw that it was an article she'd written, several years earlier.

"It is a paper that I wrote on marital therapy."

"Indeed. You state here, and I quote, 'Abuse is a circular relationship. Simply removing the abused spouse from the relationship is not a solution. In particular, when children are involved, divorce does not mean an end to the relationship, as well as being inherently damaging to the children. Rather than relying on a one-sided, one-dimensional perspective, it is critical to meet with both parties, even if separately, to adequately assess the circumstances and dynamics of the relationship. All relationships where abuse is reported will initially appear hopeless, and the clinician cannot determine options without an evaluation that includes the allegedly abusive spouse.' "

"Did you write this, Ms. McDonald?"

"Yes, I did."

"But you went ahead meeting with Ms. Rivers for month after month, never meeting Mr. Rivers to assess the dynamics, the truth of the relationship, the. . ."

He was cut off by an "Objection" from Robinson.

"Sustained. Leave *truth* out of it, Mr. Grimes," said the judge.

"Let me put it another way. Ms. McDonald, were you aware of your client's intent to divorce?" he asked.

"Of course."

"And did you guide her to methodically inventory belongings, to take pictures to verify possessions? Did you tell her to rent an apartment even before she told her husband that she wished a divorce?"

"I did encourage her to take measures, uncomfortable as they were, to insure some degree of protection."

"Did Ms. Rivers come to you with a plan or did you provide her a plan?"

"That is a difficult question." Grace was truly reflective now, caught in trying to explain what happened behind the closed doors of therapy. "It was a mutual process. Ms. Rivers would be struggling with how to proceed and we would brainstorm options. I'm sure that at some point I was offering suggestions, but I didn't have a plan."

"So you offered suggestions on how to leave her marriage." His voice was heavy with sarcasm. "With no consideration that Mr. Rivers was himself an abused child, a man trying to be a good father and husband despite his own upbringing."

"I was doing. . ."

But he cut her off, mid-sentence.

"That is all, Ms. McDonald."

She watched his back move to the table. *Asshole,* she thought.

Grace stood up, stepped down from the box, and walked out of the courtroom. Out of the corner of one eye she saw Danny Rivers hunched over as his attorney whispered in his ear. But, throughout the proceedings, she'd never looked him in the eye. She never really saw him.

The judge concluded that there was no justification to believe that Ms. Rivers was not fully competent in making this decision, and that he would proceed.

The divorce was granted about an hour later, after the lawyers haggled over the washing machine and outstanding bills. Mandy told her lawyer in a crisp whisper to just give Danny the damn washer since another fifteen minutes of attorney time cost more than the stuff they were bickering about.

"In the matter of Ms. Amanda Rivers vs. Mr. Daniel Rivers, I hereby grant a divorce. . . " The judge's voice was sonorous, rehearsed, even mechanical.

He does this every damn day, thought Mandy about the judge. These words are part of his daily routine.

Mandy found the realization comforting. She was not the only one. Tomorrow and the next day there would be more couples standing here, their pain sinking into the gray carpet of the courtroom floor, dreams dissolving at their feet.

Then she rose quickly, patted her attorney on the arm in a gesture of distracted gratitude, and walked out of the courtroom. She did not look toward Danny, but she felt his eyes following her.

Later that evening, Mandy sat sipping iced tea on the steps that led to her second-floor apartment.

A car pulled up in front. Dr. Emmesch stepped out. Then another car pulled up, with two friends from church. Then a third. The women walked toward her, their arms filled with bags.

"We're here for consolation," announced Dr. Emmesch.

"Bullshit," interjected a friend from church. "We're here to party down."

They piled up into the apartment, filling bowls with chips and salsa, uncorking wine and making margaritas. A platter was heaped with her favorite walnut brownies, rich and decadent.

During that evening, wrapped in the arms of friendship, listening to the women tell stories of their own lost loves, Mandy had her first real glimpse of what her life could be like.

She could be happy. She could be safe. She could be herself.

"He was right in some ways," Grace told her husband early that evening as they sat discussing their respective days.

"Who was right?" Gil asked.

"The husband. In court today, I had to explain that a grown woman was competent to make up her own mind about leaving her marriage."

"And was she?"

"Quite. But the bottom line is that she might never have had the guts without the therapy. She'd have spent years rationalizing and minimizing as the crap escalated. She might have left on her own, but it would have been impulsive, unplanned. And then he'd have begged, said he'd change, and she'd have gone back. They could have done that dance for years."

"So therapy helped her leave sooner?"

"Therapy helped her become a person who could make up her own mind, then act on her convictions."

"Well, you never have had too many problems in that area."

"Are you being a smart-ass with me, Gil?"

"Hell, no. I like women who make up their own minds and can act on their convictions. Like tonight, for example—I simply cannot make up my mind between a Greek salad or one of those truly greasy burgers with a side of onion rings in that back room off the pool hall. So, I could really use a woman who had a conviction one way or the other."

Later that evening, brushing her teeth, Grace smiled. They'd ended up with the burgers at the pool hall, and a couple of cold Coronas. And now, if she knew her Gil, he was putting on a CD and sliding into bed. He'd offer to scratch her back or rub her feet, and then...

6

For Mandy, the time after her divorce was unexpectedly satisfying. She relished the freedom of not having to answer to anyone. It seemed to her that much of her energy for the years of her marriage had gone into pacifying and compromising. Her moods and feelings had been connected—an emotional umbilical cord—to Danny. If he had a good day, then she had a good day. If he was in a lousy, critical mood, then...

Two months after the divorce, Mandy stopped therapy. Money was tight, her insurance wasn't nearly as good as what she'd had when married, and she felt ready to try her wings. Grace said that her door was always open.

There were, as she'd expected, conflicts with Danny over Ross. Scheduled to pick up Ross, Danny would often be hours late, leaving them to sit and wait. There was always a reason, often dramatic, usually work-related. But the result was that Mandy could never depend on Danny, could not make her own plans.

About four months after the divorce, Danny showed up several hours late and dragged a sleeping Ross from his bed. It was, after all, *his* night. Danny's excuse was an accident next county over—mangled children, no car seats. Tragic, just tragic.

After he left, Mandy found herself sitting on the couch, thinking. She got the phone and placed it in front of her on the couch. She called every emergency room in the three surrounding counties. There'd been no big accidents. No mangled children.

It was at that moment that Mandy realized she had to leave Kaw Valley if she wanted her own life. She loved her job and her friends. She was scared of leaving. But she couldn't stay here with Danny. Even divorced, she was living with his lies, still afraid to confront him. Almost daily, she would answer the ringing phone to hear silence, and then a click. She still woke in the night, cold fear climbing her throat. She'd look through her blinds. Usually the street was empty. But, sometimes, he was there, sitting in his car in the dark.

Mandy remembered once visiting a ranch on a field trip with Ross's class. There had been a large area ringed by a single wire electric fence. The wire was almost invisible in the glinting sunlight. She'd wondered out loud how the cows saw it when she barely could, and how they knew to stay clear.

"Oh, they get a few shocks, and then they don't need to see it," answered the rancher. "They sense it's there and they just stay clear."

Mandy felt she had such a fence, that she'd been shocked. And now, even if it was invisible, she could sense the parameters. She could have some small freedoms, but within boundaries. The possibility of a relationship, even a friendship, with another man was outside that fence, at least as long as Danny was watching. Mandy did not know if she wanted another relationship, but she wanted to feel free enough to choose.

Mandy began to plan another escape.

She called "800" numbers in magazine tourist ads. She called the Chamber of Commerce of dozens of towns and cities. At night, after Ross was asleep, she would spread maps out on the bed and ponder where she could go, what special place would call to her.

She waited for a sign from God.

"Did I ever mention that my brother-in-law is a vet in Colorado?" Dr. Emmesch asked as Mandy assisted her during a routine surgery one afternoon.

"No, you haven't," answered Mandy.

"It's a family joke. I became a vet, and my sister married a vet, so we both get to live vet schedules and have abandoned litters in boxes in the kitchen." Dr. Emmesch paused. "Ever been to Gunnison, Mandy?"

"No, never."

"Want to come along for Easter with me? I'm driving out Wednesday, back the next Tuesday. I'd enjoy the company."

Mandy calculated the weekends.

"I have Ross then," she concluded aloud.

"Bring him along. How much school work can a little kid miss in a few days?"

Mandy looked over the operating table at her employer, the gentle, terrifically competent woman who had given her a job, who was unwavering in her support.

"I'd like that, Dr. Emmesch."

"Call me Emily."

Mandy felt herself blush. This was a wall coming down, long overdue.

"Sure, Emily. It sounds great."

That Easter week was magical for Mandy. They drove out across the plains, through Pueblo, and into the mountains. The road followed the South Arkansas River, climbing higher and higher. They crossed the Continental Divide at Monarch Pass, and Mandy and Ross posed in front of the sign as Emily took their photo. It was early April, the snow still deep in the mountains and canyons. They wore down vests and gloves. Mandy refused to wear a hat, enjoying the feel of cold air moving through her hair. The higher they rose through the mountains, the better she felt.

Gunnison was a fine place. It had a tourist trade, but wasn't so cutesy that the natives couldn't feel at home. There was a college, an airport. Sara, Emily's sister, and her husband, Will Woodland, welcomed them all with open arms. Their sons, Tony and Mike, took Ross out to explore.

Will dealt with farm animals as well as pets. On Saturday, he asked Mandy if she'd like to join him on rounds of some ranches where he had to make calls.

It was a different world from the neat, tidy exam rooms of VetPlus. Mandy loved it. She borrowed barn boots from Sara, and plowed through the ice-caked mud like a pro. It felt good to use her muscles, to hang onto a squalling calf as Will tried to check a festering sore near its eye.

There was one ranch where they had to put down an old, wheezing horse. He was 29 and had been a part of the family for all of his life. But now he was suffering, and Will felt it unlikely he would recover. The family gathered to say goodbye to the animal lying on the floor of its stall. Mandy held the animal's head, stroked the soft spot behind its ear, and crooned as Will administered the shot. Within a few minutes he stopped breathing. Mandy felt tears on her face.

"Would you like to work for me, Mandy?" she heard Will ask.

Mandy looked up, astonished.

"What do you mean?" she asked.

"I need another assistant, full-time, to help in the clinic and on rounds."

"But I have a job, with Emily and VetPlus," she said.

"Emily mentioned you might be looking to relocate, and that I should try you out. She says you're a damn good person with animals and people both. I can see that she's right."

Then he smiled.

"I pay better than Emily, too."

That night, after dinner, Mandy went to sit by Emily in the living room. The furniture was southwestern, facing a large glass window that looked to the mountains.

"How did you know?" Mandy asked.

"Because you always seem to have a brochure from one place or another," replied Emily. "And as much as I'll miss you, you need to get away."

Mandy felt the caring in Emily's voice as a blessing.

"How much time do I have to think about it?" she asked Will the next morning.

"Take a few weeks. Nothing urgent. I'm looking for a long-term commitment."

Three months later, about one year after her divorce, Mandy arrived in Gunnison. Danny had been difficult when she first proposed moving, raging that he would never agree for Ross to go, that he would take her to court. But he'd come around. Mandy had tried an experiment, one that caused her heart to twist with fear.

"Look, maybe you're right, maybe a boy should be with his father," she'd said. "Maybe Ross should stay. But if he does, if you want him badly enough, you'll have to get another job. He's too young to be left alone. You can't call and say that you'll be home in three hours. You can't be gone at night."

"You would leave Ross?" asked Danny incredulously.

"He'd be with his Dad, not alone on the street. I'm trying to be reasonable here."

That had taken the wind out of Danny. He did not really want the day-to-day responsibilities of full-time parenting: supervising homework, preparing meals, consistent bedtimes, doctor visits and accountability.

What he'd wanted was to make Mandy stay where he could keep an eye on her.

And he did not want to change his job, to lose the rush of flying along the highway late at night, sirens wailing. He would wither up and die without his adrenaline pump.

So, he'd let them go, reluctantly. He'd have Ross half the summer and other vacations. He felt an emptiness growing inside him, and he did not see how to fill it up.

7

"When do you think you'll have the next edit finished?" Gil said into the phone. He doodled as he listened to the reply.

"Good. That will work. If it can be in my hands by December, I'll have it back to you by late January." He kept doodling. "I think you're moving in the right direction. Look forward to seeing it."

He put down the phone and reached for his jacket. His stomach was rumbling. Time for lunch.

It was a perfect autumn day—bright sun, crisp air. He'd walk the four blocks to the Paradise Grill.

Gil was tall, with brown hair graying fast, a clipped beard more silver than not. His smile was engaging.

He was an editor at a small press that published mostly academic and educational books. In his earlier days, he'd fantasized about being a great journalist, of breaking stories with international repercussions. But small-town journalism was not The Washington Post, and he'd quickly tired of working nights and making deadlines. He'd been overly meticulous, reworking stories in his head after they'd already been published.

The pace of book publishing suited him much better. Projects took months. There was time for reflection. He had a bookcase behind his desk, with signed first editions of every book he'd edited. It gave him a sense of worth to run his hands along all the books he'd helped into print. Gil liked the permanence of books, the way they smelled and felt. Newspapers were inherently transient, and they got his hands dirty.

Still, a disappointment persisted. His own aspirations were now funneled into making the dreams of others come true. He'd tried writing himself but was embarrassed by the results. He liked writing lyrics, but when he'd tried to talk to Grace, she'd laughed.

"No offense, but I think you're about 25 years too late. You missed that boat, buddy."

He hadn't brought it up again with Grace, but he'd found himself wanting to share with someone who didn't seem to have all the answers.

In the fall after Mandy moved to Gunnison, Grace started writing a column for the local newspaper. She'd done free-lance pieces for years, but *Family Matters* ran weekly. It amazed Gil that Grace could plunge ahead unencumbered by the self-criticism and anxiety that plagued his efforts.

It was early morning, after a long night shift. Danny sat in a local cafe eating breakfast. For a man who hated routine, this habit was one he seldom missed. He had a ritual: morning paper, the same booth in the corner, greeting the regulars, sometimes entertaining them with grisly details of the night shift.

Danny read the column before he noted the author's name.

"Fucking bitch is in the paper," he muttered audibly.

He'd never forgotten Grace McDonald. She was responsible for Mandy seeking a divorce. On her own, Mandy would never have left him.

Since the divorce, Danny had glossed over the negatives of his marriage. Each separate angry word or act had grown smaller and smaller, fading into insignificance. Instead he remembered the good times: swimming at the lake, having a picnic, laughing together. Danny saw himself with Mandy and Ross, walking through a gently falling snow, each holding one of Ross's hands, swinging him up at every third step.

He remembered with an aching sense of loss, scenes that had never happened.

Danny began to read Grace McDonald's column every Tuesday morning. She rarely failed to piss him off. She had so many damn opinions. Talking down to people like she knew it all.

In one column she described her home, and what she loved about it. Half way through the description, Danny knew that he'd seen this house, across town, by the river. There couldn't be too many Victorians with seven different shades of pastel.

"Walking through the door of my *Painted Lady*," she wrote, "I feel I'm home. It isn't just the physical space, but the sense of belonging. The house would be an empty shell without my partner, and it seems hard to imagine. . ."

Danny's eyes drifted from the page. He knew about empty shells. He felt a righteous urge to punish Grace McDonald.

Danny could not have said exactly how he got started watching Grace. After reading the column, he'd driven past her house a few times. Then, one morning, a car was pulling out of the driveway just as he turned the corner, and without conscious thought, he followed it.

In just a few weeks he'd learned the basics of her schedule: home, office, grocery store, some nights eating out. Rather boring, really.

With Mandy, he'd known what he was watching for—a man, a lie, her distress at knowing she was watched. He'd even felt in some sense he was protecting her. But with Grace McDonald, he was looking for something he could not name.

There was one night when Danny almost let go. It was a Friday, a warm, autumn evening, and he was watching the McDonald house. For just a moment, he saw himself as he was: a grown man hiding in the woods, peering through binoculars. He grimaced and then snorted, softly, almost laughing at himself, breaking the hold of the obsession. For that one moment, he understood that his behavior was irrational. He started to get up.

Then, out of the corner of his eye, he saw the back door open and Grace emerged. Her husband was behind her, and three other couples. They carried trays of drinks and food. They were talking and laughing. The men walked over to a grassy area, a long stretch cut smooth and close. One man carried a bag, and he turned it over and spilled red and green colored balls onto the lawn. They began to play a game, rolling one ball down the length of the grass, then another. Danny had seen this game, in a movie, but had never played it. He couldn't remember what it was called. The men hooted with every toss, and the women stopped talking long enough to cheer particular throws.

The moment froze in Danny's mind, a snapshot of all—marriage, home, friends—he did not have.

Danny felt his heart get tight and ache with his loss.

She should understand what she's done, he thought. *The bitch should pay.*

It was then that he began stalking for real.

On the first Thursday of the month, Grace varied her routine. At 9 a.m. she met her friend, Katrina, for breakfast. Their friendship had survived decades of shared holiday dinners and domestic dramas. They could gossip with abandon, without guilt or consequences.

Danny watched the two women talking and laughing through the window of the cafe. He was parked across the street.

Grace left the cafe with her friend, and they stood talking before hugging goodbye. Grace's Toyota pulled out of the lot and started down Kansas Avenue. She turned on 9th and headed across town.

But then she made an abrupt left. He pulled over, watching in his rearview mirror as she got out of her car and entered the building. It was the Kaw Valley Regional Center for Blood and Plasma.

What is she doing now, Danny wondered. He was tired of following at a distance. He wanted the rush of taking a risk. After all, he had an excuse if she saw him. He was an E.M.T. He could be there with a business question. He could be there to donate.

Danny walked through the double glass doors into a small lobby area. Through an open doorway he could see a row of reclining chairs. There were two people on the chairs, hooked up to bags that were slowly filling with blood.

He didn't hear the footsteps until it was too late. As he whirled around on his right heel, he saw the swinging door of the women's bathroom. And then he was looking right into Grace McDonald's eyes.

She glanced at him with a perfunctory smile.

"Excuse me," she chirped. "Time to get poked."

And she walked on past.

He stood, frozen, yet with clammy palms. He'd been twenty-four inches from Grace McDonald's face and there hadn't been the slightest glint of recognition in those grey-blue eyes.

Turns my life to shit, he thought, *and she doesn't even know me.* He couldn't figure it. The courtroom scene was seared into his memory. It played over and over in his head. Her condescension, like his life could just be thrown away. How she'd smoothly denied twisting Mandy's mind. How she'd taken no responsibility for the pain she caused.

And she didn't even recognize him. He was nothing to her. Nothing. A roaring sound filled his ears.

Danny spent weeks weighing the possibilities. He wanted Grace to suffer. To lose what she loved most and be blamed, just like he had. But more than that, he wanted to make sure that Grace McDonald never hurt other couples like she'd hurt him and Mandy. She'd manipulated Mandy, and he had to make sure that no one ever trusted Grace McDonald again.

But how?

Then one evening, watching Grace from the woods, Danny Rivers saw the future with vivid clarity.

Grace was relaxing in her rocker, almost invisible in the darkening light. Her husband came out and sat next to her. Through the binoculars, Danny saw her face as she looked over at her husband, her smile as she reached for his hand. And, at that precise moment of knowing, Danny wondered how it was that he had ever not known.

Danny returned to the Blood Bank the following week and inquired about part-time positions. With his training as a paramedic, he easily met the criteria for phlebotomist.

"I work ambulance night shift Sunday-Monday-Tuesday, and then one flex night, so I'd prefer Thursdays, some Fridays or Saturdays, and could do blood drives whenever they fit in," he told the administrator in his interview. He provided a list of references.

Danny started a training period with the Blood Bank just days later. He was deferential, amiable, and cooperative. Within hours, he was accepted as a new member of the team. He missed following Grace, but he knew he had to be patient, to work for a few months before moving ahead, to become a trusted and invisible part of the routine.

He was determined to find a crack in what at first appeared to be an impenetrable wall of safety procedures. When a donor first entered, they were issued a donor card. Every donation had unique barcodes, like stock at the grocery. The barcode stickers were attached to every piece of tubing and equipment used for a particular *stick*. One of the matching barcoded stickers was attached to their donor card for that day.

Safety procedures were multilayered, insuring that no blood could escape scrutiny. With every donation, blood was tested for HIV, hepatitis B and C, HTLV-1, syphilis, and more if the blood were intended for a baby. The procedures were meticulously designed to prevent contamination of the blood supply. Even *bad sticks*—when a vein was collapsing or not pumping adequately—were counted. The phlebotomist had to go to the front desk and request a new set of barcodes and enter the old barcode as a failed donation. The small amounts of blood in the pint bags and tubing were placed on a *discard shelf* in the back room, taken daily to the nearest hospital for incineration.

Danny couldn't tell if they were tallied by some supervisor, a computer reading of barcoded numbers matched against the actual materials. He assumed so.

For his plan to work, he needed Grace McDonald's blood. Discarded blood might not even work, he realized, even if he could fake a *bad stick* and later lift the blood from the discard pile without anyone noticing. There was a requirement that donations must be 450 cc in order to have the appropriate ratio of anticoagulant to blood. Anything less and the balance was skewed. The anticoagulant was premixed in the donor bags and the phlebotomist had no means of changing it. Danny understood that a bad stick would have a disproportionate ratio, given the small amount of blood collected. Not obvious to the eye, but Danny didn't know if it would be noted by a skilled technician testing the blood, or by a DNA lab. He could not take that chance.

It was several weeks before Grace McDonald returned to donate. She was a regular, every eight weeks, and had been for years. From her perspective, donating was easy volunteer work: only took an hour and might save a life.

Danny stayed in the back room, emptying boxes of supplies. He observed from a doorway how Grace lay, eyes closed, listening to headphones during the procedure. She appeared oblivious to the tech working at her side.

Danny relaxed somewhat in keeping tabs on Grace. With two jobs, his schedule was much busier. But one day, he couldn't find her. Grace, the queen of routine, was missing.

At work, Danny was distracted and anxious.

He imagined an accident on the highway. Flat tire at 70 mph. Or worse. Maybe she had seen him. Maybe she was on to him.

At noon, he called her office number.

The answering service picked up.

"When will Ms. McDonald be in?" he asked.

"I'm sorry, but Ms. McDonald is out of town at a conference until next week. Dr. Frixell is covering for her. Would you like him to return your call?"

Danny hung up.

That night, Danny watched the McDonald home from the woods. As the dark settled in around the trees, he saw lights come on in the house. Downstairs and upstairs, at the same moment. *Timers*, he thought. The husband was probably gone too.

The next evening, he waited to see if her husband came home. Then, at 6:45 p.m., he slipped through the dusk, toward the house. It was on a large lot, the woods a buffer zone. He moved close to the house, protected by the deep shadows. He took his time at each window, looking from an angle at whatever he could see through the mini-blinds. He paused, putting on surgical gloves.

Danny had a small hammer in his back pocket, but he didn't think he'd need to break one of the square panes in the kitchen door. He'd observed Grace's husband one day retrieving what he thought was a key from under an old watering can filled with ivy that sat on the deck. And he was fairly confident there was no security system. He'd watched them drive off and leave their garage open. They were not careful people.

Still, he was relieved when he picked up the watering can and saw the key in the dirt.

So predictable, he thought. *So stupid*.

The door opened easily. Once inside, he checked immediately for any sign of an alarm system. None.

He leaned against the door, waiting until his breath slowed.

He started in the kitchen, checking drawers. He wanted to make sure that there was no easily accessible gun. He assumed not, but he needed to know. Danny moved efficiently through the house. He took photos of every room, angled photos of the halls.

In ten minutes, he was done. He reached the enclosing cover of the woods by the time the lights. . .1—2—3. . . came on.

8

Grace and Gil were in Portland. Grace was attending a conference. But it was more an excuse to get away, to have seven days without being texted or phoned.

Grace felt liberated. While she liked her work, it was undeniably intrusive. There were times recently when the phone would ring and she'd flinch.

"I don't know what it is," she told Gil.

"Maybe twenty years of people's pain is wearing you down."

"Sometimes I wish I had work that stayed finished. I could look at it and see exactly what I'd accomplished. More concrete. Therapy feels more like housework."

"It would never be good enough, Gracie. You'd always want to fix one more thing. Just tweak it."

"You talking about me or you? You're the one who can't let stuff go."

"Can we just try and leave the work shit behind? Let's pretend we're independently wealthy and haven't a care in the world. . ."

After two days at the conference, they rented a car and headed north to the Olympic Peninsula.

Grace had made reservations at a lodge her parents had taken her to as a child. She remembered a low, curving building overlooking a green lawn that swept down to the bluest of lakes, so clear that each and every tree was reflected in the shimmering water. Grace did not know if the lodge and lake in her memory existed. It seemed, from her adult perspective, too cinematic to be real.

Gil drove. They listened to music and chatted.

Lake Quinault was out of the way, on the edges of the Olympic National Forest. They took the interstate to Route 12, through Elma, and had lunch in a small cafe overlooking the Pacific in Hoquiam.

The landscape changed as they drove north.

"Gil, this is it, yes, this is it," said Grace in the excited voice of a child.

They came around a bend in the forest, through walls of towering trees, sunlight barely filtering through the dense foliage. They saw the lake through the trees, a glittering expanse of deepest emerald. The entry to Lake Quinault Lodge was unassuming, a small, circular drive close to the road.

Grace bounded out of the car. She pushed open the door of the lodge, and bypassed the front desk, heading straight for the back. When Gil caught up to her, she was standing on the flagstone patio, her hands in her pockets.

"It's just like I dreamed," she said softly to him as he came up behind her and put his hands on her shoulders.

It was a step back in time. Every few yards were another pair of Adirondack chairs. In each, couples lounged, sipping cocktails or wine. They all faced west, toward the sunset.

Gil and Grace checked in and went down for dinner. Their table was nestled in a window corner, and they could see the last washes of peach and pink across the sky. They ordered Pacific salmon and ate their salads and warm, crusty French rolls with gusto. The flickering lights of many candles provided the only light.

For three days, they spent the mornings hiking trails through the rain forest, the afternoons curled up on lawn chairs, reading. Late each afternoon, they lay down for a nap, a nap that evolved into lovemaking. They were unhurried, kissing lightly, slowly. They were, for the most part, silent, knowing without words what each other would want, when to introduce some small element of surprise.

By the third afternoon, Grace actually felt sore. But it was a sensual soreness. The distance that she'd felt from Gil was gone. Her anxiety, starting when she'd discovered him smoking, was a grey cloud that had drifted away. She wondered if it had ever really been there.

Sitting side-by-side in wooden chairs on the slope, watching their last sunset, Grace counted her blessings.

While they were gone, Danny took a drive. He headed south, to Wichita, to a gun show he'd seen advertised on a poster at a pawnshop.

He planned to buy used, since new purchases were easier to trace, and there was a five-day waiting period to purchase a handgun in Kansas. Danny had done his research. He'd studied four magazine articles comparing handguns. Now, in the crowd at the gun show, he planned to get a feel for what the magazines had described.

"What can I help you with?" asked an older man, wearing overalls and a plaid flannel shirt, as Danny looked over the assortment of guns lying on the table.

"Well, I'd like something for my home, for protection," Danny answered. "It's a changing world out there."

"I agree with you there, bud. What do you have in mind?"

"I'm not sure," Danny answered. "Something that doesn't take a lot of practice, more for up close than distance."

The man picked up one model and handed it to Danny. Then he smoothly began demonstrating five different handguns. Danny listened attentively, although he'd already decided on a .38 from the articles he'd read.

"If I buy one, do I have to wait, or can I get it today?"

"Well, if you have an I.D., we can process it today. No background check or waiting period if you're buying from an individual like myself," the man replied. "That's only for dealers. That's why these shows are so popular. No government butting into your business."

The purchase itself took three minutes. Danny paid cash.

Danny went back to the motel room. He'd never had a gun before. Now, moving his fingers over the cold smooth metal, Danny felt a transient euphoria, a power. He understood how easy it could be for someone to just pull the trigger.

He felt an urge. It was like standing on the top of a high tower and looking down, feeling the call to fly, to jump. He'd avoided rooftops, cliffs, and open windows as a child, imagining that the air itself at that height could suck him out. Even a breeze could be dangerous. In his dreams, he could fly, but that was what dreams were all about—doing the impossible.

Danny lay on the bed and got used to holding his gun.

Early the next morning, he went to a shooting range outside Wichita. He needed to shoot the gun, to practice, to know the feel of it as he pulled the trigger.

"I've never shot one of these things," he told the manager. He changed his accent some, tossed his hair and affected a very slight lisp.

Later that day, the range manager would get a laugh from his buddies at the coffee shop as he imitated the blonde gay guy trying to shoot a gun with a wimpy wrist. He would not remember Danny's face, only the affectations.

Danny didn't leave the range until he put three bullets into the center of the target. He went back to his motel and packed his bag. On the way out of town, he stopped at a large medical supplies store for surgical gloves. Then he drove back to Kaw Valley.

Grace and Gil were back home. The sensuality and intimacy of the trip seemed like a pleasant dream—remembered but hard to replicate—as they slipped back into the familiar routines of work.

Danny now fixed his sights on Gil. He'd seen his name on mail he pulled one night from the mailbox. He followed Gil to work, to the health club where he played racquetball, to the Greek cafe where Gil ordered gyro sandwiches for lunch.

Overall, Gil was as predictable as Grace. They were, in Danny's estimation, very boring people. Danny noted that on Friday afternoons, Gil left the office early. He went straight home, emerging shortly in jeans and a flannel shirt. Then he raked leaves, pruned or weeded. He went into the house about 4 p.m. and Danny would see him moving about the kitchen. Grace generally came home after 5 p.m. They often sat on the deck and sipped tea or, it appeared, wine, sometimes eating supper outside.

9

"What's for supper, Mom?" Ross yelled from his loft bedroom.

"White chicken chili and cornbread," Mandy yelled back. "Then homework."

The first days in Gunnison had been difficult. Will and Sara had invited them to stay at their house while they looked for a place, but Mandy had felt too awkward. So, she and Ross stayed at the Super 8, eating too much fast food and getting on each other's nerves.

Ross had missed his Dad and his anger erupted at Mandy.

"What are we doing in this stupid place, anyway? Why did we have to leave home? This is all your fault. Dad didn't want us to go."

Mandy tried to explain, but her answers all sounded fake. And she couldn't tell Ross the real reasons, not that she wasn't tempted. She missed home too. She hadn't moved because she wanted to, but because she felt no other choice.

The first two days, they'd looked at apartments, boxy and predictable, no different from what Mandy had left in Kaw Valley. Mandy had been ready to sign a lease on one of the apartments when they'd taken a drive up into the hills. Coming around a corner, they'd seen a "For Rent" sign. It was a small A-frame, almost hidden in trees. A gravel drive led into a garage, twenty steep steps below the front door. As they clambered up, Mandy had to lean her head all the way back to see the blue sky through the towering evergreens. They stood on the deck and peered through the big windows.

Inside was an open rectangular room and a ladder going up to a loft. Under the loft area was what looked like a bedroom and a bathroom. They could see a kitchen separated from the main room by an eating bar.

When they called to inquire, the realtor said the school bus stopped right out front. If they took a two-year lease, the rent would be lower. It'd been empty for a while. It needed, the realtor added, a little TLC, but the owner was willing to knock the rent down for the right tenant.

Mandy and Ross spent a day scrubbing the floors, kitchen, and bath. With the Woodland's help, the U-Haul was unloaded, and the house set up in three hours. Mandy thought Ross should have the enclosed bedroom so she could stay up late without disturbing him. But Ross was adamant. He could sleep through anything. He wanted the loft.

"I climb better, Mom, and you don't stay up that late anyway."

He made her go up the ladder and lie down in the back corner of the loft. It was, Mandy realized, quite large and like a cozy cave under the eaves.

"Can you even see the light?" Ross called up to her. "Can you hear the TV?"

"Not when you have the sound off, sneaky."

Mandy gave in.

"But if you don't get enough sleep, we'll have to switch."

"Not to worry, Mom," he replied solemnly. "And I can sleep through anything."

The days had assumed a routine. Mandy rose before dawn. The hour before Ross awoke was her quiet time. She put on water to boil for tea, and then sat next to the large picture window in the front of the A-frame and watched the sun creep up over the mountains. Sometimes she would write in a faded, fabric covered journal, but mostly she simply sat.

Mandy felt as though she were making up for years of not thinking. To just sit, without a task or purpose, had been so opposite to how Danny had functioned that she'd never tried it.

There were other changes as well.

In the grocery store, the week after they moved into the cabin, Mandy was filling her cart with the usual stuff. It wasn't until aisle six that she looked at what was in the cart and really saw it: iceberg lettuce, American cheese, cereal, pork chops, frozen pizzas.

Mandy realized that she didn't particularly like any of it. She walked away from the cart, down the aisle, to the front of the store. She got another cart and started through the produce on aisle one.

"Do I like this?" she asked herself, mouthing the words, pausing in front of each and every item. "Do I want to eat it if I have a choice?"

The stock boys nearby stared at the muttering woman.

"I don't know what half this stuff is," Ross complained as he helped put groceries away.

"Me neither," replied Mandy, "but it can't be any worse than what we've been eating." That night she fixed a supper of mixed greens salad with feta and crab corn chowder. She baked bread from a mix.

Ross sniffed suspiciously at the feta but ate half the loaf of bread still warm from the oven.

Mandy would wait for Ross to get on the bus at 7:30 a.m. and then head for the office. After school, Ross hopped a school bus to the office, did homework in the back room, or comforted a sick animal until Mandy was ready to leave. On the weekend, they might go downtown to catch a movie, or out for supper.

Mandy was friendly with whomever she met, but also kept a certain protective distance.

Ross made friends quickly and signed up for after-school sports.

It was easier, better, than Mandy had dared hope.

10

On the first Thursday of November, Grace McDonald left home right on schedule. Danny watched her enter the cafe to meet her friend, but he did not wait. He drove straight to the blood bank, taking his white employee jacket with the big pockets and name tag from the back seat.

He'd changed the name tag for just this day, from Daniel Rivers to Daniel Rivera. It could be explained away as a typo, but he'd realized that staff had stopped seeing name tags a long time ago. He draped the jacket over his arm. He began to walk away, then remembered to retrieve the glasses he wore here, wire frames with clear glass that made him appear bookish.

Grace McDonald sailed in around 11:30 a.m. She wore some sort of poncho, and it swirled around her from the wind as she opened the door. She called hello to the director, then gave a staff person a hug and peck on the cheek.

She was, Danny thought, disgustingly familiar.

Danny had considered and discarded several possible plans for stealing some of Grace McDonald's blood. In the end, the choice was obvious.

At the end of each donation, the phlebotomist would stop the flow to the pint bag, leaving the needle in the donor's arm. The donor would often not even feel this happening. The phlebotomist then inserted four small vials, one at a time, into the attached vacutainer holder, placed in the tubing, and filled each one. Because of the vacuum suction, the vials were filled in one to two seconds each. It was a rapid, automatic, process. Phlebotomists would often put the filled vials in a jacket pocket, then remove the needle so the donor could go have some juice and cookies in the recovery area. Only then would they go label these last components of the donation, the blood that would be checked for HIV and other diseases. Even one missing vial was cause for alarm and would prevent the donated blood from ever being used.

This was his crack in the impenetrable wall constructed to screen out contaminated blood. Danny realized that he could collect an extra vial, even a few, and place them in his white jacket pocket. The pockets were deep. The blood bank was a busy and active place. There was a drawer full of empty vials.

The only other factor to consider was that the vials generally used, with red rubber tops, had no anticoagulant in them. The blood was tested, and vials discarded. But identical vials, with purple tops, had minute amounts of anticoagulant. Danny needed the blood to appear fresh and un-clotted after storage. He needed purple.

Once he understood that it could really be done, with a minimum of risk, Danny had practiced. He'd experimented with several donors, chatting with them as he took extra vials. It had taken only seconds. No one had ever noticed.

Danny watched as Vicki, one of the other phlebotomists, sat with Grace in the glass booth and asked her the required questions: "In the past four weeks, have you taken any pills, medications, Accutane or Proscar?" "In the past twelve months, have you had a tattoo, ear or skin piercing, acupuncture, mucous membrane exposure to blood or an accidental needle prick?"

He watched Vicki's lips do the litany. He got ready to make his move when she would leave Grace to get what she needed for the donation.

"I've got some space here, so if you want to take a smoke break, feel free," Danny said softly to Vicki as she came around the corner from the front desk after finishing the interview, papers and barcode stickers in hand. He put the barest edge of flirtation in his eyes and voice, a hint of sensuality.

Vicki glanced around quickly to see if the transfer would be observed or questioned. Everyone else was busy, focused.

"Sure," she replied. "I could use a quickie."

"Only an ex-smoker knows what it's like," he'd said, teasingly, the week before. He'd avoided chiding her about what her coworkers regarded as a nasty habit.

Grace was lying back, wearing headphones, on one of the reclining donor chairs facing three large picture windows. Danny went through the usual procedures to hook Grace up. His eyes were glued to the inside of her elbow, to the vein he gently prodded into visibility.

"Make a fist," he said. Grace did. He slid the needle into her vein and watched as the blood started to flow, a bright red line down the tubing.

"That's good," he murmured. "You're all set, just relax and I'll check back in a few minutes." Grace opened her eyes.

"You have very good hands," she said. "Thank you. I hardly felt the stick."

"Sure," he replied, still poking at the tube. "But you got me on a good day. You should see what the others look like."

Grace laughed, a low throaty rumble, and closed her eyes.

Danny kept busy for the ten or so minutes that Grace's blood flowed through the narrow tube and into the plastic bag hanging below her recliner. He checked a few times to make sure there were no blockages.

"How are you feeling?" Danny asked Grace softly.

"Fine," she answered, eyes still closed, barely hearing him as Vivaldi's Four Seasons filled her ears.

"You're just about done," he continued. "Just another minute and I'll get you unhooked."

Danny crouched next to the recliner and clipped off the flow. He efficiently inserted the first small vial, filling it and then capping it off in one smooth motion and placing it gently in his deep jacket pocket.

The people working in the large, airy room were busy. Danny was at the center of a whirl of activity, yet he was invisible. In twenty seconds, he filled eight vials.

Four for you, four for me, he thought.

With sure and competent hands, Danny gently removed the needle from Grace McDonald's arm. He placed a cotton ball at the point of entry. As he glanced up from her arm, he found himself looking straight into her blue-gray eyes.

There wasn't even a flicker of recognition.

"Lie here for a few more minutes, and then you can move over to the canteen for juice and cookies," he said. "Let me go label these and I'll be right back to help you."

Removing four red-topped vials from his pocket, putting on bar-coded stickers, placing them in the tray for the lab techs, Danny tried to control his heart from making hyper-accelerated leaps. He tried to breathe deeply and slowly. He felt his face must be visibly flushed, his pupils dilated.

Danny returned to Grace.

"Feeling any dizziness?" he asked.

"I'm fine," she replied.

She swiveled with one fluid motion off the recliner and picked up her purse. Then she walked over to the canteen area and poured some juice.

Danny walked out the side door and over to his car. He'd parked with the trunk facing away from the building. He opened the trunk and placed the four remaining vials in a chilled thermos, which he then put in a cooler. With one smooth motion, he took his lunch out of the cooler and closed the trunk.

As he walked back toward the front door of the blood bank, Danny realized that he might actually be hungry.

That night at home, Danny carefully placed the vials of Grace McDonald's blood in an aqua Tupperware container. He hesitated, black marker poised, considering what to label the package.

"Salsa," he printed carefully, moving aside some condiments to make room in the back of the fridge.

Danny whistled as he got ready for work.

Danny was the favorite for giving tours to school kids when they came to the station on a field trip. He had erased his erratic previous work history from his mind. How he had become a paramedic, the memory of the evening when Mandy had put the brochures down in front of him on the table and gently guided him toward his future, had been rewritten.

"I wanted to do this work since I was a little kid," he'd explain cheerfully to the school groups that came to tour the ambulances. "I always thought that saving lives was one of the most important jobs in the world."

Then he would give them his little boy grin and say in a loud whisper, "And I like the sirens, too."

The children always giggled.

One of the team, Danny routinely brought donuts to work. He volunteered to orient new staff. Everybody liked him, but nobody really knew him well. Nobody could get very close.

Since his divorce, he hadn't dated anyone steadily. If the work crews socialized, or had holiday parties, he came alone. The few attempts made to fix him up with a blind date were met with a passive resistance. He was not a significant part of anyone's life, which is how he intended it to remain, at least until after he carried out his plan.

Every few weeks Danny would drive over to a strip club in Kansas City and watch the women go through their gyrations. Occasionally, he would pick up a woman, go to her place or a cheap motel, and have sex.

But he never brought a woman back to his place.

In his own bed, waking in a half-dream state, Danny imagined Mandy. Each time the scene would be different, but the outcome was always the same. Mandy would lean against him, her eyes holding the initial wonder and delight with which she'd first greeted him years before. He would reach down and run the tips of his fingers along the side of her face, then brushing her lips. She would shiver, and he would bend his head and kiss her.

"It's time for us to go home now," he would say. "I've taken care of everything."

11

Danny settled on the Friday before Thanksgiving.

He practiced holding the gun and pulling the trigger while wearing the surgical gloves he'd purchased. He wanted to go to a local target shooting range for practice but couldn't risk being noticed. So, he looked at his photos and went over his plan. Over and over and over.

At the designated hour, Danny stood in the woods in the waning light. Through the window he could see Gil moving about in the kitchen.

He started toward the house. He wore his ambulance service uniform and already had thin surgical gloves on the hands he shoved deep into his pockets. The gun was in an inner pocket, the metal cold against his ribs even through the shirt. Danny moved swiftly along the edge of the woods, cutting over to the house at the shortest point.

He looked at an angle through the windows into the spacious living room that stretched from the front of the house clear through to the back. He needed to be sure that no one else was in the house.

The room was empty. So was the family room. So was the kitchen.

Danny started to sweat. His breathing became a quick panting.

Then the basement door leading into the kitchen opened and Gil emerged. Danny ducked instinctively. The music was familiar, classic Motown, and it made the walls vibrate.

"Hell," he muttered, "he wouldn't hear me if I waltzed in the front door."

Gil had a blue glass vase in his left hand. Danny watched as he filled it with water, took flowers from the sink and put them in the vase.

Danny had planned a spiel to talk his way into the house. But the loudness of the music provided him with a better cover. He went to the back door and rapped loudly on a glass pane. He saw Gil startle.

Gil came to the door and opened it.

"Can I help you?" he asked.

"Sorry, sir, but I knocked on the front door and no one answered.

Heard the music and figured someone was home, so I came around back." Danny gave Gil a crisp, professional smile. "Hope I didn't scare you."

"No, no." Gil relaxed. "What can I do for you?"

"Well, sir, the ambulance company is conducting a survey of neighborhoods with a high percentage of unmarked and poorly marked houses to try and make it easier for ambulance drivers to identify specific houses. Can I take a minute of your time?"

Lyrics almost drowned Danny out. . . "I heard it through the grapevine. . . No longer would you be mine. . . OHHHHH, I heard it through the grapevine. . . and I'm just about to lose my mind. . . Honey, Honey. . ."

Gil looked apologetic. He waved toward the next room.

"Sure, come on in. Just let me turn down the music." He turned toward the living room.

The black metal curve of the gun rose from Danny's jacket like a dolphin's fin curving out of the ocean. It was there, visible, and then gone. Later, Danny would have a hard time remembering what it had looked like, if it had been real.

The first bullet entered Gil's back through his left shoulder. Danny's aim, even at close range, was not as good as he'd thought. It spun Gil around and threw him against the counter. One arm flailed and the glass vase and flowers were swept into the air. Gil looked straight at Danny, into his bright blue eyes, as though for one paralyzing second memorizing Danny's face. The vase shattered, soundlessly, against the wall.

The next bullet, or the third, went through Gil's heart. In any case, his body dropped to the floor, a slow-motion tangle of arms and torso.

The music still vibrated through the house. It was still the same song. Nothing had changed except there was now a dead body on the floor. The body had blood trickling out of its mouth and from the holes in the back and chest. The blood mixed with water from the vase, forming puddles among the shards of glass on the shiny kitchen floor.

Danny felt an instinctive urge to make the blood stop, to call 911, to reach down and tilt back that head and put his mouth down to that bloody mouth and try to make it breathe. That's what he had been trained to do, what he knew best.

But he also knew when a body was gone.

Danny carefully returned the gun to his front pocket, making sure the safety was on.

He was panting again, the shallow, short pants of an animal who had run a long way, but cannot stop, not yet.

Danny reached into another pocket, this one in his shirt, under the uniform. He very slowly and carefully removed a small vial of blood. It was still cold from the refrigerator. He pried open the small rubber top and slowly inverted the vial. As gravity took hold, the blood dropped through the air until it hit the inert warm mass. He capped the first vial, took out another and repeated the process, this time extending his arm over another part of the body. It was not much blood, about a tablespoon a vial, but it was enough.

Danny was panting harder. The music was still blaring, a different song now.

He glanced at the kitchen clock over the stove. 5:10 p.m. He had to get out, had to get clear.

The phone rang, the answering machine kicking in, as Danny closed the back door.

"Gil, pick up—I know you're there somewhere. Anyway, I just ran into Joanna and we're going to have a cup of coffee. Be home in about 45 minutes. See you then."

There was a click as Grace hung up, and then a last, final beep.

Danny stood in the dark shadow of the house for a full two minutes, making sure the yard was completely empty. He edged toward the woods. He'd considered staying in the woods until Grace's car drove up, to watch, to relish the moment in which her perfect little life was destroyed. But now there was a body. There was blood. He felt tired and he wanted to go home.

Danny drove home very carefully, stopping at every corner whether there was a stop sign or not.

12

"We need to do this again," Joanna said, giving Grace a hug outside of the bakery. "We're just too damn busy for our own good."

Grace laughed, hugging back.

"How about a Kansas City shopping day before the holidays?"

"You've got a date," answered Joanna with a grin.

Grace put on National Public Radio in the car on the way home. She usually got "All Things Considered," but she was a bit late. The classical music had started.

As she drove up to the house, she could see that all the lights were on. Approaching the front door, she could hear pounding music.

"That is going off as soon as I get in," she announced to the fading geraniums that framed the front steps.

She put her key in the lock and walked in the door. She put her briefcase down by the coat-tree and hung up her coat.

"Yoo-hoo, Gil, I'm home," she called out as she walked toward the kitchen.

Grace had always imagined that she would feel some sense of warning, at least for a microsecond, before her life was transformed. She fancied that she was possessed of a hyper-vigilance, an awareness of a change in the cosmic field, much as animals can sense the coming of storms and earthquakes.

But there was no warning. She was thinking of what to tell Gil, hungry for whatever he would have fixed for supper. Her last conscious thought as she crossed the threshold from living room to kitchen was that tonight she'd open a bottle of Merlot with dinner.

Her first high-pitched scream could have been heard above the music if anyone had been close enough to hear. Her hands went to her face, one on top of the other covering her mouth. She couldn't breathe.

Gil was on the floor, part of his body propped against the cabinets. His eyes were open, but empty, so empty. The floor was covered with blood, more brownish-burgundy than red.

Grace wanted to go to Gil, to touch Gil, to see if he was breathing. But her feet would not move. Her legs began to fail her, and she slipped, clutching the wood frame of the doorway down to the floor.

Then she was eye level with Gil, and she could see that there was no life, no hope of life. She moaned, an incoherent plea.

"Oh God, Oh God, Oh God, Oh God, Oh God. . ."

She started to crawl toward Gil. But her hand slipped on the floor, slipped in the puddled blood. She turned it over and looked at it, at her palm coated with blood and tiny shards of glass. Her hands went to her face, as if to cover her eyes. Then, with a reflex both primitive and desperate, Grace wiped the bloodied hand across her skirt, hard, again and again, until the blood was gone. She tried to get to her feet, but they would not hold steady. She crawled, on all fours through the living room and out the front door, going crablike down the steps. Her palms and knees tore against the rough stones of the walk, but she was oblivious.

She put her face down against the cool evening grass and felt her stomach turn over. Hot brown bile came up her throat and onto the grass, over and over, leaving her trembling.

Bad dream, get away from bad dream, she thought. She rolled away from the vomit and was still.

About ten minutes later, a neighbor drove by and noticed the front door open, light streaming out, music throbbing. The circumstances were odd enough that he walked down the street a few minutes later to see if everything was all right. It was not until he was halfway up the winding front walk that he saw Grace McDonald's body lying in the grass.

Grace was open-eyed but unblinking, unresponsive when he called her name. The neighbor put his jacket on top of her and ran back to his own house to call 911.

The sirens could be heard long before the police car and ambulance arrived. The shrill rise and fall abruptly ceased as they pulled, first ambulance, seconds later police, around the corner and into the driveway.

Paramedic Eva Dominguez hit the ground running. She started checking ABC's—airways, breathing, circulation.

"Can you hear me?" Eva slapped lightly at the woman's face trying to get a response. There was none, although Eva thought she saw a flicker of movement deep, very deep, in the woman's pupils. There were dark streaks on her face.

"Pupils dilated, skin diaphoretic, pulse shaky. Eyes open, not responding," Eva reported to Bill, her partner.

Eva was assessing. With breathing and pulse not too out-of-line, they were not dealing with regular shock. So, how did this lady come to be catatonic? Seizures? Allergic response? Gas? Some other poison?

Eva sniffed the air for any odor, but there was only the faint stench of vomit.

She tossed the jacket aside and started a head-to-toe, pressing quickly and gently, sweeping her hands under the body, searching for soft spots, for wounds. With a fast log roll, the two paramedics got Grace onto a spine board, put on a C-collar, strapping her down.

"All I got visible now are skinned, bloodied knees and palms," noted Bill. "And some stains on the skirt and face."

"Do another vitals," Eva said. "It's more than that. Just don't know what yet."

It was Patsy Tsosie, a rookie who'd completed the police academy and officially joined the force just nine months earlier, who first walked through the open front door and into the house.

She did not have her gun drawn, assuming, as had the others, that this was a medical call. It was, after all, Kaw Valley, not Kansas City. She was thinking about turning down the music. She never smelled the blood.

Patsy's question, projected to be heard above the music, was halfway out as she turned into the kitchen.

"Anybody Hom . . e?" ended on a gasping inhalation of air.

For three, maybe four, seconds, Patsy stood frozen, uncomprehending, unable to exhale. Then she turned and stumbled back through the living room and out the front door.

"Sam!" she yelled. "Get in here, Sam."

Sam Hillard, a veteran of 21 years on the force, looked up and saw death in the young woman's eyes.

Oh fuck, he thought, *it's gonna be one hell of a long night.*

13

A homicide case is a time warp.

First everything is on fast-forward—the wail of sirens and ambulances, frantic calls for more personnel, the rush to "hold the scene," to seal the perimeter.

When the back-up officers arrived, they worked the house in pairs. They were fast but cautious, not knowing if a killer was still inside, or what they would find each time they opened a door. They walked down the sides of the hallways, almost on tiptoe, in order to disturb the environment as little as possible. The police combed the house: every closet, air duct, attic, basement. Then they carefully backed out the front door.

Everyone stopped and took a deep breath. The time warp shifted. For the next six hours, two evidence officers worked the scene. They were slow and meticulous. They took photos of each room from every angle. They did a video scan of every room, ceiling-to-floor and wall-to-wall. They photographed each piece of potential evidence in place before picking it up. Each tiny piece was packaged, sealed, numbered, and information corresponding to the number entered into a log. Blue Sheets were used to record it into the evidence system and turn it over to the evidence room officer. From that point he would be responsible for transporting evidence to labs and court, for protecting the chain of custody.

The fewer people involved on the scene, the less likelihood of any contamination of evidence. Fewer people required to testify when it came time for court. A clean chain, which is how the department liked it.

When Patsy Tsosie had discovered Gil's body, Eva Dominguez was in the middle of her assessment. Normally, paramedics do not go onto a crime scene until given an all-clear by the police, but she was already present, and no way would she back off while they checked the area.

So, during those same seconds that the police back-ups were

arriving, she and Bill were loading Grace into the ambulance.

There is protocol to be followed. Temp. A quick EKG. Start an IV line. Check blood sugar. Narcan ready in case of an overdose. Vitals—again—this time with numbers. Preliminary vitals—blood pressure, pulse and respirations—are rough estimates. In the ambulance, vitals are taken by the numbers and documented. Pulse oximetry is taken by attaching a small plastic probe to a finger, over a fingernail. In two seconds, it reads pulse and oxygen saturation, and helps to assess for carbon monoxide poisoning, asthma, anaphylaxis, and whatever else would impact blood oxygen levels.

"Shit, she's wearing polish."

Eva grabbed at a small bottle of nail polish remover and rubbed roughly at one of Grace's nails. For all its technical perfection, the machine needed a clear nail to get a reading.

All of this data was communicated directly to the Emergency Room, to prepare the triage team. Patients are color coded: green is relatively okay, yellow means urgent but not critical, red critical, blue cardiac arrest. Black is too late.

Grace was a yellow.

Lying in the grass, Grace heard the noises, the sirens. But they were so far away, and there was a dense grayness all around her. She felt hands touching her, then moving her. She was on a bed, moving through the air on the bed, then closed into a small space. Something held her wrists, held her down. Her eyes were half open, but she couldn't seem to see, or make sense of what she saw.

The sirens were all around her now, wailing like a hungry baby. In her mind, she was back with her own babies, hearing the whimpering, the ech-ech-ech that became a plaintive cry, through the nursing mother fog of torpor and exhaustion that comes from no sleep for months. She whimpered, an involuntary sound of pleading: "Not yet, please God, not yet." She could smell milk, the middle-of-the-night smell of baby and milk and just the slightest tinge of pee. She inhaled, then again, trying harder to smell it, to get it back. She wanted to smell the milk, the babies. She wanted them back.

"Take it easy," a voice said. "Almost there. You're doing fine."

This must be dying, Grace thought.

The triage team was ready: an ER physician, two nurses, techs from the lab and X-ray available.

Orders bounced off the tile walls.

"Get a head CT up here now."

"Trauma profile—CBC, Chem 16—and get her catheterized for a UA. Do a drug screen with that."

"Let's do a C-spine bedside. Call down. STAT."

"Is there anybody here with this woman?" asked the doctor.

"Nobody, Doc." Eva replied from a corner of the room, already doing the paperwork. "There was a dead body in the house, but no help there."

"Will somebody call social work? Maybe someone is still hanging around up there," asked the doctor.

"Right. Like why go home on a Friday night when you can stick around here," added a tech.

Sixty minutes and several tests later, they ruled out the *bad* stuff. No apparent damage to spine, brain, heart. No broken limbs. No signs of an overdose. Nothing funny in the blood work so far. Oxygen saturation fine.

In other words, no answers as to why Grace McDonald should be catatonic in her front yard. Except for the obvious.

The team had heard ten minutes into triage that the body on the scene was Gil McDonald, the husband of their patient. An apparent homicide. A cop had shown up at the ER with the news. His orders were to stay with the patient until she woke up and said something useful. She might be a witness.

Nurses put her clothes in an evidence bag. They dug microscopic glass shards out of her hand and put on a layer of antibiotic ointment.

"I want a close watch," said the attending. "Call ICU and tell them we're sending one up."

The cop just hoped he could get coffee and a paperback before starting his vigil.

The coroner arrived at the McDonald house about 8:30 p.m.

"Hey, Doc. Glad you could finally make it. What'd I do, drag you away from some dinner party?" Sam's voice was affectionately sarcastic as he called to the woman stepping out of a navy BMW.

Carolyn Liebowitz's eyes swept the lawn, crime scene tape ringing the perimeter of the yard. She was a slight woman, her cocoa shoulder-length hair now twisted into a neat French knot at the nape of her neck. She wore a black cocktail dress, gold chains, and large gold hoop earrings. Not the usual look for a coroner.

"T.G.I.F. at the new Dean's," she replied, turning to face Sam.

Carolyn was married to a professor at the local university, a position that required attendance at certain social functions. Getting called away was as much relief as inconvenience. But now that she was at the scene, she began to wonder if she wouldn't rather still be sipping white wine and exchanging hummus recipes with the visiting professor from Lebanon.

"What have we got?" she asked Sam.

"It's a homicide, that's for sure. Male, white, about 50. Wife found in shock lying on the lawn. Medics took her to the hospital. Haven't gotten anything out of her yet."

Carolyn started toward the door when Sam called out to her again. "Do me a favor and talk the rookie through some basics, would you? This is her first."

Carolyn nodded without stopping as she went up the steps.

The entry and door handles were already dusted for fingerprints. Patsy Tsosie was standing by the doorway to the kitchen.

"Please show me the body," Carolyn asked.

Patsy looked blankly at her, as though trying to make sense of why this sharply-dressed woman was asking to see the body. Carolyn had seen that look before, regardless of what she was wearing.

"I'm the coroner. I want to see the body. I assume you're the new officer Sam just told me about."

"Yes, ma'am, I mean Doc," Patsy replied. "Right this way."

Carolyn slipped inside the perimeter line put down by the homicide squad. She'd do nothing at this point that could interfere with their investigation, simply make some quick determinations and leave the rest for autopsy. She reached into her bag, lifted out surgical gloves, and slipped them onto her hands.

She leaned over toward the body, gently touching the jaw. She noted the discoloration in the elbow area.

"There's no rigor, so it's definitely less than four hours," she said to Patsy, motioning towards Gil's jaw. Her tone now was the one she used when teaching pathology over at the med school, detached and brisk.

"Livor, the pooling of blood in lowered places and extremities, is visible after about 30 minutes. He's clothed, so we can't get a good look, but the discoloration caused by livor can mask trauma and bruising. See that elbow area—that's livor." She paused, fingers moving swiftly yet cautiously.

"The rigor starts after about four hours, first noted in the jaw and small muscles. It is most pronounced at about 12-14 hours postmortem, and then goes away after about 24 hours. Any questions?"

Patsy's head moved sideways, then back again.

"What we have here is a recently murdered white, middle-aged man, warm, some observable livor, no rigor," Carolyn continued.

"What we have here is a fucking mess," said Sam, coming up behind Carolyn.

Patsy stayed with the body. It was standard procedure: the officer who found the body of a homicide victim stayed with the body. No chance for tampering or contamination of evidence.

Guarding a dead body was not what Patsy had in mind when she took the exam to try and get on the force. A Navaho, she'd come to Kaw Valley to attend Haskell University, known as the *Indian College*. She'd liked the town and stayed on. The first female Native American on the police force, she'd discovered that a lot of what she did as a cop was not what she'd expected.

The house was eerily quiet. In the movies, cops swarmed over a crime scene, dozens of them, each with a different task.

Right, Patsy thought, *like I can see what that would do to the evidence.*

14

Sam stared at the list posted on the inside of the kitchen cabinet. It simplified the awkward and often challenging process of whom to notify.

"Who to Call in Case of an Emergency" it read. "Executor" seemed a logical starting place.

Katrina was just getting up from the dinner table when the phone rang. "I'm trying to reach a Katrina Baptiste," the male voice said.

"If you're selling something, forget it," Katrina answered. She knew the voices of all of her friends and this was not one of them.

"Am I speaking to Katrina Baptiste?"

"Yes. Get on with it."

"I'm Officer Sam Hillard of the Kaw Valley Police Department. Your name is down as executor on a list in the home of Gil and Grace McDonald."

"Oh God. Oh my God. Are they okay? I'm a friend of Gracie. We've been friends for years. What happened?" Katrina realized that she was babbling, but she couldn't stop herself.

Shit, thought Sam, *should have stuck to procedure and had some cop show up at her door in person. Too fucking late now.*

"Ma'am," he continued, "is there someone there with you?"

"Yes," Katrina said. "Forget about me. I'll be okay. Just tell me."

Katrina felt as if she were under water, his voice a faint echo.

"Ma'am?" the voice said. "Ma'am, are you there?"

"Yes," Katrina answered, in a whisper. "Were they in a wreck? What happened?"

"Ms. McDonald is in the hospital. It would be easier to explain if we could talk to you directly. Would you prefer that we come to your home or do you want to come here?"

"I'll come there," she said. "Where exactly?"

"The police station," he said. "Do you know where that is?"

Sam put the list in his pocket, took another look around, and started for his car.

Sam Hillard was an average guy, so average he could disappear in any crowd. About 5'10", balding, he had curious dark eyes and a small paunch that spoke of his affinity for buttermilk donuts. He looked like a plumber, not a detective. And, though he would never admit it, he enjoyed his nickname, Columbo, and played into it by always asking that one last question as he was walking out the door.

Katrina told her sons she had to go out.

"I may be late, so don't wait up," she said. "No wild parties, okay?"

They nodded in unison, not looking away from the TV screen. At 14 and 12, her sons were trapped in "zit-land," as they called it, plagued by acne and adolescent angst. She saw the long evenings they spent hiding out in the basement as part of some cosmic hibernation.

Katrina forced herself to focus on driving. The police station parking lot was empty. She pushed open a glass door.

"I'm here to see a detective," she said through the sliding partition to a secretary. "But I forgot his name. He just called me."

"Is this with regards to a particular case, ma'am?"

"Yes. McDonald. Grace and Gil McDonald. Tonight. It just happened tonight."

Katrina turned to survey the metal and plastic orange chairs, the piles of old magazines. *Field and Stream*. *Mechanic Monthly*. Guy stuff.

"Mrs. Baptiste?" a voice said.

Katrina startled.

"I'm sorry, didn't mean to scare you. You've had enough of that for one night." He reached out his hand. "I'm Detective Hillard, Sam Hillard."

"Katrina Baptiste," she replied, shaking his hand. Hillard took her in: tall, graceful, maybe mid-40's, skin the color of toffee, a sure handshake.

He showed her into a small room, with two couches, a coffee table. Unlike the tile boxes of *Law and Order* or *Homicide*, it felt almost cozy.

"Is that a one-way mirror?" she asked.

"Yes, but it isn't in use. Would you like to see?"

"No. I just wondered."

Katrina shifted position to look full into the balding cop's face.

"What happened to my friends?" she asked.

"A neighbor called 911 and reported that a woman was lying in her front yard. When we arrived, we found Grace. She is now in the hospital. No obvious physical trauma, but she hasn't come around yet. Then one of our officers discovered Gil. He'd been shot."

Sam's voice was factual. He could have been describing the weather. He watched Katrina as he spoke.

"Shot?" Katrina was stunned. She'd been imagining a car wreck. "This is so hard to believe. I mean, we had concert tickets for next weekend. We're going to see. . ."

She was babbling.

"Mrs. Baptiste, is there anything going on in their lives that could possibly elicit violence? Anything at all?"

Katrina felt a knee-jerk of defensive anger. How dare this guy insinuate. . .

"What's that supposed to mean?" she blurted out.

"A request for information. Anything. A lead." Sam kept his voice calm.

"I'm sorry," Katrina said. "I'm a little jumpy."

"With good reason."

"Nothing I can imagine. Gil was a pacifist. Grace has a temper, but she mostly gets angry with institutions, corporate America, politics."

"Any drug use?"

"No. Gracie tried grass in college, but she couldn't inhale. She claims to be one of the few people who truly understood what Bill Clinton meant." *More babbling*, thought Katrina. *Stop babbling*.

"Any marital problems?"

"No. But I may not be the best one to ask. I just got divorced two years ago after twenty years. So they looked pretty damn good to me. Hell, they put up with Bernie and me when we were snippy."

"You socialized as couples?"

"Officer, we spent every Thanksgiving together. If we didn't leave town, we did Christmas."

Katrina's hand flew to her mouth as she made a connection in her brain.

"The kids?" she asked. "What have you told the kids?"

"We haven't told anyone anything, Mrs. Baptiste. We were hoping to get some guidance from you. Where are the kids?"

"Well, they aren't really kids. Alex just turned 21. Molly is 18. Both are in college."

Sam consulted his notes.

"Who are these other people?"

Katrina went down the list, explaining the tapestry of relationships that wove through the lives of her friends.

"How do you think we should proceed?" Sam asked.

"I'll call Alex. He should be the one to tell Molly. I'll ask them to get back here as soon as they can."

"And the rest?"

"I don't know. There are a few friends I can call and start a telephone tree." Katrina looked over at Sam. "This is not what I want to be doing."

"Me neither," said Sam.

"Just two nights ago we divided up Thanksgiving. She asked me to bring my sweet potatoes and a chocolate souffle. Oh, sweet Jesus. . ."

15

"There are no unsolved homicides on the books in Kaw Valley," Patsy recalled the instructor saying during training. "That's because we take it slow and careful. A dead body is in no hurry to get to the morgue."

"There is only one chance to work a crime scene," he'd reinforced, "and that's the first time. Don't screw it up."

The house was silent, leaving Patsy to contemplate the body of Gil McDonald without distraction.

Officers had finished canvassing the neighborhood. They'd knocked on every door, asking questions about any unusual activity, unfamiliar cars, strange patterns, local feuds.

At about midnight, Sam walked up behind Patsy and looked into the kitchen. They watched the evidence officer on his hands and knees on the floor. He was using what appeared to be a shiny putty knife, meticulously scraping dried blood from the floor. It looked like paint chips with glitter.

Earlier, cotton swabs had been soaked in the then, still-damp blood, and put in test tubes. Now that the blood had dried, swabs were first dipped in distilled water then gently rubbed in the dried blood and also put in vials.

The evidence guy stood up and nodded to Sam.

"Ready to bag him?" he asked.

Sam returned with some small brown paper bags and tape. He slipped on surgical gloves, moving toward the body with unexpected grace. He lifted the right hand and slipped a bag over it, then carefully wrapped tape around the bagged wrist. He repeated the procedure with the left hand.

"You use plastic and any bloody cloth will rot. Has to be paper." Sam talked to Patsy without ever looking at her. "You put all the extras, clothing, etcetera, in paper bags and let them dry out down in the evidence room. We have some vials and containers for the blood, and they'll go over to the KBI lab. This time you watch. Next time you do."

Sam and Patsy rode with the body in the ambulance. The coroner, Carolyn Liebowitz, met them at the entrance to the emergency room. She was now in jeans and a turtleneck, covered by a white, deep-pocketed smock.

They went first to X-ray for full body scans, then pushed the draped corpse down the hall, into the elevator and down to the morgue. Photos were taken of the body from every angle. Each piece of clothing was removed, carefully, so as not to disturb the bullet holes, and placed in a paper evidence bag.

They slid the draped body into a refrigerated wall crypt, then locked it carefully. Only the coroner had the key. Sam placed evidence tape across the vault to seal it. There were papers to be signed, procedures followed. They did not look back at the wall as they left the room and locked the door.

Whenever there is a homicide, the district attorney is notified immediately. If there are going to be legal questions, the cops want them handled by the top dog. Bruce Saunders had been district attorney for just nine months and was only ten years out of law school. But his name was as familiar as the daily paper, probably because his family had owned it for two generations. He was 6'2", with Nordic features and eyes that were Paul Newman-blue. He saw his future in politics.

When Bruce got the call, it was all he could do to not head for the crime scene. But he knew his place, knew not to step on toes. Too much overlap gave the impression of collusion between the DA and police, an impression he could ill afford to hear mentioned by a defense attorney in court.

He'd planned to watch his son play a Saturday morning soccer game, but now he figured he might just stroll on over to police headquarters instead. Chat up the detectives. Take a look at the evidence.

Alex pressed the pause button on the remote before he picked up the phone. Years later he would remember the fuzzy screen frozen to Woody Allen's puzzled face.

"Alex, is that you?"

He recognized the voice, but for a split second could not place it. It did not belong, did not make sense.

"Mrs. Baptiste?" he asked. "I mean, Katrina?" When he had turned 16, she'd told him that he was old enough to call her Katrina.

"Yes, Alex, it's Katrina."

"What's the matter? Why are you calling?"

"Oh, Alex. You need to come home. It's your Dad."

"Where's my mother? Why isn't she calling?"

"She's in the hospital, Alex. She's going to wake up soon, and she'll be needing you here."

"What do you mean, wake up? What the hell is going on?

Katrina's voice was a cracking whisper.

"Oh, Alex, I'm so sorry. Your dad is dead."

"What? He's the healthiest man I know. Hell, he. . ."

Katrina cut him off in mid-sentence.

"He was killed. He didn't just die."

"How? He always wears his seat belt. He hardly went out except to work."

"It appears that he was murdered. In the house."

"In our house?"

"Yes. Listen—someone needs to tell your sister. I can call her now, but I wanted to talk with you first. But someone has to call Molly. She will need to come home, too."

"I'll call her. But first tell me whatever you know."

Katrina spoke for three minutes in a low flat voice. She would say something, then repeat it. Alex didn't seem to notice.

Alex called his sister, saying words that he'd never expected he would ever have to say, crying with her on the phone. He started to make a plane reservation for the next morning but realized that he could drive home in 12 hours. Considering the layover in Dallas if he flew, the ultimate difference wouldn't be much. And driving would give him a purpose, something to do. He was on the road in thirty minutes.

It wasn't like he was going to be able to sleep.

In her dorm room, Molly sat up much of the night, surrounded by her roommates. For her friends, it was very sad but also high drama. They still felt immortal, and this was a death. At 7 a.m. they drove her down to Denver and she caught a flight to Kansas City. She'd called a friend at home to pick her up at the airport there.

Katrina went to the hospital after talking with Detective Hillard. By now, after meeting with Hillard and calling Alex, it was the middle of the night. She stood silently in the darkened room and watched Grace's body, curved in fetal position on the bed, metal sidebars pulled up like a crib. She had no idea what her friend knew or did not know. She hoped she was having one last peaceful, dreamless sleep before having to face reality.

She asked the nurses to tell Grace that she'd been here and would be back. Then she drove home. Before she crawled into bed, she stood silently in each of her son's rooms and watched them breathe.

16

At the Kaw Valley police headquarters, a room had been set aside for the investigation. The homicide team had assembled, reviewed the evidence thus far, and was ready to hypothesize. They sat around a long table, each with a yellow legal pad in front of them. They watched videotape of the scene, the yard, every room in the house, the body.

This was Sam Hillard's favorite part of an investigation—when all things were possible.

"What do we have, Sam?"

White, upper-middle class, established, local, professional," Sam replied. "Except this was no robbery, boys. This looks gang."

"You think it could be drug-related?"

"Never rule it out, but we went over that place with a fine-tooth comb and there was no sign of anything but a few prescriptions. No paraphernalia. Zip."

"What do his finances look like?"

"That's one thing we start checking into today. Plus his past history. We got no strong leads, so we just check it all. Neighbors say he was a peach of a guy who helped old ladies mow their yards. No audible domestic disputes, kids never in trouble."

"What's the wife say?"

"So far, nothing. We got an officer with her ready for when she can talk."

"She a suspect?"

"At this point, joker, you're a fuckin' suspect."

Grace was in a hospital. That she could tell from the smells, the clanking sounds of bedside barriers being lowered and raised, the voices that talked in medical jargon, the squeak of rubber soles on vinyl floors. What she didn't know, for sure, was what day it was, how she had gotten here, why she was here. And, as long as she kept her eyes closed, she could keep it that way.

She heard footsteps next to her bed and then a strong, warm hand picked up her left wrist and held it, thumb pressed gently.

Still curled in fetal position, Grace's body felt frozen, as if coated with thick layers of ice. It was how people freezing to death are toward the end—enveloped, motionless, yet drifting. A soothing paralysis.

Grace tentatively opened—just a crack—her left eye, the one not burrowed into her hands. She saw the hand of the nurse, a dark hand, and then a face moved down into her line of vision.

The face was very, very black, with startling white around the eyes. The lips were wine red, deep and full. They spread open, turning up at the corner, and white teeth emerged. It seemed that this process took minutes, long minutes, but it was actually a second.

"You're safe, ma'am," the teeth said. "Can you hear me? You can come back now. We're here to help you."

Grace closed the eye.

You can't tell color from touch, she thought.

Then she escaped into the recesses of her brain, into the soothing darkness. She never saw the cop sitting at the foot of her bed.

About 11 a.m., Grace opened her eyes, blinking, and announced in a low, hoarse voice that she had to go to the bathroom.

She sat up in the bed but could not twist her legs out because of the sidebar. Then she saw the policeman sitting at the foot.

"Would you please get this damn thing down before I pee all over myself?" she asked.

"I don't know that I'm allowed, ma'am, but. . ." He wasn't on his feet before the nurse returned.

She assessed Grace with a quick up-and-down glance, hesitated a second, then put down the side of the bed.

"I want to hold onto you now, just in case," she said, reaching to place a hand under Grace's elbow as she guided her to the bathroom. It seemed natural to be sitting on a cold toilet in a small tiled cubicle with a substantive nurse standing over her. She felt an urge to lean forward and bury her face in the white uniform.

Grace looked up and into the deep, dark eyes. They took her in, not only body, but soul. She felt her own eyes fill with tears and she turned her face away.

"Oh my, honey," the woman said. "You poor dear." And a hand tentatively stroked the top of her head.

After helping Grace back to bed, the nurse went to get her some tea and toast.

The cop cleared his throat.

"I need to ask you a few questions, ma'am," he said.

"What's your name?" Grace asked him.

He looked surprised at the question.

"Ahh, Jim," he answered. "Jim Beuler."

"Well, Jim, I'll try," she said, sinking back down under the covers.

"I'd appreciate you telling me just what happened last night," said Jim. "We can take it slow."

Last night. Last night. Last night.

The images pushed into her frontal lobes. She could feel the neurons in her brain sparking like a bad electrical connection.

Last night. Last night. . .

"I never did get any dinner," she said.

Jim looked at her and said nothing.

"I came home from work the usual time. No, no, I stopped at the Prairie Bakery for bread for supper and ran into a friend, Joanna. We had a latte. It seemed lucky, you know, to run into each other on a Friday night, and be able to sit and talk."

Grace looked at Jim for confirmation. He nodded.

"So, I got home later than usual. But I called Gil to tell him I'd be late."

"You spoke to your husband? Can you recollect what time that was?" Jim asked.

"No. I didn't talk to him. The machine picked up, we still have a landline. I left a message."

"So, you have no way of knowing if he ever got the message?"

"Not really, I guess, unless he saw the little red light flashing."

Grace heard herself talking, so normal, in a contrived, calm, dispassionate voice.

Talking to a cop. Cop. Hospital. Gil. Last night. Gil. Last night. Gil. Gil. Gil.

She looked around, her breath coming in short, heaving gasps. This was a dream. It had to be a dream.

Wake up, she silently screamed. *Dammit, wake up!*

Jim got up and walked to the side of the bed. He pushed a button, once, then again. In a second, the nurses were there.

"She's getting agitated," he said. "I think it just hit her."

Twenty minutes passed before Grace was coherent enough to go on with her statement. When she continued, her affect had flattened.

"I came home. I went to the front door. The music was loud. Gil loves to play music loud when he cooks or cleans."

Jim noted that she had not yet transitioned to past tense when speaking of her husband.

"I put in my key, went in the door, hung up my coat. Maybe—I'm not sure about that—walked to the kitchen. That's where I found Gil. He was on the floor, blood everywhere. His eyes were open."

"What did you do then, ma'am?"

"I'm not sure, but I think I fell. I don't think I passed out, but I was down on the floor. I wanted to go to him, to check, do something, but I couldn't."

Grace looked at Jim, her eyes an apology.

"And then what did you do?" he asked.

"I got out of the house. I don't remember walking. I think I crawled out the front door. I remember reaching up and opening the front door from the floor. It was so high."

"You didn't phone the police? Call 911? Were you going to a neighbor's?"

"No. I just got out." Grace put her hands over her face. "That's all I remember."

"Did you see anything unusual? Any sign that anyone else had been there?"

Grace looked at the cop as though he were an alien species.

My husband was dead on the fucking floor, she wanted to shriek. *I wasn't looking around for signs.* The words started to come up, to erupt. She choked them down.

"No," she said flatly.

Danny had a headache.

The late-night television news had been ambiguous. "Apparent homicide," they'd called it. A wide angle of the police line encircling the house. Some neighbor saying, "This is terrible, just terrible."

Danny couldn't tell if he meant they'd miss Gil, or that he was afraid of the impact on property values if the neighborhood got a bad rap.

It didn't seem real. He'd killed Gil McDonald. The culmination of so much concentrated effort, so much care. And now, in the quiet morning aftermath, watching a cardinal hopping from branch to branch in the oak outside his window, Danny was not quite sure why he'd felt so compelled, so driven.

The nurse stood next to Grace's bed. The cop was right behind her.

"The police want to get a blood sample, and a few strands of hair. Is that okay with you?"

"Why?"

"Because they can't determine what doesn't belong in the house until they know everything about the people who live there—like a baseline."

"Sure, go ahead, whatever they want." Grace turned her head away. She flinched as the needle pricked her finger.

Alex and Molly could not go home. Home was still a crime scene, sealed with neon police tape. They met at the home of friends before going to the hospital.

When they got to her room late Saturday afternoon, Grace was sitting up in bed. She gasped at seeing them, flinging her arms out toward them. In seconds they were all three on the bed, one on either side, crying together.

"Oh God," moaned Grace. "You're here. You're here."

"What happened?" asked Alex in a choked voice. "What the hell happened?"

17

In the homicide room, Sam focused on the initial test results from the KBI. There had been two blood types thus far determined at the scene. The most prevalent, as expected, was the victim's. It was O, a common type, over 44% of the population. The other type was B Negative. This was far less common, about 1.7% of the general population.

What troubled Sam was that Grace McDonald also was B Neg.

"Did we get a paraffin test on the McDonald woman?" Sam called out to Jim Beuler, who was rewriting notes in a corner of the room.

"No. Why?"

"Don't know yet. Something funny going on here."

Sam reviewed the statement taken at the hospital. She never mentioned being cut or bleeding in the house.

It didn't add up.

He put in a call to the K.B.I. headquarters over in Topeka to request a comprehensive DNA analysis of the blood samples. And he began composing a line of questioning in his mind for Grace McDonald.

Gil's autopsy was scheduled for late Saturday afternoon. Patsy Tsosie walked through the gray metal door marked "County Coroner." While Sam would also be there, she needed to be present with *her* body, *her* case, for the autopsy. It was her first.

Patsy's eyes were drawn to a plaque on the wall next to the entrance.

"Let laughter cease.
Let speech be gentle.
This is the place
where Death rejoices
to instruct those
who live."

Patsy felt the hairs on the back of her neck rise. Then the metal door opened and she heard familiar footsteps.

"Ready to go, Doc?" Sam called out.

"Just waiting for you," replied Dr. Liebowitz, appearing in a doorway. Together they took off the police tape that covered the door to the cold storage vault that contained Gil McDonald's body. They slid the wrapped body on to the gurney. Carolyn effortlessly moved the gurney through the room and through a door marked "Autopsy 2." Then they returned to the main room.

A kid in surgical scrubs appeared as if by magic.

"Go ahead and prep him," said Liebowitz.

The kid went into Autopsy 2 without a word.

"Go over the case with me, Sam?" said Liebowitz.

Patsy was half-aware of the conversation but was mostly staring through the open door into the autopsy room. Gil's body had been moved from the gurney to the long metallic autopsy table. The shoulders were propped by a wooden bar. The neck faced the ceiling, a vulnerable white, a lump of Adam's apple poking through the white skin. The face hung backward, empty eyes staring at the wall.

Gil was now naked. His skin was a grotesque mural of alabaster white and darker shades—rose, yellow, brown, navy—where blood had pooled and discolored the skin. There were holes, but they were bloodless, like pretend wounds.

The hair at his groin did not yet know it was dead. It curled, dark brown with gray swirls interspersed. Patsy knew if she touched it that it would feel alive. Nothing else about him would feel human, but that hair would. Patsy felt she could almost see it growing.

His testicles were propped up by his legs, and his penis lay at an angle as if draped across them. Together they made a very small arch up from the otherwise flat surface of his body. They looked soft and warm.

"Here, put these on," Carolyn said, handing Patsy blue booties and surgical scrubs.

They walked into the autopsy room. The kid was waiting.

"This is Mike, my diener," she said.

"Your what?" popped out before Patsy remembered her resolve to keep her mouth shut and act cool.

"Diener. From the German verb, dienen. Means helper. Somehow it's ended up meaning an autopsy assistant."

Carolyn turned to the body. In two minutes she'd taken photos of the body from every angle. She started checking orifices: mouth, ears, nose, eyes. She took swabs from each and handed them to Mike.

She turned her focus to the wounds: measuring, numbering, taking more close-up photographs. She described each observation for the tape recorder that sat on an adjacent table. She reached over to a table and picked up a narrow steel rod, two or three feet long, and gently began to insert it into the hole in Gil's chest. Careful not to push, she threaded it through the body until it encountered resistance.

"Trajectory rods," she said over her shoulder for Patsy's benefit. "Helps determine angle."

Then she took more photos. Mike moved to help her as she rolled Gil's body over and repeated the process.

This time the rod emerged from Gil's back.

"Entry on both sides," she noted. "Must have spun on the first hit."

Then she selected a small knife.

Carolyn began at one shoulder, then the other, making a V that met about six to eight inches below the throat. Then one long smooth slice from breastbone to groin. As the knife moved, the skin splayed open just a bit, so that the layers of fat and muscle were visible. Carolyn pulled at the skin that covered the chest wall, pulling it to one side. It was like peeling the skin off a chicken, only thicker, lined with more yellowy fat. Taking a different knife, she marked off a triangle over the ribs, then carefully cut through, rib by rib, until she could lift out the entire front of the chest wall. Blood was collected from the heart using a large needle and syringe.

Patsy exhaled. No longer anxious, she was now fascinated.

The diener started to work on the organs, pulling out squiggles of intestine, then carefully lifting out foot after foot of bowel—like long yellowish plastic tubing, almost transparent.

The air changed abruptly when he opened the stomach. Carolyn poked methodically through the contents of the stomach, looking for clues, for anything that would provide data. She saved the contents in a plastic cup.

Every organ was removed, weighed, examined, sliced. Sections were taken for lab study, the remains then put in a bucket. The table had holes in the metal, draining downward. There was a hose and faucets. A large cutting board rested on a corner of the table for dissecting and slicing the organs.

With the organs out, the chest area was a curving vacuum, the inside of each rib visible, blood-water puddles on either side of the spine. The back of a bullet glinted from where it was wedged in the bone.

Patsy looked around the square room. Metal shelving lined the walls. There was a box of surgical gloves. Patsy reached in and put one on.

Gil's skin was icy to her touch.

Like a rubber baby doll left outside all night, Patsy thought, her left hand softly cupping Gil's foot. And he did feel like cold rubber, somewhat pliable, so that small indentations could be made in the surface, but no more. Much of the rigor was gone, leaving as it had begun, first the small, then the large limbs.

Carolyn cut upward under the neck, peeling back that skin, digging out the larynx and trachea. The diener wiped away any blood. The insides were pink, almost glowing.

Then they were ready for the skull.

The diener took a small knife and gently cut a line around the back of the scalp, lifting Gil's hair to get a clear view. Then he grasped the scalp and pulled forward with all his weight. It was not enough.

Carolyn got on the other side and together they tugged the scalp forward until they peeled it down over the face, a tight rubber inside-out mask, where they left it. Carolyn traced a line around Gil's white bony skull from behind his left ear to behind his right ear, then from the top of each ear up and over the top of the skull. She reached backward and flipped a switch.

"This is a Stryker saw," Carolyn said to Patsy. "Remarkable tool. Won't cut soft tissue, just bone."

Carolyn held the round whirring blade up to the palm of her hand to demonstrate. Patsy flinched as the blade touched skin. But there was no blood.

Carolyn leaned over Gil's head. She leaned into the saw, putting all her body weight behind it, pushing through the bone. A white dust rose from the line moving slowly across the back of the neck, then over the top of the skull. The saw made a high piercing whine. Putting down the saw, Carolyn lifted off the top of the skull.

"Oh my God," whispered Patsy.

The brain glistened. It rested in the bottom half of the skull. It was textured, full of white and gray swirls. Soft and mushy, it looked terribly fragile.

Carolyn took a small knife and gently inserted her hand under the base of the brain. Then she cupped the brain in her two hands and carefully lifted it out. In the bottom of the skull, Patsy could see the brain stem. It was the size and pulpy whiteness of bok choy. There were distinct containers in the base of the skull, rounded, hollowed out spheres.

Looks like Tupperware, she thought. *Like a dip tray.*

"Contusion here," Carolyn pointed at a mark on the skull. "Something hit it, or it hit something pretty hard."

Patsy stared into the empty skull. She'd hoped to be *professional*, to survive her first autopsy without puking or fainting. But she hadn't been prepared to be awestruck. This was as close to miraculous as anything she'd ever witnessed.

By the end, they had measured and photographed every wound, every bruise. Carolyn had drawn pictures as well. One bullet had been pried from the spine. Every fragment of metal had been found, removed, and labeled as evidence.

All the organs remaining in the bucket were placed in an orange plastic bag and the bag unceremoniously stuffed back in the body cavity. Then the diener took a large S-shaped needle, with industrial size thread, and loosely stitched together the flaps of skin. He settled the skull back in place and pulled the scalp up and over. He stitched the skull flaps together. When he was done, it was hard to see where the line was under Gil's hair.

The diener handed a plastic bag to Patsy.

"Hold this for a minute, okay?"

It was a Pro-Tex-Mor adult size plastic shroud sheet, with a chin strap and cellulose pads, ID Tags, and ties.

Patsy wondered what Pro-Tex-Mor stood for.

18

On Saturday morning, Katrina told her boys about Gil McDonald. They were adolescent in their response, their fascination that someone they knew had been murdered alternating with awkward attempts to comfort their mother.

Katrina responded to the unreality of it all by cleaning. She started with the bathrooms and worked her way clear outside to the garage. She grunted from exertion, and could feel her shoulders ache, but she did not stop.

It was late afternoon, the light waning outside, when the phone shrilled.

"Kat, it's me."

"Gracie. Oh, dear God, Gracie. How are you?"

"I'm here. That's about it. The kids just left to get some dinner and clean up."

"I was there last night. Did they tell you?"

"Yes."

"Do you know what happened?"

"No, not really. I came home and found Gil." Her voice was shaking.

"Gracie, this is so horribly awful. I'm so sorry."

Grace was silent for a minute. Then she spoke.

"Kat, I need help here. I have to put together a funeral in the next few days, and I can't think straight. Could you take off work and come help me?"

"I can be there in an hour."

"No, not tonight. I get out of here in the morning. Come over tomorrow afternoon. I need your level head."

"Where, Gracie?"

"What?"

"Where will you be?"

"Oh, yeah, *where*. Okay, you know that little guest house behind the Simonson's, where her mother used to live?"

"Yes."

"Well, we're staying there for a while. Until the police are done with the house."

At 4 p.m. on Sunday, Grace and Katrina sat on the flagstone patio of the Simonson's guest house.

It was like a dollhouse, with white paint and blue trim and window boxes. There was a tiny living room, kitchen and bedroom downstairs, a loft space above with two twin beds. Molly and Alex had slept up there last night.

Grace wondered if she could just live here forever, sit and watch the squirrels bicker over nuts. She would ignore the nightmare in her own home. Her home had been destroyed, as surely as if a gas line had exploded it into a fireball.

Molly and Alex had left when Katrina arrived, swept off in a crowd of solicitous peers. They'd said they would bring back food, looking both guilty yet grateful for a chance to escape. Grace and Kat had been sitting for an hour, avoiding the talk.

"What do you think Gil would like in a funeral?" Kat finally asked.

It felt like a stupid question to ask, but Kat had never planned a funeral before. She'd had some input after her father died, but then it was all prescribed by religion, by custom.

"Gil hated funerals. He said everyone sounds the same, sanitized into sainthood." Grace looked across the yard. "Gil was great, but he wasn't a saint," she continued. "I think he'd want us to focus on who he really was, not some phony facade. He liked blues and oldies and Philip Glass. He read magazines and the *New York Times*. He was a good father, such a damn good father. He brought me tea in bed in the morning. He loved basketball and Greek food and. . ."

Grace stood up abruptly. Her voice was choking.

"Talk to the kids when they get back. See if they have any ideas. I need to lie down for a little bit."

She walked stiffly into the cottage.

On Monday morning at 11 a.m., Grace and Katrina were at the funeral home. Grace had never thought about picking out a casket for her husband. She preferred to look at pinstriped suits, extra-long shirts, and snazzy ties.

Not in my game plan, she thought to herself, absently listening to the soft-spoken funeral director who was trying to demonstrate the features of the various models. There were twenty or more caskets in the long, narrow room.

"Would you mind getting us that booklet that described what's included?" Katrina asked. "And I think my friend could use a few minutes alone here to just look and think, so take your time."

Thank God for Katrina, thought Grace.

The caskets seemed massive, made of colored metals and bronzes and hardwoods. They also seemed to be gender-typed, with rose and pinkish tones for females and grays and blues for males.

"You see a pine box around here anywhere, Kat?"

"Not a pine box in sight. Maybe they keep them in some back closet."

"I can't see Gil in all this silky material. He hated stuff around his face at night. I'd bury under the covers and he'd peel them back down to his shoulders."

"You have to do what feels right, Gracie."

"He loved the woods. This metal looks so cold, like a tomb."

Katrina said nothing. They were tombs, made huge and cozy because people liked the image of their loved ones surrounded by all that satin and stuffing.

"Would the pine one have just a little lining?" Grace asked.

They'd been making arrangements most of the morning, talking first to the priest, now the funeral director. Grace had sent the kids to a friend's house to put together a music mix of Gil's favorites for the funeral. That would be difficult for them but better than looking at caskets.

There were too many small decisions at a time when any decision seemed monstrous.

Grace settled on a simple, pine box.

"It's usually for our Jewish clients," said the director. "Their religious customs require a plain wooden coffin."

He explained that the pine would have to be lowered into a concrete vault at the cemetery, due to state law. Gracie signed the papers.

"We need some food," said Katrina as they left. The November air was crisp, the sky an intense cerulean blue. They could smell burning leaves.

Katrina drove to a small Greek restaurant downtown. They stared absently out the window while waiting for the food, sipping hot tea.

"Gracie, hi there," called out a voice. A large, fur-encased body moved toward the table. "Why I haven't seen you in a-a-a-ages."

Katrina took one sideways glance at Grace's face and interjected.

"I'm Katrina, a friend of Gracie's. I'm just helping her with the arrangements." She held out her hand.

The woman took a second to digest the message.

"Arrangements?"

Grace replied in a voice without affect. "Gil is dead, Marcella. He was killed last Friday."

"Oh my God. I had no idea. I just got back into town." Marcella seemed to deflate. "I'm so sorry."

"Whatever I can do." She tentatively put her hand on the top of Grace's head, then left. Grace looked over at Katrina.

"I'll be in the car. Could you just get the food to go?"

"Sure, Gracie. I'll be out in a minute."

They drove back to the Simonson's guest house in silence. Kat set the small round table. Grace sucked the tart black olives and spit out the pits. They wrapped chunks of gyros in pita and dipped them in the cucumber sauce. They were ravenous.

Grace didn't know who of the family would be coming to the funeral. All of their parents were dead. Her only sibling, a brother, was living in a group home at the moment, maybe, out in California, unless he had, once again, gone off his meds and left to go back to living on the streets. It was a crapshoot. In any case, Oliver hadn't seen Gil in years.

Oliver was schizophrenic, diagnosed when he was 20 and she was 16. Watching his struggle, and her parent's desperate attempts to care for him, had been a factor in her eventual choice of profession.

Gil had a younger sister, Mary, but her husband was in the military and they lived overseas, on Okinawa. She did not see how she could get back that fast.

Grace expected that some Missouri cousins would drive in but doubted if others would make it. They'd send flowers.

"There isn't much family," Grace said to Katrina. "We've made our own family, patched it together out of friends."

"And we'll be here," Katrina reassured her. "All of us. So many people who loved Gil."

On Monday while Grace and Katrina were looking at caskets, Sam and Patsy were doing the routine legwork of any investigation.

At 7:30 a.m. Sam and Patsy sat in an unmarked car across from the small publishing house where Gil had worked. They watched the people arriving for work. They spent the entire morning talking to employees who had worked with Gil, had shared lunches and projects.

Without a suspect or motive, the only place to start was with the victim.

Two hours later, Patsy and Sam sat over coffee at the Lotta Latte Cafe.

"Face it, Sam, the guy was a saint."

"Maybe that's just how it sounds now that he's dead. It's one thing to bitch about somebody alive and kicking, another to complain about the habits of the deceased."

19

The hooker was blonde and skinny, with a punk haircut and an Ozark twang. Danny had picked her up off Troost Avenue in Kansas City. They'd gone to a room in a sleazy motel just blocks away. He was on top, pushing into her, his eyes clenched shut. She was making moaning sounds with an overlay of words—"More. Harder. Faster. Baby. Faster." Through closed eyes, he was seeing Mandy's face. His hand reached to feel her long, soft hair. But he touched a bristle, stiff with gel. His eyes jerked open. Her eyes were filled with a bored indifference.

"What are you, a dyke?" he growled, rolling off and away from her.

"I'm no dyke, buddy. But you're just gettin' your rocks off. You don't know shit."

Danny slapped her across the face. He waited for her eyes to register rage, pain, something. He saw the red lines of fingers across her cheek.

She blinked, twice. Her eyes did not change. She rose, wiping at herself with a small, yellowed towel, pulling down the short skirt that had gathered up around her waist. She walked to the door. When it was open, she turned.

"You still don't know shit," she said. "Slapping women around just shows you're too stupid to learn."

On Wednesday at 10:45 a.m. Danny Rivers sat across from St. John the Evangelist Catholic church in his parked car. The lot was filling fast. Men dressed in dark suits stood unobtrusively under the outside corner eaves of the church. Their eyes roamed the crowd, as though looking for a missing spouse. He recognized them as cops.

Danny had not been sure he would actually go into the funeral. But now, with the police watching, he might be noticed if he drove off.

He got out and walked toward the church. He wore the same suit he'd worn to his divorce hearing. He felt it was only fitting to wear it again here. He nodded to the officer as he climbed the church steps.

Danny stood in the back of the church. Off to the left, in the choir loft, he saw two more of the dark-suited men scanning the crowd. He lowered his head and closed his eyes in an appearance of sorrowful prayer.

When he opened them, Grace McDonald was being escorted up the aisle. She wore a long, black dress, almost to her feet, and plain, gold hoops in her ears. Behind her were a young man and woman who looked to be in their early twenties. They clung to each other. Danny recognized them from photos he'd seen in the house.

Danny felt his heart pound. The girl reminded him of Mandy. She was crying silently, tears streaking her face. The boy held onto her, his face a white mask, his eyes hollow and dry, dark circles below the sockets.

Danny felt hot inside the gray suit. He'd wanted to teach the bitch how it hurt, what it felt like. But he had not figured in the kids. He felt a desperate urge to escape, to slip out. But then he would lose invisibility. The men watching the crowd from the choir loft might notice.

Music began up in the loft. It was not religious, but a Tracy Chapman tape—*All That You Have is Your Soul*. What followed was unlike any funeral Danny had ever been to.

Different people got up and walked to the front of the church. Each spoke about Gil. What Gil was *really* like. How he could make them laugh. His eccentricities, both endearing and annoying. His dreams. His accomplishments. What he enjoyed: basketball, music, his children, reading the *New York Times* on a Sunday morning with coffee and donuts. Travel. Taos. Hiking in the mountains. His loyalty to his friends. His love for his wife.

With each voice, some cracking, some solid and sure, the presence of the man who had been Gil McDonald filled the church.

When it was over, Danny exited in the first wave from the church, careful to be in the middle of a group, to not be singled out as alone.

He got in his car and put his head on the steering wheel. He did not stay to see Grace's tear-streaked face as she walked back down the aisle. He'd wanted her to suffer, but something had gone wrong.

The homicide squad came back together after the funeral. They'd taken down the license plates of all the cars parked at the church, had videotaped the entire proceedings, unobtrusively sweeping through the pews to get the faces of those present. Officers had watched for anyone that seemed to be out-of-place.

And they'd come up with a big, fat zero.

20

"Listen to this, Sam," insisted Patsy.

It was a tape of a call to the TIPS Hotline.

"I'm not sure if this information is relevant, but. . ." the voice was shaky. "I was pretty close to Gil McDonald. We had a relationship."

"Could you come down and give us a statement, Miss. . .?" a male voice asked.

"Can't I just talk on the phone?"

"Then could I get your name and number so that the detective in charge can give you a call?"

"I called the Hotline so I could stay anonymous."

"We'd try to protect your privacy," the voice reassured. "If you're not comfortable releasing your name, I'll give you a TIPS number. But it really would be simpler. . ."

"I need to think." Then a click.

Jennifer Watson called back an hour later and agreed to come in. She was 35 years old, with reddish-brown hair. She was an editor at the press.

"Why not just tell me whatever you can about Gil McDonald," Sam started.

They were seated in the interview room. Patsy was on the other side of the mirror.

"Well, Gil was a really good man." Her hands were twisting in her lap. "He was there for me when I was hurting."

"How do you mean that?"

"My husband divorced me about two years ago. We had fertility problems." Jennifer stared at her hands. "He re-married within weeks. They had a baby six months later."

"How long did your relationship with Gil last?" Sam asked.

"About seven months. Three months, then we stopped for about six weeks, then two more months. But it was over. When Gil came back from Oregon, he asked me to meet him at a motel restaurant. He told me it couldn't go on. It wasn't any big surprise."

"What did the relationship involve?"

"Mostly talk. We were at different places in our lives. We were both coming to terms with our disappointments."

"Was it sexual?" Sam asked, more directly.

"Yes." She looked at her hands again. "It was sexual, but more about getting through the hurt. I don't know how else to explain it."

"Did Mrs. McDonald know of this relationship?"

"Oh, no. When Gil broke it off, the reason was that he couldn't live with a secret from Gracie."

"Did he ever mention what her response might be if she did find out?"

"Not really. We were very discreet. There was only one time anyone ever saw us together—at lunch the day he broke it off for good."

"Do you know who that person was?"

"I'd never seen her before. I think Gil introduced her as Katrina."

"For the record. Ms. Watson, where were you around the time Gil McDonald was killed?"

"I worked until 5 p.m. and then went directly to a TGIF with the women from my therapy group. It's not quite a *happy hour*, but we're trying. I was with the group until about 8 p.m. and I can give you their names and numbers."

"Thank you, Ms. Watson. Here's my card if there's anything else that you think of."

Sam showed Jennifer out and came back to the interview room, to the other side of the one-way mirror.

"Motive," announced Sam to Patsy. "We've just uncovered possible motive." He should have been exultant, but he sounded depressed.

"I think I'll give Mrs. Baptiste a call."

Katrina sat again in the interview room at police headquarters.

"Mrs. Baptiste," Sam was saying. "The last time you were in, I asked if you were aware of any marital struggles with the McDonalds."

"Don't mess with my head, Officer."

"We have a woman who says she had a relationship with Mr. McDonald. She was introduced by Mr. McDonald, at a motel restaurant, to a friend called Katrina. Would you happen to be that Katrina?"

Katrina looked past Sam's left shoulder. The words settled.

"I believe I may be," she replied.

"Were you aware that Mr. McDonald had an affair?"

"Yes."

"But you failed to tell us?"

"Look, Officer, the affair, as you call it, was over. Gil told me so himself. I didn't see any reason to bring it up when it would serve no purpose."

"What did Gil tell you?"

"He called me after I saw him at the restaurant. He said he'd had a brief relationship. A mid-life crisis. He didn't want to lose his marriage. He said he wanted to be with Grace until he died."

The words echoed, hollow.

"And what was your response?"

"I told him that my primary loyalty was to Grace, not him. If it was over, I wouldn't say anything. But if I ever found he was lying, I'd tell Gracie."

"And his response?"

"He was grateful."

"Whom were you protecting by keeping this secret?"

"Their marriage. It really was a good marriage."

"How did Grace discover the affair? Who told her?"

Katrina looked confused.

"Nobody," she replied. "She doesn't know. I would have heard."

"Even if Gil had told her that you'd known and kept his secret?"

Katrina did not answer.

"Mrs. Baptiste, I'm going to give you ten minutes to consider whether there's anything else you've forgotten to mention."

Sam got up.

"Oh," he said, turning from the door, "Have I mentioned that withholding information in a homicide investigation is a criminal act?"

In her memory, Katrina could see Gil so clearly, leaning over the table, talking to the woman. If she hadn't known him for years, she would only have seen a man and woman having a business lunch. But she knew, without words, that it was more than that—the tilt of his head, the way he was leaning forward, looking into the woman's eyes. One minute Kat was scanning the room for the lawyer she was meeting to discuss a case—and the next. . .

If she'd turned at that first second, she might have been able to pretend. But she'd stared. He'd looked up. His face had flushed. He'd introduced the woman as an editor at the press.

Gil had called her that night. He'd made no pretense, did not deny what she'd seen. He'd asked for her complicity, for Grace's sake.

It had seemed the sensible choice.

The day after the funeral was Thanksgiving.

Kat asked Grace and the kids to come to her house for turkey and fixings. But the look Grace gave her, akin to dread, had squelched that.

In the past, Grace had often hosted expansive gatherings. But now she lay in the dark bedroom of the guest house. Alex and Molly tried to cajole her into getting up.

"I think I have a virus or something," she said. "Why don't you go over to your friends for a while? Please? I know you have invitations. And you have to eat. It's okay, really. I can't move."

She tried to keep her voice maternal, reassuring.

"Are you sure?" asked Molly.

"Yes. You are not abandoning me. Go. Out with you."

They each leaned over and kissed her forehead, loud smooches that echoed the goodnight kisses she'd given them for so many years. She sensed in them that same relief that she'd felt in tucking them in, softly closing their bedroom doors, temporarily liberated from the responsibility of caring.

Listening to the closing front door, Grace felt relief also. She went into the tiny kitchen, put on a pot of water for tea. The wind was up and neat piles of leaves were being blown about. Gil always bagged his leaves as soon as he had a pile. Gil was cautious.

"What the hell happened?" she spoke to the air, to the invisible spirit of her husband.

Then she was sobbing.

"What the fuck happened? How could you get killed?" Her voice rose and cracked. "We spend twenty years living in Kansas because it's so fucking safe! We could have been in New York City for all the damn difference it made."

For an hour, Grace ranted. Then she found herself on the floor, her back against the couch, keening softly, longing for her mother.

On Friday night, Grace pushed Molly and Alex to return to school, to finish the semester. She knew they were hurting but shadowing her would not help their grief.

"It makes no sense to lose a semester's work or get stuck with five incompletes. Go, finish up, take your exams, and then come back," she said. "I do not need you to sit here and hold my hand."

They left on Saturday afternoon, Alex taking Molly to the airport before he headed down I-35 to Austin. "We'll talk every day," they promised.

The police released the *crime scene* the day after Thanksgiving. Grace felt like a refugee, forced to flee with only a few clothes. Everything she owned was just a few blocks away, inside that front door, but she could not imagine how she could ever return.

In the tiny, borrowed guesthouse, she curled up to lick her wounds.

21

In the DNA lab of the Kansas Bureau of Investigation in Topeka, the sounds of the various machines made a low humming. To Ellen Woods, lab supervisor, the sound was as familiar and reassuring as the coursing of blood through her veins.

To Ellen, the procedures had lives of their own.

DNA testing was not simply a matter of comparing samples of blood and tissue, but patiently waiting for the samples to declare themselves, to make the invisible visible. At any given time, the lab was in the middle of a dozen different analyses. Semen, blood, hair, tissue—the minute particles of flesh found underneath the fingernails of a strangled child. To take this and turn it into tangible evidence, to make the evidence irrefutable, and then to make it easily understood by the average juror, was Ellen's challenge.

"DNA, deoxyribonucleic acid, produces a profile, a type. Each person has a unique type, like the way that we think of snowflakes coming down—they look alike, but every one is distinct in some way," she would explain, oversimplifying, to cops-in-training, or to jurors.

"This profile is contained in your blood, tissue, organs, whatever has cells. It's consistent throughout the body. And the only way that two people have the same DNA profile is if they are identical twins."

By the time that Ellen finished with explaining RFLP (Restriction Fragment Length Polymerase), PCR (Polymorphase Chain Reaction)—which she called a molecular Xerox—and HLA-DQ (one hell of a lot faster in terms of analysis time required but less absolute in terms of power of discrimination), and Polymarker systems and D1S80, her audiences had a primer of the basics.

Ellen was a good teacher. She made a great witness at trials, explaining complex scientific testing in such a way that a jury could see, understand, and trust the evidence.

But her love was her lab, her tanks.

And tanks could not be rushed, no matter who was doing the talking.

"I don't give a shit how long the lab says it's going to take," Saunders said impatiently into the phone. "You tell them I need that evidence now."

He hung up the phone. Through his office windows he could see the park, the gazebo in the middle of gardens. There was a feathery dusting of snow.

"Norman Rockwell lives on," he muttered.

Around the room were six tall bookcases, shelves piled with folders and papers. Everywhere he looked were case files. But no murder cases. No high visibility cases. Not one damn case that would bring him any decent media coverage.

He punched another number into the phone.

"Sam Hillard," he said, and waited, tapping his fingers.

"Sam. Bruce Saunders. What have we got on the McDonald case? I want to move on this."

He grimaced as he listened to Sam's reply.

"Look, I'm not inclined to wait. It looks like favoritism if we hold back just because of the holidays. And I disagree that she isn't likely to run. She gets wind that we're holding her out as a suspect and she could be out of here."

Bruce's fingers tapped more rapidly now.

"Yes, I recognize it's circumstantial at this point. But the facts and what the woman says are inconsistent. To me, that's incriminating."

He listened again.

"You do your job. But get her in and ask whatever damn questions you have to because I want an indictment before Christmas."

In Gunnison, Mandy was reading a letter from Emily Emmesch. She cherished her letters from Emily, whom she saw as something between a surrogate mother and a secular guardian angel. A clipping fell out, but Mandy went for the letter itself. Emily described the latest in the clinic, trouble with the new receptionist, the gossip around town, a new parrot that was now a fixture in the waiting room. But then—

"I have some bad news. I've enclosed something from the paper.

Remember Grace McDonald? Well, her husband was murdered. I thought you might want to know."

Remember Grace? Of course she remembered Grace. If it weren't for Grace, Mandy knew she'd never have had the courage to leave.

She picked up the clipping from the floor and read it once. Then again. There was no reason for this to happen. She heard Grace's voice in her head. *There is nothing you did to deserve this, Mandy. You are trying to find logic in the senseless.*

And now Grace was face-to-face with the senseless.

"Oh God," muttered Mandy. "Oh my God."

It had been five days since Alex and Molly had left. Closing the door of the cottage after hugging them goodbye, Grace had cried with exhausted relief.

For the first three days, Grace cocooned herself. Her hair became matted. She could not sit or lie without closing up into a fetal position, knees to chest, chin down, hands tucked up against her mouth as though warming them with her hot breath. She gnawed softly, a suckling, on the smooth place where her thumb met her hand.

Grace dreamed of the children, nightmare fantasies of their dying, their heads tipped back at unnatural angles. She was trying to reach them or warn them. She would jerk awake, to lie sweating and panting in the darkness.

On the fourth day, Grace stood in the shower for a very long time. She washed her hair twice, then, forgetting, she washed it again. She put on a pair of jeans that were hanging in the closet, and a sweater. They fit her. She didn't know how they'd gotten there.

She stepped outside the cottage. The tree limbs were now barren, stark brown sticks against a sharp blue sky. The last time she'd looked, leaves remained. The ground was cold against her bare feet.

She walked through the grass, the leaves, and inhaled the winter air. She felt the cold against her skin. She smelled leaves burning somewhere close. She was alive.

She did not will it, did not want to face it, but she was alive.

Back in the cottage, Grace made coffee. She found her purse, her appointment book, the pad where she kept the lists she relied on to tell her what to do next.

She was having a very hard time seeing *next*. Her life had been organized, since the kids left, around work and Gil. But now Grace could not see herself working.

"It's like an emotional transfusion sometimes," she remembered explaining to a class of graduate students, trying to help them see beneath the theories. "I can use logic, challenge cognitive distortions, analyze behavioral patterns, provide substitute thoughts and acts, and connect it all to family history and experience. But all that is useless crap unless this feeling is there, this absolute belief that they can heal and grow. I have to believe enough for both of us at the beginning until they're strong enough to feel it, to nurture it along."

But now Grace could not feel anything. She had nothing to give. And who in their right mind would go to a therapist mired in grief?

Grace stared at the open appointment book, the whiteness of the blank pages. The ring of the phone was almost a reprieve.

"Ms. McDonald?" a man's voice inquired.

"Yes."

"This is Detective Hillard. I'm sorry to bother you, but we were wondering if you could come down to the station house and go over a few things with us."

"I've told you whatever I know, Detective."

"How about 2 p.m.?"

"Okay, I'll be there." Her voice grew stronger, as if simply agreeing to be somewhere provided her with some small sense of direction, of purpose, of *next*.

Sam hung up the phone and looked over at Patsy Tsosie. Patsy stared back impassively.

"She doesn't sound worried," said Sam.

"Maybe she has nothing to be worried about," said Tsosie.

"And maybe all the politicians in Washington are selfless public servants with no personal agendas who vote for the good of the country," said Sam.

"Ms. McDonald, we'd like to go over the sequence of events on the evening of your husband's death once again."

Sam was seated across from Grace in the small room where he had first met with Katrina Baptiste. Next to him, taking notes, was Patsy Tsosie. Behind the mirror were two more detectives.

"All right. I had an appointment from 4 to 5 p.m. and then. . ."

"And who was that with?" Sam interrupted.

"Officer, I can't tell you that. I'm bound by confidentiality."

Her voice was almost reproving, as if Sam were a child who had reached for candy without permission. "I left right around 5 p.m. but I stopped at the bakery and bumped into Joanna. I called Gil to tell him I'd be late."

"And what time was that?" asked Sam.

"About 5:15, I think."

"And you spoke to Gil?"

"No. I got the machine. . ." Grace looked at Sam. "Don't you know all this already?"

"Well, yes, but I'm in charge of the investigation and it helps to hear it directly from you, so that I can ask any questions and fill in any holes."

Holes, Grace thought. *I'd like to fill in a few holes myself.*

"I left a message on the machine. I had a cup of coffee with Joanna. I drove home."

"And what time was that?"

"Six-ish."

"Could you be more specific?"

"*All Things Considered* was over. Classical was on. So it had to be after 6 p.m.—but not too much after. Six-ish."

"And when you reached your home?"

"I got out of the car. . ." Grace's voice faded. She took a slow breath. "I got out of the car. I walked up to the front door. I think I used my key. The music was loud. I hung up my coat. I figured Gil was cooking, so I went to the kitchen. That's when I saw Gil. He was on the floor, against the cabinet. His eyes were open. There was blood."

"And then you?" Sam asked softly.

"I wanted to touch him, to be sure he was dead. But my legs wouldn't move. I think I fell down. I got blood on my hand, and I couldn't go on."

"Did you ever go into the center of the kitchen?"

"No," answered Grace.

"How did you get outside? Did you go out the back door?"

"No, I didn't go any further into the kitchen than my arm could reach from the doorway."

"How then do you explain our findings of your blood on your husband's body?" Sam's voice dropped to just above a whisper.

She's not stunned, thought Sam. She did not have the trapped-in-headlights frozen fear look.

She looked puzzled. Simply puzzled.

"Whatever are you talking about?" she asked.

"Your blood, Ms. McDonald. Your blood has been matched to samples found on the body of your dead husband. Not by the door, but on the other side of the kitchen, the far side. And what troubles us is that we cannot explain how that blood got there."

Grace looked confused, almost stupid. Her jaw dropped open a half-inch and a small bit of saliva began to pool in the corner of her lips and mouth.

"My blood?" she asked.

"Yes."

"But I wasn't bleeding. What you're describing is impossible."

"We have the samples, Ms. McDonald. They were taken from the scene."

"Where? How? When did you get my blood to match?"

"You gave permission for samples to be taken in the hospital."

Grace's face twisted in concentration, trying to remember. The young officer in the hospital room. . .nurses poking at her. . .the kitchen floor.

She made a gesture, lifting both palms hands-up in the air.

"I don't know."

"Could you tell me about your husband, Ms. McDonald?"

Grace inhaled, then slowly exhaled.

"Gil was just a good guy. He liked his work. He doted on the kids. For a long time, the kids were at the center of how we organized our lives. But with them both away in college, we were relaxing, enjoying ourselves more."

She stopped, and her eyes filled with tears.

"I loved him. We had our differences, but it was a good marriage."

Shit. Oscar-caliber performance, thought Sam.

He waited a moment, then continued in a conversational tone.

"And where does his affair fit into that picture?"

"She sure looked surprised," commented Sam the next day to the task force.

"Or she'd prepared herself, knew it was coming," said another detective.

Four cops started arguing at once.

Sam butted in.

"Okay, you guys, let's look at what we have. Do we hand this over to the DA now or do we need more to go on?"

Patsy Tsosie hesitated. The rookie, she was grateful simply to be included on the task force. But she wanted to be more than an observer.

"Is there any way that we're moving in too fast on one suspect and not looking at alternatives?"

"Such as?" asked Sam.

"What about this girl he had an affair with? The victim broke up with her. Doesn't that deserve a second look?"

"We've got signs of a fight, her blood is like 8-9 feet from where she says she was, and her husband was having an affair she says she didn't know about," rebutted another detective.

"Look, the woman has a profession, friends, home. Nothing in her past. Why do you assume that an affair or even threat of divorce would lead to murder?" Patsy retorted.

"Like maybe it wouldn't look so good for the marriage therapist's husband to be foolin' around or walkin' out. Or maybe she just got pissed off."

"Simmer down, people," Sam cut in, then turned to Patsy.

"If you want to take another look at this other woman as a suspect, bring her in for questioning. Check out her alibi. See if there is anyone in her life who might be overly protective. We turn this over to the DA with any loopholes and the defense will have a field day."

Sam looked around the table.

"We're taking 48 hours to wrap this up. Go over every piece of shit. Every interview. Come up with ten alternate theories of how Gil McDonald got murdered in his own pretty little kitchen, and then follow up on 'em like they're our only hope. Any questions?"

Patsy Tsosie asked Jennifer Watson to come down to the station again. Her story was the same.

No, she could not think of anyone who would want to get revenge. Gil had been a good friend. Gil had never told his wife.

"It wasn't about sex," Jennifer said.

"Could you explain that?" asked Tsosie.

"We both felt like we'd failed, me with my marriage, Gil with his writing. We talked it out. But Gil didn't want to be with me." Jennifer looked into Tsosie's eyes. "Gil wanted to be with Gracie. And I was ready to move on, too."

22

"Katrina. Call as soon as you get in."

Hearing the voice, Katrina knew. It was all coming out.

For some ridiculous reason she had hoped that the secret of the affair could remain buried, with Gil, six feet under.

At the time, keeping Gil's secret had seemed so logical. She'd felt a distorted sense of power: she could turn her friend's life upside down in the name of honesty or allow her to remain oblivious and happy. Like a blindfolded doll of justice, Katrina had weighed the right and wrong of it. In the end, she'd done what Gill had asked.

For the sake of Grace.

"What was I thinking," Katrina moaned. "Grace is gonna fucking hate me if she doesn't kill me first."

The door to the Simonson's guest house was open when Katrina arrived. Grace was waiting in the living room.

"Gracie, I'm so sorry. I never meant to hurt you, it was like. . ."

Grace raised her eyebrows, her eyes stopping Katrina in mid-sentence.

"I need you to tell me everything you know, starting at the beginning," Grace said tightly. "Let's not worry about hurting my delicate feelings, okay? Just lay it out."

Kat nodded.

"I was meeting a lawyer from out-of-town about a case. She was at the Holiday Inn. Gil was having lunch with someone in that restaurant off the lobby."

"And?" prompted Grace.

"He'd been talking intently. He looked up and he saw me. And that would have been it if he'd just waved or called me over. But he flushed. Then he introduced me, and I found my attorney in the lobby and left."

"And based on that you tell the police my husband was having an affair?" Grace was almost spitting the words.

"No. Gil called me. He didn't deny that I'd seen something. He said he'd had a brief relationship, but that it was over. He wanted to be with you for the rest of his life. It was some mid-life craziness. He asked me not to say anything, that he didn't want to hurt you."

"And you agreed?"

"Gracie, it was so hard. But I really felt Gil was telling the truth, that it was over, that you were the most important person in his life. I didn't want to spoil what you had."

"What about truth and friendship and loyalty?" Grace's voice shook. "Huh, Kat? What about not keeping secrets at the expense of your friends? What—poor Gracie can't handle reality, so we better not tell her? Did you really think that it would be better for me to find out this way?"

"I didn't know he'd *die*, Grace. I just saw us growing old together, all of us, friends. I figured in five years I wouldn't even remember. Like a bad dream. Maybe it was just me. Maybe I couldn't cope with any more loss and telling you might have meant that."

As she said the words, Katrina realized that this was the real truth. Ultimately, she'd kept Gil's secret to protect herself, to preserve her friends, because she, not Grace, couldn't deal with it.

And, watching the look, the pain, that washed over her friend's face, Grace understood. And at the same moment she realized that she needed her friend more than she needed to be angry.

At least for now. Plenty of time to get angry later, she thought.

"Kat, I felt like such an idiot, like those wives on the TV talk shows when the smart-ass host tells them that their husband is a flaming bigamist. I've just finished telling him that our marriage was good, that we had no real problems, and he tells me my husband had an affair."

"Oh, Gracie, I'm so sorry. But when they called me in, they already knew. . ."

Grace cut her off.

"Now the police are saying that my blood was found on Gil's body. It makes no sense. I never really went into the kitchen. And I wasn't cut at that point. As near as I can tell, I cut my knees and hands on the gravel, later, crawling."

Kat looked confused. "Grace, what in the name of God are you talking about?"

"The police are acting like I'm a suspect. They say my *story* does not explain the presence of my *blood* on my husband's *body*. And then they spring the affair on me. That detective asked me if Gil had had previous affairs, if I'd had affairs, if I'd ever threatened Gil. It was made-for-TV- movie dialogue, and I could not change the channel."

Katrina was blank. None of this made any sense.

"Then the detective said that I might want to consider legal counsel. And he requested that I not leave town. I told him that it was all ridiculous, that this was a very sick joke, but he wasn't laughing."

Grace paused to breathe.

"So, you know any good criminal lawyers?"

23

It was December 15th. Danny was leaving soon to drive out to Gunnison and get Ross for the holidays. He was supposed to just pick him up and bring him back to Kaw Valley, but he had another idea. He was going to surprise Mandy by arriving with presents. Maybe, just maybe, they would spend the holidays together, like a family should.

He was having his breakfast, reading the paper. Some cop was quoted in the paper, "We are following up some serious leads, but we cannot compromise the investigation by revealing specifics."

Danny didn't expect that Grace would be charged. But neither she nor the police would be able to explain how her blood got there. Her precious reputation would be tainted. She'd never be trusted again. She wouldn't be able to tear apart other families, and she'd be haunted by the unsolved mystery.

Danny did not feel the elation he'd expected. Instead, it was as if the entire episode had nothing to do with him, was just something that he might see on the 6 o'clock news.

The 48 hours that Sam had given his team to look for any lead in any direction that did not point to Grace McDonald was almost up. The small room with the one-way mirror was getting a lot of use. There was something about the change in venue, thought Sam. People acted like they'd stumbled on to a movie set and were trying to figure out their lines. They came up with details, otherwise irrelevant.

"It was a joke," the one chubby woman had earnestly explained. "We all knew that at the time."

"But now—you wonder?" asked Tsosie.

"No. I mean, not really. It's just that, given the circumstances, it seems—just a bit. . ." Her voice trailed off. She looked down at her fingernails, where she had picked the pink polish off in neat tiny horseshoes all along the cuticles.

"Well, it was late, at this party, and we were joking about middle-aged men going off with bimbos, you know, much younger women. And Grace said that if Gil ever wanted to go off with a bimbo, he was welcome to. Then she said, this was the joke, that of course he wouldn't get far with a bullet in his back. Then Gil said something like, 'Well, gee, thanks, Gracie, for that therapeutic response.' And Gracie said how it would be compassionate compared with what else she'd dish out if he took off with a bimbo. And we laughed."

"That he wouldn't get far with a bullet in his back?" repeated Tsosie, her voice flat.

"Yes, but it sounds serious and it wasn't. We were all drinking and laughing."

"Do you remember how much Grace McDonald had been drinking?"

"Well, gosh, no. I mean, she isn't a heavy drinker or anything, but I'd think she'd had a few. And we finished off a few bottles of wine at dinner."

"And do you think that anyone else would recall this particular incident?"

"It wasn't an incident," the woman said. "It was a joke. But yes, there were at least a dozen of us."

"Could you give me their names?"

"Look, I said I'd cut my husband's pecker off if he fooled around on me. We were just in that sort of mood. It didn't mean anything."

Tsosie said nothing.

The woman sighed. "Jill and Harry Wingate, Mary and Ted. . ."

In the observation room, Sam flipped the switch for the mike.

He did not doubt that it had been a joke. But he heard it through cop ears, as it would be heard by a jury. He heard the twisted echo of premeditation, of intent.

The woman's husband still had his pecker.

But Gil McDonald was dead.

All jokes were off.

Bruce Saunders was tired of waiting. He wanted grounds for an indictment. And he wanted them now.

"Sam, I am as prudent as the next guy, but I think our town would sleep easier this holiday season knowing there is not some gun-toting homicidal maniac wandering the streets," Saunders argued into the phone. "This case has generated considerable public anxiety. I do not want to rush into anything, but I believe that we have evidence sufficient to charge."

He tapped his fingers, listening.

"Yes, we could wait for the final DNA, but we both know what that will say. The enzyme patterns came back a match. What does that narrow it down to, huh, Sam? Like one-in-ten-thou or less? Listen to me—we've got motive, opportunity, and a suspect lying through her teeth."

Saunders ran his fingers through his hair, listening again.

"I know we have no gun. But I have a feeling that the lady will roll over when she sees the complexity of her situation."

He grimaced as Sam responded.

"Let's meet tomorrow morning. I'm not going to charge unless I'm damn sure I can make it stick."

"Doesn't a grand jury have to indict?" Patsy asked Sam after his chat with Saunders.

"Nah. That's big city format. We investigate, put together a case, bring it to the DA If he thinks it will fly, he asks a judge for a warrant."

"So, how fast could this happen?"

"The way Saunders is, like this is his freakin' Christmas present, it could take all of an hour."

"Aren't you satisfied with the investigation?"

"I'm satisfied with the process, I just don't like the way it turned out. I like it better when my hunches play out. I got sideswiped by this one."

Tsosie was silent, thinking that it felt good to have this balding, chunky white man talking about hunches.

"It doesn't feel right for me either, Sam," Tsosie replied.

The DA was feeling flush.

He'd prepared the affidavit setting forth probable cause and brought it to the judge. It took him ten minutes to go through it. . .dead body. . . gunshot wounds. . .crime scene investigated. . .evidence samples taken… two blood types identified. . .one a match for the wife, found in different locations around the room...further tests in process...statements taken... the affair...the smashed vase...evidence of an altercation...her wounds...glass slivers from a broken vase found on her hand, on her clothes...the wife's explanation inconsistent with the physical evidence..

"Weapon recovered?" asked the judge.

"No."

"Why such a high bond request?"

"Judge, this woman has assets. She could be a flight risk."

"But she didn't leave town since the crime?"

"No. But she didn't know she was a suspect, either."

"Okay, you have your warrant. I'm sure the defense will put in for a bond reduction, but I'll deal with that at first appearance."

After Saunders left, Judge Hugh Johnson sat quietly. He ran his hand over his bald head. He'd come to appreciate the sensory experience of touching skin rather than hair these last few years, once he'd come to terms with its absence.

Hugh had known Grace McDonald for about 15 years. He'd listened to her testify in his own courtroom. The McDonalds were one of those couples that, over the years, his wife had mentioned they should try and have over for dinner sometime. So he should be feeling horrified, but instead he was puzzled.

What he did know was that this was one case he'd recuse himself from if and when it ever came to trial.

24

Grace parked the car in front of the Hy-Vee. She was reaching across the seat for the grocery list when she noticed the two cops strolling over. She thought momentarily that she'd parked wrong, maybe not within the lines. Or had she not come to a complete stop at the last corner? She waited until they were beside her window.

"Please get out of the car, ma'am. Slowly. Out. Now."

But the tone was wrong. Before the words made any literal sense to her, she felt puzzled at the tone. Then she saw the gun. It was held low, not obvious, but she could see right into the dark hole of the barrel.

"Get. Out. Of. The. Car." The words came again.

Grace very slowly turned her legs sideways and lifted her body out of the car. As she turned, she felt hard metal scrape against her wrists, a loud snapping sound, as her arms were jerked tightly behind her back.

"You are under arrest for the murder of Gil McDonald," the young man's voice changed tone, tinged with relief that this had gone so easily. He continued, sing-song, through the memorized Miranda, but Grace heard nothing but the roar of confusion that filled her head.

"Can you tell me what in the name of God is going on here?" Grace demanded.

There was no reply. She amended her tone.

"Where you are taking me?" She was perched in the back seat of the patrol car, unable to lean back because her arms were behind her, in handcuffs.

One of the young cops looked back over the seat, through the mesh screen.

"To the jail, ma'am," a female voice replied.

"Then what happens?"

"Then we take you upstairs and book you."

Grace had had many clients over the years who had been in trouble with the law. Mostly that meant they'd smoked marijuana, or found their alcoholism exposed after getting a D.U.I. There had been adolescent shoplifters, cases of domestic abuse. But Grace's involvement had always been limited to the carpeted courtrooms or judges' chambers.

Never the jail.

This is just fucking nuts, she thought. *What idiots are running this circus?*

The police car turned into the parking lot and then swerved sharply down into an underground garage and parked. Two hands reached into the back seat for her, as if anticipating that she would resist getting out.

"I can do it myself." Her tone was petulant.

There was an elevator, direct from the garage to the third floor. The two officers escorted Grace to a chair in a beige, tiled room. A woman came in, different uniform. The other two left.

"Let me get those off of you," the new cop said, reaching behind Grace to release the handcuffs.

"Thank you." Grace massaged her wrists.

The woman went behind a desk and pulled out a packet of forms. She began asking Grace questions, as if this were a doctor's office: age; address; height; weight; eye color; hair color; medical issues.

"Tattoos?" inquired the cop.

I've never been asked that one before, Grace thought.

"Sure. There's this dragon on my left thigh. And curling snake that wiggles when I flex the muscle in my upper arm." Grace heard a tinge of hysteria in her own voice.

The cop was not smiling.

"I'm sorry, officer. No—no tattoos."

"Scars?"

"Just from C-sections. Do you have children?"

The woman shook her head, *no*, even as she asked the next question.

"Previous arrests?"

Grace was led down the hall to a small room to be fingerprinted.

It reminded her of when her children played with stamp sets, their fingers as coated as the stamps. She was placed against a white backdrop for photos, both front and side.

Then back to the desk.

"According to the arrest warrant, your bond is $250,000," the jail cop said.

Grace inhaled sharply.

Bond. How one word could made this so real, she thought. She really could not leave without paying a bribe. At least that is what it felt like. She was a hostage.

"I need a quarter of a million dollars to get out of here?"

"Yes, ma'am. Bond is set high for capital crimes."

"How do I get it arranged if I can't leave here to do it?"

"You use a bonding company. For a 10% fee, they'll post bond."

"You mean they keep the 10%?"

"Yeah. That's how they make their money."

"So to walk out the door I need to fork over $25,000? Which I never get back?"

"Looks that way."

"Well, then, I may be staying for a day or so, during which time I hope somebody figures out what the hell is going on. Because this is one hell of a mistake."

"Do you want to call someone?"

Grace called Katrina and asked her to call the kids. "But wait until tomorrow morning, in case. . ." she added.

She called the lawyer who had done their wills and asked for the name of a competent criminal attorney. Then she called the criminal attorney and left an "Urgent. Please return ASAP," with her name and the jail number. She was furious with herself for not taking steps to prepare after Sam's bombshell that she was a suspect.

She felt a brief flash of gratitude that she had not returned to work. Those were calls she was spared. "Hi, this is your therapist. Need to postpone our appointment because I'm in jail. Try and make it to your ACOA group in the meantime, okay?"

Alex startled awake at the first ring, but in that semi-state of not being sure if he was still dreaming.

"Alex, this is Katrina. Were you sleeping?"

"Katrina?" he asked. "From home?"

"Alex, your mom. . ." Katrina's voice cracked. She choked on the words.

"Is Mom okay? What happened?"

"Your mom's been arrested."

"That's insane."

"Yes, it's nuts, Alex, but I think you need to get home."

"Where is Mom now?"

"In jail. I'll bet that's an excuse the professors haven't heard much."

Alex felt the dumb shock of a cow as the stun gun connects.

"Do you want to call your sister?" asked Katrina.

"No." His voice choked. "You do it. I'll try to get home tonight, late."

"Okay. Call now for a late afternoon flight. Don't drive."

"Where do I go?"

"What do you mean?"

"Mom wasn't back in the house yet. She was staying in that cottage. Where do I go?"

"You can stay with me, Alex. We'll figure it out."

The cell could use some freshening up, thought Grace. It was about seven feet by nine feet, with a cot, toilet, and sink. The ceilings were high, with a recessed light that she could not turn off. There were no bars, just a steel door with a small window and an opening large enough for a meal tray. The color was one the kids would describe as "barf beige."

She sat on the edge of the bed, hunched over, rocking as if she were rocking a child to sleep, only faster and more desperate.

When it became clear that she wouldn't be buying herself out immediately, she'd been "processed" further. They'd made a list of her personal property. She'd been escorted into a small windowless room with a bench, shower, toilet. She was told to undress and given a loose-fitting orange top and bottom, and rubber sandals. She'd passed her clothes through an opening in the wall to an invisible someone. It felt as if she were handing her real self out with her clothes. She wondered if her *self* would be waiting in the carefully folded creases of her skirt and blouse when she got them back.

25

Danny was in the ER, waiting to do a transport to the university medical center in Kansas City, when the cop he was chatting with got a call.

"Yeah. Yeah. Okay. Yeah. Hey thanks," was his side of the conversation.

"That was my partner. You know that guy they found shot in his kitchen a few weeks ago?" the cop asked, but not stopping for a reply. "They arrested the wife. I coulda' told them that right off. Been doing too damn many domestics. Want to toss them all in a hole and walk away for a week, come back and see who's still standing. . ." The cop's voice rattled on, but Danny did not hear. His heart had stopped at the first line and it took two more lines to start breathing again.

Grace McDonald arrested? How could there be enough evidence? For a minute, Danny felt like he needed to do something, needed to explain. . .

But there was nothing he could do. This was like a sign from God that it was all out of his control. He had done what he needed to do and now he could step back.

It was almost midnight, and while. Danny had worked a 3-11 shift, he was still wired. He planned to drive to Colorado Springs the next day, then across the Divide and into Gunnison to pick up Ross on Sunday.

Danny sat at his kitchen table, surrounded by wrapping paper, ribbon, scissors, and scotch tape. He was wrapping presents to bring to Mandy and Ross, and to put under the tree from Santa for Ross. He was looking forward to the drive to Gunnison. He wanted to see where Mandy lived, to get his foot in the door.

Since she'd moved to Gunnison, he had not been there. Each time visitation was scheduled with Ross, Mandy had made the travel arrangements.

"Danny," she'd said, "as long as I'm going to be in Denver anyway for the vet conference, I might as well just put Ross on the plane." Or, "Danny, guess what? My old boss is coming to visit her brother and she's volunteered to drive Ross back with her for spring break."

He couldn't argue with her, but he'd felt her desire to avoid him, to keep her new life separate.

For over a year he hadn't even known where she lived. He had a phone number to call Ross, and a P.O. box to send mail. But, last visit, he'd gotten Ross talking about the A-frame and the mountain roads. Danny had casually brought out a map of Gunnison from his desk drawer.

"Can you show me your school on here, buddy?" he'd asked.

Ross had been so proud of his map-reading skills, of his ability to show Dad exactly where his school was, where Mom's work was, where in the twisting maze of mountain roads was the exact spot upon which stood his house. Danny had carefully marked an "X" at each point.

The plan was that Mandy would bring Ross to the Ramada Inn on Sunday evening. But Danny planned to show up early.

In his mind, Danny saw it clearly. Mandy would be surprised. He'd be in the doorway, bearing holiday gifts and wearing his bashful smile.

"You really are too much," she'd say. "Never a dull moment with my boy Danny." Then she would step aside and gesture toward the living room. "Come on in before you get chilled to the bone. I'll make some hot cocoa."

They'd sit down next to the tree. Mandy would go to the kitchen to make the cocoa. He'd bring out the CD of holiday music that Mandy had always loved, the one he'd told her was lost, and whisper to Ross to put it on. Mandy would come out of the kitchen when she heard it. Her eyes would glisten just a bit at his thoughtfulness.

Then they would sit together and drink cocoa, and it would get later and later but they wouldn't notice because they would be having such a good time talking. And then? Anything could happen.

Danny whistled *Jingle Bells* as the scissors made a perfectly straight cut across the wrapping paper.

In the visiting room of the jail, there were five stools screwed to the floor in the small cement room. There was a partial wall, with wire mesh to prevent physical contact between visitor and inmate. Katrina sat down carefully on the stool at the far end and waited for Grace to be brought from her cell.

Katrina had passed through a metal detector to get this far, explaining her relationship to Grace, presenting a photo ID. She'd tried to come immediately after Grace's call. But visiting hours were Sunday mornings at 11 a.m. for female inmates. No exceptions.

The rest of the stools for visitors were filled now, with women mostly. Everyone looked ahead—at the screens—not at each other.

Grace was the last one escorted in. She was being held in a separate cell, not in the women's group cell area. On the phone she'd said it was because they had her on suicide watch.

Katrina tried very hard to keep her face composed, but without success. Grace had been in jail for two nights. She looked like shit. Her eyes were hollow. She was haggard and pale.

Grace spoke first.

"When do I get out of here?" she asked in a hoarse whisper.

"The attorney you want is out of town. He'll be here first thing in the morning." Katrina talked fast and low. "He'll request a lower bond tomorrow. Then we find a way to post bond. So, I need to know how to get to the title to the house, the car titles. . ."

Grace stared past Katrina.

"Gracie, you have to help me on this."

"This is not going away, is it?"

"No, Gracie, it isn't going away."

"Most documents are in the safe deposit box. The key is in a little yellow envelope, in the bottom drawer of my desk at home. Under the boxes of new checks. There is a list of everything in the box in that same drawer. I put you on the list of people to have access, just in case. I never considered this, more like if Gil and I were overseas traveling and there was some emergency. . ."

Grace swallowed hard, then continued.

"The money seems less important than it did Friday. If it takes a bondsman to get me out, just do it. If the attorney can get the bail lowered, I'll clear out my savings and pay the fucking fee."

"Wait until you talk to your attorney, okay? Now, Grace, the kids are here. They're waiting outside."

Grace's head shook abruptly.

"No, No, No. I don't want them to see me like this, in this outfit, caged. No."

"Gracie, they need to see you. They're scared too."

"This will only make them worse. It'll be an image they'll never forget. Tell them I love them and that I'll be out tomorrow. We'll get through this together."

"Okay, Grace. Are you sure?"

"Yes, dammit, I'm sure."

Alex and Molly sat huddled over their table in the Paradise Grill. It was late Sunday afternoon. Their mother was in jail and wouldn't let them see her. There was nothing they could do. It was all too—too bizarre.

They'd just said goodbye to Katrina, giving her hard hugs of confused grief. She had to get home to her boys. Alex had assured Katrina that he and Molly would be just fine. They planned to go home.

"We need to do it sometime, Katrina," he'd explained. "We haven't really been there, just to get some clothes for the funeral, and that was with a cop standing over us."

Now he wasn't so sure. He'd driven up the day before from Austin. Late Saturday night, he'd picked up Molly at the airport. Neither could face going back home in the middle of the night. They'd gotten a motel room near the airport with two double beds and collapsed.

When Molly had awakened, she'd been disoriented. She'd heard her brother's faint snores but could not place where she was. For an instant she'd felt she was back in the big hexagon tent that the family had taken on camping trips, all four of them lined up in their sleeping bags. She'd often awakened first, staying perfectly still, listening to the snores of her father and brother, the morning sounds of birds in the woods. It'd been so peaceful, so safe.

"I wonder if anyone has been in to clean the house," Alex now said.

"Haven't a clue. Would Mom have arranged it?"

"Never asked. What do I say, like, 'Mom, have you hired someone to clean up that mess after Dad was murdered?' "

Molly kicked her brother under the table.

"You are one sick puppy."

"I can't stay there if it hasn't been cleaned," said Alex.

"Me neither. Maybe we could just open the door and check it out."

Molly's hands were wrapped around her coffee cup, clenched, as she spoke. Alex reached across the table, placing his larger, rougher hands, over hers.

"This sucks. Absolutely sucks. But we will get through this, Molly. We will make sick jokes and be as pissy as we need to. You got that?"

There was no small talk as they drove to the house. Alex parked in the driveway.

"Looks the same from here," commented Molly. "Let's walk around back."

The yard was shrouded in winter, the grass a dull brown. The trees were stark against the sky. The air felt brittle. Alex walked to the back door and peered through the window.

"Kitchen is clean," he announced. "Let's try the front."

The key in the lock made the familiar, double-clicking sound. They pushed the door open. All the shades had been drawn, but otherwise the room looked the same.

They walked through the house together, opening every room, every closet. They saved the kitchen for last.

"I'll make some coffee," said Molly.

She reached into the cupboard for filters. She was very precise as she measured.

"This is so fucking weird," said Alex, sitting at the kitchen table. "We never even locked the doors. Nobody gets murdered in this town."

Molly didn't answer. She stared out the back window into the yard.

"Alex, I can't see the bocce court. It always stood out, like a green rectangle in the middle of the rest of the lawn. I can't see it now." Molly's voice sounded as if she were about to cry.

Alex got up and put his hands on her shoulders. He looked where she pointed.

"It fades every winter, Molly. You just never noticed."

26

Scraping the icy windshield, Mandy anticipated her day. There would be farm visits all morning, then office hours. She was bottle-nursing a motherless litter of Australian shepherd pups in a corner of the office. She'd decided to give one to Ross for Christmas. Money was tight, and there could be no better present than a squirming, licking puppy. And she sure didn't have to worry about vet bills. She had one picked out, a saucy female with black spots on her gray rump. She'd wait until Ross got back from his Dad's to give it to him.

They'd been in Gunnison now for almost a year and a half. There were rough times, when she'd second-guessed the decision to move or been paralyzed with anxiety about the future. And Ross had had days, the first six months mostly, when he'd pouted and yelled, blaming her, saying he wanted to go home. But it had gotten easier, and she'd felt stronger with every passing month. Ross had made friends. He had joined some sports teams.

Danny was coming tomorrow to pick him up for Christmas break.

Mandy climbed into her truck. She'd traded in the small car that got stuck in the snowy roads of the mountains for a slightly younger and more reliable 4-wheel-drive truck. She was making regular payments for the difference. Ross thought she looked "totally cool" driving it. She sang *Joy To The World* at the top of her lungs all the way down the mountain.

Danny spent Saturday night at a motel outside of Colorado Springs. He had take-out fried chicken for supper in front of the television.

He was up early the next morning, heading for Gunnison. He'd moved the presents to the front seat, and he looked over at the bright holiday wrappings every few minutes. Outside of Gunnison, he stopped to once more consult his map.

It was mid-Sunday afternoon when he came within sight of the A-frame nestled in the trees. A truck was parked in the drive.

Danny frowned. He didn't recognize the truck and didn't see Mandy's car. He briefly wondered if he had the right house. He looked at the map Ross had marked, at the detailed notes he'd taken. It had to be the place.

Danny parked far enough down the road that he was not likely to be observed from the house. He took the shopping bag of gifts. He walked up the incline through the woods instead of taking the stairs from the drive. As he got closer, he heard Gregorian chant coming from the house.

Danny smiled. Mandy was home.

He went to the front door. It was painted a glossy sky blue, the blue he'd seen on postcards of doors in New Mexico. He knocked.

When Mandy opened the door, she was grinning. She wore an apron over jeans and a white turtleneck. Her hair was tied up in a ponytail.

He smiled his bashful smile, extending the bag in front of him. "Merry Christmas!" he said.

Mandy's face contorted, as if she could not make the adjustment from expectation to reality. Then the grin was gone. Her jaw locked. Her eyes narrowed.

"How did you find me?" she asked.

"Just followed the directions Ross gave me," answered Danny. "He wanted to show me his house and his room."

"Ross isn't here right now. He'll be back in a little while. I'll bring him down to the hotel like I said I would."

"Aren't you going to invite me in? You don't have to entertain me, but I would like to use the bathroom."

Mandy felt stuck. She'd felt terror at the idea that Danny would do this, just show up on her doorstep. But now that he was here, that terror seemed out of place. It seemed ridiculous to tell her ex-husband, her son's father, that he couldn't use the bathroom.

She stepped back from the doorway and motioned him in.

"The bathroom is right over there, under the loft, first door," she said.

"Thanks."

Danny put the bag down by the door. He looked around. There was a red chair by the window, a green carpet on the hardwood floor. A huge print of sunflowers in a white pitcher hung over the fireplace. Three bookcases, painted the same yellow as the sunflowers, lined one wall. They were filled with books. Danny couldn't remember so many books at their old apartment. A compact fir tree, shining with mini-lights, was angled in the corner.

He walked to the bathroom and closed the door.

Mandy leaned against the outside door. She wished that she had ten minutes to think this through.

She did not want Danny here, but neither did she want to have a scene, not out here, alone. And if she told him to get out, there could be a scene. Just thinking it made her heart pump faster. And Ross would be home at any minute.

Just be calm, she thought. Let Ross show Danny his room. Then they'll leave. She could pack Ross' stuff later and bring it down to the hotel as planned. She'd "make nice-nice" as her mother used to say. Put up a front.

Danny took his time in the bathroom. He washed his hands and looked inside the medicine cabinet. He let his eyes go shelf to shelf: a few dated prescriptions, Tylenol, Midol, and cough syrup. Nothing new. No birth control.

When he came out, he stood still, listening to the sounds coming from the kitchen area. Then he took two steps and stopped, looking into what must be her bedroom.

There was an old pine dresser, a canning jar filled with pine sprays on top. The double bed was covered by a patchwork quilt. A small table next to the bed was piled with books.

"Do you want to wait for Ross?"

Mandy stood in the doorway to the kitchen. She did not comment on his perusal of her bedroom.

"Sure, Mandy," he said. "I really wanted to surprise him."

"He'll be happy to see you. He's been excited about going back to Kaw Valley, about seeing his old friends."

"What about you?" Danny knew he was pushing, but he wanted to get a reaction from her.

"Ross will be happy. It doesn't matter what I feel."

"It matters to me."

Mandy took a breath. If there was going to be a scene, so be it. But she couldn't play this game anymore.

"No, I'm not happy to see you. You've shown up here without any warning. I'm trying to be civil. I expect you to do the same."

Danny felt his neck flush.

"Civil?" he rebutted. "Showing up with presents in an effort to generate a little good will, a little holiday friendliness, that doesn't meet your definition of civil? Trying to show our son that his parents can be decent with each other despite differences isn't civil?"

Mandy felt the words swirl around her. This was how it used to be, how he would turn what she said inside out, until the only logical recourse was to agree or apologize.

She didn't answer. She turned and went to the kitchen, leaving him standing there, his arms extended to demonstrate his goodwill.

She picked up where she'd left off, pounding and kneading the soft mounds of dough. She did not look up when she heard him come to the kitchen doorway.

"I'm sorry, Mandy. Not calling first was stupid. I just wanted to surprise Ross." Danny's voice was contrite.

"If you look out the front window, you'll see Ross when he comes," Mandy said.

"Aren't you even going to accept my apology?"

"Look, I don't want an apology. I don't want anything at all from you."

"Jesus, Mandy, what's happened to you? Huh? You never used to be this cold, not until you started seeing that therapist." Danny paused. "She twisted everything. And you never saw that she was screwed up."

"What are you talking about?" Mandy did not look up but pushed hard into the dough with each syllable.

"She's in jail, Mandy. For killing her husband. What does that tell you?"

Danny's words hung in the air between them.

"I don't know what kind of mind-game you think you're playing here, but it's over. Just get out of my house."

Danny took a step forward.

"Stop right there." Mandy's voice was low, almost venomous.

Danny realized that she was holding a knife in her right hand. A large butcher knife. He had not seen her go for it, had not seen movement. But it was there, glinting.

Danny stopped. He put both hands palms up in front of his chest, a play gesture of defeat and submission.

"Mandy, please." His tone was placating. "Look at yourself. This isn't you."

"Get out of my house."

"I didn't want it to be like this, really. I just wanted to talk," he pleaded. "This is all her doing. She must have been unbalanced all along."

"Get out of my house."

"Mandy, she manipulated you, and you trusted her. We could have worked it out. Just think about it, okay? Just tell me that you'll think about it."

"Yeah. I'll think about it. Now, get out of my house."

The cold air and noise hit them at the same moment as they heard Ross coming in the front door. He wore his backpack and his arms were filled with books and toys.

"Mom," he called out, "There's a car outside that looks like Dad's. Do you think he could. . ."

He stopped abruptly, then whooped with delight at the sight of his father.

"Daddy," he yelled, rushing to get a hug.

Danny grabbed Ross up and swung him around. They danced around the kitchen.

Standing by the counter, Mandy watched.

27

With a grating noise, early Monday morning, the door to Grace's cell swung back.

"Your lawyer is here," said the guard.

Grace was escorted to a small, windowless room with a table and four chairs. A man stood up as she entered. He stood eye to eye with Grace. Wire-rimmed glasses perched on the top of his head, held in place by curling salt-and-pepper hair. His suit, she noted, was well-fitted and probably high-end.

"I'm Miguel Leticio." He held out his hand.

His grip was firm. His brown eyes were assessing.

"Do have a seat, Ms. McDonald. Would you care for some coffee?" As he spoke, he brought out a thermos from his briefcase. "It has a bit of vanilla flavoring, if you don't mind." His voice had a melodious accent.

"Yes. Thank you."

Miguel was silent as he pulled two small cups from his briefcase, then poured, passing her a cup.

"I regret the lack of amenities, but I did grab a few of these on my way up," he said, reaching into his pocket and pulling out two, tiny containers of cold Half & Half. He extended his hand to Grace.

She took the cream and mixed it with her coffee. The aroma was strong, vanilla blending with dark roast. She inhaled slowly.

They sat that way, quiet, holding their coffee under their noses, not yet sipping. Miguel Leticio was not uncomfortable with silence. Indeed, he generally found what he learned from silence to be as useful as what came from speech. So he sat, allowing his prospective client some time to adjust.

"Can you tell me what the hell is going on?" Grace asked.

"I will tell you what I know thus far," responded Miguel. "You will be charged this afternoon with the premeditated murder of your husband. According to the district attorney, there is evidence linking you to the crime scene, evidence inconsistent with your account. There is a presumed motive, based on the assumption that you discovered an infidelity."

"The detective told me that my blood was found on Gil's body. Is that the evidence?"

"I believe so."

"That's impossible. I think I skinned my knees crawling across the gravel walk. But that was after finding Gil. There must be some mistake."

"Ms. McDonald, I certainly hope that there has been a mistake, but we are not in a position to sit and wait. You will go before a judge this afternoon for what is called a first appearance. I will argue, persuasively, for a reduction in bond. Our first and most immediate concern is to get you out of jail."

"Lay out the options."

"You have two choices. With the bail bonding company, you forfeit 10%, which will be a considerable sum, for their fee. Or you can try to meet the full bond yourself."

"Will the court take a bank's assurance of equity in the house or car titles?"

"No. They require cash or cashier's check. They are not willing to sell homes or auction cars to collect their bond."

"So I really don't have any choice here. Not unless I sit in jail and wait for the insurance company to pay up on Gil's life insurance. And I can't see them paying out when I'm accused. . ." Grace's voice trailed off. "What if they don't lower the bond?"

"In my experience, the bond will be lowered. I expect to about $100,000."

"So, assuming you get the bond lowered to $100,000, I am out $10,000 to not spend another night in jail."

"Think in terms of more than one night. It will be months before your trial. You need to be out not only for your mental health, but so that you can most effectively participate in planning your defense."

"My defense?" Grace's voice was cracking under the sheer weight of her pain and fear. "Finding my husband murdered is not awful enough? Now I need a defense? What am I supposed to say? I was in Hawaii? Bullshit. I was there. I found him. That's my defense."

Miguel waited for a moment after Grace finished.

"Ms. McDonald, there will be an explanation."

Grace looked into Miguel's eyes, holding them for a silent moment.

"My husband is dead. I don't think any explanation will fix that."

She crossed her arms and straightened in her chair.

"Between my business and home accounts, I think I can make it. I had funds put aside to pay taxes. If you can get my checkbooks from the jail people, I'll write you a check."

"I will make every effort, Ms. McDonald."

"Look, you better start calling me Grace."

"Certainly. And I am Miguel."

"Where are you from, Miguel?"

"Originally?"

"Yes, originally."

"El Salvador."

"And when did you come here, to the U.S?"

"When I was 15. My mother sent me to stay with relatives when it became clear that there would be civil war."

"And you did not go back?"

"No, I was granted asylum a few years later."

"And your family?"

"My parents were killed. They were academics and seen as a threat. My sister is in a convent in Costa Rica."

"You would have been killed? Is that why they granted you asylum?"

"Not really. But I had a very good lawyer."

They sat looking at each other. Evaluating.

"When do I get my clothes back to get changed for this hearing?" asked Grace.

Miguel cleared his throat.

"You do not get your clothes back. You attend the hearing as is."

Grace came out of her chair.

"No! They can't make me go like this." Her voice was that of a pleading, desperate adolescent. "Make them give me back my clothes. Please."

"I am very sorry, but that is the policy."

"Do I have to be there?"

"You must be present. To ensure that you understand the charges against you."

Grace slid slowly down on to the chair. Her head dropped forward to the table.

"I look like some criminal. It is impossible to wear an orange jumpsuit and rubber slippers and not look guilty."

"It will just be a few minutes. You will be seated in a row with several others. Everyone will be in the same clothing. There is no assumption of innocence or guilt based on appearance."

"Then why can't we look innocent if we're presumed innocent?"

"Grace, please listen." He paused, considering his words. When he spoke it was with a quiet urgency.

"How you look today means nothing. To survive this process will demand much strength of character, an ability to not succumb to the attack of the press, to the accusations of the prosecutor. You need to begin this now, to wear your character in your bearing, on your face. You must hold your innocence in your heart, and let it come from you in your eyes, in your walk, in your willingness to meet others directly. You must do this today, from this first appearance."

Miguel was silent for a minute, allowing his words to register.

"So, go back to the cell and prepare. Focus on the injustice that this should happen in your life. There is no shame in being the victim of injustice. There must be no shame in you this afternoon. Do you hear what I am saying?"

Grace slowly lifted her head, and looked into his eyes, holding nothing back.

"I'll try."

Saunders was preparing for the first appearances at 3 p.m. Usually this was a task delegated to one of the less experienced assistants, but today he wanted to do it himself.

Saunders reviewed his arguments against bond reduction. He knew that, in this county, for a woman with no priors, the judge would reduce bond. But he still liked to make his points, especially if someone from the press was there. He assumed they would be, given the anonymous tip that the reporter who covered the courthouse had received on Saturday recommending a close look at the Friday arrests.

Opening the door to the courtroom, Katrina saw Alex and Molly. They sat together, third row on the right, not talking. She went over and sat down next to Molly.

"Have you seen Mom?" asked Molly.

"Not since yesterday," Katrina replied. "But the attorney met with her this morning."

"How did Mom figure out who to get?"

"She asked her lawyer. He said this guy is the best defense attorney around."

The best *criminal* attorney was what she almost said. But she stopped herself. *Criminal* was such a guilty-sounding word.

Others were coming into the courtroom, women mostly. They huddled together, whispering. Attorneys joined the huddles, sometimes putting a reassuring hand on a shoulder, patting a back.

The attorneys, whether men or women, wore suits. The rest of the people were in jeans, sweaters, their winter coats unzipped.

The back door to the courtroom opened. Two guards came first, standing to one side as the accused were directed to the first row. There were nine men, one woman—and Grace. The men looked scruffy, with unkempt hair and stubble. Some walked with a street swagger. They'd been here before. Two appeared uncertain, apprehensive. Novices to the system. The woman chewed on the nail of a nicotine-stained finger. They all wore the same orange jumpsuits, the same rubber slippers.

Molly's inhalation was audible. Alex's face went white.

Grace was last in line. There were no handcuffs. But it was as if the accused were shackled together, by guilt if not by chains.

Grace looked around the courtroom, stopping when she came to Alex and Molly. She attempted a tight smile.

"All rise," announced the clerk.

They stood. The judge came through a door off to the left. He wore a black robe and carried a stack of manila folders. As he sat down, so followed the courtroom.

"Shall we proceed, Mr. Saunders?" he asked of the District Attorney seated at the long counsel table to the right.

Saunders stood.

"Yes, your Honor. First case to be called is #10245, The State of Kansas against. . ."

As each charge was filed, the accused was called to a podium to respond to questions from the judge as to whether he understood the nature of the charges against him, and whether he had representation.

Finally, it was Grace's turn.

Grace had often stood behind just such a podium, lecturing at the university or at professional conferences. Her hands instinctively went up to grip both sides, and she glanced down as if looking for her notes.

The DA began. "On or about the 20th day of November, in the County of Douglas, State of Kansas, one Grace McDonald did then and there, feloniously, unlawfully, intentionally, and with premeditation, kill a human being, to wit, Gil McDonald, all in violation of KSA 21-3401, subsection A, contrary to the form of the statutes, in such cases made and provided and against the peace and dignity of the state of Kansas."

"Do you understand the nature of the charges being brought before you at this time, Mrs. McDonald?"

"Yes, sir, I do."

"And Mr. Leticio will represent you?" He gestured at Miguel.

"Yes, sir."

Leticio spoke.

"Your Honor, I wish at this time to request a reduction of the bond amount. This woman has no previous record, not so much as a speeding ticket, and she is a long-term community resident. The current bond is impossible to meet, thus depriving her of her rights to assist fully in the formation of her own defense," said Leticio.

"It is because of the nature of this charge that I requested the current bond amount, Your Honor," countered Saunders. "The state contends that Grace McDonald is a flight risk, and that she has the assets to enable such flight."

"That is ridiculous. Mrs. McDonald is going nowhere. She has a home, family, employment, all here in Kaw Valley. A quarter million-dollar bond is, in effect, an assumption of guilt prior to trial. I request reduction to $100,000, a sum that reflects both the nature of the charge and the prior history of my client."

"I have the picture, gentlemen," said the judge. "Bond reduced to $100,000."

"May we have a stipulation that the accused is not to leave this jurisdiction without prior approval of the court?" asked Saunders.

"So stipulated."

"Now, let's get a trial date set, shall we?"

The judge studied his calendar.

"Let's move quickly on the preliminary hearing, say January 3rd? Then there's a week for trial open March 29."

The negotiations continued. . .

Molly and Alex huddled together outside the courthouse.

Leticio had turned over a certified check for $10,000 to Bill's Bonding. Later, Leticio had explained, they'd need to provide Bill titles to property, etc., to hold in his safe in case Grace should disappear.

"She looked like shit," said Alex.

"Yeah, it was definitely a bad hair day," said Molly.

"Cut it out, Molly. This is serious. They don't go around charging people with nothing to base it on."

"What the hell are you getting at, Alex? Mom did not kill Dad. The evidence must be circumstantial, and they have it wrong."

"Right, some cop came up with a hypothesis. 'The wife did it.' But they need *some* evidence. Why Mom?"

"I have no fucking idea, asshole. Why don't you go buddy up to the DA and ask him?"

Alex turned away, looking out over the park next to the courthouse.

"I just don't understand why this is happening."

"There isn't a reason why. Dad getting killed was crazy-making enough for one lifetime. Now Mom's indicted. Our lives, the ones we used to have, the nice, ordinary, middle-class, predictable, 'Come-home-for-Thanksgiving-and-bring-a-few-friends 'cause there's always room at the table.' You know? How she always told us that? Well, that life is kaput. We have exited from the ranks of the normal."

"Well, the whole fucking thing is fucked."

"Has anyone ever told you that you have a real knack for language?"

"Don't fucking mess with me," Alex said, cutting her off.

"God forbid, Alex, that I should ever fucking mess with you. . ."

Grace was in the changing room, that windowless cell where she had first relinquished her clothes and donned the orange jumpsuit. She dressed carefully, ritualistically. She touched the soft fabric of her sweater before pulling it over her head. She inserted each earring carefully.

She took a small bit of hair gel from a tube in her purse and ran it through her hair. Lip gloss. A scarf draped around her neck.

Leticio was waiting.

"Hold your head up. If there are any press, you can make eye contact, not angry, just look them in the eye," he said, as they walked toward the elevator.

When Leticio escorted Grace out into the cold, dank December afternoon, Katrina, Alex, and Molly were waiting for her in Katrina's car. There was only one reporter. Miguel barked an abrupt "No comment" in passing.

Leticio opened the car door for her, saying "I will call you in a day or so." Grace grimaced, but she grabbed his hand and squeezed it for an instant before he closed the door.

"Let's get the hell out of here," she said.

Katrina looked over her shoulder, then turned into the traffic.

"Mom—are you okay?" Molly asked in a small voice.

"I have no idea how I am right now, honey. Give me a few hours, a hot shower, and a stiff drink. Then ask."

They headed through the back roads.

Grace looked out the window. "Where are we going?" she asked.

"We're going home, Mom. We need to go home. That's where we still live," Alex answered.

"I'm not ready. Take me to the cottage. You can go, but. . ."

Alex cut her off. "The cottage is occupied. Their relatives are here for the holidays. We have your stuff."

"Then take me to a damn motel!"

"Mom, please," begged Molly.

"Grace," said Katrina, "Just give it a try. I know this sucks. But you have to face it some time. If it's too much, you can come home with me. Really."

Grace covered her face with her hands.

28

Alex and Molly had prepared the house. All the lights were on. The holiday wreath that Grace and the children had made years earlier, covered with tiny silver bells and ornaments, was on the door.

Grace stopped on the gravel walk. She could feel her heart pounding. Bile rose in her throat, or memory of bile, of that night.

"Are you gonna make it, Mom?" Alex asked.

Grace turned to her son. He sounded scared. It reminded her of when he was a child, when she had the power to make the hurts go away. She had not had that power for a long time, not since he turned into a lanky, distant adolescent.

"Yes," she said, looking him right in the eyes. "I will make it. But I may need to hold on to you."

And that was how they entered their home, Grace in the middle, Alex and Molly on either side, holding tight.

The kids made chili for supper, serving it in the dining room. Grace avoided the kitchen. *Maybe tomorrow,* she thought.

"Look, Gracie, there is no way that this is going to be easy," said Kat a few hours later. They were sitting on the double bed in the guest room. Alex and Molly had changed the sheets, turned down the covers.

"I never realized how big our bed is. I mean, I knew it was a king size, but it never felt big with Gil. I cannot imagine sleeping there alone."

"You don't have to, Gracie. You can order a new bed over the phone. Tomorrow. Or you can put this double in your room."

"But it's the room too. I can't stand it, but—I went into his closet before, when you were downstairs, and closed the door. I just wanted to smell him. I stood there in the dark with my eyes closed and just inhaled. It was like he was there, breathing. I filled myself with his smell. I rubbed my face against his gray sweater. I wanted to feel something scratchy like his beard, like how it felt to rub against his face."

Tears rolled silently down Grace's face. "I miss him. I keep wanting Gil here to help me get through this, to help me think straight. I know that I looked organized, in control, but it's because he was here for me."

"Oh, Gracie. I'm so sorry."

"Leticio and Brown. May I direct your call?" a voice said briskly.

"Mr. Leticio, please."

Alex waited.

"Miguel Leticio." The accent was thicker than Alex remembered.

"Yes, sir, I'm Alex McDonald. You're representing my mother."

"Of course, Alex. What can I do for you?"

"I need you to answer some questions for me."

"Have you spoken with your mother?"

"I've tried, but it's like she's trying to protect us."

"I will need her release. Given that, I see no problem."

"When can I come in?"

"I have a court appearance this morning. Will 4 p.m. work for you?"

Leticio called Grace.

"Your son wishes to speak to me. I require your permission to do so."

"Why—" Grace stopped. "Yes, of course. Thank you. Talk with him, Miguel."

Alex paused to collect himself before entering Miguel's office. It was in a renovated church building, a compact limestone structure with wood plank floors. The waiting room was simply furnished, an oak church pew along one wall, sage green chairs on a print rug.

A secretary smiled at Alex as he took off his coat and gloves.

"Can I help you?" she asked.

A few minutes later, Miguel came down a short hallway, extending his hand toward Alex. His office was square, a massive desk on one side, two armchairs on the other.

"Let's sit here where it is more comfortable," Miguel said, motioning toward the chairs. "How can I help you?"

"I need to understand why my mother is accused of murdering my father. There must be evidence."

Miguel rubbed at his chin.

"The crux of the prosecutor's case hinges on the discrepancy between your mother's account of the sequence of her behaviors upon discovering your father's body and contradictory physical evidence. There are also factors which contribute to alleged motivation. There is no weapon, and clearly no witnesses to corroborate or contradict any accounts or assumptions."

"Could you spell that out? What discrepancies? What evidence? What factors?"

Quietly, Miguel explained.

"But why? There's no motive," Alex argued.

"Your father had an affair in the year prior to his death. Your mother contends that she had no knowledge of that affair, but the prosecutor regards it as possible motive."

Alex did not move, his heart having slammed against his chest wall and stopped.

"Alex?" inquired Miguel in a soft voice.

"My father had an affair?"

"It appears to have been brief, with a woman from his workplace. It was concluded some months before his death."

"Couldn't the blood be from someone else with the same blood type?"

"The blood is an enzyme match. Further DNA tests are being conducted, to produce definitive evidence. But, given the results so far, I am not anticipating different findings."

"They really believe my mother shot my father."

"Yes."

"With what? We never had a gun in the house. They were big supporters of the Brady bill."

"The murder weapon has not been found. It remains a significant question."

Alex was having a hard time breathing.

"My mother could not have killed my father."

"I will provide your mother the very best legal representation I can, Alex."

"What is your plan?"

"I am not yet prepared to discuss strategy, Alex. This is the stage of discovery. All strategy is contingent upon what we uncover."

"Like a gun with prints on it? And if we don't get lucky?"

"We have not yet had the preliminary hearing. We don't know what will be presented. To define a defense at this point will only distract us."

"Distract us? What else do we have to do?"

"We have to seek the truth. To uncover plausible alternative explanations for why someone would kill your father. We have to uncover a basis for reasonable doubt."

"That's your defense? Just spread some doubt around and hope a jury agrees?"

Alex slumped in the chair. He knew he was getting antagonistic.

"I'm sorry. I just can't stand this. I want it over."

"Of course. However, without the recovery of a weapon with someone else's prints or the spontaneous confession of some as yet unidentified stranger, it will not be over for quite a while."

Alex abruptly stood up. His body swayed slightly, then steadied. "I need to go," he said.

Without looking back, he went out the door.

"Then what did he say?" asked Molly.

They were sitting in the car, parked a few blocks from the house. Alex had asked Molly to do some shopping with him, had gotten her out of the house, and was talking, now, in a low tone, as though someone might overhear.

He felt like a conspirator.

"He said that some of the blood was Mom's, but that Mom has no idea how it got there."

"So maybe she freaked out. People do block out awful experiences, you know."

"The police think they have a motive." Alex had held off on this, as if a few more moments of his sister's innocence were to be guarded, protected.

"That's ridiculous. What kind of motive?"

"An affair. Dad had an affair."

Molly heard the words, but they did not compute. Other kids' parents had affairs. Not hers. As a child, hearing her parents argue, she'd asked, "Are you going to get a divorce?" Her mother had gently cradled Molly's face in her hands. "We're just arguing," she'd said. "It's normal for parents to disagree. Don't worry. We love each other very much. It's the people who don't argue that are in deep trouble. We're fine."

"With who?"

"Someone from work."

"Why would Dad have an affair?"

"How the hell should I know, Molly? I'm starting to feel that I don't really know my own family, that maybe I was living in some phony dream world. Everything I counted on is gone. Dad is dead and Mom may have killed him."

There. He had said it out loud. The horrific suspicion that had gripped him in the lawyer's office was now spoken.

Molly's head jerked around.

"What kind of stupid asshole thing is that to say? These idiots are attacking Mom and you're already on their side?"

"No, I'm not. . ."

Molly cut him off with a gesture.

"Just shut up before you do more damage. Okay?" She started pounding on the inside of the car door. "Just shut up."

Alex started to reach for her, then stopped. He looked out the car window, at all the pretty houses. It was dusk and some holiday lights had come on, blinking, on-off-on-off-on-off. He thought nothing. He felt nothing. All his attention focused on the tiny, blinking lights.

29

"*Hello, Emily? This is Mandy.*"

"Mandy! So good to hear your voice," replied Emily. "Are you calling about Christmas? I'm flying out tomorrow morning. Sara and Will told me you're joining us."

"I'm really looking forward to seeing you, too. But that's not why I'm calling. This is going to sound crazy but Danny showed up here Sunday to get Ross for visitation. He told me that Grace McDonald was arrested for killing her husband. I figure that's him messing with my mind."

There was silence at Emily's end of the line.

"Emily? Are you there?"

"Yes. Mandy, it was in the papers this morning. And someone at the office said there was a mention in the Saturday police notes."

"That's crazy."

"Look, I'll see what I can find out, and I'll bring the newspapers."

"Please. Thanks."

Mandy put the phone down. She felt disturbed. How could this happen to the woman who had helped her find her life? But more, a profound uneasiness, as if there was something she was missing.

Patsy Tsosie was dreaming.

In her dream, the air was warm, the trees green and leafy. A park. Children were chasing one another. Patsy sat on a park bench, in the dappled sunlight. Some mothers were gathered across the park, blankets spread on the grass, picnic supplies around them. They were talking, glancing over to check on their children in between bites of sandwiches and sips of iced tea.

A small round girl in a flowered sundress, barefoot, came down the slide too fast. Unable to grasp the sides to slow her descent, she landed on all fours in the gravel that lined the path next to the play area.

She did not cry out, but climbed unsteadily to her feet, then looked down. She'd skinned her knees, and a trickle of blood was making its way down the front of her leg.

Patsy did not run to help her, but sat, mesmerized, watching the thin line of blood move in slow motion, a dark red magic marker against white skin. The girl herself seemed transfixed. The blood oozed slowly until, at last, it reached her foot. Only then did the girl rouse herself. Inhaling sharply, she exhaled all the breath in her body in one long wail.

Patsy jerked awake, startled, still seeing the trickle of blood in her mind's eye. So slowly it moved, so very, very slowly.

Sam sat at his desk. He rubbed his temple with his thumb, digging at the start of a headache.

"Hey, Sam, you got a minute?"

Patsy Tsosie stood in the doorway.

"Sure. What's up?"

"I know we're about wrapped up on the McDonald case. Case closed. But my gut doesn't feel right."

"So what's the point here, Tsosie?"

"Once this is turned over to the district attorney, are we off the case? Like, can we work it, maybe in our spare time? It's not like I have a plan, but. . ." Her voice trailed off.

"Well, Tsosie, I see two possible agendas. One is to find the murder weapon, or to find additional evidence that will build the prosecutor's case. Then you got this gut feeling. I would say that any investigating damn well better look like you're working to support the DA Unless, of course, you came across something that proves we're prosecuting the wrong person. Then you'd have to speak up. But it better be substantive."

"Low profile. Just tying up loose ends. Is that it?"

"Anybody asks me what Tsosie's doing, that's it. No talk about feelings."

"Got it. Thanks, Sam. I didn't want to screw myself or you by asking a few questions. And I know I've got a lot to learn. It's just that. . ."

Some things you learn on the job, and some you had before you got here. You need 'em all. Now, get back to work, Tsosie."

Christmas was in three days and Katrina was in over-functioning mode. Nothing in her experience, not even the personal anguish of her own divorce, had felt this awful. She'd realized last night that she wasn't going to be able to pull off a traditional Christmas. No way in hell.

"Guys," she'd said, after sitting her sons down at the kitchen table, "this has been a shitty month. I love you totally, but I am not thinking straight. If I go shopping for you, especially at this late date, I will make lousy choices. So, here's what I propose. Tomorrow night, we all go to the mall. You each get a hundred bucks. You go buy yourself some nifty presents. Then we come home, and you wrap them. Tell me nothing. And I will get to be, for the first time ever, surprised big time on Christmas morning. And, really, a good surprise is all I want for Christmas."

The boys looked at each other, sizing up the situation.

"Mom," said the oldest, "I'm not sure where your head is, but, like, one hundred bucks does not cover much ground these days. Is that figure negotiable?"

So here she was sitting at a table in the mall food court, sipping hot tea, with an assortment of papers and lists spread out in front of her. And the boys were off, having negotiated $200 each, going for broke.

Start with a menu, she told herself. *We have to eat.*

"Roast beef," she wrote. "Garlic mashed potatoes. Green beans and mushrooms. Salad. Chocolate mousse."

It was a start.

In her bedroom, Grace was making her own list.

    1) Weapon—where is it?
    2) Arrange referrals for remaining clients.
    3) Talk to kids about holidays. We need a plan.
    4) Who hates us?

Grace looked at her list. It was the most bizarre combination she'd ever seen. She remembered an incident from last year, a harried afternoon when she'd felt exhausted from juggling work, shopping, cooking—all the myriad details that went into creating even a pseudo-Martha Stewart Christmas for the family. She'd had a hissy fit, yelling at the walls, at Gil.

"I am never going to *do* another Christmas like this. No more super-woman. Next year either you do half, or it isn't getting done."

So incredibly innocent, she thought now, *and so stupid*. She'd give anything to have it be that way again. To have too many presents to buy, too many cookies to bake, a husband to talk with.

"I want normal crap," she whispered to the air.

Ross was a happy boy. He had his Dad all to himself. And they had the whole Christmas break together. And he would see his old friends in Kaw Valley.

Danny was trying to be upbeat, but he was disappointed. He could not understand Mandy. After all the times she'd complained that he wasn't thoughtful. And now, when he went out of his way to show he still cared? When he brought her presents? And it meant nothing to her?

That bitch poisoned her mind, he reasoned. It was just going to take a little more time.

But that was okay. He had patience.

He hadn't meant to tell Mandy about Grace McDonald. But seeing her name in the small print of the Saturday morning police report had made her arrest more real. "Picked up without incident. Being held pending arraignment." Just two short lines.

The entire *incident* had taken on a fuzzy quality for Danny. When he replayed it in his mind, it was as if he were watching a movie clip. He could understand Grace being questioned, see the police trying to figure out the mystery, see her credibility undermined. But indicted?

Whatever happened from now on was out of his hands.

Ross's voice interrupted his thoughts.

"After we see Garden of the Gods, can we go up Pike's Peak?"

"We'll see. Could be darn cold up there."

"I like cold. I'm used to it now."

They'd left Gunnison at dawn and would be in Colorado Springs for lunch. Danny figured they could play tourist, then crash at a motel. By tomorrow night they'd be back in Kaw Valley.

"Doesn't my life count? Over forty years of being a good person? Doesn't that count for anything?" Grace protested.

She was in Leticio's office. It was December 23, and Grace and Miguel were having their first meeting since she was released on bond.

"Of course it does, and we will have character witnesses. But we must explain how your blood got to be on your husband's body. We cannot erase evidence with character. We must provide explanations or other evidence."

"What do you want me to do? Lie? Take back what I told the police?"

"You were in shock. You blanked out from the horror of finding Gil. You told the police what you could remember. Now, as time has passed, more is coming back. Is this not possible, Grace? Shock-induced amnesia?"

"If I had shock-induced amnesia then, I've still got it."

"Could you not have crawled out of the house, felt like it was a nightmare, that it was not possible to have witnessed what you did, and thus gone back in?"

"No. But just saying I did like you said, wouldn't there be blood somewhere else, like on the steps, or the front hall?"

"All right. We'll come back to this later. Now, we have Joanna from the cafe to account for your time from after work until you left the bakery. Next, I need names of people who can testify to your commitment to anti-gun legislation. . ."

At the courthouse, Winona Banks fiddled at her computer, preparing the lists of registered voters who would be receiving their call to jury duty in the mail in the next few weeks.

The initial questionnaire was brief, covering the basic criteria to serve. Can you read, write, and speak English? Are you a citizen? At least 19 years old? It asked about education, marital status, employment, felony convictions, pending lawsuits. When the prospective jurors arrived, they would be asked more questions. Depending on the nature of the trial, the questions could be personal. Their prejudices and life experiences were subject to scrutiny. They would be verbally prodded and poked until the attorneys felt some sense of knowing who they were, what they thought, how they reached decisions. It could be an uncomfortable process for the uninitiated.

The noise of the printer clicked on, the list slowly appearing from the white box. The people who would make decisions about the lives of their fellow citizens. The people who would determine liability, accountability, innocence or guilt.

The jurors.

30

Alex pulled into the driveway, the trunk of the car bulging from a Douglas fir. It was the morning of December 24th.

He hadn't intended to buy a tree, but he'd been driving down 6th street and stopped at a light. A tree lot sat on the corner. Two men seemed to be gathering the few remaining trees, as if they were preparing to close up shop. Alex had abruptly turned in, walked up to the men, and held out his hand. As if by prearranged signal, one of the men picked up a tree leaning against the fence and handed it to him.

"How much?" asked Alex.

"Ten bucks. It was going to be mulch."

Alex half-carried and half-dragged the tree to the front door. He laid it down and went to the basement, pushing and pulling at boxes until he found an old tree stand. That was his Dad: "You never know when something might come in handy," he'd say, while Grace would be yelling, "Just throw the damn thing out." For fifteen years they'd had an artificial tree and still he'd never thrown out the real tree stand. And now, sure enough, it was going to come in handy.

Alex placed the stand in the living room window, on top of a plastic garbage bag and a few towels. Then he hauled in the tree. He got it upright in the stand and started screwing it in. But it was hard to get perspective when he was lying underneath.

"What are you doing?"

It was Molly's voice, incredulous, above him.

"What do you think, you with the amazing powers of perception?"

"Where did you get that thing?"

"Shut up. You'll hurt its feelings. Rescuing it was an act of mercy."

"You can say that again. This is one lopsided tree."

"Which you could remedy if you'd be so kind as to hold the top straight so I can get these damn screws in."

When the tree was in place, they stepped back to check it out: six feet tall, with skinny branches sticking out at odd angles. Not so much a triangle shape as a square with a few sticks poking up on top.

"Ugly but serviceable," Alex commented.

"Let's get the lights and ornaments," Molly replied. "It needs some dressing up."

They worked in silence, stringing the lights, draping the tree with gold garlands. Molly put down a quilted tree skirt. They methodically put on ornaments, bigger ones at the bottom, smaller at the top. When finished, they carried the boxes back down stairs. Molly swept up the needles from the hardwood floor. It'd taken less than an hour.

Alex sat on the couch and picked through holiday music. "Sesame Street? Perry Como? Caribbean carols? The Judds? We have what you call an eclectic collection here, sister."

"Just not somebody dead."

When Grace came downstairs hours later, the house was empty. She'd been taking a sleeping pill at night to overcome the insomnia. What she didn't tell the kids was that she was taking another at 4 a.m. when she awoke in a panic—heart pounding. At this point, every hour spent asleep was an hour she didn't have to think.

Vivaldi played softly. As she came around the corner, she stopped abruptly. There was a tree in the living room. Not their usual, perfectly shaped, artificial tree. This one tilted, but it was lit, and covered with familiar ornaments.

"Oh," she whispered. "How did you get here?"

Grace was curled up on the sofa sipping tea when the kids got back from the store an hour later. They carried in the groceries, walking through the living room. After putting away the food, they came in with mugs of cocoa and plunked down on either side of Grace on the sofa.

"Are you two responsible for this?" Grace asked.

Alex and Molly simultaneously pointed at each other, their voices overlapping, lapsing into whiny, New York accents.

"It was all his idea." "No, she started it." "Don't pin this on me, butthead."

Grace laughed. Not her usual deep, resonating laugh, more of a limp chortle.

"So, are you pissed or what?" Molly asked.

"No, decidedly not pissed. Amazed. Grateful. So, what's for Christmas dinner?"

Molly and Alex grinned. "Pasta!" they said in unison.

Later that afternoon, Molly initiated a walk along the Kaw River. They tromped along the path, feeling the cold air through their jackets. They walked, as if following orders, down to the two-mile post, then turned back. As if by unspoken contract, it was understood that anyone could cry at any time without being asked why, that their shared holiday goal was not joy but survival.

Pizza was delivered around 7 p.m. and they ate it sitting on the floor in the living room around the coffee table. Alex opened a few beers and Grace took two long swigs.

"I'm going to Midnight Mass," said Molly. "Can you handle it?"

Ironing clothes, taking showers, getting dressed, gave them a focus, a task. Once at church, they did not sit in their customary spot toward the front, but off to the side. Grace wanted to be able to slip out a side door if she felt overwhelmed.

But she never got to that point. Instead, she found herself calmed by the Mass. It provided perspective, this ritual that had been going on for two thousand years, through wars, famines, floods and plagues. At the sacred moment of transubstantiation, of "Do this in memory of me," Grace felt a moment of peace.

"Only say the word and I shall be healed," she murmured, and felt her eyes fill with tears.

It was 1:30 a.m. by the time they got back to the house. They hugged. They could not use the word *merry*, but each said "I love you" before going to their rooms.

They slept long and deeply, as if willing themselves to miss the early morning, to bypass those hours when they would have been laughing, giggling, opening presents. Those hours, with Gil, when they'd been a family.

When Grace awoke, sunlight filtered through the blinds, making patterns across her quilt. She heard music playing softly on the stereo downstairs and smelled the aroma of cinnamon. She looked at her bedside clock. She'd slept for nine hours without a sleeping pill. She extended her hands, reaching toward the ceiling, stretching, then headed for the shower.

When she got downstairs, Molly was bent over a cutting board, chopping peppers, red and green, and tossing them in olive oil. The smell of garlic had replaced that of cinnamon.

"Good morning, sweetie," Grace said into her ear. "Is there any coffee around here?"

Molly pointed to a carafe on the table.

"Under the foil are apple-raisin-cinnamon muffins. Still warm."

Grace poured her coffee, put a muffin on a plate. In the living room, Alex sat cross-legged on the floor, a jigsaw puzzle taking shape in front of him on the coffee table.

"God, this muffin is wonderful. Have you had one?" she asked.

"One? Mom, have I ever stopped at *one*? I had four."

"When did you get up?"

"About ten. Molly was already in baking mode, so I lucked right into the muffins."

"So where's the paper?" Grace asked.

Two hours passed easily. Molly cooked. Grace read, sipping her coffee. Alex worked on the puzzle, stopping only to start a fire in the fireplace.

The ring of the phone startled them all. Grace answered.

"Gracie? Listen, how are you guys doing? My boys are done with their presents and they don't care what table we eat at as long there's food. Be there in an hour. Just say the word."

"We're okay, Kat. Honest. I don't mean to be rude, but it would be too hard. Trying to make it like it used to be."

"I get the picture. Can I call you later?"

"Tomorrow. Okay?"

Grace hung up the phone. In the back of her mind she'd half-expected Katrina to just show up, loaded with presents and food, overly determined to cheer them up. And she could not have told her to leave, but it would have been unbearable.

And Katrina, at her end, felt guilty for the relief that swept over her. She did not have to go to the rescue. She could set the table and feed her boys until they were too stuffed to stand upright. Then they would lie on the living room floor and watch corny holiday videos, and she would fall asleep on the couch reading one of the novels she'd unwrapped just hours earlier.

Molly sautéed garlic until the house reeked. She tossed the pasta with shrimp and crab, mushrooms and peppers. There was a salad of wild greens, bread baked with spicy, black olives. The merlot was smooth, and they finished off a bottle. Dessert was Godiva chocolates and espresso with steamed milk.

"To Dad," toasted Alex.

"To Dad," added Molly. "I miss you."

Grace raised her glass, clicking it gently against the glasses of her children. Then she took a long swallow, closing her eyes as they blurred with tears.

31

"*Explain to me why you wish to subject yourself* to a polygraph, Grace?" inquired Leticio in a clipped voice. They were seated in his office. It was January 5th, and the winter light played across his desk.

"I read all the information you supplied me, the KBI lab reports, and police reports," replied Grace. "I know that there is some kind of horrific mistake. But it would be normal, only human, to assume that the evidence is correct. I want some evidence on my side."

"For whom are you doing this?"

"For me, dammit. I just want something I can point to, something I can touch." Grace's voice cracked.

"I ask again, Grace. For whom are you doing this?"

She looked at him, her face a bleak mask of despair.

"For my son, Miguel. For Alex. He doesn't believe me."

In the week after Christmas, Grace had immersed herself in novels, pure escapism. She called no one, did not return calls. Molly took over the shopping and cooking. Alex made lists of fix-it jobs, each of which required its own trip to the hardware store. And somewhere in there, on a date that Grace would never remember, the nightmare got worse.

Grace had been sleeping, but without the sleeping pill she frequently turned to. She awakened to the sound of voices. She rose quietly and went to her door. It was cracked open, and she squinted out through the space and into the hall. It was dark, empty. Grace held her flannel nightie close to her body and walked in bare feet to the top of the stairs.

The voices came from the kitchen. She understood that they were her children's voices, but they did not sound like her children. They sounded old.

"Look, Molly, I can't keep it in anymore. It's like we're living in some fuckin' fantasyland here. We're just putzin' around, and nobody is talking about what's coming. Mom is doing nothing. It's like she's given up, living in La-La Land until it's time to go to jail."

"You know, you can be such a royal-ass prick sometimes, Alex. What the hell do you expect her to do? Canvass door-to-door and ask if anybody saw anything suspicious the day Dad was killed? She has an attorney. He's in charge."

"Yeah. And what do you see him doing? Not a whole hell of a lot. And maybe, just maybe, it's because there isn't a hell of a lot to do. Unless you buy into some conspiracy theory, like the police and KBI and God knows who else are out to get Mom, then what you have is a lie. Maybe it isn't an intentional lie. Maybe she has some kind of protective amnesia. But it doesn't add up. It just doesn't fucking make sense."

"I don't know what's going on either, but I know that Mom is innocent. I can feel it in my bones."

"Your bones? Maybe that's where you have to feel it because you sure as hell can't know it in your head. Step back from your new domestic goddess role and stop chopping veggies long enough to see what we're up against."

"Alex, think. Think about all their years together. They had their fights, but they really, really loved each other."

"But maybe it was all just an act. Molly—Dad had an affair. People who love each other don't have affairs. Maybe it wasn't the first. And maybe Mom did find out and lost it. Like if he was leaving."

"Who said anything about leaving?"

"What if he wanted out and she couldn't face it? It doesn't look good after all her little lectures on *How to build a strong and healthy-marriage* for the husband to cut out."

"Mom kills Dad because she doesn't want to lose face? If Dad ever had left her, business would boom." Molly's voice went into parody, "Here's a woman who knows the pain I'm going through."

"Well maybe she wasn't thinking so logically. Maybe she was hurt. Maybe she fucked up. One out of control moment. Bang-bang."

There was silence, then. . .

"You really do believe it, don't you? You think Mom killed Dad?" Molly asked, so softly Grace could barely hear.

"Yeah," Alex whispered. Grace could hear that he was crying.

"Well, I can't, Alex. Not without giving up everything I've ever believed in. I don't care what the evidence is, or what a jury says. Unless Mom looks me in the eye and says she did it, I can't. I won't."

There was movement, perhaps gathering bowls or plates, and moving them to the sink. Perhaps Molly rested her hand on Alex's shoulder. Perhaps Alex whispered *I'm sorry* in a voice too low for Grace to hear. Perhaps a look passed between them that was a contract of silence. Or perhaps nothing.

Grace would never know.

She did not wait but slipped back to her bed and crawled under the quilt. She lay there, eyes compulsively blinking, until there were no more sounds, no running water, no toilet flushing, nothing but the silence of the deep night.

Miguel cleared his throat, and Grace looked up.

"Alex believes that I killed Gil. My own child thinks that I am capable of murder. All those years, caring, worrying, and he — my son. . ."

"And you want to give him something to help him believe?"

"Yes. I've been naive. I'm expecting friends to believe me and my own son. . ."

"Perhaps it is easier to think the worst, to prepare and brace for the worst."

"Great explanation, Miguel, but excuses aren't cutting it. Can we get the police to do it?"

"I think not, but I will inquire."

"Why not? They're so sure I'm guilty. . ."

"It is rare that a DA will stipulate to admit evidence in advance that may not be to his advantage. So, I expect that we will have to seek a private examination with someone whose credentials are excellent, where we stand some chance of getting it admitted."

"You mean that it might not even be admissible?"

"It is at the discretion of the judge. If you clearly pass, the DA will argue most vehemently. We must lay the proper foundation. Even then it is a crapshoot."

"You used the word 'if' Miguel. 'If' I pass."

"Polygraphs have limitations. Even if it proves inconclusive, I will provide you the same representation."

"That's bullshit, Miguel. I didn't kill my husband, and I need to be represented by someone who knows that in his gut."

Miguel did not reply. She was right. He did feel a different energy when he knew, in his gut, that an accused client was unjustly accused. He could taste the injustice like blood on his tongue, and he moved differently in the courtroom.

"I'll make the arrangements," he said.

32

When Mickey Donahue conducted seminars on the uses and abuses of the polygraph, he was thorough. He covered the major theories and strategies used in the Reid method; Department of Defense; R & I (relevant and irrelevant); MGQT (Modified General Question Test); and, his favorite, the zone comparison testing. Mickey felt that polygraph got a bad rap. It was perpetually misunderstood by the media. Because its validity depends on the expertise of the examiner, it had a mixed record of being admitted in court. And after the Frye decision in '23?

"Never has a science come under so much scrutiny as polygraph," he'd explain when he lectured.

It pissed Mickey off that there were idiots claiming to be examiners who didn't know squat, who did tests for Quik Shops, or used to anyway until that case ruling in '88 restricted pre-employment screenings. He'd heard of tests that lasted ten minutes, about as valid as the Inquisition.

Mickey's exams lasted two hours, or longer. Hardly any of that time was actually asking questions. It was setting the scene, explaining the process. And he never went in blind. He studied the file, selected a strategy, determined questions and sequence— neutral questions, symptomatic questions, the wording of the relevant questions—then wrapped up with a few control questions. His exams often consisted of 10-12 questions, but that was all that was necessary if he was thorough and precise in his pre-test component.

Polygraph works on the fear of detection. Lying in other circumstances would not elicit the same metabolic, measurable response. If someone were in a conversation and lied, comfortably confident that they would never be discovered, or, more importantly, with no real consequences attached to being discovered lying, their bio-chemical responses would be minimal.

Setting the stage is critical.

"We can lie to our friends. We can lie to detectives. And no one will ever really know whether or not we're lying," Mickey would explain before an exam. "But you can't lie to yourself. You may appear cool, but inside you're ready for action. You may look about to fall asleep on your feet, but you're like a tiger, ready to leap."

Mickey would wait until he had them nodding in agreement.

He'd carefully place the blood pressure cuff around their arm, always asking if it were comfortable. He'd bring the wires around the chest area for the pneumo and attach the skin sensors for the GSR (galvanic skin response) readings.

"This is just practice," he'd say.

He'd ask them to secretly write down a number on a piece of paper between 1 and 8. He told them to answer "No" every time he asked "Did you write the number 1? Did you write the number 2? Did you. . ."

Then Mickey would show them the paper, ask them to point out which squiggly line looked different, and explain how that was the one and only lie. It was then, understanding that they could not bluff, that clients would sometimes freak out. He'd had some rip off the sensors and storm out. He'd had them weep confessions.

Mickey felt affection for his machine. The new computer whiz-kids considered it an antique because the examiner had to do all the interpreting, but he thought of it as a classic. The Factfinder.

Leticio checked with the DA and got the anticipated response. So Leticio and Grace were driving to Donahue's office in Kansas City. Grace did not make small talk. She made no comments on the foraging cows, the lone frisky colt skittering sideways across a pasture. She saw everything, took in everything. But she did not speak.

Donahue's office was a tidy suite in a small brick building. The P.I. office didn't look the way Grace has expected it to. There was nothing externally to distinguish it from the insurance office next door or the investment firm down the hall. A simple: "Donahue & Associates." Mickey ushered them into the inner office. One wall was lined with books. A large desk was covered with neat piles of manila folders. There were five chairs. And the polygraph.

Grace had never seen a polygraph machine. It was surprisingly compact and looked like her old Singer sewing machine.

Leticio excused himself, saying that he had a few errands to attend to. Grace and Mickey sized each other up. Decades in their respective professions had left them with sharp intuitive edges.

"How do you feel?" asked Mickey.

"Terrified," Grace said. "If I fail—well, then maybe I am crazy."

"Why do you think you're crazy?" Mickey asked.

"Because the police are wrong or I am."

"Let me explain to you about how polygraph works," he began.

The exam was relatively painless. When he first hooked her up, and she felt the blood pressure cuff tighten on her arm, the pneumo lines around her chest, the sensors in her palm, she felt herself freeze.

"This isn't a trap," Mickey explained. "But you need to relax. Just stay quietly still, no movements because they throw it off. Center yourself. Count if that helps. Let me know when you're ready."

When he got to the core of the exam—the questions that mattered—after all the preparation, they were almost anti-climactic.

They were words, mere words.

"Yes." "No." "No." "No." Then she closed her eyes.

When she opened them, Donahue was sitting there with her print-out. Grace looked at the lines. They were all about the same. No jumps, no wild gyrations, no surprises. And she felt the truth, the warmth and rightness of her truth, wrap around her like a warm woolen blanket on a cold night. She reached out to touch the truth, running her fingers along the wavering lines. She sat, touching the edge of the paper, while Donahue went out of the room.

Leticio was waiting.

"Far as I can see, she's telling the truth," Donahue told Miguel.

"Any sense that she's delusional, that she believes it so she can make the poly work for her?"

"No. She didn't kill her husband."

"But, then how did her blood. . ."

"I know. Doesn't make sense. But I've been doing this for thirty years, and I'd wager my retirement that she ain't lying."

"Say that on the stand and we may have a chance," replied Miguel, staring past Mickey at the blank wall.

"You thought she did it, didn't you?" asked Mickey. "You thought that the test would help her see clear to plea this thing out."

"Sometimes, Mickey, evidence can be persuasive. I wanted to believe Grace McDonald. I was willing to provide her the best possible representation. But. . ."

"And now?"

"I'm thinking, Mickey. I'm thinking."

Grace was suffused with relief. She'd actually started to wonder if perhaps she was schizoid, if what she believed and remembered was fiction. As if her life had become a short story like that one by Kafka where the man wakes up and finds himself transformed into a giant cockroach.

"I am not crazy," she said out loud in the car.

"No," responded Miguel.

"But for a while there, after hearing Alex, trying to find a logical explanation for the blood, I questioned my own sanity. . ."

"And now?"

"It's nuts, but I'm not."

Grace turned sideways in the front seat to look at Leticio.

"So," she asked, "What will it take for you to believe me?"

"I believe you, Grace. But we still have to persuade a jury."

She did not reply.

"Alex returned to school, did he not?" asked Miguel.

"Yes."

"And did you discuss this before he left?"

"No. We never did."

33

Actually, they didn't "discuss" much of anything. The morning after hearing the kids talking in the middle of the night, Grace had wondered if it had all been a very bad dream. Alex had appeared normal.

Overly polite, but normal.

Molly had been the one to bring up returning to school.

"Mom," she'd started, hesitantly, "we need to talk about school."

"Of course. When do classes start up? I've been in a daze."

"We're all in a weird place, Mom. But it's now January 12th and classes start the 17th. I'm thinking of laying out a semester. It's not a big deal."

"Laying out?"

"Yeah, Mom. I think I need to stay home."

"Why?"

"Why? Because Dad's dead, you're going on trial, and my life sucks. Might be hard to concentrate."

"Would you be staying home for you or to take care of me?"

"Can't it be a little of both?"

"Sure, honey. But how much of each? 50-50? 80-20?"

"I can't give you numbers."

"Screw the numbers, then, sweetie. But think about it. Do that old heads-or-tails routine that Dad always did. Can you do that?"

Molly remembered heads-or-tails. It was not to force a choice, but to flush out the hidden feelings. Molly could see her father now, as if he were right with her, at the table. "Okay," he'd say. "So you're trying to figure out whether to go back to school or stay here with Mom. Heads, you go back. Tails, you lay out." Molly saw the imaginary quarter turning in slow motion, rolling end over end, landing with a small bounce in his extended hand. "Tails. You're laying out. Quick—what are you feeling? Happy? Relieved?"

No. She felt trapped. She desperately wanted to escape to the familiar routine of classes and friends, a world where she was not the daughter of a murdered father and an accused mother. But she couldn't leave her mother. Molly felt tears fill her eyes and she swiped at them with an angry motion.

"Oh shit," she said softly.

"Is that a decision?"

"I can't leave you," Molly replied.

"But you want to get back?"

"Not an option."

"Can we at least talk about it?"

"There's nothing to say."

"Well, I have a compromise. You could return to school for now and then come back for the trial. There is nothing you can do now, really. And with the scheduling, the trial may even include spring break."

"And leave you alone until then?"

"I'm not alone. I have Kat. I have my attorney. I have friends. I'd feel better if you were back in school."

"You're just saying that."

"No. It's easier for me to not have to have anyone else to think about. And then, after the trial, we'll have all summer together."

"Yeah, right, sure—assuming that they don't lock you up and we never get to be together again."

Grace suddenly looked stunned. It was as if that particular piece of the horror had not occurred to her. Her fear had revolved around the physical reality of jail. That these weeks might be the last to spend with her children, in her home?

Grace's hand flew to her face, covering her mouth.

In one motion, Molly was next to Grace, arms wrapped around her shoulders.

"It's okay, Mom. I'm not going anywhere."

Alex and Molly must have had a conference, because it seemed to be settled that Alex would return to Texas and come back for the trial. Molly would stay. When he left, he hugged Grace awkwardly, a bag in one hand. "Call if you need anything," he said.

Patsy Tsosie had been quietly following her gut for two weeks. She'd gone to the McDonald's street a few nights before, parking under a towering elm a few houses down. In the moonlight, she sat, watching, hoping to feel something, anything. She sat there for two hours. Nothing.

Patsy called Eva Dominguez and asked if she could get together. "Off the record."

"All the facts are in my report," Eva had said.

"It's a thorough report. I'm more wanting your impressions."

"Okay," Eva said. "Let's do lunch."

They met at 1 p.m. at the Paradise Grill. After a few minutes of preliminary chit-chat, they ordered soup and salads.

"So, ask some questions," said Eva.

"I'm not even sure where to start. It's more that I feel that something is missing."

"Like the gun?"

"Yeah. Just take me through every step, what you noticed."

"Dispatch got the call from the guy, all weirded out. Said his neighbor was unconscious in her front yard. He'd tried to wake her. He ran home and called 911."

"Okay. Then what?"

"When we got to her, she was out of it. Skin clammy. Pupils dilated. Shock response but breathing and pulse not too far out of whack."

"Bleeding?"

"Some. Raw knees and palms. Oozing."

"Was there a deeper wound? Something that might really gush?"

"No. More surface. Some gouges. What are you getting at?"

"How long would she have had to stand there for her blood to have dribbled down?"

"A long time but could have had a nose-bleed. That would gush. She had stains on her face and skirt, but I don't know whose blood it was."

"Do you feel like she could have been faking her symptoms?" Patsy probed.

"No. Maybe with a med. And they'd pick that up with the lab work at the ER. Shit, it's a hell of a lot easier to fake hysteria if she wanted to fake something."

"Did she seem like somebody who'd just committed a murder?"

"I don't know how to answer that. If she went bonko, shot him, then flipped out when she realized what she'd done? Yeah, she might go into a shock response, even block out the whole thing. That's possible."

"Then what about the weapon? How could she hide a weapon if she was in shock? We've been through every nook with metal detectors, almost dug up the yard."

"That's your job, not mine. But it doesn't add up."

They chewed quietly, thinking it through.

"Look, I find my hubby dead, I think I'd call 911," said Eva.

"Yeah, that's what they've been telling me down at the station."

Eva moved her fork around on her plate, pushing bits of salad from left to right, thinking. Then she spoke. "When I heard they arrested the woman, I was blindsided. But I'm the EMT, not the cop. So, what are you going to do now?"

"No idea. Hey, thanks for talking with me."

"Sorry I couldn't be more helpful."

"You were. I'm not sure how yet, but you were."

On Friday afternoon, Tsosie waited for the neighbor to come home. When he drove up, Patsy got out of her car. The man was short and thin. Patsy remembered that he was an accountant.

"Sir? Sorry to bother you, but I have a few questions about the McDonald incident."

"Incident? Having my neighbor murdered is not what I'd call an incident."

"Sorry. Poor choice of words. I meant no disrespect."

"Oh, never mind. Not your fault. I'm just testy as hell since it happened. Thought it was a random burglary gone sour. Thought I'd feel better after someone was arrested and charged. But I feel sick. We've been neighbors for twenty years. My stomach turns over every time. . ."

"Sir, did you see Grace McDonald on the lawn when you first drove past?"

"No. I told the police this already. Saw the door wide open, lights on, loud music coming out. Just hit me funny. So, I walked down. When I got to the edge of the lawn, I saw Grace. It was kind of dark by then. I went to her, shook her shoulder a little, but she didn't respond. I wanted to pick her up, but I remembered that first aid stuff about not moving people in case there's a neck injury. Put my jacket over her. She had no coat on and it was cold."

"Do you recall why you came all the way back to your own house to call 911?"

"Didn't have my cell."

"Did you think to go into the house? The door was wide open."

The man was silent. In his mind, he was back on the lawn, the light from the door casting a beam toward Grace's body.

"I don't even know how to talk about this. I deal with numbers, facts. And I have thought about it."

"But?"

"I couldn't go in that door. I felt something—something *evil*."

"*Evil?*"

"Doesn't make any logical sense. I know that. But I felt it."

"Well, sir, not logical sense, but it makes sense. At least to me."

Bruce Saunders was preparing for trial.

He had lists of exhibits, each tallied and labeled. He had pictures and diagrams of the kitchen. They showed where the body was and the exact spots where Grace's blood was found. He was lining up witnesses, setting appointments to review testimony. He'd double-checked the chain of custody so that there would be no surprises in court. He had that woman from the K.B.I. to explain what the hell she did in the DNA lab. Sam was going over court procedures with the rookie who'd discovered the body. He had the woman who'd had the affair. Hell, he even had the friend who'd found out about the affair. Had to subpoena all of them, and the last as a hostile witness.

Saunders saw it all in his mind's eye: Grace coming home from work. Discovering the affair. Or maybe she'd known and then heard Gil on the phone with the other woman. They argue. They say unforgivable things. He says he's leaving, that he can't stand her anymore. Did she slap him first?

He saw Gil slapping Grace, sees her nose start to bleed as she leans over, dazed with shooting pain, unbelieving. The vase is thrown across the room, shattering. Gil pushes her. She falls, shards of glass embedding in her hand.

Grace is enraged. Blood is streaked across her face. He could see her reaching into a drawer, pulling out the gun, pulling the trigger. Gil spinning. Then another shot. Then another. Then Grace standing, unbelieving, her nose still bleeding, her cut hand oozing as she reaches down to touch the dead body of her husband.

Open and shut, Bruce thought. Drops of her blood on his torso, on his arms, on the floor. Fresh blood. On the far side of the kitchen from where she insists she was. On the other side of the body. *Might as well be the other side of the moon,* he thought. Blood doesn't lie. People lie. And they lie to cover up.

He wished they'd found the gun, but DNA was enough.

Open and shut.

That's what Bruce saw, and every time he played the tape in his head, it got clearer and clearer. He just knew it. And that's what he would make the jury see and believe. Hell, if he were the defense attorney, he'd be arguing self-defense. At least then there would be a chance of getting her off. Then they could try and plea it out.

Miguel Leticio sat at his desk, softly drumming his fingers together. He had six weeks remaining to prepare for the McDonald trial. He had outlines for his *storyboard* where he would show that the time sequence made it impossible for Grace to have murdered her husband and then so effectively hidden the gun that countless police searches had failed to find it. He planned to hammer away at the missing gun, the lack of forensics evidence, how Grace McDonald had never held a gun let alone owned one or shot one.

He had no intention of refuting the testimony of the DNA expert. She was honest, professional, competent. He could introduce doubt in the minds of the jury if he got the polygraph admitted. He'd researched every precedent of polygraph admissibility.

Miguel hated cases where he had to pray for mistakes to surface during trial. He liked to be in control of the evidence, to draw a clear and compelling picture, a picture of innocence. For this one he needed more than mere prayer. He needed candles lit, whispered promises, and midnight sacrifices.

Danny found himself humming a Beatle's tune as he drove the ambulance down the turnpike. It was a routine transfer. No sirens.

Danny had been trying to analyze why Mandy had been so

vulnerable to the bitch, and what needed to be different. He was working on a plan. First, they would move, someplace where nobody knew them. Have a fresh start. He'd find a small house, with a garden. And Mandy could stay home. *She doesn't really like working,* he thought.

She would just love to stay home and be a mom and wife. No worries about making money. He'd make sure she had a decent allowance. And he'd really try to make it home when he was supposed to. He'd sit down with them at the table. He saw them together, laughing.

Danny had had a good enough Christmas break with Ross, taking him to see the lights on the Plaza in Kansas City, to holiday movies, to a friend's home for a sleepover. They'd eaten out almost every night and Danny could tell it was a treat for Ross. He'd tried casually pumping Ross for info about his mom, but Ross had not given up much of anything—Mom stayed home; Mom read; Mom cooked.

Danny suspected that Mandy had told him to keep a tight lip about her activities. Danny wondered if she really did have something to hide. He couldn't imagine Mandy with another man.

"Take good care of your mother," he told Ross as he put him on the plane to Colorado Springs.

Every morning, Danny read the newspaper for any word on the upcoming trial. He had fantasies of going to the trial. He could change his looks again somehow, just enough to throw her off. Not that she'd be looking. She'd be so freaked out she wouldn't see anyone but the judge and jury. And he was entitled. He was, after all, the aggrieved party.

The confusion he'd felt at the funeral had abated. Danny understood now the detachment he'd observed in suspects on television. Not that he was anything like them, not at all. They were criminals, acting out of greed. But he'd acted out of justice. He'd righted a wrong. And then, for Grace to have cut herself, so that instead of living under a cloud of suspicion, she was indicted—that was the hand of God, a sign of absolution.

34

Grace was in the grocery store, picking through the red peppers. Katrina was coming over for supper. It was the first time she'd shopped in a while. Molly had taken over that chore.

When Grace looked up, she saw Beverly, a woman she knew from church. She instinctively smiled and waved. Beverly did not wave back. She stared at Grace, her eyes unsmiling. Then she turned her back, put a bag of oranges in her cart, and went in the opposite direction.

Grace felt her face flush. Leticio had told her to be prepared, that people would be different. But she had imagined an awkwardness in conversation, not anything so blatant or so cold.

Grace almost ran after the woman. "Listen to me," she'd plead. She saw herself telling everyone, aisle after aisle, "I didn't kill my husband. Honestly. It's all a mistake."

She turned to leave the store, to run away. But then she stopped.

"Shit," she muttered. "Might as well finish the shopping."

But she kept her face down and read a magazine in the check-out line. She made eye contact with no one.

"I felt guilty," she explained that night to Katrina as they ate angel hair pasta and sipped wine. "Some woman from church snubs me, acts rude, and what happens? It's that Catholic girl guilt crap."

"Of course, Gracie. But you can't give in to it. Look 'em in the eye. Make them be accountable for how they act."

"Right," Grace answered, twirling her fork. "It's now my job to educate the universe on why they shouldn't jump to conclusions."

Katrina did not reply. Her mouth was full.

"I thought I was a person with a lot of friends, but I'm not," Grace mused. "I used to be, but haven't been for a while."

"I don't get it."

"Neither does Miguel."

"So explain it."

"When the kids were young, I was over-involved. School board. Carpooling. I knew everybody. Picking up the kids from school could be a 30-minute process because I kept talking to people. When Molly graduated junior high, it was a relief to pull back. So, while I have tons of acquaintances, and I've been on committees and in groups with half of the town, I haven't invested in forming real friendships. And some that might have been friends kind of drifted away because what we shared most were our kids."

"But couldn't you reach out? Just give a call?"

"It's too late. I got calls and cards when Gil was killed, but I was too depressed to respond. Now it feels self-serving—'Thank you for your sympathy. And now that I'm indicted, I could use a few more friends. So, are you free for coffee?' "

"What about church? Those people have known you for decades. You gave your soul to that place."

"Is that a joke?"

"Maybe a little."

"No, it's the same thing. I've been a lot less involved. Like not at all. And, really, it's hard enough taking sides when a couple gets divorced—but a murder? Everybody's waiting to see what happens."

They chewed in silence. While they'd never discussed it, each felt an unspoken gratitude that their friendship had survived the crisis.

"Maybe I could just do the hermit thing for a while," said Grace. "Which actually is what I've been doing."

"But that's letting them win."

"I may need to save up whatever shreds of dignity and self-worth I can to face the trial."

"Maybe you need to see it as training. Each time you survive a snub, you're better prepared for the trial. How's that for a re-frame?"

"Not bad for an amateur. But I still prefer hermit mode. Less likelihood I'll blow up in public."

Kat giggled at a memory.

"Remember the time you started yelling at the biker who took your parking place? You were in his face: 'Your mother would be so ashamed of your behavior.' The guy is 6'5," with multiple tattoos, hardware hanging from his eyebrows, and you're yelling at him about his mother.

I'm sure that had a profound impact."

"I saw the flicker of guilt in his eyes. He knew he'd done me wrong."

"You're lucky he didn't have a knife."

"And your point?"

"No public nuisance charges on top of homicide. Makes you appear a tad less credible."

"You are no fun, Katrina. No fun at all."

"Yeah. That's what my ex-husband used to say when I declined to participate in group sexual encounters with total strangers."

"You lie. He never had that much imagination."

"Hey, Joanna, it's Grace. My life is extremely crazy right now, and I could use lunch with a friend. Please call me." Grace hung up slowly after leaving the message.

Three days later, Joanna called back.

"Grace, I don't think I can do lunch. I have to testify at the trial, and I talked to this lawyer and he said that it isn't a good idea to socialize."

"It's just lunch, Joanna. And all you have to testify to is that we met, had coffee, and for how long. Not like I told you I was gonna' go home and shoot Gil."

Joanna inhaled sharply.

Oops, Grace thought, *maybe not the best choice of words.*

"Just having to go to court makes me anxious," said Joanna. "I've never had to testify. I hate being in the middle like this."

"In the middle of what?"

"Look, Grace, I just can't do lunch now, okay? I should think you'd understand."

"Yeah, Joanna. I understand. I won't call you again."

Alex was back in Austin. He was being circumspect in what he shared.

"My father died and my mother is having a very difficult time," was how he put it to his professors. "If the situation deteriorates, I may have to go home for a while. In that case, I'll make up the work as soon as possible."

As a child, Alex tended to be anxious, to worry what people thought. When kids cheated on tests, copied each other's homework, he went ballistic. Even team sports could get him worked up.

"They're breaking the rules," he'd tell his father.

"Just do your best, and don't worry what the other guys are doing," Gil had advised. "You can't change the world."

Sound advice, but difficult for Alex to follow. His heart was that of a scientist: consider, evaluate, measure, conclude. He held himself to certain standards and expected others to measure up. He was often disappointed.

Nothing in his life had prepared him for this. Now Alex could barely get out of bed in the morning. He isolated himself from friends. He told no one the truth.

Grace read the letter from her editor at the newspaper. On some level she'd been expecting it. She'd asked for a leave of absence after Gil's death. And the owner of the paper was, after all, the DA's father.

"Given the circumstances, it would not be appropriate for us to continue to carry your column, or any other feature articles. While we have a contract, we are prepared to defend this decision in court should you elect to seek legal remedy."

So much for innocent until proven guilty. Years of a pleasant working relationship wiped out in one memo. The coldness made her shiver.

They must really believe I did it, she thought.

"It would be most helpful for me to review your clinical files. It might lead to something," said Leticio.

He and Grace were preparing for the trial.

"That's impossible, Miguel. All my files are confidential. I can no more hand over the names of my clients than you can."

"I understand the nature of client-therapist confidentiality. But these are exceptional circumstances. I am looking for something, anything, to help us."

"And if you find something, you'll want to use it, no? To give the jury another suspect?"

"If we were to discover something, then yes."

"You'll use my client as a bone for the jury to chew on. Then I'm in deep shit with the Regulatory Board and lose my license. Not to mention that it is unethical."

"Licenses are not terribly useful in prison, Grace."

"Sorry, Miguel. No can do."

Leticio sighed. "This could be a very short defense, Grace. If the polygraph isn't admitted. . ."

Miguel looked out the window. There was a fine coating of ice on the branches of the trees, and in the morning sunlight they glinted and refracted as if crystallized.

"Grace, the police have never identified a single other suspect. One angle I can play here is that their premature fixation on you precluded the investigation that would have turned up someone else. I need possibilities, motives, grudges, whatever. I need to give the jury reason to doubt."

"Look, I cannot just turn over my client folders. But I will go through them. If I see anything that concerns me, any red flag. . ."

"All right, Grace. But soon. Yesterday. And now the larger question—"

"What?"

"How your blood got on Gil's body."

Grace actually chuckled.

"This is not funny."

"But it is so *X-Files*."

Miguel did not respond.

"Jesus, Miguel, I've racked my brains. I wasn't bleeding. So it can't be there. So what then? Some twisted Scott Turow frame? But how did they get it? Somebody snuck in my house and took my blood when I wasn't looking? The vampire theory?"

"Get on the files, Grace. Now."

35

Danny was doing research. He'd been unable to erase the incident with the hooker from his mind. Her words had stung. And so he was back in Kansas City, in a quiet corner of a Barnes and Noble. Between his armchair and the wall was a hidden pile of books. No one would be able to see what he was reading unless they snuck up behind him and looked over his shoulder.

This stuff is better than porn, he thought. Danny had never *studied* sex before. Whatever he knew had come from the locker room and the street—how hard you got, how hard you pushed, how you got off.

Now, reading, he recalled Mandy's whispered entreaties. "Slow down." "Softer, honey, please." "You're being too rough, Danny."

He remembered her hand taking his as she tried to show him how to touch her. He remembered getting angry.

"It's distracting when you do that. I'm not some puppet."

After two hours, Danny settled on three books to purchase. Judging by the hard-on he'd had since he started reading, he was on to something here.

I may not know shit, he thought, *but I am not too fucking stupid to fucking learn.*

Molly was hanging on, but just barely. The future that she'd taken for granted now tormented her.

Walking through the park, she saw a grandfather pushing a toddler on a swing, and awareness rose up, tidal in intensity. *My child, my children, will not have a grandfather.*

Then a high school friend who'd married young had a baby shower.

"Go," Grace said. "It will be good for you to see some friends."

But it was awful. Her friend was glowing. Her mother doted over her, bringing her tea, explaining how she'd be babysitting after the baby was born. They exclaimed with delight over each gift.

Molly heard screaming in her head: *My father is dead. My mother will die in prison. I will never have this. I will be alone.*

She pleaded a migraine and left the shower early.

Despite years in a parochial elementary school, faith had always been a struggle for Molly. She yearned for a faith that was pure and uncomplicated. She'd even envied Alex's agnostic certainty. She remembered Alex challenging transubstantiation: "If it's ritual, that's fine. But to say that a piece of bread, a cup of wine, actually becomes the body and blood of Christ? Signify, yes. But become? No way."

"You think your minuscule brain matter is the final judge?" she'd countered. "Maybe there's a process here that supersedes logic. Maybe that's where faith comes in." But even then she was trying to convince herself.

In the weeks before the trial, Molly would wake before dawn, shaken. She often felt tears on her face before her first thoughts had fully formed.

She began going to the early daily Mass.

"Free me from all anxiety," she would say softly along with the priest. She did not really hear the scripture reading, the brief homily. She came for Eucharist, seeking strength and solace.

At times she thought of going to confession. It had been a very long time. "Bless me, Father, but I seem to have misplaced hope. I am so afraid. I need my mother and father. I am not ready for this. Please hold me."

But she could not imagine herself saying what she really felt. And it made no sense to go unless she could.

"What sort of jurist profile would be logical yet empathic, use common sense, yet be critical of scientific absolutes?" ruminated Leticio as he perused the menu at La Parilla.

"Tostada and coffee for me," said Liz Foster to the waitress. "He'll end up with chicken enchiladas. He always does."

Liz put her menu aside. She was a tall woman and had been skilled at playing college basketball.

"Off one court and onto another," she'd joke. "Same game: play rough, foul, pretend you didn't mean it."

Liz was a prosecutor in Kansas City. She and Miguel had become friends in law school. He'd appreciated her sharp intelligence and not been distracted by her height. She'd gotten past his accent, the pauses as he groped for the right word. Now they called on each other when stumped. Since they worked in different judicial districts, there was no conflict of interest.

Miguel laid out the facts of the case for Liz as they waited for their meals. She interrupted a few times to ask for clarification. When he was finished, she doodled for a minute on the corner of the page, then looked up.

"If you don't point a convincing finger elsewhere, you're screwed."

"That I already know. I am looking for one of your brilliant insights, a strategy that will circumvent the evidence."

"Well, I'm drawing a blank. Unless she changes her story. Emphasize shock, amnesia."

"Which Saunders can then twist to show that she could just as easily have done it, realized, then hit the shock amnesia phase. Which makes more logical sense for how her blood got on the body."

"Do you trust the polygraph?" asked Liz.

"Yes, I do. But if she truly is delusional, then the polygraph might not reflect deception."

"What's your gut take on it?"

"I do not believe that Grace McDonald killed her husband. But I also do not believe that the evidence has been tampered with."

"Which means you have squat."

"Such a rich use of language, Liz, especially for a jock."

"Jury selection is critical. You need a few people who have felt betrayed by the system."

"Sure. And the moment they declare themselves, Saunders targets them. I'll see their backs as they leave."

"That's the key. To know who has such experiences but doesn't say."

"As in mind reading?"

"Saunders' experience is limited. He could be swayed by demographics, by appearance. You'll need to see deeper."

"My intuition is not so reliable."

"It may be your best shot."

36

February in Kansas can be brutal. Winds blow across the plains, arctic fronts surge in, storms come and go unpredictably. But this February was different. The sun shone, and temperatures warmed to unusual levels. A few bulbs slipped up green shoots and purple blooms. While snow mounds lingered, there was a feel of spring. People knew that winter was only taking a brief hiatus, but the respite was welcomed. Every conversation started with a comment on the weather, with murmurs of gratitude.

Spring had always been a good season for Grace and Gil. They'd gravitated to the outdoors, Grace with a head full of projects, Gil an agreeable collaborator. They'd work, side-by-side, then stop to sip coffee and admire what they'd accomplished.

This was the spring when they'd planned, maybe, to dig a pond. Just large enough for a few water plants, some koi, a trickle of water bubbling up through a hole in a rock. It was the sound that Grace desired. But there would be no pond, no more projects. Grace felt a sharp, pointed pain. She could not imagine gardening alone.

So when the spring catalogue arrived from K. Van Bourgondien & Sons, Grace was surprised at her response. She turned the pages over and over as her mind floated off in idle designs of caladiums and hostas, coral bells and lobelia.

Molly saw no purpose in making her mother face the unthinkable, that she could be in prison, not her garden, by summer. Molly herself could not even think it without feeling a sudden desperate need for air. So, she colluded with her mother's fantasy life, looking at the sketches, making suggestions.

"I know it's all fantasy," Molly told Katrina one night on the phone, one of many nights that Katrina would call to see how Grace was doing, how Molly was managing, if there was anything that they needed. "But it's a hell of a lot better than abject depression or alcohol."

In Gunnison, there was still a thick layer of snow on the ground. Yet Mandy too dreamed of a garden. She'd started one the previous spring, trying a few tomato plants in the sunny spots between the trees. But they'd died, never getting the strength of the full sun. This year she'd stick to shade flowers; ferns and hostas. She wanted to terrace the walkway, to leave a permanent mark even if it was a rented house. It was her home, and she was, in countless ways, claiming it.

"How many square feet?" Danny asked the real estate agent. He was at an open house. He'd started going to open houses on Sundays, just to get familiar with the market. He'd even talked to a banker about what it would take to qualify. Every paycheck from his second job, the blood bank, went into a special savings account for a down payment. He was amazed how quickly it was accumulating.

He'd also discovered the magazines at the grocery store with pictures of floor plans and "how-to" renovation guides. Sometimes he'd sit on the floor of the living room and spread them out. His favorites were the ones where there was a big fireplace in the middle, where the kitchen and living and dining areas were all open. He liked the idea of being able to see whatever was going on, of everyone within his reach.

The week before Valentine's Day, at the station, one of the other paramedics had covered a table with red paper hearts, glue, white lacy edging. In between runs, she was pasting collages.

"For my kids," she explained. "It's a tradition."

Danny took her leftovers home. The next day he found himself cutting pictures from his magazines and gluing them to a large red heart. There were rooms, gardens, and happy people eating meals around large tables. He put on edging. He drew an arrow through a heart. By the time he finished, it was a picture of all he wanted from life. He put the red heart in a large manila envelope and mailed it unsigned.

Leticio was drafting questions for voir dire, in pencil, on a long legal pad.

In theory, the goal of voir dire, or jury selection, is to seat people who will be impartial, able to make a thoughtful evaluation of the evidence presented within the dictates of the law. And, in theory, the process of voir dire is to gather sufficient information to allow judge and attorneys to assess juror prejudices, to reveal attitudes.

In reality, voir dire is much more. For Leticio and Saunders, it would not only be their first look at the jury pool, but the first time potential jurors got a look at them. It's a time to make a positive impression, establish rapport. If jurors sense that an attorney is trustworthy, that trust can extrapolate to the trial itself. If a jury first perceives a lawyer as objective, they are more likely to believe later what is presented.

It's also a time to educate jurors as to what is expected of them and what they can expect in their new role. Legal terms must be explained, made accessible, but in a manner that respectfully includes them, makes them feel an essential and valued part of the process.

And all, Miguel recognized—the information gathering, the rapport, the educating—all must be done in such a way as to subconsciously position jurors to see the case, the evidence, through his eyes. It must also be done in so subtle a manner that neither judge nor prosecutor could find fault, could make sustainable objection. If he could manage it, this invisible, microscopic transition would make all the difference.

And in this case, Leticio understood, more than almost any other he had ever tried, the jury selection would determine outcome.

37

Grace carried the mail into the living room. She opened a letter with a P.O. Box return she did not recognize.

Dear Grace,

I can't quite imagine what you're going through, but, after all the support and help you gave me, I needed to say something. I don't understand what's going on, but I'm thinking of you and praying that this will all work out for you. I am so very sorry for your loss. I know from the way that you spoke of your husband how much you loved him.

You may not even remember me, but I was your client a few years ago. You helped me to make some hard choices. My life is much better now. I live in Gunnison, work in a veterinarian's office, and I'm taking a college class. Ross has made a good adjustment. His Dad had Ross back in Kaw Valley for Christmas.

That's all. Just remember that there are a lot of us out here who remember you and are grateful.

Mandy

Grace looked out the window. Of course she remembered Mandy. The tentative smile, the self-depreciation, the growing resolve. And the photos of the son that Mandy had pulled from her purse: sturdy, round faced, with serious eyes that looked right into the camera. There had been that messiness, having to testify in court, but it'd been over in an hour. The husband had needed a scapegoat, someone to blame. But once the judge ruled, he'd settled down.

Grace dropped the letter on the pile of magazines by the coffee table. She walked to the back door and looked out. In her mind, she saw the expanded garden, curving along the edge of the woods, maybe a dogwood tree. She'd call a nursery tomorrow and ask about dogwoods. There must be varieties that could tolerate cold winters.

Patsy Tsosie was on her hands and knees, peering under a bush in the wooded area behind the McDonald home, when she heard a twig snap. She looked up, startled to see Grace McDonald standing perhaps fifteen feet away.

"May I help you?" inquired Grace in a tone both polite and sarcastic.

Patsy scrambled to her feet, brushing away leaves and dirt. She walked toward Grace, extending her hand. Only then did Grace recognize her as a cop.

"I'm Patsy Tsosie, ma'am. I met you at the courthouse. Didn't mean to intrude."

"Perhaps I can be of assistance?" The sarcasm won out.

"I doubt it," Patsy said. "I don't even know what I'm looking for."

"Is this some kind of mind-game, detective?"

Patsy snorted.

"No, ma'am. I'm not even officially working now. I'm on my own time."

"On your own time?" Grace echoed, now confused.

"Yes. Look, I'd better go."

"Wait a minute. Really, what are you doing here?"

Patsy weighed the rules against her own sense of justice. *Oh, hell, maybe I'm not cut out for being a cop anyway,* she thought.

"Our official investigation is done, but I don't feel right about it. So I'm just following up on some loose ends. Hunches is more like it."

"And do your superiors know about these hunches?"

"Sam Hillard. But he told me to keep a low profile."

This came as a surprise. Hillard supporting a hunch?

"This is not some ploy to get me to divulge something that could be used against me?"

"I don't see what else you could say. Unless, of course, you casually mentioned where that missing gun disappeared to."

Grace paused, thinking.

"Would you like a cup of coffee?"

"I'd better decline. I'm not exactly going by the book here."

Grace returned to the house, walking slowly, considering what she'd just heard. A cop, even if she was a rookie, wasn't completely satisfied. And she'd implied that Sam Hillard wasn't either. Grace found it all somehow liberating.

Mandy was at work, trying to persuade a hyperactive Dalmatian puppy to be still long enough for her to give him a vaccination, when the receptionist called out. "You have a call on line two."

"Get a number and I'll call back," Mandy replied.

An hour later, with morning appointments wrapped up, Mandy grabbed her messages. Two were local follow up calls about their pets.

The last was from Danny. Mandy felt her stomach constrict. She punched in the ten digits.

She got his recording. "Hi. I'm out saving lives." Beep. Beep. Beep. Mandy left her message.

It was 10 p.m. when Danny called back. Mandy was already in bed, reading a textbook before falling asleep.

"Hello," she answered, yawning in the middle of the word.

"Hey, it's me. Do you want me to call back tomorrow?"

"No. I'm awake."

"You sure?"

"It's okay, Danny. Let's get it over with."

"Well, it isn't exactly something we have to get over with. Our son is not. . ."

Mandy cut him off. "Poor choice of words. What's up?"

"Spring break. It's only a month off. I've got time off. Thought I'd come out there instead of Ross flying back here. Maybe camp, at least at the lower elevations. Visit Silverton, do the gold mine tour, try the hot springs at Ouray."

"Well, Ross has been talking about seeing his friends in Kaw Valley, but I think he could be persuaded. There's still skiing then and Ross would love that."

"Ross can ski?" Danny asked.

"Just started in January. He's taking lessons up the road in Crested Butte. I imagine he'd like to try somewhere else."

"Do you ski?"

"Barely. I fall down more than stay up. But the last time I got all the way down the easy slope without pitching into the snow."

"That's amazing. Really. You like skiing."

"I didn't say I liked it. I said I did it. But actually, I'm getting into it.

It's magical. And it takes so much focus that you forget everything else."

Mandy realized that she was talking to Danny as if he were just an ordinary person from whom she had nothing to fear.

"Hey, Mandy? You know how you've changed? Well, I've changed, too," Danny was saying. "So, could you do me a favor? Would you just think about the possibility of coming skiing with us for a few days? Ross would love it. Not the whole week, just a day or two. Just think about it?"

Mandy was silent. In her mind, she could almost see it, the three of them laughing, stumbling down the slope. Hot chocolate in front of a big lodge stone fireplace. Ross grinning. God, it would make Ross happy.

"I'll think about it."

Mandy held the phone in her hand, listening to the dial tone, before putting it down.

She had changed since the divorce. But could Danny really be different? The scene last Christmas. . .

Mandy thought about it. He'd arrived unannounced, with presents. She'd seen it as controlling and presumptuous. But what if he had been trying to make a gesture? What if he'd just wanted to see where his son lived, and knew that if he asked, she'd say no. And she would have. So he came, taking the risk. And, predictably, they'd argued. But he hadn't touched her. He'd been angry, but she'd been the one to hold up the knife, to threaten. He'd backed down immediately. Or was it that Ross had come home? She couldn't quite remember.

Then there was that anonymous Valentine. At first she'd thought it was from Ross, something they had the kids do at school, but then she'd noticed the Kaw Valley postmark. It had seemed so out of character, and, well, creepy. It might have been sweet five years ago, when they were married. But now?

But maybe it was possible. If she'd changed, perhaps Danny had also. Perhaps he now had his priorities straight, understood what it meant to respect a partner. Or at least was willing to learn.

Grace sat on the floor of her office, surrounded by files. There had been something in her accidental contact with the rookie cop that cracked open the cocoon she'd been hiding in. If someone she didn't even know was trying, on her own time, to find something that might help in her defense, then she, Grace McDonald, needed to get off her sorry ass and do likewise. She'd always been a person who took charge. The paralysis that had gripped her was an aberrance.

Grace started with her current files. She read through her notes, looking for any history of rage. She tried to remember the tone of their voices, their inflections and her responses.

Five hours later, she methodically alphabetized the files back in the drawers. She had some names, family members who had served jail time, a kid with pending drug charges, some shoplifting and DUI's. But she felt they wouldn't pan out. Her clients tended to be men and women who struggled with depression, anxiety, obsessive compulsive disorders—neurotic rather than psychotic. They were good people. They worried a lot. And worried, caring people did not murder.

Grace had figured out a way to balance her professional ethics with her attorney's requests. Mickey Donahue. He had the means to access all sorts of information while preserving confidentiality. She'd pay Donahue herself to do follow-up, computer stuff mostly, looking for any red flags. If he found something—well, then she could decide whether to let her ethics float away down the stream of self-preservation.

Grace stood up and stretched. Her neck and back were stiff. Enough for now. After she gave these names to Mickey, she'd start on the *back closet*, the boxes of case files from the past.

"Something's changed, Kat, but I'm clueless as to what started it," Molly told Katrina on the phone. "She got dressed and went into the office yesterday, spent most of the day, said she was checking files. Today she drove to Kansas City. Said she needed to talk to 'the man.'"

"Hey, any movement is good here." Katrina paused. "Could she actually have thought of something useful?"

"I doubt it. If there was anything specific, I'd have heard."

"Well, keep me posted."

Molly hung up the phone.

Over the past months, Katrina had become not just her mother's friend but her friend as well. It was the first time that Molly had ever talked with direct, blunt honesty to a woman her mother's age. With the narcissistic self-absorption of adolescence, she'd been dismissive of her parents, their relationships.

Now she counted on Katrina, counted on her for day-to-day contact, if only phone calls. There was a comfortable familiarity. And she realized that this was the nature of her mother's friendship with Katrina, that this was what they'd shared for decades.

For the first time, Molly found herself looking more closely, differently, at all the *older* people, taking them out of the mental boxes to which she had relegated them in the past.

God, Molly thought, *am I like the only jerk or are all kids this way?*

38

The trial loomed, a storm cloud on his mental horizon. Leticio could not escape it now. Each morning, no matter how blue and clear the sky, how bright the sun, he felt a sense of dread. He went over and over his notes, looking for another angle, a way to work this defense. But he had nothing. No other suspects. No plausible theories. Only character, time frames, reasonable doubt.

He'd filed motions. But none of them had gone anywhere. He'd done everything he could think to do. And as he engaged in mental arguments, taking first his position, then the State's, he knew the State's was stronger. He could introduce doubt, but they had DNA.

"How did you get through Valentine's Day?" Mickey Donahue asked Grace.

They were meeting to discuss her case.

"I don't get out much. Avoided the cards and candy so it just slipped right by."

"Good. It was a bitch for me after my wife died. It was just one of those days we used to make a big deal out of."

Grace looked at Mickey, seeing him as a person, not just someone whose skills might help her. "I'm sorry." she said. "How long has it been?"

"Four years," he said. "Car hit her broadside. Just a drunk kid. Not a bad kid, just made a bad choice to get behind the wheel that night. I wish I'd been driving but I'm still here, still going through the motions."

"Does it get any better?"

"Sometimes. Then there are days when I almost forget. I'll get real involved at work, come home, have a beer, relax, almost have a good time."

"Almost?"

"Maybe in four or five more years I'll have a whole day where I don't remember. Of course, then I'll probably feel guilty."

"At least no one is after you for killing her."

"I wanted to. She was brain dead but in a coma for a few weeks. I got them to turn off the ventilator, but damn if she didn't keep breathing. Then she caught some virus and by then we had the DNR order in place. Didn't treat it and she died."

Donahue stared out the window at the trees. Then he reached for the manila folder that Grace had put down on his desk when she walked in.

"Let's see what you need me to do," he said.

Grace punched in the number written on the yellow slip of paper, then hung up before it even rang. *Shit,* she thought, *I have got to get a grip.* She punched it in again.

A woman's voice answered on the third ring.

"I'm trying to reach Jennifer Watson," Grace said.

"This is Jennifer. Can I help you?"

"Jennifer, this is Grace McDonald. Please don't hang up. I need to talk to you."

There was absolute quiet.

"Jennifer?" Grace asked. "Are you there?"

"Yes, I'm here. I'm sorry. I just don't know what to say."

"What do you mean?"

"Oh, everything. I told the truth and now it's gotten all twisted."

"I feel pretty much the same way. Look, Jennifer, I'd like to talk to you." Grace's voice was quaking. "I didn't shoot Gil. I've been waiting for the police to figure it out. That isn't going to happen. And you probably know nothing, but maybe there is something. Can we meet and talk?"

They met in a small-town cafe ten miles from Kaw Valley. As Grace entered, a woman waved to her from a back booth.

Jennifer extended her hand and Grace shook it, sliding into the booth. Then they looked at each other, eyes holding. It was as if they needed to connect what they heard about the other with the reality, the flesh, of the person sitting across.

Jennifer spoke first.

"Mrs. McDonald, I never intended to hurt you."

"Look, when I first heard, I would have ripped your face off," Grace replied bluntly. "But now I need your help. I'm not over being hurt, but I just can't let it get in the way right now."

"What can I do?"

"Tell me about Gil. I have all these fantasies, like he'd gotten into gambling, some kind of trouble. When the police told me about you, I felt as if I didn't know Gil at all, that everything had been a lie. That there are more secrets. Do you understand what I'm trying to say? Perhaps, just perhaps, there is something that can help us make sense of what happened."

Jennifer did not answer at once, but sat, quiet.

"I understand. But I don't think I'll be of much use. He just got lost for a little while, and that was probably mostly pity for me. Gil was kind. He listened. I was a little in love with him. And I started it."

Grace felt her stomach twist.

"Was he disappointed in his marriage?" Grace forced herself to ask.

"No. More disappointment in himself. We talked about it as editors, that we were having to re-write the ways we'd dreamed our life-stories would turn out. I couldn't make a baby. He couldn't write."

"But he never really tried to write."

"He tried, but he said it was trash. He threw it away."

"Did he show you?"

"He just told me."

Grace knew, with sudden ice-water honesty, why he hadn't shared his angst with her. She had empathy with her clients, but that understanding often didn't extend to her own family. With them she was often impatient, less understanding. "Stop moaning and just do it," she'd have said. "And if you aren't any good, then drop it. It's not the end of the world."

Grace and Jennifer talked for two hours, dissecting Gil's moods, behaviors, habits. Forgetting who they were, they joined together in a common cause. And they came up with—nothing.

There were no secrets. No leads.

Files littered the floor of Grace's office. She'd asked Katrina to help.

Screw the ethics, she thought. Miguel is right. *Damn license isn't going to do me any good in prison.*

For seven hours they poured through files, stopping only to call out for pizza.

"Everything but jalapenos and anchovies," Katrina ordered. "Double cheese. Pile on the toppings." She gave the address and grinned. "I love it when you're paying," she said to Grace.

They located nine more possibilities, remote though they were. Two were court-ordered custody disputes which Grace had mediated, getting nowhere but managing to piss off everyone in the process; one in which she'd testified about a man's molestation of his 14 year old stepdaughter; a borderline personality disorder fiasco; three divorce cases where her testimony had reversed residential custody; two cases where she'd been abruptly fired by her clients for reasons unknown (which meant they might have other imaginary grudges).

Mandy River's file was in the middle of a pile against the back wall. It never made it out of the first round.

Grace now spent every waking moment working. She was tormented by her earlier lethargy. What had she been thinking? How could she have been so passive when it was her future at stake?

The passivity, she'd realized, was the end result of a middle-class life in which the really bad things, the awful things, happened to other people. She'd been waiting to be rescued, for someone else to fix this. Because this felt too crazy, like it had to be fiction, not real life. Not her life.

Grace provided Mickey with data to do background checks on everyone who might remotely have a grudge against her. Jennifer brought her lists of the projects Gil had worked on over the years, and whatever gossip she could find out about anyone who had not liked working with Gil.

A lead emerged that looked promising.

Gil had edited a book a few years before in which the author had challenged every suggestion. It was as if the writer felt Gil's criticisms were intended to sabotage the true nature of the book. In frustration, Gil requested a change of editor be made, but the publisher had instead dropped the book entirely. The author had been bitter and had left several acrimonious messages and letters. "You'll pay for this" had been one. And, "You were out to get me from the start."

"I checked him out, Grace, but no," Donahue reported. "He was in a classroom in San Jose the afternoon of the day Gil was shot."

As the trial approached, Grace became more frantic.

Miguel Leticio was immersed in his preparation.

"We do not have to prove your innocence, Grace. The State must prove your guilt. We will hammer away at each piece of evidence they present, demonstrating that it is all circumstantial. Lacking witnesses or a weapon, there exists significant reasonable doubt."

"And the DNA?"

"Our biggest challenge, certainly. But there are many cases where juries have opted to discount convincing DNA evidence. Do you recall O.J. Simpson?"

"I am not a black football hero in Los Angeles. There are no conveniently racist cops nor conspiracy theories, and I don't have any gloves or alibis."

"Grace, for one last time. It is not too late. Could you have found Gil, crawled out of the house, felt trapped in some macabre nightmare, and gone back inside after you cut your knees?"

"You don't give up, do you?"

39

The morning of March 29th dawned gray and blustery. There was a dank chill in the air, a chill that cut to the bone, making noses run on contact. Grace showered and dressed slowly in a somber navy dress with matching jacket, just a touch of pale lipstick, gold stud earrings. Leticio had nixed her usual style and had torn a picture from a Vogue magazine in his waiting room the week before to show what he wanted.

"Your appearance is too counterculture. Those bright skirts. The dangling earrings. You look like a gypsy," he'd said, pronouncing gypsy as if the *g* was silent. "You have to appear solid, a woman of substance and calm demeanor. In mourning. Incapable of violence."

"This has nothing to do with my clothes. Everyone will know I'm pretending."

"The jury will not."

"Whatever you say. I can play dress-up. I'll even practice walking on heels so I don't appear wobbly."

Looking in the mirror, she realized she'd forgotten something.

"Shit," she muttered, trying to pull the pantyhose up over her hips, "who the hell invented these things?"

Molly insisted on driving. They parked near the courthouse. Leticio had prepared Grace. He'd mentioned that a legal intern would be helping out, and a colleague from Kansas City would be watching from the gallery, consulting with him during breaks.

Alex had not yet returned. He had an exam, a paper due. He'd assured Grace that he would be there if she wanted, but he could use an extra few days. He'd be up by Wednesday.

Katrina had received a subpoena from the DA. As a witness, she wouldn't be allowed to sit in the courtroom, but have to remain outside. Especially as a hostile witness, which she felt was a fairly accurate description. She'd initially told Saunders to screw off. Saunders had then explained about contempt citations.

Grace walked into the courthouse, holding her body stiffly, as if it might shatter. Without moving her head, not making eye contact, she saw everything. She saw the frayed cuffs on the shirt of the old man seated on a hallway bench. She saw the yellowed teeth of a woman chewing a wad of gum. She saw the wiry, young man with the camera equipment slouched in a shadowed corner and how his arm extended upward with one fluid movement as she passed and—click—took her picture as her face involuntarily twitched.

She felt that she could see with the pores of her skin.

Miguel was already at the table, folders neatly piled, briefcase opened, his head down as he studied a sheet of yellow legal pad. At the end of the table, a young woman was immersed in jury questionnaires.

As Grace approached, Miguel looked up. He held out his hand.

Grace looked at it for a moment, then extended her own. Miguel took it and just held it. Their eyes met.

"Where should Molly sit, Miguel?" Grace asked.

Miguel gestured. "Right behind us is fine." He looked into Grace's eyes. "Any last questions?"

"None that you have answers for."

Miguel had told her that her role for today was to say nothing, to simply listen, to not show personal reactions on her face or in any other manner of body language, to make eye contact with prospective jurors if they seemed to want to make eye contact, to not stare or appear intimidating or threatening by holding the eye contact for too long, to not appear worried or overly tense—all in all, Grace was to do whatever she could to communicate her innocence. A polite and deferential innocence.

It was a long and complicated list and Grace already felt the strain of having to contain herself, for hours, of not being allowed to pound the oak table and scream that this was a horrific injustice in which she, not only Gil, was a victim.

"All rise. Hear ye, Hear ye, the court of the Honorable Judge Jordan Fisher is now in session. You may be seated," the bailiff announced.

As the potential jurors entered, Leticio sat, back erect, hands on the table neatly crossed. These people, so ordinary, that he might not have looked at twice on the street, were now the most important people in his world. And it might only take one juror, with opinions and the ability to persuade, for a jury to be like so many dominoes, lined up and then falling. He needed that juror on his side.

Bruce Saunders leaned back in his chair, legs crossed, a picture of relaxed authority. Next to him was an assistant D.A, Georgia Lawson, a woman in her 40's who had gone back to law school when her kids were out of the house. Bruce had figured that a middle-aged woman with him at the table could balance out some of the sympathy factor. Georgia knew that she'd been selected by Saunders more for her graying hair than her strategic mind, but she didn't care. Experience was experience, and her age and gender had been liabilities long enough that a few perks were appreciated.

"Ladies and gentlemen of the jury, we will begin the process of voir dire. It is your obligation to consider seriously and respond honestly to all questions asked. You are not to make any judgments about the case based on the questions being asked," the judge spoke clearly, in a level voice. Grace felt the atmosphere in the courtroom shift. It was time for work.

Saunders stood. He walked toward the jury, extending both hands, a gesture of welcome, of inclusion.

"Ladies and gentlemen of the jury, I am about to ask you questions, questions that may at times seem to you to be personal, even inappropriate. Let me assure you that it is never my intention to embarrass you. But this is a case that causes many of us to respond more emotionally than we might otherwise. So, as we inquire into your history, your attitudes, your beliefs, you must have the courage to speak out. It is essential for this process that you do so. We rely on your integrity."

The jury was with him, Grace saw, following every word, nodding their understanding and agreement. If this earnest young man was relying on them to be truthful, they would do it. Or at least some would. But a few sat with their arms crossed or held the sides of their chairs a tad too rigidly. While Grace could see these polarities, she did not know what to make of them.

Saunders was still speaking.

"Do you feel that a police officer could make a mistake while performing his duties?"

He asked the question, then stopped, looking at the faces in front of him for some response. He glanced down at his list of jurors for a name.

"Mrs. Gardner, what do you think?"

It went on like that for the entire morning. Did the police work for the prosecution or for the people? Were scientific labs credible? Have you ever been misdiagnosed for a medical condition? Had that misdiagnosis involved lab results? Do you have friends who are cops? Attorneys? Have you ever been a victim of violent crime? Do you own a gun?

Saunders asked if anyone knew the defendant, pointing to Grace. A few were perhaps faces that she'd passed in the grocery store. But she knew no one.

"Do you watch the T.V. news most nights?" Hands went up.

"Have you seen coverage of this case?" More hands.

"Do you read a daily newspaper?" Many hands.

"Have you talked with friends about this case?"

"Have you expressed an opinion?"

Leticio's pen moved fluidly over paper, taking notes, making connections, yet his eyes never looked down. As Saunders paced and talked, Leticio's eyes were on the jury—how each sat, the moment they shifted, whether they looked at Grace.

Several rows behind the prosecution table, Liz was doing likewise. She'd chosen a different vantage point, as if the angle might possibly generate a revelation.

Lunch was a welcome break. They slipped across the street to Miguel's office. Sandwiches magically appeared. Miguel spent the hour looking at notes, conferring with Liz. Katrina, Molly, and Grace said little to each other.

When they returned to the courtroom, and the prospective jurors returned, it was Miguel's turn.

"Were I to be on a jury, I would not be capable of objectivity in several areas. For example, having lost a close friend in an accident involving a drunk driver, I react strongly. I do not represent drunk drivers, and I would make a biased juror for such a case. I have had jurors tell me that they could not be objective in cases of child abuse. I commend them for their courage and self-awareness. As Mr. Saunders noted earlier today, we rely on your integrity."

"Are you ready to proceed?"

Miguel waited, his head moving along the rows of jurors, making momentary eye contact with each until he had a nod, a movement of the eyes, a silently mouthed "Yes." Two refused to respond, simply sat and stared. They, Leticio noted, would have to be cut.

"How do you understand the principle that a defendant is innocent until proven guilty?" he asked. Within thirty minutes, jurors were interrupting each other. They were focused on what was happening among them, less aware of the audience. By fostering such a process, Leticio hoped to observe how they might function in deliberations.

"Come now," he said to one older woman, "you have a good brain, and common sense. Just say what you think. If you saw someone being arrested in the parking lot of the grocery store, wouldn't you think that they'd done something wrong?"

"What if I don't do a darn thing all week except cross-examine? Do I have to do something for you to regard Grace McDonald as innocent?"

"Beyond reasonable doubt to a moral certainty—that's what the law says. Not 'probably.' Or 'makes sense.' Or 'can't figure out another explanation.' But 'moral certainty.' What examples can you give me of moral certainty?"

Grace sat, seeing which panelists might look her way. There were some people she felt she might trust, but it was nothing she could explain.

The judge called for voir dire to conclude. The attorneys huddled around a table next to the bench, going down the list in front of the judge, citing cause when appropriate, using their preemptories when needed.

As the judge announced those who were dismissed, panelists filed from the courtroom. The remaining 12 and the 3 alternates regarded each other with curiosity, smugness, or resignation.

Then the judge banged a gavel, they all rose, and everyone went home.

So what do you do the night before you go on trial for murder? Molly asked herself. Then she realized there was only one possible answer.

Whatever the fuck you want.

Katrina stayed over, she and Grace acting like rapid-cycling manic depressives, one minute half-comatose or crying, the next laughing hysterically and planning a trip to Greece as soon as the trial was over.

They opened a bottle of red wine. Then another.

"Vino is good for what ails you," intoned Katrina.

"If I keep this up, I'm gonna have a headache tomorrow," said Grace.

"Oh, like you wouldn't have one anyway?" countered Katrina.

"I see your point. Pour me another glass."

"It's not like you have to think on your feet. You just have to sit there and look innocent, appalled at the injustice of it all," Katrina said as she poured.

"You two are fruitcakes, wacko, on top of drunk," said Molly.

Grace and Kat looked at each other, then clinked their glasses in a toast.

"To wackos," said Katrina.

"Long live fruitcakes," added Grace.

40

Grace had never been to a murder trial. Neither had Katrina or Molly. But Leticio had warned them that there might be a full house.

When Miguel saw them entering the courthouse, he gestured them into a small conference room off the hallway.

"You did very well yesterday. Just try and maintain that today," he said to Grace. "It will be more difficult as you listen to the prosecutor to not feel intense reactions to what he is saying. But it will not help you to display those reactions. The jury will not think, 'Ah, see how upset she is, the prosecutor must be lying.' They will think, 'She cannot control her emotions, even now.' So, shall we go in?"

The courtroom seemed to be filling fast. Leticio had told her that other than reporters, there would be the curious. The regulars. Apparently, there were people for whom going to trials was a form of entertainment, a diversion. Like real TV.

"Don't they have jobs to go to?" Grace had asked.

"I have no idea what their circumstances are, but they seem to fixate on mayhem and murder. There is one that brings her knitting, wears a brown coat even in summer, always sits in the third row."

Remembering, Grace turned to see if the woman was there. And, yes, on the aisle in the third row was a woman in a brown coat, her hands moving in her lap.

Inexplicably, Grace was filled with a yearning for Gil. He'd always been there for her, to talk her through the rough times. *He should be here now,* she thought. *I need his hand to hold, to lean my head against his shoulder. I want to tell him about the woman in the brown coat. I cannot endure this alone. I cannot. . .*

The first time Danny had thought, *I could go to the trial,* had been a rush. A rational slice of brain told him to stay away. But he felt entitled. After all, his marriage had ended in a courtroom. It was only right that he be there.

So, for the past several weeks, he'd been growing out a beard. His hair, almost bushy last fall, was military short. He'd sat in the lobby at the law school and observed how the law students dressed. He now wore beige Dockers, a denim button shirt, hiking boots, and carried a soft-sided black briefcase from Land's End. He had yellow legal pads in it, a book on criminal procedure. No glasses.

Now he sat in the back, head bent over the textbook. He'd prepared an explanation in case he ran into anyone he knew. "I'm playing around with the idea of law school," he'd say. "Thought I might chase ambulances instead of driving them."

The sound level of the courtroom abruptly dropped when Grace entered. He watched her walk down the short aisle. She looked like some Republican matron. Then the daughter came in. He hadn't seen her since the funeral. Her face, not swollen now with tears and grief, was thinner.

He started to feel anxious, visible, but then calmed himself. He was, he told himself, an anonymous face in the courtroom crowd.

The door to the jury room opened and the jury started to file in. On the other side the judge entered.

"All rise," said the bailiff. "The court of the Honorable Judge Jordan Fisher is now in session."

The judge began a list of instructions to the jury, clarifying how they were not to speak about the case with anyone, not watch television or read newspaper coverage of the case, not. . .

Danny crossed his legs, took out a yellow legal pad, and got ready for the show.

Bruce Saunders slowly walked over to face the jury box. He arched his head back and looked at the ceiling. He took a deep breath. By the time he actually spoke, the courtroom was in absolute silence, the jury riveted.

"We don't like to think that murder, calculated and deliberate murder, can happen here. Murder is what happens on television, or maybe over in Kansas City. But in Kaw Valley? In our community?" He exhaled. "And we don't like to think that ordinary people are capable of that kind of violence. We want murderers to wear some sort of sign, to be able to tell them apart from the rest of us. They don't, of course, but that's what we want in order to feel safe. We may even deny the facts in order to preserve our precious need for safety."

"But this is a case where our desire to deny will be challenged. The defendant is not from out-of-town. There was no drunken bar scene. There are no drugs involved. It is murder, plain and simple. Committed by a well-respected community member. We have theories why she did it, but, in the end, the theories won't really matter. Because, in the end, it comes down to the facts. Tangible, visible, measurable, scientifically validated, and absolute. Facts that refute Grace McDonald's account of the events of that evening."

"The prosecution will present witnesses: police, EMT personnel, the coroner, a DNA expert from the KBI lab over in Topeka. They testify because it is their job. But we will also call on others who do not come willingly, but reluctantly. In the end, after listening to the witnesses, hearing the evidence, you will separate fact from fiction. This is your responsibility. You are no longer allowed the luxury of denial. You are a jury now."

Saunders stood, hands together and fingers extended in a gesture that was almost like prayer, his eyes making a second of connection with each and every juror. Then he turned, walked to the prosecution table and sat down. He had not looked, even once, at Grace.

Miguel stood, and walked slowly to the front of the jury box.

"If Gil McDonald were here, he would tell you the facts. That is what Mr. Saunders said, and I agree. Gil would tell you about his wife, their relationship, and those last moments of life in which an unknown killer shot him, murdered him, in his own home. He might even tell you about the gun, the murder weapon that the police have never found. It has evaporated, perhaps discarded by the real murderer, perhaps still in the possession of the person who did kill Gil McDonald, a person who sits comfortably because he knows that the police have charged the wrong person..."

Danny sat absolutely still, eyes closed. His pulse raced. *This was a stupid, stupid idea,* he thought. Why the fuck had he been so intent on coming? Any moment Leticio would turn around and point at him.

But nothing happened. He opened his eyes. No one was looking at him. Leticio was still talking.

"Grace McDonald abhors guns. She's never owned one and doesn't know how to use one. She has no history of violence. In her work, she mediates disputes, advocates for the peaceful resolution of differences. The prosecution will attempt to establish motive, but they will fail."

"So why is Grace McDonald on trial? No confession, no witnesses, no weapon, nothing but a trace of blood—and the prosecution's insistence that not remembering equates to murder."

"Yes, the prosecution will present witness after witness. And they will describe how Gil McDonald was murdered, in awful and horrifying detail. We do not dispute any of it."

Miguel talked for ten minutes, but Grace heard only sounds, as if listening to a foreign language.

"Just as the prosecution asked you to do your job, so do I. Because the real killer is still out there. We cannot send someone to prison just because we have not been able to find the murder weapon, or the real murderer, and we want the security and satisfaction of a conviction."

Danny kept his face blank, his eyes lowered. *They don't know a thing,* he told himself. *It's just words. Don't make a move.* But his left hand started to twitch. He reached for his briefcase and put it on his lap, over the twitching hand.

Defense attorneys contend that the system gives unfair advantages to the prosecution. The prosecutor gets to give opening arguments first, present evidence first, and gets first and last closing arguments.

Prosecutors say it doesn't really matter, that jurors make decisions based on evidence. Defense attorneys argue that it damn well does matter, and if it doesn't matter, then change the order. No prosecutor in his or her right mind would do that. Social scientists agree with the defense. Most people are subject to a "recency effect," in which arguments heard most recently have more influence. In addition, there is a "primacy effect," in which the first information heard about a person often weighs in heavier. Overall, jurors tend to remember the beginnings and endings of trials better than they do the middles.

"The State calls Eva Dominguez to the stand."

Grace had no memory of Eva Dominguez. As Eva spoke, Grace felt that she was hearing about someone else—pupils dilated, skin diaphoretic, non-responsive, appearance of shock, pulpy knees, and scrapes and contusions on the inside of hands. Eva described tests conducted in the ambulance and oxygen saturation levels.

"One last question, Ms. Dominguez," Saunders was asking. "Was Grace McDonald bleeding?"

"Not copiously. Surface."

"Yes or no. Was Grace McDonald bleeding?"

"Yes."

"And did you note in your report that there were streaks on her face that appeared to be blood?"

"Yes."

"And what happened to those streaks?"

"Excuse me?"

"At the hospital, Ms. Dominguez. What happened to the streaks?"

"They were washed off when she was cleaned up."

"They were never tested? No samples were taken for analysis?"

"No, not that I know of."

"And so there is no way to say today whether the blood streaks on her face were her husband's blood or her own blood?"

"No. I'm not even absolutely certain they were blood."

"But you made that observation at the time, isn't that correct?"

"Yes."

Leticio stood and walked around the table.

"Ms. Dominguez, do you believe the patient was faking symptoms of shock?"

"No."

"Why not?"

"Because she was not conscious. I slapped her to get a response."

"And what did you think upon hearing that Grace McDonald was charged with shooting her husband?"

"It didn't add up for me."

"Thank you."

But then Saunders was back, challenging Dominguez's ability to make such distinctions, looking for exceptions. Grace felt her mind drifting until she heard a familiar name.

"The State calls Officer Patsy Tsosie to the stand."

Saunders covered the basics—were you working at such-and-such a time on such-and-such a date? What did you observe? When did you first find the body? Where was Grace? What did you observe prior to entering the house? What procedures were followed?

Then it was Leticio's turn.

"Officer Tsosie, your testimony has been thorough and professional. However, was any evidence found that night, weapon or otherwise, that would point to my client as the perpetrator of that crime?"

"Objection," said Saunders. "Evidence was present but not yet identified."

"Your Honor, I simply wish to point out the narrow parameters of that evidence and the lack of anything else discovered at the crime scene during the police investigation," replied Miguel.

"I'll allow it," said the Judge.

"No," Tsosie answered. "Nothing was discovered in the house, yard, or surrounding areas that incriminated Grace McDonald."

Tsosie was giving Miguel more than he asked for.

"Hypothesis and conjecture aside, has the investigation uncovered any concrete evidence other than my client's blood?" asked Miguel.

"Objection, Your Honor. This witness is not an experienced detective in a position to evaluate the relevance or significance of evidence," said Saunders.

"Well," countered Leticio, "She's your witness and a police officer. Who would you prefer to make such discriminations?"

"I'll allow it," commented Judge Fisher.

"No. No other physical evidence."

Tsosie didn't look at Saunders as she stepped down from the stand, but she felt strongly that she'd just moved to his shit list.

Sam Hillard and some other cop were also sworn in and asked much the same questions.

When the coroner was called to testify, after the lunch break, Grace found herself detaching. Dr. Carolyn Liebowitz, silky hair in a French knot at the nape of her neck, calmly explained in the most graphic detail how Gil died. Exactly how the bullets entered his body, what organs they destroyed. How bone causes bullets to spin. How time of death is established.

It hurt too much to listen. Grace closed her eyes to escape.

In the early years of their marriage, when Gil was late, Grace had imagined a policeman at their door. "I'm sorry, ma'am, but your husband's been in an accident," he would say. She'd conducted mental disaster drills: how she'd get to the hospital, who she'd call to watch the two small children asleep upstairs. It was as if by imagining the worst she could prevent it. If she braced for awful possibilities, they would never happen.

And they never had. Gil had inevitably returned home safe. Together, they would check their sleeping children, his arm around her shoulder, then fall asleep talking. The system had worked well for twenty-five years.

"How tall was the person who killed Gil McDonald?" Saunders was asking.

"From the trajectory, and where the bullets entered his body, shorter than Mr. McDonald. The bullets entered rather straight, not angled, indicating that Mr. McDonald was standing, as was the person holding the weapon. Depending on how the gun was being held, I would estimate 6 to 12 inches shorter."

Wednesday started off with the DNA specialist from the KBI.

Molly took notes. Not that anybody cared, or would use them, but it gave her something to do. It kept her from chewing apart the inside of her cheek.

Ellen Woods had charts, diagrams, tri-colored illustrations. She couldn't just say, "Our lab did a bunch of tests. We found two types of blood, the victim's and his wife's. Trust me. I run a tight lab."

No. Woods had to explain every step of the scientific process, from why and how DNA is unique, to how certain tests prove DNA matches, etcetera, etcetera, etcetera. Wife's blood on husband's body. Husband's blood on wife's skirt. Her professionalism and dedication gave the evidence an increased weight, a credibility that it might not have had from someone less committed.

Which, Molly realized, was not the least bit helpful for her mother.

The courtroom perked up after lunch, when the emphasis moved from science to sex.

Jennifer Watson took the stand. She looked trapped.

"Would you please state your name, occupation, and your professional relationship with the deceased," intoned Saunders.

"I'm Jennifer Watson. I'm an editor at Free State Publishing. I worked with Gil McDonald for seven years."

"And when did the nature of your relationship with Mr. McDonald change?"

"After I was divorced, I was very depressed. Gil was supportive. He was willing to listen, and we talked a lot."

"Did you have an affair with Gil McDonald?"

"I suppose you could say that, but it didn't start out that way."

"Were you sexually intimate with Gil McDonald?"

Jennifer paled. "Yes," she replied softly.

"To the best of your knowledge, did his wife know about this affair?"

"No."

"Was that because Gil McDonald was afraid. . ."

Miguel was on his feet. "Objection, Your Honor."

In the back of the courtroom, Danny's jaw had dropped. It was cosmic justice. Gil had screwed around on the bitch. The perfect marriage was a sham. He'd been right all along.

His mind started spinning. When it stopped, Leticio was addressing the witness.

"Ms. Watson, in your many, many hours with Gil McDonald, did you ever hear anything from him to make you think that there had ever been any physical altercations in his marriage?"

"Never," she replied. "Gil was struggling with his own issues, but he loved his wife. That's why he ended our relationship. He never said anything that made me ever think that they couldn't work out any problems that came up."

Katrina was called to the stand. Obviously distressed, she said that, yes, she'd once seen Gil with Jennifer Watson, later talked to Gil, and never told her best friend about the affair. Her attempts to explain were cut off by Saunders. Leticio asked questions that allowed her to describe Gil and Grace's relationship, but her credibility was shot. She was too clearly allied with Grace.

It didn't get any better.

There was the *friend* who reluctantly explained that Grace McDonald had said, out loud, at a party, that she would shoot her husband in the back if she ever caught him messing around. And while the woman admitted—under cross from Leticio—that she'd said she'd cut her own husband's pecker off, Grace's threat seemed to hang there in the air.

On that note, the prosecution rested.

Leticio needed to get the polygraph admitted. He had nothing to balance against the hours of Ellen Woods and DNA. He hadn't challenged Woods. He'd made that mistake once before, in a prior case, trying to allege mistakes in the lab, a possible cover-up. Big mistake. What could fly in Los Angeles did not fly here. With good reason. Ellen Woods ran a tight, honest lab. She didn't take sides. She reported results.

He was up against a wall. His attempt to get the polygraph admitted in pre-trial had failed. But his client could not take the stand and have any credibility without the support of the polygraph.

Leticio took the plunge.

"Your Honor, at this time, prior to presenting our defense, I request that you reconsider the admissibility of the polygraph exam which my client. . ."

He didn't get to finish the sentence, what with Saunders leaping up to object.

"Your Honor, that matter was ruled on pre-trial. It is hardly. . ."

The judge cut him off with a wave.

"In chambers, gentlemen. Now."

In the judge's chambers, Leticio and Saunders did a familiar dance.

"Your Honor, polygraph has been admissible only when both parties have stipulated to admission prior to the taking of the test. . ." started Saunders.

"A request that you denied, if you recall, Mr. Saunders," Leticio continued. "Your Honor, this case is hinging on a few drops of blood against the word of my client. Given the hours of scientific testimony provided in support of the validity of the blood samples taken from the scene, cannot some small measure of scientific validity be accorded to my client, to bolster her only means of defense, which is her word? You do have that discretion, even in the absence of stipulation, and. . ."

"I'm well aware of what discretion I have, counsel," the judge interjected.

"Of course, your Honor. But to deny the admissibility of polygraph is to deny my client the right to a defense. My client requested a polygraph exam by an expert, neutral professional and she passed without question. The jury has a right to hear that. Mr. Saunders is quite willing to stipulate to the validity of a polygraph exam when it suits his purposes. Indeed, he argued for its admissibility four months ago in State v. Hutchings."

The last remark was one Leticio had been saving. Saunders had used polygraph to convict. Miguel had read the transcript.

"There were extenuating circumstances. . ." Saunders rebutted, but the judge stopped him with a wave.

"I'll allow it."

The judge looked at Miguel. "When will your expert witness be able to be here?"

"He's in the hall waiting, your Honor."

"How convenient, Mr. Leticio."

Mickey Donahue took the stand. He was dressed in a dark suit. He appeared conservative, scientific, neutral. Under questioning from Miguel, Donahue explained his own professional background and experience. Then he explained how a polygraph worked, the underlying principles, the standards, the application process.

"And what conclusions did you reach after a comprehensive examination of Grace McDonald?"

"That she was telling the truth when she stated that she did not kill her husband."

"Was there anything in those test results to suggest ambiguity?"

"Nothing whatsoever. It was as clean an exam as I've ever seen."

"Thank you."

Saunders stood.

"But there are exams that are not clean, Mr. Donahue?"

"Yes. But in such cases. . ."

Saunders interrupted. "Yes or no will be sufficient, thank you. There are cases where people have been known to manipulate the polygraph exam, is that not correct?"

"Yes."

"And the polygraph could be less reliable with individuals who believed that they were telling the truth, who were, to use a general term, delusional?"

"Could be. Hard to say."

"And you were paid by Grace McDonald to conduct this polygraph exam?"

"I'm a professional. I get paid for my work, the same as you. I don't slant results based on. . ."

"Just answer the question: Yes or no."

"Yes."

"Thank you," said Saunders, as he turned to face the bench. "That will be all."

Miguel proceeded methodically.

He started with a timeline. He had Joanna testify as to when she and Grace had met at Prairie Bakery, at what time they had parted. He had telephone logs of when she'd left the message. He played the telephone message she'd left for Gil, Grace's cheerful voice echoing in the courtroom.

Leticio recalled Tsosie and Hillard. The timeline poster was five feet high and it stayed in front of the jury, off to one side, the entire time. Leticio hammered in that the timeframe did not allow for Grace to race home from coffee, shoot her husband, hide the gun so well that countless police searches could not find it, and then lie down and pretend to be in shock on the front lawn. He had maps showing the extent of the police search, yet no weapon had ever been recovered. If Grace McDonald killed her husband, logic dictated that there would be a weapon. It could not have disappeared into thin air. But if someone else killed Gil McDonald, then, of course, there would be no weapon found. He asked the police why a paraffin test, to determine if there was gunpowder residue on her hand, had never been conducted on Grace when she was in the hospital. Such a test would have exonerated his client, he stressed, and the absence of such a test should not be construed otherwise. Miguel questioned the narrow focus of the investigation, the drive to find a suspect, the premature fixation on Grace McDonald.

There was an expert witness, a psychiatrist on fugue states, to explain how Grace McDonald could have found the body, cut herself falling, stood up and then remained frozen. That would account for the blood. And amnesia is not uncommon in such circumstances.

Then Leticio moved to Grace's character. Grace McDonald had never owned or used a gun. He called witnesses from her assorted peace projects. He put on a forensic psychologist who cited statistics of how very remote the possibility that a previously non-violent marriage, with no record of altercations, would turn deadly.

With every witness, Saunders cross-examined. He left the psychiatrist in tatters by harping on how he was a paid witness, that he made a good part of his income being a paid expert witness. When he said "paid," Saunders twisted his mouth so that it was impossible not to hear "bought."

And the forensic psychologist? He hadn't even met "the couple." Plus, if domestic violence was closeted, which it often was, the statistics were worthless.

But Saunders did not attack Molly. When Leticio put her on, she described how her parents had loved each other, how they never really fought but talked things out.

"They never fought?" Saunders asked gently.

"Well, they argued."

"Did they raise their voices? Did they express anger?"

Molly looked trapped.

"Yes, but that's arguing."

"And you've been away at college for two years now?"

Yes, but I'm home summers. I knew my parent's relationship."

"Yes. Of course. It's clear you love your mother very much."

"The defense calls Grace McDonald to the stand," said Leticio. There was a slight buzz in the courtroom.

Grace stood and walked to the front of the witness stand. She raised her right hand and swore to tell the truth, the whole truth, and nothing but the truth.

Then she sat down.

The initial questions from Miguel were easy.

As Grace answered, she tried to look at the jurors. She described being a mom, running carpool, being on the school board, helping out with Scouts. She talked about her marriage. She felt that she had to justify her life, to make these strangers understand who she was and how impossible it was that she could ever have shot Gil.

"Can you tell us now what you remember of the events of that Friday in November?"

"I finished work at about 5 p.m. and closed up the office. I stopped for bread." Grace quietly told of the November afternoon.

"And when you got home?"

"I walked into the house. The music was on loud. I put my coat and bag down and walked to the kitchen to see Gil." Grace stopped and took a deep breath.

"And you saw. . .?"

"It was horrible. Gil was lying on the floor. There was blood all over the floor. I screamed, and then my legs just sort of gave way. I remember grabbing on to the doorframe to steady myself. But I just slid down."

"And then?"

"I think I reached for Gil. Just to be sure he was dead. His eyes were half-open but empty. I remember crawling out of the house. I must have crawled over the gravel and rock entry and path, but I don't really remember any of it. I woke up in the hospital."

"You say that 'I must have crawled, but I don't remember any of it.' Is it possible that you stood there, paralyzed, in denial? Is it possible that you cut yourself falling?"

"Yes, it is possible. I wish that I did remember more clearly."

"Did you kill your husband?"

"No. I loved my husband deeply."

"Were you aware that your husband had had an affair?"

"Not until Officer Hillard informed me."

"Have you ever owned a gun?"

"No. Never."

"Have you ever shot a gun?"

"No. Never."

"Thank you," said Leticio.

Bruce Saunders just sat behind the prosecution table for a few long seconds looking at Grace. Then he stood up and came toward the witness stand.

"Among your many accomplishments, Mrs. McDonald, did you ever have any starring roles? Because that was quite a performance."

"Objection, Your Honor," thundered Leticio.

"Withdrawn," countered Saunders.

"Ever had a nose bleed, Mrs. McDonald?" Saunders queried.

"Yes. Infrequently, but yes."

"Did you have a nose bleed the night in question? Or is that something else you can't quite remember?"

"I did not have a nose bleed."

"Because a nose bleed would explain a lot. In fact, I'm surprised that defense counsel didn't bring it up. Of course, then there might be a question of how it got started bleeding, whether as a result of being hit. But I'm still surprised defense counsel didn't introduce the possibility of a spontaneous nosebleed. Because that's a lot more believable than the conjecture of some fugue state followed by amnesia."

"Objection. Is there a question here?" Leticio asked.

"Stay on task, Mr. Saunders," the judge responded.

"The medic testified that she observed dark streaks on your face. Bloody streaks. Do you know how they got there?"

"I think that I reached out to touch Gil, then wiped my skirt. Maybe I wiped my face also."

"Mrs. McDonald, how many times have you testified in court?"

"I don't know."

"More than ten times? More than fifty?"

Grace considered.

"Somewhere between the two numbers."

"Enough so that you know your way around a courtroom?"

"How do you mean?"

"Just that you know how to cover yourself. . ."

"Objection, Your Honor." Leticio sounded truly exasperated.

"Sustained. Mr Saunders, please refrain. . ."

But he did not refrain.

"Did you and your husband fight?"

"Yes. We disagreed. That's normal."

"Not disagreed. Fight. Did you fight?"

"Not physical fights. But we did argue."

"You never hit him? Not once in decades of marriage did you lose your temper?"

Grace paused. There had been a rough patch, when the kids were early teens, when everything Gil did grated on her nerves. Things got volatile. She'd slapped his face one night. She'd broken his glasses.

"I've lost my temper. But I did not kill my husband."

"You haven't answered my question."

Bruce Saunders was pushing her, wanting her to explode, wanting the jury to see. Grace felt the bile rising in her throat.

"Have you ever had an affair?" Saunders asked.

"No." Grace's voice was tight.

"At the time of your husband's murder, were you having an affair?"

"No."

"So, the reason that the police have never found the weapon could not have been that you passed it off to an accomplice, that you had someone. . ."

"Objection!" shouted Miguel.

"I am attempting to show, Your Honor, that there can be many explanations for not finding the murder weapon, in addition to those explanations provided by the defense," Saunders rebutted.

"I'll allow it."

"How long does it take you to drive from your house to the river?" Saunders asked.

"What?" Grace responded.

"The Kaw. The river that passes just one-half mile from your front door."

"A few minutes, I guess."

"And that little wooden bridge, the shortcut to the turnpike?"

"About five minutes."

"So, you could have easily driven to the bridge, which gets hardly any traffic, disposed of the gun and then. . ."

Miguel was on his feet, spitting out his objection.

Grace's face went slack. This was what Leticio had meant when he said that taking the stand might not be advisable, that it could work against her.

By the time Grace stepped down from the stand she was trembling. She felt enraged and impotent, but the jury didn't know that. She just looked shaken.

Closing arguments were set for the next morning.

"The wife did it." Miguel intoned. "Why not? It's worked before. At least they have an arrest. But it is up to the jury," he continued, "a jury with some common sense, to not let this travesty of justice continue."

"Reasonable doubt," he said. "A woman lives her entire life without incident, a respected professional. A good wife. A good mother. A good woman caught up in a horrific mistake." Miguel's voice was soft.

"There is no weapon. Family members and friends clearly state that Grace McDonald abhorred guns, did not know how to use one, had never owned one. Yet the State contends that she had a gun stashed away, that she shot her husband at close range, and that she then managed to hide the weapon so effectively that police searches turned up nothing. But where is their proof? Neither police or KBI has found any purchase of a weapon. Is this reasonable?"

Miguel was passionate. Lacking a suspect, the police had created one. The prosecution's attempt to establish motive was a witch hunt. They'd never proven that Grace McDonald knew about the affair until told by Officer Hillard. Doubt. Doubt. Doubt. He hammered at the timeline. This was a case of conjecture. Grace McDonald was in the courtroom because she couldn't remember if she could have cut herself when she discovered her husband's body, couldn't remember. . .

"As the expert testimony explained in this courtroom, Grace McDonald clearly passed a lie detector test. And that is because Grace McDonald is not lying. She is telling the truth and has always told the truth."

"Someone else killed Gil McDonald," Miguel continued. "Someone else. And he is still out there."

Leticio was convincing. His belief in the innocence of his client was palpable. Grace could see the jury following every word, nodding in agreement.

Then it was Saunders' turn.

Grace McDonald was sick. Truly delusional people did not hold themselves accountable. She believed the lies she told herself, which allowed her to pass that polygraph. If she even had, if the results of a paid examiner could be trusted. Her performance on the witness stand had been commendable, but it was just that—a performance. None of us really know what goes on behind closed doors, and now her husband isn't here to back up her pretty picture of the perfect marriage, the perfect family. All we know is that it wasn't so perfect for him. He'd had an affair. And maybe she'd had one too. Maybe that's where the gun was. If not, then certainly there was room in the timeline for a drive (he'd timed it) to the river: three minutes over, three back, toss the gun.

All Grace McDonald has to defend herself are words, Saunders argued. Believe me, she pleads, I'm a nice person, just like you. But words are not the basis for reasonable doubt. Reasonable doubt requires facts. *I don't remember* does not excuse behavior. Especially when the *I don't remember* is self-serving. She cannot remember to call 911? She cannot remember where she went in her own kitchen?

There were secrets here. There were signs of a fight. A vase full of flowers heaved across the room. Signs of a nosebleed. Dark streaks on her face. Shards of glass in her hand, on her skirt.

His blood on her skirt.

Her blood on his body.

Grace stopped hearing after Saunders mentioned the vase. The vase was her secret. She hadn't realized until sometime in January that the vase in the police reports was her anniversary present from Gil. She never told anyone. The truth would only be twisted.

Danny was riveted by Saunders' description. He could see it so clearly as Saunders spoke—Grace coming home, something ticking her off, angry words, the vase being hurled across the room and shattering. He could see Gil slapping Grace across the face, see the blood gush from her nose, see the rage in her eyes. Now it was her hand that held the gun, her arm extended, her fingers pulling. . .releasing. . .pulling. . .releasing. This was how it happened. Really.

The prosecution had irrefutable facts, Saunders continued to explain. No matter how much the defense wanted these facts to disappear, they would not. Grace McDonald had lied to cover up a murder and then she got trapped in the web with her own lies. Maybe the murder was impulsive, maybe it was planned. That wasn't the issue. Gil was dead—and Grace lied. No matter how much they, the jury, wanted to excuse Grace McDonald, in the end it all came back to the blood. Irrefutable and absolute.

DNA doesn't lie.

Only people lie.

Which is why, no matter how uncomfortable it made them, they had to convict.

Saunders returned to his seat and started fiddling with some papers.

Molly looked around, as if waking from a dream.

The judge was giving instructions to the jury. Then everyone stood, the entire courtroom, as the jury filed out.

Want to go over to that new Italian place for lunch?" Molly heard one woman in the row behind her ask another. "I hear their foccacia and artichoke salads are to die for."

"What do we do now, Miguel?" Molly heard her mother asking.

"We wait. Go home, Grace. I doubt there will be a verdict before Monday. If they come back early, I'll call. Be prepared to come quickly. They have agreed to allow 30 minutes notice, which is generous, for us to reconvene."

"You did the best job any attorney could have done."

"I rarely feel that way, Grace, and I certainly do not right now."

"I didn't help. I felt that the truth—I may have been terribly mistaken."

"Second guessing will make us both nuts, Grace."

41

Grace, Molly, and Katrina left the courthouse by the back door and drove home. It was not even noon. By 1 p.m. Grace was in the backyard. She squinted at the sunlight, bright without the leaves on the trees. The air was warm enough to work without a jacket. She wore jeans and a sweatshirt and she made her mind go blank as she raked up the dead leaves remaining from last fall.

In the upstairs bathroom, in Katrina's arms, Molly was incoherent, sobbing. "It could be her last weekend," she said, choking on the words.

"We don't know that. Look, you have a choice here. If it is her last weekend, what kind of memories do you want to have? Sitting on a toilet seat with wadded up Kleenex up your nose or doing something with your mom? I figure we follow her lead on what she wants to do. And she is not going to want to sit around crying."

"How can you be so calm?"

"I'm not. I'll cry myself to sleep tonight. I feel like when my mother died, only even worse because that was a natural act and this is so fucking insane."

"If and when I ever see that asshole brother of mine, I'm gonna wring his fucking neck."

Alex hadn't returned for the trial. He'd called Tuesday night, saying he'd prefer to wait. He didn't know if he could face it.

Molly had refused to beg.

Grace had been a mother, even then.

"Listen. Alex, it's okay. There isn't anything you can do. We'll call if we need you." But when she'd hung up the phone, Grace's mouth was twisted as if trying not to cry.

Leticio had written Alex earlier, in February, saying he thought he might like to know that Grace had requested a polygraph test and had passed.

There had been no reply.

Danny was shopping for Mandy. It was a first in some ways. He'd always bought presents at the last minute, running into a store, buying whatever was advertised or what the clerk said was "hot" or "in." But this time he was thinking of Mandy, her house, her picture of sunflowers in a white porcelain pitcher.

He'd decided to find her a real white pitcher, even if it took all weekend.

In the garden, Grace was not ignorant of the precariousness of her situation. She was not in denial. Time felt precious. She wanted to soak up the essentials. Immerse herself in the ordinary. Feel the earth.

The weather cooperated. The women gardened, cooked, napped, reminisced. They listened only to music.

In a three-ring binder, Grace made lists for Molly and Alex: what was in the safe deposit boxes; when to pay bills; which bank accounts were for what. Gil's insurance should be coming soon. The children had been listed as beneficiaries as well as she. Miguel would help them with the finances. She'd talked to a colleague about closing out her practice and moving her records into safe storage or having them destroyed. Grace knew what to do. Over the years, she'd helped several clients prepare for death. Doing this now, she marveled at her own ability to procrastinate, how she had avoided, as dying people often did, facing the unthinkable.

On Monday morning, they were back at Miguel's office, trying to maintain the illusion of doing something, anything. But what they were doing was waiting, waiting as families wait during surgeries of loved ones when the outcome is terribly uncertain but presumed bad. Waiting with a desperate urgency, hoping for a miracle. They were each, internally, choking with fear. They functioned with robotic precision. They were beyond the comfort of words.

The call came a little after 3 p.m.

"All rise," the bailiff said. The judge entered the courtroom, then the jury. Everyone sat.

"Ladies and gentlemen of the jury," the judge queried, "Have you reached a verdict?"

"We have, your Honor."

The judge gestured to the bailiff.

"The defendant will rise for the verdict," intoned the bailiff.

The bailiff took the verdict from the hand of the presiding juror and brought it over to the judge, who read it, face impassive, then handed it back to the bailiff. The bailiff turned, faced the courtroom, and read aloud.

"We, the jury, on the count of murder in the first degree, find the defendant, Grace McDonald, guilty."

The roaring in Grace's ears blocked out the hubbub of the courtroom, the keening in her heart louder than the sound of the gavel pounding. "Order," a distant voice was saying. "Order." Grace's hands were on the table, bracing herself, and there were hands on both her shoulders. It felt like Gil's hands, solid and hard.

But when she opened her eyes, it was Miguel, his eyes wild with anger and defeat.

"Sentencing is set for 30 days hence," said the judge. "This will allow court services adequate time for their pre-sentence evaluation and to make recommendations. Mr. Leticio, you have ten days in which to make any motion for a new trial. The defendant is remanded to the custody of the county sheriff until sentencing. I believe that concludes our business for today."

He turned to the jury.

"Thank you for your service. You are dismissed."

Then Molly was sobbing, pawing like a two-year old trying to get mommy's attention, as two men in uniforms each gently took one of Grace's elbows, guiding her out of the courtroom through a side door.

Grace never looked back.

42

"I'm goin' to Graceland, Graceland. . ." Danny sang along with the CD at full blast. His right hand pounded the dashboard, his left smoothly steadying the wheel. It was Tuesday. Moving at 75 mph, Danny was headed to Gunnison. He felt liberated, vindicated.

Clean slate, he thought to himself.

He'd been in the courtroom yesterday for the verdict. It had been a moment of intolerable tension, and then—release.

He'd gone home and shaved the beard he'd grown for the trial. He'd already taken the week off. It was Ross's spring break.

Danny had left Kaw Valley early that morning. He'd called Mandy about noon to say that he was en route, leaving a message. "On my way. Can't wait to see you guys." It was intentionally ambiguous.

It was 9:30 p.m. when he finally swung around the last curve in the mountain road that passed Mandy's cabin. He parked at the base of the stairs that led up to her door. He could see lights on through the half-opened curtains.

He reached for the backpack on the seat next to him. Not a suitcase, which would have been too obvious, but it had all that he'd need if he spent the night. On the floor of the car was a white porcelain pitcher filled with flowers. He'd stopped in Colorado Springs and bought flowers to put in it, then propped the vase between some books and a small cooler so it wouldn't spill.

Danny felt anxious, like a kid getting ready for a date.

Mandy answered his soft knock. She was wrapped in a floor-length, peach chenille robe tied at the waist. She looked surprised. Not angry, just surprised. A puppy scrambled around her feet.

"I didn't expect you tonight," she said softly. "You must have driven like a maniac."

"I moved right along," Danny answered. "Can I come in? Just wanted to say hi to Ross. I've missed him a bunch."

"Shhh. He's asleep. He went hiking today with some buddies, then helped out at the clinic. It wore the kid out." She gestured to the darkened loft upstairs.

Danny said nothing. Mandy noticed the vase he was balancing in the crook of his left arm.

"Alstroemerias," Mandy whispered.

She looked up at Danny, his face highlighted against the dark night. He was trying to please her, she realized. It had always been her trying to win his affection. But now...

"Hey," she said. "Come in for a minute and catch your breath."

She reached for the puppy.

"C'mon, Cloudy, it's your bedtime."

They stood in the kitchen, chatting, in low tones. Classical music played softly, a backdrop so that Ross would not wake. She fixed Danny a turkey sandwich after asking if he'd stopped for dinner. Danny asked her questions about her work. She told him, not censoring what she said, just talking. He listened intently.

At the kitchen table, Mandy watched Danny eat. He'd always been a gulper, inhaling his food. But now he moved slowly, taking a bite, putting it down. Asking another question.

When he finished, Danny stood up and carried his plate to the sink. It was that gesture that caused something in Mandy to turn, to open. Their entire marriage, he'd left his messes behind, expecting her to clean them up. But now he was standing at the sink, rinsing off a dish, putting it in the wooden rack on the counter, wiping his hands on the towel, placing it back on the hook. Mandy noted each and every step with detached amazement.

"Would you like a glass of wine?" she heard herself say.

Later on, when Mandy looked back that night, it would always have a dream-like quality. They sat on the couch, their voices at a whisper. They sipped the wine. They talked with the easy and comfortable familiarity of old friends reunited after a long absence. She told him about getting the puppy and how Ross was learning dog training at 4-H. She asked Danny about his work. He answered with no trace of the defensiveness she remembered from their marriage.

And then, at some point, he reached over and very gently placed his hand along the side of her face. He moved two fingers down the side of her cheek. When she did not pull away, he leaned over, slowly, and kissed her. It was a whisper of a kiss. He moved his face so that their cheeks were touching, then softly kissed her cheeks, her forehead, and nuzzled down into the curve of her neck.

They were like a gift, these kisses. She stayed very, very still, her eyes closed. With the slowest of movements, his hand brushed through her hair, his lips moved on her neck. Then he stopped, his cheek against hers, hand nestled in her hair. Mandy felt as if she were floating.

When Danny moved back against the couch, his eyes were glistening.

"Danny?" Mandy whispered. "What is it?"

He said nothing, just reached for her hand and placed it against his cheek. And she felt her hand moving, as if a separate entity, up the side of his face, touching his hair, his lips, the fingers of a blind woman learning the face of a new lover.

It was she who stood, reaching for his hand, leading him into her bedroom. She who closed the door. She who stood perfectly still, eyes half-closed, and felt gentle hands untying the robe, hands moving down to circle her waist, unhurried.

Mandy was wearing a long, flannel nightgown, so worn from washing that the colors had muted. There were six buttons down the front. Danny's hands moved from her hair, over her shoulders, to the top button. He hesitated, then moved his hands back up to her face, lifting her chin to look into her eyes. His eyebrows crinkled into an unvoiced question. Mandy's lips lifted into the softest of smiles.

"Yes," she murmured. "Yes."

His response was a low groan of anticipation and relief. He pulled her to him and simply held her, enfolded her, saying nothing.

There was a moment when Mandy saw herself from above, from the ceiling, aghast at her own recklessness. A voice, deep in her brain, cautioned—*Stop! Don't do this.*—but the dream prevailed.

Danny opened the buttons. One button, then a touch, a kiss. The next button—after the last button, he pushed the fabric over, and with a tenderness that made her catch her breath, cupped her breast. His fingers moved with infinite slowness to circle her nipple. He leaned forward and kissed the top of her breast.

Mandy felt her nipples harden. She never could recall where her own hands had been before that point, but they then began to move. She touched Danny's shoulders, moving her fingers across his neck, down his back. She could feel his muscles arch under the ever so slight pressure of her fingers.

He reached for her hands, holding them together for just a second, then stepped back. He undressed, fluidly, and she watched as his shirt dropped to the floor, then jeans. Naked, he stepped back toward her, almost touching. He sank down, effortlessly, on one knee, and slowly pushed up the fabric of her nightie, laying his head against her thighs. As he stood, he lifted the nightie up and over her head.

Then he reached out his hand, palm up, a gesture both formal and intimate. It was as if he were about to lead her onto a dance floor. She extended her arm. He took her hand, delicately, and led her the few feet to the bed.

It was his slowness, his pace, that aroused her. Danny was not touching her simply as a preliminary. It was as if the stroking was everything, that his being able to touch her was enough.

His hands were warm. They played down her back in small ripples. They moved up the insides of her thighs. Then they were on her buns, massaging. She felt herself shudder. He turned her, slowly, his hands never leaving her body. She inhaled sharply as they brushed her pubic hair, not probing, but slowly brushing back and forth, a hand on soft, spring grass. He leaned forward and kissed her breasts, his tongue circling her nipples, lingering over the right, then shifting to the left, kissing ever so gently as he moved back and forth. She moaned. She had never felt such an ache of desire, of longing.

When his hand came to a slow stop between her legs, she felt her breath stop also. He pulled back to look at her, as if memorizing her face as it looked in this moment. Still looking, he moved his hand in the gentlest of circles over her mound. She felt her back arch upwards, her pelvis tighten.

And then he started all over, touching, kissing. No rush, no hurry, no end in sight. It was she who reached for him, took him in her hand, leading, moving him into her. When he was inside of her, he stopped, staying absolutely still. He moved with infinite slowness, deep into her, then almost out. And again. And again. Then he slid to one side, pulling her with him, so they were lying on their sides, facing each other. When he moved inside of her again, his thumb was on her clitoris, ever so lightly, circling in synchrony.

The intensity of the sensations caught her by surprise, and she heard herself whimpering, her breathing ragged. He watched her, holding himself back, waiting until the moment when she was coming. Only then did he loosen, quicken, plunge with abandon, moving to release.

They lay, panting, as the ripples subsided. She could feel him, heavy and limp, inside of her. She felt a paralysis engulf her, immobilize her. She wanted to talk but her tongue felt too thick.

And then she was asleep.

Danny lay awake, also immobile. He wanted to stay inside Mandy for as long as he could. He had started out to seduce, but he had been swept into deep emotional waters by the seduction. It was, for Danny, perhaps the first time he had ever truly made love.

All those years of fucking, he thought, *and I never had a clue.*

When Mandy woke, she felt disoriented, swimming upward into the light. The awareness of what had transpired the night before came to her in layers. It felt more dream-like than real, and so it was a shock to roll over and see Danny sleeping, a bare leg curved over the comforter.

Danny. In her bed. Naked.

Mandy shivered.

Oh shit, she thought. *What have I done?*

"Danny, wake up," she whispered.

His eyes opened and he took her in with a smile.

"Hi there," he said.

"Danny, please get up. I don't want Ross to find you here. It would be just too confusing for him. Hell, it's confusing for me and I'm the one in the bed. So, just go sack out on the sofa. That I can explain. Okay?"

"Hey, Mandy, relax. Ross will understand. Heck, Ross has probably been praying for this day."

"Danny, we have a lot to get through here, and I don't want to mess with Ross's head."

"Sure we do, baby. But we'll do it together."

"What do you mean?"

"I mean, we're a family. Whatever's ahead, we'll face it together."

"Danny, I never said anything about getting back together. Not a word."

Danny looked shaken. Then his eyes narrowed.

"Then what was all this about?" he asked, gesturing to the bed, the clothes on the floor.

"I don't know. Not yet. I need time to think. And I don't want Ross worrying. So please, just put on your clothes."

"Okay, I'll put on my clothes. But you better start thinking. What happened last night—Mandy, we belong together."

"Look, there's plenty of reasons we split. They don't just disappear because we had sex. I'm sorry if you got that idea. But it takes more to make a marriage. We'd have a lot to work through before we could even think of getting back together."

"Like what?"

"I can't answer that in one sentence. It would take hours."

"Look, I know I wasn't very family focused before. But I've changed. I want to take care of you. We can live wherever you want. You don't have to work some dead-end job anymore. We can have another baby. We'll buy a house. You can have a garden."

Mandy felt a flutter of panic, the drowning sensation of her nightmares.

"Look, Danny, don't plan my future for me. First off, I love my work. I'm back in college and plan to finish. Right now I've got plenty going on in my life without trading it all for a picket fence and diapers. I really am sorry if you thought this meant more than it did. But nothing today is different than yesterday."

Danny felt disbelief, then rage, flooding his body.

"Yeah, Mandy, there is something different." His voice was a growl. "Grace McDonald was convicted. God only knows how many marriages she destroyed. She sure turned you against me."

Mandy sat cross-legged on the bed, her mouth open.

"Grace was convicted?" she whispered.

"Yeah. It proves what I've been trying to tell you all along. She twisted your mind, Mandy. And she never gave me a chance."

Mandy didn't respond. Her mind was filling with images of Grace, Grace asking her questions, so many questions, and not minding at all when Mandy did not have answers. She could hear Grace's voice, prodding, confronting.

Danny was so wrong. Grace had never told her what to do, never twisted her mind. But she had helped Mandy find the self-respect to make her own decision.

Grace wanted to give you a chance, Mandy wanted to tell Danny. *I was the one who said no.* But the words stuck in her throat.

Danny was still talking. "I'll get dressed now, and I won't say anything to Ross. But you better do some thinking. We're a family, Mandy, and I'm not going to settle for anything less. Not after all I've done to get you back."

By the time Ross climbed down from the loft in his pajamas, Danny and Mandy were dressed and coffee was brewing. Ross whooped with excitement at seeing his father, and Danny scooped him up into a big bear hug.

"Ready to go play, my man?" Danny asked.

"You betcha!" yelled Ross. "I can get dressed in five minutes."

"Want some cereal, honey?" Mandy asked Ross.

"Hey, don't bother," Danny replied. "We'll grab breakfast at one of those local cafes Ross tells me are so good." He turned to Ross. "You have a favorite?"

There was a twenty-minute flurry, as Mandy double-checked Ross' bag for underwear, put in extra toothpaste. She reminded Danny to put sunscreen on Ross when heading for the slopes. She fussed until Danny and Ross swept out the door, arms full of bags and skis, Ross leaping down the steps after giving Cloudy ten hugs good-bye.

Danny turned to her as he left. "I'll do anything to make you happy. We'll be back in four days, and then we can talk."

Mandy said nothing, just watched his back as he went down the steps.

Mandy closed the front door. The silence was heavy. She poured another cup of coffee and sat in her armchair by the window. What the hell happened? How did she end up in bed with Danny?

It had something to do with entitlement, she thought. After those awful years with Danny, she'd felt entitled to be desired. And maybe, also, a touch of revenge. Danny had always considered himself a stud, expecting to be cared for sexually. But last night he'd been focused on her.

It was everything she'd wanted from him years ago.

But now? Did she want it now?

43

At work that morning, Mandy was distracted. She asked the pet owners the same questions twice and missed an obvious case of kennel cough. By lunch she was ready for a break.

Mandy ate her sandwich in the staff room with Will. They'd become friends, partners, more than boss and employee.

When Will asked "What's the matter?" Mandy started to say "Nothing." But then she realized that was what the old Mandy did, afraid of being judged.

"You sure you want to know?" she asked.

"Yeah. I asked and I do."

She told him in an uncensored rush. How Danny had been nicer—for months now—the unsigned Valentine, wondering if he'd really changed, then showing up late at her door last night, the wine, the talking, how it felt like a dream, the sex, waking up and wondering what the hell she'd done, Danny's assumption that it meant they were reconciled, Danny telling her that Grace McDonald had been convicted. Mandy spoke for fifteen minutes straight, looking mostly at the weathered wood of the old oak table.

Will cleared his throat.

"It's no crime to sleep with your ex, Mandy. Lots of people do it, for all kinds of reasons."

"But I don't like my reasons, Will. It's like getting back at him more than wanting him. But last night, in that moment, he seemed so different, like he was finally offering everything I'd ever wanted from him."

"Well, Danny didn't just show up to say goodnight to Ross, not with flowers. He wants you back. What you have to figure out is if you want him back. Out of all the men in the universe, do you want to spend the rest of your life with Danny Rivers?"

The question startled her. The rest of her life? Even if Danny had changed, could she ever really trust him? Could one night of sex, albeit physically gratifying sex, erase years of running her down, of not listening, not even trying to know her? And, now, did he even know *her*, want *her*, or some image he had of her to put in his fantasy house, the one with the garden and baby?

"No," Mandy said.

"Take your time, now. It's a big question."

"The answer is the same. I could never trust Danny. I wish I could do it for Ross, to make him happy. But for me? No."

"Then you've got to tell him when he gets back."

"Yeah, I know. And he'll probably try and figure out how to pin this one on Grace McDonald too."

"He really has a thing for this therapist, huh?"

"Yeah. He blamed her for my leaving. Now he's gloating like her conviction proves something."

"Well, sometimes decent people go nuts and do things they regret."

Mandy went straight home after work and crashed before 9 p.m. She was back in the clinic by 7:30 the next morning.

She was in the middle of giving an injection to a golden retriever when she felt a wave of nausea, intense and uncontrollable, along with something else. Fear? Terror?

"I think I'm sick," she told the woman. "Be right back."

Will found her in the back room, doubled over the big sink, heaving.

"What's the matter? Got a bug or something?"

"I don't know. Just hit me hard. Can you finish up with the golden?"

"Yeah. Sure. I'll check back in a few minutes."

Mandy could not stop retching, long after the contents of her stomach were gone. Dry heaves shook her frame.

It was in the middle of a heave that a single thought hit her.

"Go with your gut."

And then the terror was back, gripping her with a cold, clammy hand. And she heard Danny's voice from yesterday.

"After all I've done to get you back. . .After all I've done. . ."

Oh God, Danny, she thought, *what the fuck did you do now?*

44

Sometimes otherwise rational and cautious people behave in ways they themselves find inexplicable.

Mandy told Will she needed some time off, that she needed to go to Kaw Valley. She drove home, called the local airport for the next flight to Denver, and booked it plus a connection to Kansas City. Then she climbed up to the loft and surveyed Ross's room. She started going through his junk, looking for his treasure box. It was under his bed. Inside was the leather chain with a key to his Dad's apartment. He'd shown her when he returned from his last visit.

"Dad said I needed my own key. Because it's my home too," Ross had said.

"Put it somewhere special," she'd cautioned, keeping her voice neutral.

She dropped the puppy off at Will's on the way to the airport. She expected Will to advise her to calm down, take some Valium, and soak in a hot tub. Instead, he handed her an envelope of cash.

"Just in case. We'll cover here. Do what you need to do," he said. "I've called Emily to pick you up."

Emily met her flight in Kansas City.

"What's going on?" Emily asked. "Will made no sense when he tried to explain why you were coming out."

"I don't know. I think I'm nuts. But maybe, just maybe, Danny has done something. I'm really hoping he didn't do anything. But I couldn't stop puking, and then I had this thought, and next thing I'm on a plane. Am I psychotic? Is this a psychotic break?"

Emily looked her over.

"Dearie, you are making no sense whatsoever. No matter. When we get you back to my place, you're going to tell me every detail so we can sort this all out."

They talked past midnight, not that it made much more sense. The next morning, Mandy was still in her pajamas when Emily left for the office.

"I'll call you at lunch. Then we can decide what to do. Just wait for me, okay? Now, here are the car keys to the Honda in case you want to see how the town has changed. I'll take the truck."

After Emily left, Mandy got another cup of coffee and sat to think. She didn't know what she was looking for. But she did know that she didn't want to involve Emily in something that was illegal. And she was pretty sure that searching someone's home without permission, even if you did have a borrowed key, was against the law. She just hoped the key worked because she didn't want to think about having to break a window.

"I am certifiably crazy," she muttered.

Mandy drove past Danny's complex, or what she assumed was the right complex from the address. She parked a block away and walked back. She wore jeans and sneakers. In her purse she had a notebook, pens, wallet, comb, lip gloss, and three pairs of surgical gloves she'd lifted from the emergency medical kit that Emily kept in every car. The key on the leather chain was gripped in her right hand.

The apartments were more like townhomes, clustered around a central courtyard. #507 faced the courtyard. There was a privacy fence around a small, cement slab patio to the left of the door. Two lawn chairs were folded against the fence.

Mandy knocked briskly on the door. She did not expect a response, but there was always the remote possibility that someone was staying there while Danny was away.

She knocked again.

Then she slid the key into the lock and tried to turn it. It didn't move. She jiggled the key. She took it out. She inserted it again, holding the door handle steady. The key turned, the lock clicking. She pushed open the door.

"Yoo-hoo," she called out. "I'm here."

It was silent. Only then did she feel the sweat trickling between her shoulder blades.

The house was chilly. Mandy looked at the bottom of her shoes, first one, then the other, to see if she'd brought in any dirt. Satisfied, she began walking slowly around, getting a feel for the place.

The living room was divided by a breakfast bar from the kitchen. A short hall led from the living room, ending in a bathroom. On either side of the hall was a bedroom. In one a double bed, dresser, chair, bedside tables, desk. In the other a desk and bulletin board, twin bed against one wall. Over the bed was a poster of dinosaurs.

A small table held a framed photo—Ross and Danny, grinning, each making a thumbs-up gesture.

Mandy squatted in front of the photo and stared. Then she abruptly got up and went into the living room.

Her purse sat on the rug by the door. She reached in for the gloves and carefully put them on.

She began in the living room, looking under the furniture, lifting the cushions of the couch. She sifted through the magazines. She glanced behind the pictures hanging on the wall. She realized that she was doing what she'd seen people do in movies but that she had no idea what else to do.

In Danny's bedroom, Mandy started in the dresser, gently lifting his underwear, his shirts, to look underneath. She meticulously replaced them exactly as they were, resisting the old urge to organize. She looked between the mattress and the box spring from either side. In the small closet, she went through every piece of clothing, checking the pockets of the jackets, reaching inside the shoes and boots. She found grocery receipts, a few pens, a crumpled handkerchief.

Then, in the pocket of a white lab coat, she found a blue I.D. badge. Daniel Rivers. Regional Center for Blood and Plasma.

She looked at the badge in her hand. Since when?

She put the badge back in the jacket pocket and moved on.

In the third drawer of the desk, Mandy found an envelope of photos. They were of the inside of a big house, with hardwood floors and bookcases filled with books and plants. She went through them slowly, wondering where on earth Danny could have taken them, and why. None of his friends would have a house like this. The final shots were of the outside—a deck and backyard. Mandy went through the small stack once again, looking for meaning.

She resumed her search.

In the second bedroom, on the top closet shelf, underneath an old quilt, Mandy found a lock box. It was about two feet long, twelve inches wide and eight inches deep. She shook it gently and heard the movement of papers.

Shit, she thought. *Now what do I do?*

If she opened it, or if she took it, Danny would know someone had been here. He'd call the police. There would be an investigation. What if she'd been noticed? What if a neighbor could describe her? She could go to jail. Lose custody. Lose Ross.

Mandy sat on the floor, staring at the box in front of her. It was gunmetal gray, with a built-in lock. She had no idea how she could break it open.

This is fucking insane, she thought. *I'm sitting in my ex-husband's apartment, wearing surgical gloves, looking for—I don't know what.*

"I'm going home before I do something really stupid," she announced to the air.

She stood up. She carefully put the box back on the closet shelf, quilt on top. Mandy walked toward the living room. Each step felt heavier, slower.

The terror, like vomit, was inching up her throat.

Go with your gut.

NO. NO. NO. She couldn't risk it. It was probably just birth certificates, family records, maybe a will. She'd just slip out now. Disturb nothing. She could fly back to Gunnison tonight and pretend like this whole nutty episode never happened.

But her feet didn't move.

If she went back without looking in the box, she'd never know.

"Never know what?" she muttered out loud.

What could possibly be in that box that would be worth the shitload of trouble I could be in if I break it open, she questioned to herself.

Go with your gut.

"This one's for you, Grace. It better be worth it." The loud bang of the hammer first striking the metal corner of the lock-box made her jump.

Mandy had found the hammer in a container of household tools under the sink. She'd spread a pillowcase on the floor, put the lock box in the middle. She'd figured she had a better chance smashing at a back corner, bashing it in, then prying it open.

She wrapped a towel around the hammer to deaden the noise. She raised her arm and smashed again. Again. Again. She felt the back giving way. Using the largest screwdriver like a crowbar, Mandy pried open the back of the box and slid out the contents.

There was a notebook and two manila envelopes. She opened one envelope and dumped it.

Grace McDonald's face looked up at her. Through a window in a restaurant. Walking along the street. Raking leaves, a house in the background.

It was, she realized, the same house as the stack of photos in the drawer. The same exterior colors. The same deck and wrought iron furniture.

Mandy's hands trembled as she picked open the metal clasp of the next envelope. Newspaper clippings.

"Local Man Murdered." "Investigation Continues." "Local Therapist Indicted For Murder."

This must be every article published on the case, she thought.

Mandy opened the notebook. It was Danny's handwriting. There were dates, times, notes. She flipped through. "M" it referred to. That was it. When "M" left. Where "M" went. What "M" did.

Then "M" stopped, and "M-2" started. There were comments in the margins. "Evaluate various windows of opportunity," was scribbled toward the end. "Friday p.m. looks like best option." It stopped.

Mandy looked at the date of the last entry. She pawed through the clippings, looking for one, for the date of the one that said "Local Man Murdered."

The diary ended the day before Gil McDonald was killed.

"Is it possible to talk to someone who's involved with the McDonald murder investigation?" she heard herself saying in a flat tone to the receptionist at the police station.

"That case is closed, ma'am."

"Yes, I know it's over, but is there someone there who was involved? I'd really appreciate it"

She heard voices in the background.

"Try Tsosie. She's in the break room, I think," someone called out.

The voice came back.

"The detective in charge is unavailable, but someone will be with you shortly."

"Officer Tsosie here," said the next voice. "Can I help you?"

It was a woman. Mandy looked at the phone, stupidly, then answered.

"I hope so. I think that I may have found something relevant to the investigation. I need for someone to check it out."

"Relevant to which investigation?"

"The McDonald case,"

There was a pause.

"That case is closed," the cop said.

"But I don't know what to do with what I've found. Please, couldn't you just give me ten minutes?"

"Give me the address. I'll come on over."

"Thank you," Mandy said.

It took Patsy just three minutes to get out of the station house.

"I'm going to go talk to this lady. I'm not sure why yet," she said to the desk.

"Want anybody to go along?"

"Nah. I'll call if it's anything."

Mandy opened the door on the first knock. Patsy stepped in. Mandy closed the door, quickly. Too quickly.

Tsosie watched her, seeing the fear in the jerky movements of her arm, the clenching of her jaw.

"Thank you for coming," Mandy said.

"Why don't you tell me what's going on?"

"I'm not sure I can. Maybe it's all in my head. I came all the way here because I had this feeling. But it's not like I really knew anything. I don't know what to think. But I just felt I had to. I'm terrified to think what it could mean if it does, then. . ."

Tsosie interrupted, not rudely, but as if to turn off a faucet that would never otherwise shut off by itself.

"Where did you come from?"

"Gunnison, Colorado."

"You don't live here?"

"No."

"Who does live here?"

"My ex-husband."

"How did you get in?"

"I have a key." It was almost the truth.

"And then?"

"I found all of this stuff. . .It makes no sense why he would. . ."

"But you think it has to do with the McDonald case?"

"Yes."

"Did you know Gil McDonald?"

"No. But Grace McDonald was my therapist. My ex-husband blames her for our divorce. And then I moved away."

Patsy took a few seconds to process this. *Just when I thought it was over. Let's take this nice and slow.* "Can you show me what you found?"

"It's in the back room," said Mandy, turning to walk down the hall.

"Oh," said Mandy, stopping halfway, extending her hand, not even noticing she still wore surgical gloves. "I forgot my manners. I'm Mandy Rivers."

Patsy shook. "And I'm Officer Patsy Tsosie."

Mandy had spread out her findings. The lab coat hung on the door, the phlebotomist I.D. on the front. The photos of the house were on the bed. On the floor was the lock-box, the envelopes, and diary. Mandy had put the hammer back under the sink.

Patsy saw the photos and froze.

"Where did these come from?" she asked.

"I found them in an envelope in the desk."

"Do you recognize them?"

"Not at first. But then I found photos of Grace McDonald sitting in back of the same house. At least it looks. . ."

"It's the McDonald's all right. I know that house as well as my mama's."

"I thought it might be Grace's house."

"Can you explain why your ex-husband. . ."

"I don't know," Mandy interrupted. "But there's more. A diary. Newspaper clippings. Like he was obsessed or something."

Patsy inhaled slowly. This was getting way over her head. It was time to call Sam. But Sam was testifying over in Kansas City on another case. It would be late afternoon before he'd be back.

"I'll just look this over," Patsy asked. "Do you have another pair of those surgical gloves?"

"Sure, in my purse," said Mandy. "Anything else?"

"I could use a glass of water."

Mandy returned with the gloves, then walked to the kitchen. She opened a cabinet and took down two glasses. She didn't even wonder where they would be, she just knew. The logic of placement.

She opened the freezer to get some ice. Pretty empty. Danny never had been one for advance meal planning. And he wasn't into leftovers either. But maybe she was wrong. In the freezer was what looked like a big roast all wrapped in foil and some stuff in Tupperware.

She put ice cubes in the two glasses, filled them with water and walked back down the hall.

Tsosie was on the floor, going through the photos, being careful to keep them in order. The diary was open next to her. She wore the surgical gloves.

"I think my boss needs to see this," said Patsy, shaking her head. "So, find anything in the kitchen?"

"Just that my non-cooking ex-husband has a big roast in the freezer. Nothing incriminating." It was a poor attempt at levity.

Patsy felt a spark of electricity in her brain, a charge before there was room for a thought to form.

"Ever see him cook a roast?" she asked.

"A burger, maybe, with tater tots. Maybe chili."

"Humor me. Go open that roast up real careful and see what kind it is. Okay?"

Mandy walked back to the kitchen, opened the freezer, took out the roast. It was light for such a big hunk of meat. She peeled back the many layers of wrapping, slowly, carefully, until, with one layer left, she could make out a shape.

Her hands froze. She stepped back, fingers still extended.

"You better get in here," she yelled.

Mandy watched as Patsy turned back the last layer of paper.

"It's a thirty-eight," Patsy said. "They're pretty common, but it's the same kind that killed Gil McDonald." Patsy looked up.

Mandy had slid down the counter to the floor. She was hunched over, her face in her hands. Tsosie reached out a hand and touched her shoulder. When Mandy looked up, her face was bleak.

"He has my son," she whimpered. "Sweet Jesus, he has my son."

45

It was the best time Ross had ever had with his Dad.

Ross had shown off how he could ski, proud of his new skill. He'd never been better at anything than his father. Danny had signed up for a morning of lessons, and within a day, they were going down the easier slopes together.

Danny tried to call Mandy a few times, but she wasn't home. Danny leaned over toward Ross, who was licking the whipped cream off the top of his cocoa.

"Did I tell you how much I want us to be a family again, little buddy? I really miss you and your mom. We'll have to figure out how to help her see this our way."

Ross nodded, cheeks still red from the cold, lips covered with whipped cream.

Grace McDonald was starting to grasp the meaning of Gethsemene. To be facing a horrific future, to fully comprehend all that one is losing, how hopeless escape, how futile all attempts on one's own behalf.

Her mind formed thoughts that were somewhere between prayer and desperation.

Miguel had been up to assure her that he would file an appeal, on what basis he did not yet know. She could not see Molly or Katrina until Sunday, visiting day. She did not know if she could face seeing them. She was beginning to think that the only way to survive was to pretend to be dead. For her family to pretend she was dead. To walk, eat, sleep, even read—but as a dead person. If she let herself think about what she was cut off from—children, friends, earth, home, sky, life—she would start screaming and never stop.

She was in the women's group cell now. Four small cells with a central area in the middle. In the corner, attached to a wall, was a television. It stayed on all day, from the time the skinny blonde woman in for cooking up meth in her kitchen got up at 6 a.m. until they all went to bed. There were six other women, all incarcerated for drugs, bad checks, shoplifting. Mostly "chick crimes" as one put it. Most were serving their sentences here at County. Grace had been told she would be here only until she was formally sentenced, when she would be moved to the state penitentiary.

For the rest of her life.

The women kept a certain distance from Grace, as if sensing that she could come unglued at any moment. She got her own cell at night while the others doubled up. When she tried to pick at the bland cafeteria food, her throat refused to swallow. She did not join in the conversations, did not play cards. Reading was futile. The words ran together on the page.

Her only release was a small window, with bars, at the corner of the cell. Grace stood by the hour, staring at the park below. She could see the gazebo where she and Gil had taken the children every summer for concerts. She remembered how the setting sun reflected off the copper roof of the gazebo as the children danced in circles to the music. She remembered the smell of summer grass.

She wanted to feel the righteous indignation of the unjustly accused, to feel rage, to feel anything but this despair. But she couldn't.

Grace willed herself to die.

Tsosie left the apartment number on Sam's pager.

Sam called within fifteen minutes.

"What's going on?" he asked.

"You got to see it. I think we have evidence here on the real killer."

"What are you talking about?"

"The McDonald case. Found a gun. At least I think it's the gun. I mean, it could be the gun."

"Where are you?"

"A townhome belonging to a Danny Rivers. It's in one of those developments back behind the hospital."

"How'd you get there?"

"His ex-wife called, asked for a cop. There's photos, a diary, a .38."

"Jesus Christ, Tsosie. You got a warrant?"

"Ah, no. Not yet. I was calling you for what to do next. Thought you might like to see this first."

"I don't want to see anything without a warrant. If you got something, the last thing we need is for it not to be admissible because of procedural foul-up."

"Look, Sam, no way I came in here without permission. I mean, the lady called and asked for a cop. Said she needed someone to look at stuff."

"Yeah. But does she have that authority if she doesn't live there? Hell, we'll leave that one for the judge to figure." Sam paused. "Look, don't move anything. Just stay put until you hear from me. And don't let the woman out of your sight."

"Her name is Mandy Rivers. Grace McDonald was her therapist."

"Damn. I'll be back in Kaw Valley in an hour and we'll go straight to the judge for a warrant. No, better yet—keep the ex-wife with you and go to the courthouse. Don't talk to anyone. Meet me outside Judge Fisher's chambers."

"Sam, I'm sorry if I screwed up, but I had no idea what I was walking into."

"That's what I'm counting on. Accidental discovery. You were asked to come over, not a violation of this guy's Fourth Amendment rights."

"Okay, I'll be waiting at the courthouse. Thanks, Sam."

Mandy had heard just one side of the conversation.

"So what do we do now?" she asked Patsy.

"We go to the courthouse, wait for my boss, try and get a search warrant."

"And then?"

"Come back here and do a real search. Then see what we got."

"What about my son, Ross? He's skiing with his Dad." Mandy's voice broke.

"When do they come back?"

"This weekend, I think. Danny hates to be pinned down, so it's hard to tell."

"Is there any reason he'd suspect something?"

"I don't know."

"Would he hurt Ross? Has he been abusive?"

"To me, yes. Not to Ross. And he's been this perfect Disneylanddaddy since the divorce. But when he finds out I broke into. . ."

"Hold it," Tsosie said, holding up a palm. "Are you saying that your ex-husband did not give you a key?"

"He gave it to our son. I took it. Danny has no idea I'm here."

"You didn't tell me that."

"You didn't ask. Am I in trouble?"

By the time they parked the squad car and got to the judge's chambers, twenty more minutes had passed.

When Sam arrived, he gestured to Tsosie to step outside the door. After five minutes, they re-entered.

Sam looked grim.

"Margie," he asked the assistant, "What's his schedule look like this afternoon?"

"You're in luck today, Sam. Had a continuance on some burglary case so he's doing paperwork. Let me check."

Margie knocked softly, then poked her head into the inner chambers. She turned back with a smile.

Sam did the talking. He laid it out succinctly: how Tsosie had been called, how a "citizen" had discovered what appeared to be critical evidence, how a warrant was required to fully search the premises and collect evidence.

Then the judge turned to Mandy.

"What started this?"

"Something my ex-husband said, how he was acting."

"And you have access to his home?"

"I have a key."

Mandy made no eye contact with Tsosie. She was not sure what the eventual consequence might be for being less than fully truthful with a judge, but she'd decided to deal with that later. Now she needed the police to help her get Ross.

"What made you call the police?"

As Mandy replied, the judge's eyes widened. Mandy did not mention using a hammer on the lock-box.

"And where is your ex-husband now?"

"With our son, in Colorado, skiing."

Sam interrupted.

"Judge, that's one reason why we have to move fast. If this guy did murder Gil McDonald and he finds out we're on to him, he could do something crazy or take off with the kid. He may just be some weirdo stalker who never acted. But if he is dangerous. . ."

Mandy heard Sam speaking in a serious, urgent tone about her worst nightmare. Ross in danger. Ross abducted. Through the fog of fear that swallowed her up, she heard voices but could not make out the words. Then she felt Tsosie's hand on her arm.

"We have the warrant. It's being written up now. Can you come back with us in case we need your help?"

It wasn't until 5 p.m. that Mandy remembered Emily. When she called, Emily's voice was frantic.

"Where in God's name are you?" she asked.

"With the police. They have a warrant. They went through Danny's apartment. It's out of my hands now."

"Why didn't you wait for me?"

"I'll tell you later. We can have a stiff drink and I'll tell you everything."

Two small glass vials found in the Tupperware container in the freezer were the only surprise of the official police search. The contents looked black, but they knew what color it would be when it thawed.

The DNA would take time, but the gun was another matter.

KBI ballistics reported back by 10 a.m. the next day, just minutes before Bruce Saunders called Sam.

Bruce wasted no time on formalities.

"You want to tell me what's going on over there? I heard you're back on McDonald. That case is done."

"Didn't want to bother you until we had something concrete."

"What blind alleys are you running down this time?"

"We recovered a gun, Bruce."

"*A* gun or *the* gun?"

"*The* gun. KBI ballistics said it is a match."

"You got a report already?"

"I called in an IOU."

"What else?" asked Bruce.

"Stalker shit—a diary, photos, clippings—and a phlebotomist I.D.

badge."

"What's that got to do with it?"

Sam paused. He was going to savor this moment.

"This guy is an EMT, but he worked part-time at the blood bank. Got that off a W-2 we found in a desk drawer. Tsosie checked out his work records. Did you know Grace McDonald was a regular donor? We have at least two and maybe three times that this guy worked the same day that Grace McDonald donated."

"Are you saying that this guy took McDonald's blood? They run those places like vaults."

"We found vials of blood in the guy's freezer. Drove it to the KBI last night myself. Same vials used by the blood bank. Initial typing indicates the contents are B negative. Only 1.7% of the population, I recall you saying."

Saunders felt his face flush. Sweat trickled down his back under his Brooks Brothers suit.

"But why? What was the motive?"

"Grace McDonald was his ex-wife's therapist a few years ago. He apparently blamed her for his wife leaving, to the point that he got her subpoenaed. McDonald said on the stand that he'd been abusive. That much we got from the ex-wife. Tsosie is over at the courthouse now pulling transcripts from that hearing."

"And McDonald never even mentioned this guy as a possible?"

"Not that I know of. She has no idea any of this is going down."

"Have you talked to Leticio?"

"No. I'd prefer to wait just a while."

"Have you picked the guy up yet?"

"No. He's out-of-state—Colorado—skiing with his son for spring break. He gets wind and he might just disappear on us with the kid."

"Keep me posted." Saunder's voice was faint.

Sam was back in the judge's chambers an hour later.

He laid out the ballistics report, blood type match, blood bank vial, overlapping work and donation schedules, and possible motivation. He left with a warrant.

How to execute the warrant without tipping off Danny Rivers was another matter. Finding him would be a first step. Breckenridge was filled with hotels, lodges, and condos, if they were even there. Sam had a sense that Danny was the suspicious type, that one false move and he would sense something. Stalkers tended to develop hyper-vigilance, constantly watching their backs.

So, concluded Sam, it might be better to let him come to them. Sit and wait.

"Tsosie," he called, "get Mandy Rivers back in here now."

Mandy had been up half the night. After the police had dropped her back at Emily's, she'd told Emily everything. But her fears for Ross had made it hard to breathe, let alone sleep.

When had Danny turned into some wacko stalker? But even as she asked herself the question, she felt stupid. She remembered seeing Danny sitting in his car in the middle of the night outside her apartment after they separated. She remembered her neighbor telling her that Danny had been by to leave something in her mailbox. But when she looked, the mailbox was empty. She now recalled things Danny had said in a different light.

And the more she got into Danny's head, the scarier it was to be his ex-wife.

The phone was jarring.

"Hello?" Mandy answered before the second ring.

"It's Patsy Tsosie. Could you come down to the station?"

"Can Emily come with me?"

"Yes."

"Are you going after Danny?"

"That's what we need to discuss. But we have an arrest warrant. And the gun in the freezer? It's a match. It's the gun that was used to kill Gil McDonald."

Mandy's heart clutched. Until this moment, there had still been that chance that Danny was obsessed but not dangerous, not a murderer.

"I'm coming," she said.

Emily had canceled her appointments for the day. Mandy needed someone with her, to drive, to help her stay focused.

They were shown into a room at the station. There was a large, wooden square table, with a dozen chairs around it. Papers were spread across the table.

Sam looked up.

"Thanks for coming down," he said to Mandy. He stood, extending his hand.

"I'm Sam Hillard," he said. "You must be Dr. Emmesch."

"Emily, please."

Mandy spoke. "Can you tell me what the plan is?"

"We have a warrant for the arrest of your ex-husband. But we don't want to do anything to tip him off or to cause your son to be in any danger. So, we're looking at going back with you to Gunnison and waiting for him to return." Sam paused. "Have you checked whether you have any messages from him?"

"No. He just has the number for the landline, but I can retrieve them."

There were three for Ross, one for her from an old friend, two from Danny. No number to call back, just "Hey, where are you? You're not at work. You aren't playing hooky, are you? I'll try back later. Ross and I may come back a day or two early. I'll try again to let you know when." Then. . ."Where are you, Mandy? You're not at work, you're not at home. Is there something you aren't telling me? Oh, never mind that. Hope you're okay. I'll try again."

Mandy called Will. He reported that there had been two anonymous calls at work for her from a man, and that the receptionist had just said that she was out sick.

Mandy felt her stomach turn as she listened.

"He knows," she said.

"What do you mean?" asked Sam.

"He knows how predictable I am. He'll smell something fishy."

"We can deal with that. What we need to do is get you to Gunnison pronto—to be there when he returns. We'll think of an excuse for you on the way."

Sam put his head in his hands, taking a long pause.

"Go pack. We'll figure out who all is going from this end, get some coordination started with Gunnison police, and pick you up in an hour," said Sam.

"Does that include me?" asked Emily.

"No. We don't know what we're dealing with. Danny could have someone keeping an eye on his place here. He could be hearing right now that there's a police line across the entrance and that the place was crawling with cops yesterday afternoon."

Mandy choked on the water she was swallowing. She hadn't thought of that possibility. Danny's coworkers were all EMTs. They were like coon dogs with a scent when it came to what was going on in town. If they knew how to reach Danny...

"We've got his license plate and car description put out with the police in the Breckenridge area. The orders are not to stop him, just to report back where it was seen, so we can track him," Sam added.

Ninety minutes later, Mandy was in a small private twin-engine four-seater with Sam Hillard and Patsy Tsosie. Sam was up next to Charlie, the pilot. Mandy was crammed in next to Tsosie. They had to almost yell to be heard above the drone.

"How'd he get this so quick?" Mandy asked Patsy.

"I heard him say something like, 'Charlie, it's payback time.' Then he said that a plane was waiting for us at the airport."

"It's not police-owned?"

Tsosie laughed. "We buy our own uniforms. How they gonna buy a plane?"

Under ordinary circumstances, Mandy would have been nervous about flying in a small plane. She was scared of heights. Now flying was the least of her worries. All Mandy could think of was Ross. Images crowded her mind: Ross as a baby, nursing in the middle of the night, crawling, waving as he walked into school, holding his Christmas puppy for the first time.

She felt herself praying, a formless, desperate begging...*when this is all over, let me go back to my life with my son.* She felt her need pushing through the metal side of the plane, breaking apart the clouds.

An unmarked police car met them at the Gunnison airport. The first stop was the local police station. They asked Mandy to wait while they talked strategy.

46

Danny sensed something. Nothing he could put his finger on, but something. But first there was the question of Mandy.

Where the hell was Mandy?

She usually had to be really ill to stay home from work. He remembered her going in with sore throats and colds that he would've gladly used as an excuse. He'd even called the hospital in Gunnison last night.

He sent Ross to the heated, indoor pool for a swim and sat down at the table in the corner of the room to make a plan.

The police made a decision. They would take Mandy to her truck, still parked in the airport parking lot, and she would drive to the cabin with Patsy in case Danny was already watching. Patsy could pass as a friend. Sam and three local officers would situate themselves in the woods at various points off the road and watch for Danny. They had his license number, a description of his car, and an old photo. If he called, Mandy would ask him to come home, saying she was sick. She would ask for a number so she could call him.

"We regard him as armed and dangerous," one of the local cops said.

Mandy started to protest. "He doesn't have a gun. I'm sure of it."

In the silence that followed, she realized how naive and stupid she sounded. Danny had had a gun, and he'd already killed someone. Why couldn't he have another? But no matter how stupid it sounded, she felt she was right.

By 6 p.m., everyone was in place. Mandy pulled the curtains. Tsosie would stay away from windows and head for the bedroom if there was a knock.

Hours passed. Mandy and Patsy read. Music played softly. Mandy yearned to turn the music up loud to block out the sounds that caused her to twitch. But Tsosie was adamant. No music was preferable, very soft the only other option.

By 9 p.m., Mandy felt herself starting to unravel. "I'm going to make some soup," she announced. "I've got to do something."

The men did not make special note of the black Jeep that drove past about 10 p.m. It was neither the make, model, or license plate they were looking for. And when one officer stepped out from the trees after it passed, to make sure it didn't turn into the cabin drive, he didn't know he was seen by the driver watching closely in his rear-view mirror.

In the rented Jeep Wagoneer, Danny's lips curled into a tight, bitter smile. Something was happening. He didn't know exactly what, but something. But before he dealt with it, he wanted his wife back.

He'd studied a detailed Gunnison map, from the Forest Service, with the logging roads and trails that few people knew existed. There was a logging road just a half-mile up Arapahoe Trail from Mandy's cabin. It had a sign that said "No Trespassing" and a chain loosely draped across the entrance. But it angled up past the back of Mandy's A-frame and could get him within a few hundred yards of her back door. He cut his lights and braked, turning off the road. Within seconds he'd lowered the chain and was back in the car. The moon was full enough that despite the woods, he could almost see with his dim lights. He watched the odometer, and when he hit 1/2 mile, he stopped.

Danny reached for a flashlight, a hunting knife, a compass. He held still, listening for any noise. Before he left, he checked the back, carefully tucking a quilt around the curled shape in the down sleeping bag that covered the entire seat. It took Danny a few minutes to orient himself to the darkness of the forest. The last snow had melted in a spring thaw. A carpet of pine needles lay on top of the damp earth. Danny made no sound as he moved in the direction of Mandy's cabin.

Within minutes, he saw the flickering of her kitchen light. Then he saw her through the window. Her hair was pulled up in a ponytail, and she was wearing a blue-checked flannel shirt. He stood in the last stand of trees before the small expanse of yard and simply watched.

Mandy was cooking. He could tell from her movements. She was going to the refrigerator, to the sink, to the stove. He saw her back curve over the counter, and her head moving slightly, as if in tune with her hands. In his mind's eye, he could see her chopping.

Danny wanted to be in the cabin with Mandy, to sit at the table with a hot cup of coffee, to talk with his wife as she prepared their supper. He felt his heart twist with yearning. They'd been married for ten years, but he had so rarely made time for the simple domestic intimacy he now craved.

Get Mandy and leave with her. That was what he needed to do. He could smell danger here. People were out to take away his family again. He needed to take Mandy someplace where they could talk it all out, where he would have the time to make her understand. That was all he needed. If he could get her away, if it were just the two of them, and Ross, he could make it work.

He circled the back of the cabin, stopping with each step to listen. The back door was just one step up. It was an old fashioned wooden door, with a large glass pane in the top half. He stood in the shadows, watching her go to the fridge, pull out some carrots, turn to the chopping block. He could hear a flute playing in the background.

Danny tapped on the glass, three quick taps. Mandy jumped, dropping the carrots she'd been holding, and jerked around to face the door. Her eyes were huge.

Danny smiled and waved at her.

He made a gesture to her to open the door, but she just stood there. He put up his index finger and motioned for her to come closer. She did. Then he pointed at the door handle. She looked at it, then reached down and turned the lock and opened the door.

"Hi," he said. "What's cooking?"

Mandy did not breathe from the sound of that first tap to Danny's walking into the kitchen. That she could have screamed, run out of the kitchen into the other room and had Tsosie radio for help, never occurred to her.

But the normalcy in his voice, the mundane nature of the question, brought her back.

"Jesus, you scared me to death," she said, in a voice twice her usual volume. She wasn't taking any chances as far as Tsosie hearing.

"Sorry. Didn't mean to."

"Where's Ross?"

"He's asleep in the back seat. That kid got totally worn out skiing.

Then he got a cold. I loaded him up with Benadryl, and you know how he gets with that. Two alarm clocks couldn't wake him."

"Let's get him in here. He'll get chilled."

"In a bit. He's in a down bag, so he's warm enough."

"Why did you use the back door? Where is your car?"

"Mandy, I was worried about you. I called here and no answer. Work said you were out sick. I even called the hospital. What's going on?"

"I was sick, some stomach bug, and I stayed with a friend for a few nights. That's about it."

"What friend?"

"What is this, the Inquisition?"

Mandy heard her anxious, defensive tone. *This is not a time to piss him off,* she told herself. *Get a grip.*

"Danny, let's go get Ross and put him to bed. Then I'll fix you some nice, hot soup. We can talk. We'll have wine in the living room in front of the fire. Really. I'd like a quiet evening to talk," she said in the measured tone she'd used when Ross was an irrational toddler—*stop climbing the stairs and throwing toys and I'll make you a nice lunchie, okay? That's a good boy.*

Danny heard it too. He felt suspicious and yet gratified. He wanted so much to just sit down, to watch Mandy ladle steaming soup into the earthenware bowls she'd stacked on the open shelf. He wanted to sit in front of the fire, to watch the shine of her hair in the soft light. He so wanted to sink into the security of the picture she described. But. . .

"Get your coat. It's a ways to the car."

"Where is it?"

"Out back through the woods."

"What do you mean? There's nothing back there."

"Sure there is. The old logging road."

"Why didn't you just pull into the drive?"

"I'm just taking care of myself, Mandy. I'll explain later."

"Explain what?"

"Just get your coat." His voice tightened. She was annoying him with her questions. Why couldn't she just come like he asked without all the fuss? Why did he have to justify every decision he made?

Mandy paused. She was frightened to leave with him, to disappear into the night woods. But she was more frightened not to. She needed to hold Ross, to know he was safe. She felt this need in her teeth, in her bones.

"Okay. Give me a minute, I have to pee."

Mandy went into the bedroom, toward the half-open closet door. Patsy stood inside, out of view but not out of hearing, gun in hand. Mandy tried to make noise taking down a hat and gloves from the shelf.

"Do nothing until I have Ross safe," she mouthed. "Danny won't hurt me."

She grabbed her coat from the hook behind the door. She went into the bathroom to pee. She really *did* have to go. She left the door open like she used to when they were married. *Make him feel accepted,* she thought. *Show him I trust him.*

When she got back, he was waiting by the door. They stepped into the dark night. He closed the door behind them, and she heard the lock click.

"Jesus, Danny, I don't think I have my keys." She dug frantically through her pockets. "What did you do that for?"

She was speaking to his back, as he took three strides across the small yard and into the trees. Then he turned and she saw the white teeth of his smile in the moonlight, his uplifted hand, keys dangling from two fingers.

"They were on the hook by the back door," he said.

Stay calm, Mandy thought. *Stay calm.*

"How far is this, Danny? I left that soup cooking on the stove."

"I turned it off," Danny said.

Mandy felt herself go numb as the meaning of his words registered. But—*I'm coming, Ross*—was her only thought as she followed Danny into the woods.

They'd walked just a few minutes when Danny abruptly stopped, holding a finger up to his mouth. He listened. Then there was a faint sound of movement.

"It's nothing, Danny, just a deer." She spoke out loud, in a normal tone, as if this were a casual stroll in the woods.

"Shut up," Danny whispered.

"Danny, c'mon. Let's just get Ross. Stop worrying about every little noise. . ." She didn't finish the sentence. His hand whipped out and grabbed her, covering her mouth with his hand in one movement and jerking her body against his.

Then they both heard it: the slap-slap-slap-slap of boots running on damp earth.

Danny twisted Mandy's neck up, hand still covering her mouth. His eyes were inches away.

"Who is it?" he demanded. He moved his hand from her mouth.

"Stop, Danny. You're hurting me."

"What have you done?"

"Danny, please, I don't know what you're. . ."

"You don't understand anything," he said. "I was making it right again."

"Danny, please. Just give me Ross. Danny. Please."

"You should've thought of that before you started all this."

His hand dropped from her neck as he pushed her away, both hands hard against her chest. Then he was gone. Sprinting through the forest, dodging branches, and—gone.

Suddenly, Sam Hillard was there. Then one of the Gunnison cops.

Sam grabbed her. "Which way?" he blurted.

"Too late. He has a car. On the logging road."

Mandy ran, panting, back toward the house, to her car. It was closer to the house than the logging road, so maybe she could get to it, get her truck, cut Danny off. There was only one way out of the logging road, one way back to the highway.

Her breath came in hoarse gasps. She stumbled, almost fell, but kept running. She heard the cops behind her, following her lead.

Mandy ran past the cabin and toward her car. Then she realized—Danny had her keys. Where were the extra keys?

Sam had her arm. He was propelling her past her car, down the drive to the road. Another car waited, engine turning, Tsosie at the wheel. They hurled themselves in, Sam in front, Mandy in back. A Gunnison cop dropped in next to her and the car peeled off even as he tried to slam his door.

"It's just up here on the right," the Gunnison cop said. "Hard to find at night. I don't know how in hell he got past us."

In their rear-view mirror, they could see the headlights of the other Gunnison cop behind them. Then, dead ahead, hurtling from the woods, sprang the black Jeep. Tsosie slammed on the brakes. Their car spun out in a wide arc, its back wheels sliding sideways into the culvert that lined the mountain road. The Jeep roared past.

The cop behind them went to block the road, spinning his car sideways, but the Jeep did a quick veer. Then it was gone, around a curve, the sound of the engine fading.

Their car was sharply angled in the culvert, stuck in the spring mud, and it took a minute to open the doors and get out. For Mandy, the seconds were infinite. Her mind had gone blank, dissociating from her terror. She clambered up, then stood in the middle of the road. Again, it was Sam's arm that grabbed her, pushing her into the back seat of the other unmarked police car.

A Gunnison cop was driving. Sam next to him. Mandy and Tsosie were in back. The other local was left standing by the disabled car, calling down to headquarters for assistance.

Mandy had never moved so fast down her mountain road. Even clinging to the middle of the road, their back wheels slid out with every twist and turn.

"Ross," Mandy said in a hoarse whisper. "He has Ross with him."

"In the car?" asked Sam, incredulously, turning around to look at her.

"Yes. Back seat. Sleeping. He said he gave him Benadryl, but maybe he drugged him. He can get drugs at work. He seemed real sure he'd stay asleep."

"Oh shit," muttered Sam.

The Gunnison cop now had his radio in one hand and was shouting into it.

"Attention. All units. All units. Fugitive in late model black Jeep Wagoneer should be coming down #1-35 into and through Gunnison. Don't shoot. Don't blockade. Clear intersections. There is a child in the car. Repeat. Do not cause accident. Observe and report. Observe and report only. Repeat. Child in car."

"Would he go north?" Sam asked the local cop, his sentence broken in half as they swung through a curve.

"Could, but he'd get stuck or slowed down. Still a lot of snow on the mountain passes. This guy seems like he's real careful, studies his situation. He'd know that north would be slow going, fewer ways out."

The cop paused. "Not that south is that much better."

"He knows it's over," Mandy said. "He turned off the soup. He locked the door. He was taking me away with him."

"Where?" asked Tsosie.

"I have no idea. Somewhere in his dreams."

Danny saw himself driving the black Jeep down the mountain road as if he were on a movie screen. It felt like when he dreamed he could fly, able to feel the sensations of flying, knowing that he would not fall, would wake up safe in his own bed.

A large stop sign loomed. Rt. #1-35. Barely slowing, he slid across the road and headed south. There was no one behind him.

Then he was going through the town. He slowed some. He was on Main Street, passing Ruby, Gothic, Ohio, Georgia, Virginia, to Tomichi. Here he swung right, to the west.

A left would take him east.

Toward Kansas. Toward home. But he couldn't go there anymore.

He flew past a police car sitting on the side of the road. He knew he was speeding, but the cop did nothing. He just sat there.

Maybe I am dreaming, he thought.

In his rearview mirror he could see a line of cars, a half-dozen at least, trailing him.

There was a turn off for #92 but he remembered from the map that it was a twisting, mountain road. He stayed on #50.

The cars behind him were inching up. Not like they wanted to pass, just get a little closer. It was annoying. He sped up, watching the small arrow in the dashboard move right.

They were dropping back. In the dark, in his rearview mirror, he could hardly see them anymore. They were giving up. He couldn't make out any headlights. He leaned his head outside the car and tried to listen. All he could hear was the wind.

Then he saw the sign for the Black Canyon of the Gunnison. Ross had told him about it, how it was the Grand Canyon of Colorado, with sheer black rock walls soaring 2,000 feet, so narrow in spots that the sun hardly ever reached the bottom.

He checked the rearview. Nothing in sight. He looked ahead. Ditto. He slowed down, then turned north toward the canyon.

In the car, Sam leaned forward, as if those few extra inches would allow him to see across the distance that separated him from Danny. Next to him, the Gunnison cop was on the radio, checking in with police in the towns ahead who had been warned. Mandy had slumped against the seat when they pulled back and Danny went out of sight. She was looking with blind eyes out the window into the darkness. Tsosie sat beside her, one arm touching Mandy's shoulder.

"He turned off," barked the Gunnison cop. "Had somebody driving east from Montrose and he hasn't gone past. Would have by now."

"You have any ideas?" asked Sam.

"Could be a farmhouse, but they're hard to see from the road. Probably took the Black Canyon road." His eyes shifted to Mandy in the rearview mirror.

"Ma'am, how well does he know these roads and all? You have any idea?"

"No," Mandy whispered. "But he must have studied Gunnison to know about the logging road."

"Well, if he took the Canyon road, he'll have to be some kind of magician to escape. It dead-ends at the Black Canyon and there is no crossing that one."

"What if he tries to take Ross and go cross-country?" Mandy asked. "Could we find them?"

"Tracking dogs might do it. But as cold as it gets at night up here..." The cop's voice trailed off.

The cops talked in low voices. Tsosie leaned forward to listen.

It was decided in a minute. Local cops from Gunnison and Montrose would check the places on #50 that Danny could have turned in. There really were only a few miles where he'd been out of sight. Three squad cars, including the one with Sam, Mandy, and Tsosie, would start up the road to the Black Canyon.

State highway patrol was on the way.

Mandy saw the sign in the headlights. "Black Canyon of the Gunnison National Monument." She'd been here with Ross during their first months in Colorado, in September. Even then the air was cool. There were trails along the canyon, out to certain points and overlooks with decks. She'd clung to the wooden bars and railings when a wave of vertigo overcame her. Mandy had been afraid, even in the bright autumn sunlight, for Ross to walk ahead on the paths. There were too many places where a person could actually fall, tumble like a tossed rock over the precipice and into the depths of the canyon. She could not imagine trying to navigate any of those trails in the darkness. And snow? The trails would be ice-crusted, slippery, with no defined markers.

"There's a ranger station up ahead, and a campground that's seasonal," the Gunnison cop explained to Sam. "The one turnoff just circles the campground areas, then back to this road. This eventually dead-ends. If a car goes up, it has to come back."

The chain was still across the campground turnoff. Sam and the Gunnison cop looked at each other. Sam softly pulled his gun from its holster. The Gunnison cop gestured with his chin toward a rifle on the floor. Patsy did not take out her gun, but she felt its weight under her arm. The car continued, slowly. Two others followed.

"I want to try and talk to him," Mandy said.

"Let's see what we've got first," said Sam. "Talking might be the best approach. But he might not even be here. He could be on some side road or in a barn."

At that moment they heard the whine of an engine, revving as it does when stuck. Surge, subside, surge, subside. . .

Sam looked over his shoulder at Tsosie. *Be ready,* the look said. *This may be it.*

They cut their lights, braking softly. They left two of the cars along the side of the road, while a Gunnison cop in a third car did a three-point turn to face south.

"Stay in the car," Sam whispered to Mandy.

She looked at him like he was crazy. Stay in the car? Ross could be close enough to grab and she should stay in the car? She was the only one who knew Danny, the only one who might be able to talk sense into him.

"Shoot me first," she hissed.

They moved through the night under the full moon toward the curve in the road. The elevation here was higher than Gunnison, and the spring thaws had not yet come. Snow covered the ground, thick crusted, pushed by the plows to form white, icy walls on the sides of the road. They timed their steps to the surging of the motor, stopping in the pauses.

But just as they were almost to the bend, the whine shifted. Wheels stopped spinning, caught something solid, and they heard the Jeep grabbing at the hard surface of the road.

Danny had felt some relief when he no longer could see the string of cars in his rearview mirror. Turning up the canyon road, he'd felt a sense of reprieve. Exhaustion was catching up to him. He was running on adrenaline. His mind was losing focus.

He couldn't see where he was going now, not the road but the future. He was being chased, but he wasn't sure why. He just wanted to be sitting at a kitchen table, watching his wife cook their supper, his son playing in the next room.

When the road came to a cul-de-sac, turning on itself, Danny understood that he'd made a strategic error. He'd turned down a road that went nowhere, and now there was nowhere to go but back. In frustration, he gunned the motor. Spinning out a bit, he gripped the wheel of the Jeep. It was then that the back wheels slipped sideways, sinking into a snow bank at the side of the road.

For a few seconds, Danny did not understand that he was really stuck. When he stepped out to inspect, he saw wheels buried to the axle. It was a serious problem, but Danny almost welcomed it. It gave him something to fix.

He moved quickly, taking a cardboard box from the back of the Jeep and layered the cardboard under the wheels. Then he got back in the car and tried the engine. When that failed, he took out an extra blanket. He hacked at it with his hunting knife to make two long strips of multi-layered fabric and then pushed at the snow to get the material under the wheels. The entire time he was working, his mind was focused. He felt almost peaceful.

The blanket did the trick. At last, the whining of the engine changed as the wheels caught and the Jeep jerked forward. He hit the pavement moving at a good clip, glancing back to see the chewed up material lying in the snow.

In the microsecond after the wheels grabbed the road, and Danny's eyes flicked back from the rearview mirror, he saw them, dead ahead, a straight shot, caught in the high beams of the Jeep. Figures dived for the side of the road, head-first into the snow.

Except for Mandy.

She stood, paralyzed, in the middle of the road, her eyes the glistening moist brown of a trapped doe.

He could hit her. She had hurt him, rejected him, betrayed him. He could try to go around her, but he'd probably slide right back into the banked snow.

Move, dammit, move! He heard screaming in his brain but there was no time to form the words. And then his arms were moving, responding, yanking at the steering wheel—around, around, around, around. His foot jammed the pedal to the floor.

The Jeep spun in a quarter circle, missing Mandy by inches. It moved as if from a catapult, rising over the snow, almost airborne, across the flat, open terrain, a median really, toward the canyon edge.

And then Danny was flying. The Jeep did not descend head first, but seemed to float, a Road Runner cartoon, in a moment of suspended animation before gravity took hold.

What came next was pure sound, a sonic boom that emanated from the depths of the canyon. The explosion reverberated, the intensity of the fire illuminating the depths of the canyon floor, the black walls of the canyon, roaring upward.

And above it all, under a cold and merciless moon, an anguished howl filled the night. More than the explosion, it was Mandy's scream that would haunt the listeners' dreams.

There had been no time for the cops to make a move. Danny was flying even as they tried to lift themselves from the snow. They stood in stunned disbelief looking outward at where the Jeep used to be.

By the time they got to the edge, there was nothing to see but fire. It was a conflagration, the intensity, flames, and smoke of a fuel tank explosion. There was nothing to do but stand, helpless, shaken, and watch the fire consume itself and anything near it 2,000 feet below.

47

Morning found Patsy Tsosie poking at the embers in the cabin fireplace with a metal rod. She added some wadded-up newspaper, a few sticks, and a log from an adjacent basket. She lit a match and held it to the newspaper in three different spots.

It'd been 3 a.m. by the time she and Sam had returned to the cabin with Mandy. They'd stopped first at the Gunnison ER for some medication to help Mandy sleep. Their concern was partly selfish. In a litany of grief, Mandy had been hoarsely moaning the name of her son, over and over. "Ross. Oh, God. Ross. Ross."

At one point, in the car returning to Gunnison, Mandy had looked at Patsy through her tears and said, "I killed my son. It's my fault. I started all of this. Danny was right." Then she turned away, moaning his name again. With each moan, Patsy felt herself slipping closer to a breakdown of her own.

Mandy's sleep, when it came, was a relief for everyone.

It was now almost 9 a.m. Mandy was asleep in her bedroom. Sam was still sacked out on the floor of the loft. Patsy had tossed and turned on the couch for a few hours before giving it up.

Patsy imagined she and Sam would have to get back to Kaw Valley, but she didn't know if that would be today or tomorrow. They had to find someone to be with Mandy.

Then there were the funerals. Separate? Together? Patsy shuddered. Were there relatives to notify? Didn't they need remains first? Would she and Sam have to hike down into that godforsaken canyon and witness the search?

Patsy's mind would not stop churning.

What did this mean for Grace McDonald? Would the evidence be enough to overturn her conviction?

Shit, she thought, that process had been known to take years. And then there was the *technicality* of whether it had been a legal search

What she needed, she thought, was to make more coffee and get Sam up.

Patsy startled at the intrusive ring of the phone. She jumped, grabbing it before it had a chance to ring again.

"Hello?" she said, thickly.

"Hello? Who is this?" a small voice asked.

"I'm Patsy. This is the Rivers' residence. Can I help you?"

"Where's my mom?" the voice asked.

Patsy heard the words, but they did not compute.

"Who, honey?" she asked, falling into the familiar tone she used with her own nieces and nephews.

"My mom."

"Who are you?"

Now the voice quavered.

"I'm Ross. I live there."

"Oh God. Oh, Ross, honey, where are you?"

"I want to talk to my mom."

"I know, honey. I'll get your mom for you. She's asleep. Just give me a few minutes to wake her up."

"Is she sick? Daddy said she was sick and he had to go home and get her. But he said he'd be back. He said he'd be here when I woke up, but he isn't. So, I thought I'd better call Mom. Was my mom in the hospital?"

"Oh, no, honey, no, she was sick, but she'll be fine. She'll be just wonderful. You have no idea how much she misses you. Ross, I need you to tell me where you are and then I'll go wake up your mommy. Okay? Can you do that for me?"

"I'm in Breckenridge, but Daddy checked out of the lodge we were staying in 'cause they had too many people and he rented a condo." Ross's voice wasn't quavering any more. "It's real nice, with a bedroom and kitchen and balcony. I can see the houses in the town."

"Can you look out the window and see a sign with a name on it?"

"Let me check." There was the clicking of small footsteps on tile. "No, I don't see a sign."

"Okay, Ross, you're doing a great job. Look at the phone you have. Is there a number on it?"

Patsy realized that Sam was standing in front of her. She hadn't heard him come down, but he must have awakened at the ring. And now he was standing in front of her, eyes still crusty with sleep, wearing nothing but his shorts and the most incredible, shit-eating grin she'd ever seen.

"The kid?" he whispered. "Is that the kid?"

Patsy nodded.

And with her nod, tears started rolling down Sam Hillard's weathered, middle-aged, ordinary face.

Ross gave Patsy the number. Sam called the Gunnison police on his cell. Within ten minutes, Breckenridge police had matched it to an address and were pulling into the lot of the Whitehaven Condominiums, heading for Unit #407 that had been rented yesterday to a Mr. Brown.

Patsy kept Ross on the line. Chatting.

"Listen, Ross, good work. Now, your Mom really wants to see you, and she can't drive up to Breckenridge right now. So we're going to ask some policemen to bring you back home. All right? I'm going to stay on the line until they get there."

"Where's my dad?" Ross asked. "Can I talk to my dad?"

"I'm not sure, honey, but maybe your mom knows. She can tell you."

"Please, I want to talk to my mom. She would want you to wake her up, I'm sure. Really." The quaver was back.

"Okay, Ross. Just don't hang up. I'm going to put on a friend of mine to talk to you while I go wake up your mom. Just talk to him for a minute. His name is Sam."

With that she handed the phone to Sam and walked shakily toward the bedroom.

"Ross? Hi. Hey, I hear that you're quite something on the slopes," she heard Sam saying. "When did you learn to ski?...Really?...That's not so long ago at all. So, what's the best part about skiing? 'Cause I've never done it but I sure would like to try one of these days..."

Patsy Tsosie stood over the bed, watching Mandy sleep. She was curled up tight, hands clutching each other in what could be mistaken for prayer. The room was dark.

"Mandy," Patsy said softly, touching Mandy's shoulder. "Mandy, wake up. I have something to tell you. It's good news. So, c'mon, try and wake up."

Mandy's eyelids fluttered with effort. The sleeping pills were still working.

"What?" Her voice was a hoarse croak.

"Mandy, Ross wasn't in the car. Can you hear me?"

Mandy heard, but the words were moving through water. It was if the synapses of her brain were in slow motion, struggling to make the connection, the logical sequence. If Ross wasn't in the car, then. . .

"Ross?" she breathed. "Ross is. . ."

"Mandy, he's on the phone. He wants to talk to you. He wants his mommy."

Mandy tried to push back the covers, to get out of the bed, but her arm was shaking too much. Patsy grabbed the covers, pulling them back, then helped Mandy up, bracing her with both of her hands. Arms intertwined, they stumbled out of the darkness and into the soft morning light.

Ten minutes later, Sam and Patsy had to pry the phone out of Mandy's hand, after countless assurances that the police, who were by then inside Ross's room, could not bring him home until she stopped talking and hung up.

"Honey, you go with the police," Mandy finally agreed. "Get your stuff. Daddy? Daddy's car got stuck in the snow. So, you need to come home. I'm waiting for you."

Sam got on, explaining to the Breckenridge police that the condo might contain evidence needed for a homicide investigation, and that a thorough search would be appreciated after the kid left.

The Breckenridge cops would drive Ross to Salida where they'd hand him over to a Gunnison unit. Ross would be home in a matter of hours. Sam and Patsy would coordinate from Mandy's house.

Patsy guided Mandy toward the bathroom and pushed her into the shower. She was in there a long time. Sam and Patsy heard surges of manic laughter alternating with segments of the Hallelujah Chorus.

Patsy handed-in jeans and a sweater. Mandy emerged, running a brush through her wet hair. She was radiant, her entire body and face transformed with joy. Tsosie positioned her on a chair by the window in the living room, putting a hot cup of tea in her hand to sip. For two hours, she sat—immobile, watching and waiting.

It was as close to a resurrection as Sam or Patsy had ever seen.

They heard the sirens before they saw the cars. When they came around the last curve, there were two police cars, with Will and Sara's truck pulling up the rear. It was a small town. Word had gotten out.

Patsy knew that she would never forget the image of Mandy, hair streaming, running down the steps and sweeping her son into her arms, then whirling, whirling, until they fell down in a dizzy heap under the pines.

Before Ross arrived, Mandy had spoken once.

"I don't want to tell him today that his father is dead. Tomorrow I will, when we're alone, when he can have some time and privacy to absorb it. Today, if he asks, I'm sticking to the story I gave on the phone. I don't know if this is the best plan, but it's what I need to do. Understand?"

Sam and Patsy nodded.

Somehow, by early afternoon, the day became ordinary and domestic. The local police left. Will and his boys carried up groceries from his truck. Everyone was introduced. Sara put a mostly-cooked turkey in the oven to heat up. Tantalizing smells filled the cabin. Music played.

It was, after all, as Will and Sara reminded them, Easter Sunday.

The adults sat in the living room, or perched on kitchen chairs, sipping wine or mugs of coffee. They kept smiling, huge, goofy smiles. The kids, oblivious, played Monopoly on the living room floor. There was no table big enough, so they ate dinner sprawled on the floor of the living room, encircling a large tablecloth covered with food. Then they all went for a walk on a path by a stream.

Calls came for Sam from the different police departments, and he took them in the bedroom. There was nothing but charred, twisted metal left at the bottom of the canyon. It would take a lab to sort it out and they had no idea how they would ever get it up from the canyon floor. The Breckenridge cops found nothing at the condo but clothes and ski stuff. They boxed up everything.

Around 4:30 p.m. Sam took Patsy aside.

"I just called the airport. We can get on a flight out of Gunnison to Denver at 6:30 p.m., then a connection to Kansas City at 9:00. You up for that?"

"Sure, Sam. I think we're done here."

"Agreed. I want to swing by the Gunnison station first, make sure we got all their paperwork done."

Will volunteered to run them down to the Gunnison station. They left in a flurry of coats and bags and hugs. As the truck pulled out of the drive, Patsy looked back at the small cabin. Mandy stood just outside the front door, framed in the pines. Her arm was draped protectively over her son.

Between flights at the Denver airport, Sam called Leticio.

"Miguel, Sam Hillard here. Sorry to bother you on a holiday but I thought this is something you'd want to know."

"Sam? What's up?"

"Miguel, this is an off-the-record call. You got that?"

"Most clearly. Go ahead."

"I just want you to be available tomorrow. Keep that calendar flexible."

"Don't play games with me, Sam."

"No games. You may be drafting a motion for a new trial based on newly discovered exculpatory evidence. If you haven't heard from Saunders by mid-afternoon, call and tell Saunders there is a rumor. . ."

"Sam?" Miguel's voice was pleading. "This is for real?"

"I think Grace McDonald will be coming home."

"Jesus Christ, Sam. What have you found?"

"The gun for starters. And a lot more."

"I've prayed for this moment."

"Yeah, well, I didn't go that far but I came close. Never felt right to me."

"Thank you, Sam. Off the record. Got it."

48

Bruce Saunders felt like shit. He'd been down to the police station on Saturday. The evidence gathered from Danny Rivers' apartment was spread all over the table in the special case squad room, carefully labeled and inventoried. Even a cursory look had made him feel ill.

Bruce had been sure that Grace McDonald killed her husband. He'd seen it in her eyes. He'd believed it with every fiber of his being. He'd felt that he'd done the community a great service in putting her behind bars.

And it had been a nice high-profile career boost, too.

If he'd been totally wrong, and Grace McDonald was a truthful, do-gooder social worker and not a murderer? Well, he'd need more than a few Jack Daniels to get through this one. In any case, he'd keep his mouth shut until Hillard got back and they had a chance to fully evaluate. No need to bring in Leticio until he knew what he was dealing with.

"Bruce? Miguel here."

It was 1 p.m. Monday.

"Listen, there are rumors floating that some new evidence has surfaced in the McDonald case."

"What rumors?"

"Ah, Bruce. Such a close community. We have no secrets from each other. When were you planning on informing me?"

"We need to get clear on just what we have, Miguel. It could take some time."

"But that is a problem, Bruce. Time is running out for my motion for a new trial. I need whatever new information that could be exculpatory in nature in order to proceed. I need it yesterday, Bruce."

"Meet me at the station tomorrow about noon?"

"Today. Can we meet there in, say, an hour?"

"Yeah, well, I'd prefer to get a better handle. . ."

"Bruce. An innocent woman sits in our jail thinking she will be imprisoned for the rest of her life."

"Okay, Miguel. 3 p.m. I'll call over and get Hillard to meet with us."

After ten minutes in the case room with the evidence, Miguel knew there was a God.

Sam methodically presented each finding. Patsy Tsosie sat to one side, prepared to answer questions. They went through the events of Friday and Saturday, from initial phone call to search warrant to arrest warrant to high-speed chase to self-immolation.

A confirmed ballistics match would have been sufficient.

But the pictures, the log, the blood?

"Excellent work, Officers. I cannot begin to express what your investigation will mean for my client." Miguel stopped, reflecting. "I am requesting an immediate hearing with Judge Fisher. I would like all of you there. I will present my motion for a new trial based on newly discovered evidence. And I will definitely be requesting that my client be released on her own recognizance pending the outcome."

"Look, Miguel, we don't even know how much of this evidence will be admissible. Aren't you getting a little ahead of yourself here?" asked Saunders.

"It is not my problem whether it is admissible for prosecution, a point that is moot given that the assumed defendant is deceased. As exculpatory evidence, it is quite adequate. Different standards apply. But why am I telling you this? You know it better than I do. We must also remember that no one will be petitioning to dismiss it." Leticio paused. "And if ever there was just cause to accelerate a hearing, it is now. I trust that you will not oppose?"

Saunders did not answer. He just wanted to go home and drink himself into a stupor.

Miguel knew that if he told Grace tonight that there was to be a hearing tomorrow she would not sleep but tremble with fearful anticipation all night. But to allow her to spend another night in despair was unthinkable.

He went straight from the police station to the jail.

Grace was escorted to the same small room where he'd first met her, when he'd brought her coffee. Leticio sat across the table, his hands folded so that he would not bang them on the table in impatience.

Grace looked terrible. Her hair was flat against her skull and her eyes were dull. Orange was not her color.

"Miguel, what is it? Did something happen with the kids?" Her voice was anxious, frightened.

"Grace, sit down. Nothing is wrong with the children. Sit."

Grace sat.

"Do you remember a client named Mandy Rivers? A few years ago?"

"Yeah, sure. She got divorced, then moved away. What's this all about?"

"Her husband. Danny Rivers. Do you remember him?"

"Not really. I had to testify at their divorce. He was pretty much in denial. Needed somebody to blame."

"The police have some new evidence. They recovered the gun that killed Gil. And more. There is hopefully going to be a hearing tomorrow. I am requesting a new trial. But I am also requesting that you be released pending a decision on my motion."

Grace was trying to track what Miguel was saying, but it wasn't making any sense.

"They found the gun?"

"Yes. In Danny Rivers' apartment."

"So what are you saying? That Danny Rivers killed Gil?"

"That is what we believe."

"Why? Was it a robbery?"

"No. It's a long story. Danny may have been stalking you for some time. He worked part-time at the blood bank."

"The blood bank?" Grace's tongue was thick.

"Yes."

"But that's impossible. How could he take. . ."

"We are looking into that. Grace, you may be going home."

"For how long?"

"For good. We have motions to file, but I think for good."

Tears welled up in Grace's eyes, and then spilled, silently, down her cheeks.

"Tomorrow, for the hearing, can I wear my real clothes?"

"Yes. In this case, I think they will allow it. They should still have them here. Or do you want me to call Molly and get new ones?"

"No." Grace was insistent. "No. Don't call Molly or Katrina. Don't tell them. Don't tell anyone. I can't bear to have them disappointed. Let's wait until it's over."

She reached across the table to grip his hands, squeezing hard. "This is real? I won't wake up and find I've dreamed it?"

"No, Grace. This is real. It is the nightmare that is ending."

49

Leticio didn't have to twist arms to get an immediate hearing. Judge Fisher was not one to let an innocent person sit in jail even if it meant throwing the schedule out the window.

Grace was escorted into the courtroom through the side door by two guards. No handcuffs. Jail staff had heard the case developments the night before, courtesy of a phone call by Sam. Grace had abruptly moved from the category of *inmate* to *one of us*. That an innocent citizen could actually be indicted and convicted unsettled everyone in the system.

Grace had been asked when she wished to shower and when she wanted to get dressed. A woman guard asked if she'd like to borrow some make-up.

"No, but I sure could use some hair gel if there's any around," Grace replied. "And my purse had some lipstick."

New gel and lipstick were waiting with her clothes, which looked like they'd been freshly cleaned and ironed.

Entering the courtroom, Grace looked different.

In the months leading to the trial, accusations and slander had taken their toll. Her posture had become vigilant and defensive, like a child bracing for an expected blow. She'd avoided eye contact. It was only now, seeing her with her neck straight, eyes open, that the difference was apparent.

Leticio took her by both shoulders and looked her in the eyes.

"It is so good to see you, Grace."

"All rise," announced the bailiff.

And they turned to face the judge.

"This is, as you are aware, a hearing to address a motion for a new trial based on newly-discovered evidence," the judge said. "There is also a motion to postpone sentencing pending the ruling."

He paused.

"Gentlemen, shall we proceed?"

Leticio stood.

"There has been a grave miscarriage of justice. My client is wrongfully imprisoned. It would compound this travesty to force her to remain in jail for one more day, one more hour, simply because of procedures. The evidence presented at this hearing will support my claim and exonerate my client. I ask that Detective Sam Hillard be called."

Sam took the stand. In a methodical voice, he explained the evidence, from the KBI ballistics match on the gun, to the vial in the refrigerator of human blood. . .

There was a hubbub in the courtroom. It was only partially full, but the press was there. They'd been tipped off by an anonymous source, sure as hell not the DA's office this time.

"Order," said the judge, lightly pounding the gavel.

"Detective Hillard, is there any doubt in your mind that this new evidence exonerates the defendant, Grace McDonald?" asked the judge.

"None."

"Thank you, Detective. You are excused."

The judge turned to Saunders.

"Mr. Saunders, has the State yet determined, should the motion for a new trial be granted, whether they will seek a new trial?"

"The State is waiting for the complete DNA results from the KBI. Until that time, we agree to postpone sentencing."

"Agreed. Now, Mr. Saunders, you have not objected to Mr. Leticio's request for release of his client pending my ruling on his motion. Do you wish to at this time?"

"No, Your Honor."

"That's a first," muttered the judge.

The Judge pushed his glasses up his nose and looked out at the courtroom.

"Fortunately, this evidence has surfaced at a time prior to sentencing, when I have discretion. Moreover, the nature of this new evidence is substantive and compelling. I will consider the motion for a new trial. Ms. McDonald, you are hereby released on your own recognizance, pending ruling on this motion."

And then they all stood up as the Judge exited the courtroom.

Grace looked bewildered. The entire process had taken under forty minutes. She looked at Miguel.

He was holding out his arm.

"May I have the honor of escorting you home?" he asked.

As they turned to leave the courtroom, Bruce Saunders was waiting.

"Ms. McDonald, I just wanted to say. . ."

"Don't bother," interrupted Grace.

"I was just doing my job," Saunders said.

"Really? You actually believe your own bullshit?"

"Grace," admonished Miguel.

But she was not about to stop.

"Mr. Saunders, you decided I was guilty and then constructed a case: I had motive, there was a fight, I had a secret gun, I got rid of the gun in the river or handed it off to my hypothetical accomplice—oh yeah, the guy I was having an affair with—and I was a psychopath who could fake shock and beat a polygraph. Where did all that come from? Did you ever question yourself?"

"I'm sorry, but. . ."

"Just watch what you say at parties, Mr. Saunders. It may come back to haunt you."

"Grace," said Leticio as they headed for the front door of the courthouse, "I believe you have recovered your spunk. How do you feel about facing the press?"

"Face them or slug them?" Grace asked.

"Discretion, please, Grace. No battery charges quite yet."

The air smelled of spring, loamy and rich, under an intense blue sky. But Molly couldn't go out. To enjoy it felt like betrayal. She was sorting magazines in the living room when she heard a car pull into the driveway. She went to the front window.

It was Miguel.

I wonder what he wants, she thought.

Miguel was walking around to the other side of the car, opening the door, extending his hand.

"Mommy?" Molly whispered. "Mommy?" She made the whimpering sounds of a child waking in the dark.

Molly ran to the front door, flinging it open, leaping down the steps and across the lawn. And then they were in each other's arms, hugging, grabbing, touching hair and face, crying and laughing at the same time.

"What's happening?" gasped Molly.

"I'm home, honey. They found the man who killed your Dad. They have the gun," said Grace shakily.

"How? When?"

"Over the last five days I think. I'll tell you everything I know. But first, I need a stiff drink, maybe a few stiff drinks, even if it is a weekday afternoon. And we have to call Kat."

Grace turned to Miguel. "Can you come in?"

"No, I need to be going," Miguel said, smiling. "I have work waiting, another case." He lifted an eyebrow. "I'll call tomorrow. And until then—*please* Grace—be nice to the reporters. Deal?"

Grace made a gesture with her middle finger.

"If you insist," she said. "But I cannot be held responsible if they come to my home."

"What's that about?" asked Molly.

"Minor altercation. I exchanged a few choice words. Didn't come to blows. Miguel was too quick."

"You tried to slug a reporter? For real?"

Grace cut her off and took her arm, turning toward the house.

"Not to worry. Now c'mon. I want lunch. Something yummy that doesn't taste like cardboard. We can eat outside. It is such a damn beautiful day. Don't want to waste it. Maybe we could. . ."

As Miguel started his car, he watched them, arms around each other's waists, walk through the front door and into the house.

I think I'll go home and surprise my wife, he thought. *The office can wait. We can have lunch on the deck.*

It was, as Grace had said, too beautiful a day to waste.

50

In the growing darkness, Grace and Mandy sipped iced tea on the deck behind Grace's house. It was now June, a soft and balmy evening, with just a hint of breeze.

Grace had written Mandy to thank her. Without her gut-twisting intuition and reckless intervention, Grace would be serving 25-to-life at the state penitentiary.

When Mandy wrote back saying that she and Ross would be in Kaw Valley for a week in June, Grace had asked them for dinner.

Grace understood that she was ignoring yet another ethical guideline of her profession, the one that said no *dual relationships*—no friendships, with clients or former clients. But Grace didn't really give a shit anymore. So many of the guidelines and social niceties that had dictated her behavior in the past now seemed pointless. She'd been a good girl all her life, played by the rules, lived by the Golden Rule, and what had it gotten her?

Plus, she didn't know if she'd ever be going back to her former profession.

So now they sat, sipping mint tea and talking, as Ross kicked a soccer ball around the yard and Molly cleared the supper table.

"How is Ross coping with losing his Dad?" Grace asked.

"It's tough on him and even harder since he got more facts. I left it that Daddy was in an accident at first. But then I realized that sooner or later he'd be hearing different."

"What did you tell him?"

"That his Daddy got really confused about love. That he hurt someone thinking that it was a way to fix his own problems. That he was mixed-up, but that he loved Ross very, very much."

"That about covers it."

"It's hard for him to take his Daddy down from the pedestal. He takes it out on me sometimes, but that's to be expected. What I didn't expect is that I'd also be grieving. And what he did, the people he hurt—Grace, I feel responsible."

Grace looked Mandy in the eyes. "You may feel it, but that doesn't make it true. Danny made really bad choices. He may have been twisted in his head for much longer than you realize."

"But I should have seen that, I should have. . ."

"Patsy Tsosie came over one afternoon and told me the whole story. How you flew to Kaw Valley, methodically checked every inch of his house, found the lockbox, pounded it open—all of it. How you called the cops here, then let yourself be the bait. What you did to save Ross. You could have said 'not my problem' or passed the buck with a phone call from your cozy living room. And nothing would have come of it. But you didn't. All of that took courage."

"But I was so afraid the whole time. That's hardly. . ."

"That's some macho guy myth—that courage means not being afraid. It's bullshit. Real courage is knowing everything that can go wrong, all the possible dangers and consequences, feeling the fear, and still acting on your principles or your gut, still doing what you think is right."

"Well I sure felt the fear. I thought I was nuts."

"Of course. It *was* nuts. What you did went against every bit of your *good girl-nice girl* socialization. It all came from inside you, your head and heart. So, here's my take—if you need to feel responsible take responsibility for what *you* did. *Your* actions. *Your* choices."

They sat in silence for a few minutes, then Mandy spoke.

"What about your son? I don't mean to pry, but Molly told me he never came to the trial, that he. . ." her voice drifted off.

"It'll take time. On some level, I understand how hard it was for him to believe me. But he's my son, and I expected. . ." Her voice cracked. "I needed. . ." Grace looked away. "I think he's waiting for me to forgive without his asking or to act like it didn't happen. But I can't do that. I think I've spent my whole life overlooking a lot to keep the peace, pretending like everything was just fine. But I've lost that skill."

"Yeah, I get that," Mandy replied.

Ross ran up to them, panting with exertion.

"Mom, I just saw some fireflies. They are way cool. Can I catch some, please?"

"Go ask Molly for a jar," answered Grace. "Make sure you have holes in the top so they can breathe."

They watched Ross as he ran into the house.

"Is it terribly hard without Gil?" Mandy asked. "I know it's a stupid question."

"No, it's a good question, one few people bother to ask. To be blunt, it's awful without Gil. In many ways it's harder than right after he died. I didn't have time to grieve before I was arrested, then I was all caught up in defending myself. Now, living without him day-to-day—it's hard to get out of bed."

"Are you working again?"

"No. I don't know if I can ever go back, to have the necessary empathy and patience. It's a complete illusion that we have any real control in our lives. I think now that I was naive and insulated."

"That would be a shame. I think you did really good work."

"Perhaps. Hard to say. Now I think I missed a lot."

"What will you do?"

"I don't know. The life I knew and had is gone. And I'm starting to realize that I can't stay here."

"You're leaving Kaw Valley?"

"I'd never planned to. But now? I used to have a place in this community. Maybe low profile, but respected. But that's gone. People I thought were my friends disappeared when I was indicted. I can't just forget that. I can't forgive either. Now strangers stare at me in the grocery store. I'm that *woman who didn't murder her husband after all.*"

"Where will you go?"

"I may just put stuff in storage and go live somewhere for a year. I don't know where for sure. But I need to see who I am when I'm not here."

"That's what I did with Gunnison. Now it's home."

Then Ross was back, a jar with seven small flashing bugs clutched in his hand. "I'm gonna take these back to Gunnison, Mom, and show them to my friends. Then I'll let them loose so we can have fireflies there too!"

"It won't work, Ross. They can't live that long," replied Mandy.

Grace agreed, nodding. "They only live at certain altitudes, in particular temperatures. It takes a certain climate to survive."

"So what do I do with these?" asked Ross.

"Just let them go, honey," answered Mandy.

Grace stood up. "Hold on," she said. "I'll be right back."

When she came back out of the house, she carried a large quilt and several pillows.

"Follow me," she said.

Grace walked to the middle of the yard, the open grassy area where no trees blocked the sky, and spread the quilt. She looked up at the sky and then picked a side for the pillows.

"C'mon. Lie down."

The lights in the back of the house went out and they heard the back door closing. Then Molly joined them.

"It's better with no other lights on," Molly said.

They lay on the quilt, pillows under their heads. In the quiet, they could hear all the sounds of the night: birds turning in their nests; insects buzzing softly; the whirr of the cicadas.

"*Now*, Ross," Grace whispered.

"Now what?" asked Ross.

"Now let them go. Their lives are so short, over in a heartbeat. They deserve to be free."

"Okay," agreed Ross, opening the top of the jar. He tapped the jar lightly on the ground. One by one the fireflies darted into the open air.

Mandy, Ross, Grace, and Molly lay on the quilt as fireflies, many more fireflies, danced above their bodies. They watched the full moon rise toward the stars in the night sky.

"We haven't done this for years, Mom," whispered Molly. "Did you do this when you were a kid?"

"No," Grace whispered back. "Your father showed me. He called it a cheap date. And I have to tell you, there were nights we never did pay much attention to the stars."

Molly giggled. Then Mandy. Then Ross.

And then they were laughing, at nothing, at everything, at life.

Book Group Discussion Questions

1) Consider the quote from Grace that opens the novel: "Some marriages end with a bang, some with a whimper. But in all marriages, without exception, the beginning of the end is a secret." What are the different secrets that are the "beginning of the end" for the marriages in *Fall from Grace*?

2) As a society, we're struggling to understand how ordinary people can turn violent. Does the author present a believable picture of how hurt and anger fester into blame and can lead to retribution?

3) The novel is told in the third person, with shifting points of view. Does this work for you? How would the novel differ if told from Grace's perspective only?

4) The novel looks at how a few drops of DNA can be a powerful force in forming public opinion and consequently erase decades of living with integrity within a community. In our age of social media, someone's *reputation* is more fragile than ever before. Do you find this disturbing? Do you identify with Grace? How do you see yourself reacting if a friend of yours was similarly accused —and there was *evidence*?

5) Grace McDonald is not a typical protagonist for a mystery series. She isn't the one who solves the crime. At times she seems almost more victim than protagonist. Readers may feel impatient with her denial of

her situation and her more vulnerable and human response to loss. Does this make her less admirable? How do you see Grace changing throughout the novel? Based on how she has changed in this book, how do you predict that she will be different as a protagonist in future books?

6) Mandy may be the character who changes most significantly in the book. What adjectives would you use to describe her at the beginning, and then at the end?

7) Danny Rivers is a complex character. How did your reactions or responses to him change over the course of the novel? Do you see him as emotionally disturbed? Are you troubled by his lack of remorse? What specifically allowed you to feel compassion? How did the author create such a dichotomy in one character?

8) Katrina makes a choice to not tell her best friend the secret. Have you been faced with choices where truth could hurt someone you love and where silence seemed to be the more caring choice? How do we decide what makes a decision such as Katrina faced right or wrong?

9) Which of the minor characters of *Fall from Grace* do you find most memorable? Are there any with whom you feel a stronger connection? Why? What does the author do, or fail to do, to make the minor characters more *real*?

10) There are multiple wives and mothers in *Fall from Grace*. How do the women experience their roles and responsibilities as wives and mothers? Compare and contrast to how you see your own roles in your own life.

11) *Fall from Grace* has been described as "Kafkaesque." In what ways do you see that as accurate or not?

12) Writers are often advised to "write what you know." Author Susan Kraus is a therapist. Do you think it helps to "write what you know," or better to have more distance?

13) Mandy and Grace have different experiences of their client-

therapist relationship. How does the therapy process impact Mandy's life? Do you feel it is a reasonable representation of a therapeutic process? Do you think that Mandy would have acted on her decision without the support of Grace?

14) Mandy refuses to allow Danny to know about or join in the counseling process. Do you feel she should have? Could Danny have changed? What do you feel are *good enough* reasons to divorce?

15) Kraus weaves a variety of social and political themes throughout the novel. Are there any that resonate with you?

16) The timeline on this book extends over a few years. Was it easy to track or do you prefer more compressed timelines?

17) In many books, the characters know things that the readers do not. In *Fall from Grace*, the readers know critical facts before the characters. Does this work? How can there be literary tension when the reader knows "who done it?"

18) Grace seems to believe that bad things will not happen to good people if they follow all the rules and *play safe*. But the plot disputes that as a naïve, middle-class assumption that fosters a false sense of security. What do you think? How does your own upbringing, neighborhood, community, religion, race and ethnicity impact your sense of security? What about your trust in the legal system?

19) Does *Fall from Grace* fit within any specific genre? Is it a thriller? A family drama? What elements do you see that reflect a genre? Which do not?

20) Grace and Katrina have forged a friendship that is more surrogate family. Do you have family-substitutes in your own life? How are they different from *real* families?

21) There is a sex scene with Mandy and Danny. Do you find it believable? Do you think it is more erotic for women than for men? Why? Did you feel judgmental of Mandy? Do you think that women are

more judgmental of other women than of men when it comes to extra-marital or post-marital sex?

22) Mandy has always been a *good girl* who followed the rules. Yet she feels compelled to follow her gut and takes significant risks. Have you ever had experiences where your intuition—your *gut*—was telling you to do something that seemed crazy? Do you feel that intuition is depreciated in our culture compared to many other cultures?

23) Did you laugh at any particular place in the book? Did you cry? What exactly elicited a strong emotional response and why?

24) The ending is not conventionally happy. Do you feel it was ambiguous? Or did the loose ends come together? What makes a good ending for you as a reader?

25) If you could ask the author a question—any question—what would you like to know?

Acknowledgments

It takes a village to create a book, plus a lot of strangers who graciously answer questions and share their expertise. Those who helped educate and guide me through the legal and scientific issues of this book include: The Community Blood Center of Topeka; Jackson County Medical Examiner's Office of Kansas City, Missouri; the Kansas Bureau of Investigation; attorneys David Brown and Pedro Iregonegaray; Judge Jean Shepherd; Judge Kay Huff; the Lawrence Police Department, in particular their skilled polygraph examiners.

My gratitude to Thea Rademacher, JD, of Flint Hills Publishing, for her insight, enthusiasm, patience, and pragmatism. Also, Nathan Pettengill, editor at Sunflower Publishing, for many years of support; Ashley Honey, cover graphic artist; Jen Sharp, web design.

In my village, I was fortunate to have many fine friends and cheerleaders: Emily Kofron, Michelle and Mel Berg, Jeffrey Ann Goudie and Tom Averill, Harriet and Steve Lerner, Alice Lieberman and Tom McDonald, Margaret and Will Severson, Marcia Cebulska and Tom Prasch, Karen Rowinsky, and many more; Greg Woodland, past manager of the Lied Lodge in Nebraska City, Nebraska, for supporting a writing retreat years ago; the gifted and prolific women of my writers' group for their kind words and gentle nudges; Dairy Hollow Writers' Colony in Eureka Springs, Arkansas for providing such a nurturing space to write.

My extended family: Anne Kraus; Marjorie Rothermund and Amy Spahn; Kate, Mark, Ross, Tess and Zoe Brilakis; John Barthell; Nancy, Danny, Alyson, Lindsey and Megan Fox; Antonio, Pamela and Joel Dominguez.

My children, Sarah and Ben, who I hope will see that tenacity is a useful trait, and while some dreams can be shelved, they should never be buried.

Most of all, my husband, Frank Barthell, my most trusted reader/editor/critic, for walking beside me on the long and winding road of a 40-plus year relationship, for always supporting my dreams, and for never letting go of my hand.

About the Author:

Susan Kraus is a therapist, mediator, and writer. Taking to heart the adage, "Write what you know," Kraus uses her decades of professional experience to take readers behind the closed doors of therapy, mediation, and intimate family relationships. Her novels tackle polarizing social and political issues, always raising more questions as she makes the political personal. But, mostly, Susan just likes to write stories about ordinary people trying to manage the challenges of ordinary life. Not strictly genre, her books may or may not have a murder, because, as she puts it, "Sometimes dying is the easy way out. It's living that takes guts."

Susan has written non-fiction for over 25 years and is an award-winning travel writer. She is the author of *Fall from Grace (The Grace McDonald Series Book 1)*, *All God's Children (The Grace McDonald Series Book 2)* and *Insufficient Evidence (The Grace McDonald Series Book 3)*.

www.susankraus.com

www.ingramcontent.com/pod-product-compliance
Lightning Source LLC
LaVergne TN
LVHW040136080526
838202LV00042B/2928